OUTLAWS

THE KING & SLATER SERIES BOOK FOUR

MATT ROGERS

Follow me on Facebook!
https://www.facebook.com/mattrogersbooks

Expect regular updates, cover reveals, giveaways, and more. I love interacting with fans. Feel free to send me a private message with any questions or comments. Looking forward to having you!

BOOKS BY MATT ROGERS

THE JASON KING SERIES

Isolated (Book 1)

Imprisoned (Book 2)

Reloaded (Book 3)

Betrayed (Book 4)

Corrupted (Book 5)

Hunted (Book 6)

THE JASON KING FILES

Cartel (Book 1)

Warrior (Book 2)

Savages (Book 3)

THE WILL SLATER SERIES

Wolf (Book 1)

Lion (Book 2)

Bear (Book 3)

Lynx (Book 4)

Bull (Book 5)

Hawk (Book 6)

THE KING & SLATER SERIES

Weapons (Book 1)

Contracts (Book 2)

Ciphers (Book 3)

Outlaws (Book 4)

LYNX SHORTS

Blood Money (Book 1)

BLACK FORCE SHORTS

The Victor (Book 1)

The Chimera (Book 2)

The Tribe (Book 3)

The Hidden (Book 4)

The Coast (Book 5)

The Storm (Book 6)

The Wicked (Book 7)

The King (Book 8)

The Joker (Book 9)

The Ruins (Book 10)

PROLOGUE

Quinn Chapman had a good life.

He wasn't quite sure how he'd got here, or what he'd done to deserve such blessings, but he chalked it up to the simple explanation that sometimes the stars aligned. They were out tonight, shimmering above the Port of Los Angeles, casting a wide net over the dark swirling water of the harbour. He wore dark clothing in turn — a black short-sleeved shirt tucked into slate-grey slacks — because that's what had been requested.

When requests were made, he had to abide if he wanted to continue reaping the blessings.

It allowed him to maintain the Cali lifestyle.

Take today, for instance: a morning surf at a hidden cove to the south of Laguna Beach, followed by lunch at the Coyote Grill overlooking the Pacific (an appetiser, an outlandishly expensive main course, and a trio of Coronas back-to-back-to-back, all glistening with condensation like you see in the commercials.) Then back to the house in Emerald Bay for a little admin with his business partners, prepping for the gig tonight, but that wasn't anything to complain about.

The jobs were always simple, straightforward, never too complicated. Find the right container, load it up, pay the respective port officials to look the other way, coast smoothly off Terminal Island, deliver the cargo to its intended destination.

Never — under any circumstances — look inside the containers.

Because that *would* make it complicated.

Then he'd have to worry about all those tricky feelings he'd rather avoid — guilt, doubt, fear.

Why would you deliberately let yourself feel like that?

Why not ignore where the cargo ends up, or what happens to it, or what you're contributing to, or what kind of people you're aiding, and just focus on the money that comes rolling in, allowing you to surf and drink and eat and play to your heart's content?

To Quinn, that was the obvious choice.

There *were* doubts, of course. He'd been raised a libertarian by hippie parents whose primary hobby involved shouting the horrors of capitalism from the rooftops, so when he had time alone to really think about it, his mind went down the obvious route.

This money you and your friends are using to live in a multi-million dollar house facing the water has to come from some-where. You know bad people are paying you for your services. Every day you spend ignoring that fact is another day you're complicit. You don't look in the shipping containers, but you know what's in them — roughly speaking. How much suffering are you contributing to? How much longer can this go on?

For obvious reasons, he didn't spend much time alone with his thoughts. If he ended up dwelling on the morality of it, he just told himself he wasn't the ringleader and left it at that. His boss (and oldest friend) was a generous man, and Quinn was fortunate for the privilege of working for him.

Questioning how much immorality he was contributing to the world made no sense.

That's not what life was about.

So, broadly speaking, Quinn Chapman had a good life ... as long as he didn't think about what he'd done to get it.

Now he stood alongside his brothers, his friends, his colleagues — all of them dressed similarly. There were six of them in total, and together they ran a smooth operation.

There was an elephant in the room but Quinn ignored it, as did the rest of his co-workers. Namely, the fact that Roman — the seventh member — wasn't around anymore. Their boss had told them he'd run off. Quinn didn't believe that. Roman wasn't the running type. If he'd fucked up, he would have stayed and face it like a man. Which is probably what he'd done — faced their boss like a man — and that explained why he wasn't around anymore.

Quinn didn't like to think about that, either.

You have a good life.

He said it to himself, over and over again.

The longer he masked the truth, the better.

The crew took up their established positions within the cargo zone. Two of Quinn's buddies peeled off to settle into scouting locations by the entrance so they could keep an eye out for witnesses. It used to be a three-man gig, before ... well ...

Quinn watched the boss locate the specific container and nod to the remaining men. Quinn and the last two guys set to work manoeuvring the tractor-trailer truck in the concrete bay, backing the empty trailer into the correct position. Then they used a giant yellow shipping container handler — like an oversized forklift — to lift up the refrigerated container, detach it from its plug, and guide it into the gaping maw of the open trailer.

Quinn watched all this from a dozen feet away. They'd streamlined the process. Cal handled the forklift, and Kurt shouted directions.

This time, there was a slight difference. Quinn's gaze wandered over the ridged exterior of the container as it caught the moonlight. He noticed a small cylindrical hole cut into the metal, maybe the size of a golf ball, no larger. There was something solid and grey on the other side of the hole, but Quinn watched it peel away before his very eyes, and realised it was packaging tape.

Then a wide eye pressed to the hole from within, barely illuminated by the moonlight.

It spotted him.

He saw primal fear in the pupil.

The eye vanished, replaced immediately by the tape.

Quinn shifted from foot to foot, his stomach churning. He knew he was breaking out in an uncomfortable sweat, but there was nothing he could do to prevent it. The night was humid and clammy, and as soon as adrenaline fired, his system did the rest. He wiped his brow and hoped nobody noticed his discomfort. He gave thanks that they were skilled enough as a crew to do this by moonlight alone. He'd hate for his face to be lit up for all to see.

The container disappeared into the semi-trailer — out of sight, out of mind.

He repeated it, over and over.

Out of sight, out of mind.

Out of sight, out of mind.

Out of sight, out of mind.

You saw nothing.

They beckoned him up onto the tractor unit, and he leapt onto the step below the closed passenger's door, attaching himself to the outside of the truck. He looped an arm in through the open window and gripped the inside of the door lining for stability. Kurt, now behind the wheel, accelerated out of the cargo zone, and the two scouts came running out of the darkness. They leapt aboard too.

With all six of them either inside or outside the tractor unit, Kurt steered the truck toward the opposite end of the gargantuan berth.

A couple of seconds later, headlights hit them front-on, fully illuminating the trio hanging off the doors. It didn't automatically incriminate them, but it sure looked suspicious. The oncoming truck barrelled past, heading further away from shore, toward distant berths.

When it was out of sight, they all sighed with relief.

It was a clear oversight on the scouts' part.

Kurt drove all the way to the edge of Terminal Island in the dead of night, passing three separate officials they'd paid off. He slowed the truck alongside an open-topped jeep parked alone in shadow, and Quinn leapt down. It was his ride out of here. Only Kurt and Vince would stay with the truck.

The boss leapt down off the same door and landed on the concrete alongside him. He was a tall man, with blond dreadlocks and a tanned wiry frame.

Your typical California surfer on the surface.

Underneath, not so much.

The boss said, 'That was close.'

Quinn said, 'Yeah.'

'We might need a seventh member for the next gig after all. We worked better with three scouts. What do you think?'

Quinn tried to steady his racing pulse.

He thought of Roman's unknown whereabouts.

He thought of the eye in the container, bloodshot in the moonlight.

He said, 'Yeah, maybe.'

He climbed aboard the jeep, realising he didn't have a good life after all.

1

Jason King heard his employer order a murder through the closed door.

Their hotel resided within the Garden Ring, overlooking the Moskva River. The suite had unobstructed views of both the Kremlin and St. Basil's Cathedral across the water. King stared out at the landmarks from an antechamber within the suite. It was a circular space, ornately furnished, that led through to a huge private office currently occupied by the man he had come to Russia to protect.

Sam Donati.

The head of an American conglomerate that ran transportation and shipping for half the globe.

Outside, it was grey and overcast. Rain drizzled — not enough to qualify as a downpour, but enough to put a considerable dampener on the mood within the suite. He already had a dozen reservations about being here, but the weak light in the antechamber and the dreary conditions outside combined to churn his gut. The rain was all he was paying attention to when the muffled voice resonated through the wood, coming from within the office.

He figured he wasn't supposed to be within earshot.

Which didn't matter.

He heard what he heard, and the rest of the world fell away.

Donati said, 'You're sure she's alone?'

Silence.

Donati said, 'Okay. Do it. Make it quick.'

King stopped. He'd been pacing, restless after a long flight from New York and a considerable lack of sleep, but now all of that became superficial. He zoned in, listening for anything that might indicate he'd misinterpreted what he'd heard.

Donati said, 'I don't care. You know what this is worth. Be discreet. Get it done.'

What this is worth.

King knew.

He reflexively reached for his appendix holster. Milliseconds later he remembered it was empty, and his hand froze along its trajectory. He glanced at the other end of the antechamber, through to the main room of the suite. The six-man team from Veloce Security Services were somewhere out there, out of sight, probably pacing too. They compromised the entirety of Donati's personal security crew.

Like King, all of them were weaponless.

They'd flown in privately, but it wouldn't have been prudent to try to smuggle an arsenal of firepower past customs. Not without the governmental stamp of approval, which King knew he'd never get for a civilian gig.

Now, an arms dealer was en route to the hotel from

further north, in tow with all the weapons they could ask for. One of Donati's team had found him on the dark web and exchanged the particulars.

But the guy wasn't here yet. That's what they were all waiting for.

So King didn't have a gun.

Doesn't matter. You can't let this slide.

The rigidly moral voice in his head. It had followed him his whole career. He knew the stakes. Fail to listen to it once, and you open the floodgates. Obeying it put his wellbeing at risk, over and over and over again. But the alternative was losing his soul, and that wasn't a sacrifice he was willing to make.

He stepped forward, twisted the door handle, and stepped into the office.

Donati looked up, surprised. Frazzled. A little angry.

Which was to be expected.

King was an outlier within the man's usual inner circle. A late addition to the party. An enigma. Donati had kept him at arm's length for the entire trip, valuing his unrivalled amount of experience but hesitant to open up to an independent contractor he'd only just met. It was an odd predicament all round.

Now, it was odder.

Donati squared up, the surprise dissipating, the anger amplifying. He was a large man, a couple of inches taller than King, sporting deeply tanned skin of Italian origin, and he was perhaps best characterised by the stubborn refusal to accept the fact he was going bald. The thick curly hair framing either side of his big head was his defining characteristic, making him stand out in a crowd. There was almost nothing left on top, but he'd be damned if he was going to admit it and start shaving his head.

He was a stubborn man through and through, and if he decided on something he stuck to it no matter what it entailed.

In that way, he and King were the same.

Donati jabbed a fat finger at the phone pressed to his ear and said, 'I'm on a call.'

King took another step forward, crossing the threshold, committing to the interruption. The action carried with it a measure of finality. There was no going back. Without taking his eyes off Donati he reached back and gently closed the door.

Sealing them in.

Donati cocked his head to one side, which could mean he was listening to whoever was on the other end of the line, but more than likely meant he'd finally registered King as a threat.

King said, 'Hang the phone up.'

Donati's eyes flared with rage, and he pointed to the closed door. 'Get the *fuck* out of my office.'

King didn't budge.

He stared the man right in the eyes and simply said, 'No.'

Donati didn't respond.

But a little of the flame died down.

Smart, King thought.

The man wouldn't win this one with intimidation. Making use of his impressive size and smouldering intensity had probably won him hundreds of business negotiations in the past.

This was not a business negotiation.

And whatever he could do to intimidate, King could do twice as well.

Donati ended the call without another word. Which was

a significant problem. King had expected a '*Wait one,*' or a '*Stand down for now,*' but instead Donati simply took the phone away from his ear, thumbed the touchscreen, and placed it face-down on the desk. He stayed fixed to the spot and crossed his giant hands in front of the gut bulging against his tucked-in shirt.

He said, 'What are we doing here, Jason?'

'Call your man back, and tell him to stand down.'

Donati raised an eyebrow. 'This is quite the change of allegiance.'

'It is.'

'Are you going to explain why you decided to interfere?'

'No.'

'You'd better start talking—'

King ratcheted his gaze up a notch. Put a bit of his own smouldering intensity into it. It made Donati shut his mouth halfway through the sentence. The atmosphere shifted. King knew why. Donati was only just now beginning to understand that the man he was facing could snap him in half with his bare hands.

King had experienced that dynamic many times before.

The sudden *thud* of realisation in an adversary.

Donati said, 'Whatever you think you heard, you're mistaken.'

'Am I?'

'I don't have to explain myself to you.'

King nodded. 'You're right. You don't. All you have to do is pick up the phone and call off the hit.'

Donati's mouth sealed into a hard, firm line.

King said, 'It's the girl from the surveillance photo, isn't it?'

'Yes.'

'Who is she really?'

'Does it matter?'

'Yes.'

'Look...' Donati said, and wiped a palm across his goatee in rumination. 'Is it money you want?'

'No.'

'This isn't something I can reverse. But I can compensate you. To keep quiet. A hundred thousand?'

'No.'

'Five hundred thousand.'

'No.'

'A million flat. You know I can wire you the money like *that*,' — he snapped his fingers — 'and you'll have it tomorrow.'

King stared. 'You don't get it.'

'What's not to get?'

'I have more money than I need for fifty lifetimes,' King said. 'But I could be worth a penny and I still wouldn't accept.'

Silence.

'You don't need money?' Donati said.

King shook his head.

'Then why are you here?'

'Because I owe someone. This was never about money.'

Donati squirmed.

The one thing he could wield like a sword — bribery.

The crux of his success.

Now useless.

'Pick up the phone,' King said. 'And call off the hit.'

'I can't do that.'

'Then we're going to have a problem.'

A vein pulsed on Donati's temple, and redness crept into his throat. The skin across his neck had the texture of sandpaper. King noticed every dry patch, every crack, every crevasse. He felt like he could see through to the man's vocal chords.

He knew what was coming.

Donati roared, '*Help!*' at the top of his lungs.

King turned, steeled himself, and waited for six beefed-up private security thugs to come bursting through the door.

2

_____

Manhattan
Four days earlier...

Will Slater was plagued by indecision.

And not because he was in a bar.

He no longer had the impulsive reflex to dull his racing mind. He hadn't touched a drink in nearly two months. Which was relatively normal for your everyday civilian, but for Slater it might as well have been the achievement of a lifetime. He couldn't remember the last time he'd spent this long sober. The mind needs balance, and he'd always needed to tip the scales back toward hedonism, given the intensity of his career. Train to his physical and mental limits, throw his life on the line for his country, get beat and cut and shot to pieces, lay low and recuperate, then do it all over again.

You had to do *something* to take your mind off the savagery of the lifestyle.

In Slater's case, he'd found the answer in the bottom of a bottle. Drink, dull the mind, suppress the bad thoughts (and the good ones too), wake up the next morning with a splitting headache, sweat it out, get back to training. It wasn't ideal for longevity or health, but nothing in his life was.

He'd never understood how Jason King had resisted the urge to do the same.

Now, he got it.

It was all habit. He'd conditioned his brain to operate on autopilot. Downtime? Open a beer. Pour a whiskey on the rocks. It had become automatic, an unconscious primitive response to his circumstances. As soon as he'd changed the script, the urge had fallen away. It hadn't been easy. But there was someone new in his life, and she'd helped him through the uncertainty.

Despite decades of meditation, for the first time in his life he was truly at peace.

Now he sat across from King in a familiar speakeasy-style bar in Koreatown. King had a pint of craft beer in front of him, the glass dewing with condensation.

Slater had a glass of water. It barely fazed him.

King looked down at the water, and then over to his own beer. He shook his head.

Slater said, 'What?'

'You classed yourself as an alcoholic, but you practically fixed yourself overnight.'

Slater shrugged. 'I used to rely on it. So that's definitely what I was.'

'You never even struggled to get out of the woods.'

'Yes, I did.'

'You found the right girl, and it was like booze had never existed.'

'It wasn't because of her. That was just good timing.'

'Still, I never saw you struggle.'

'No shit.'

King paused, ruminated on it, then nodded. Slater was grateful. They didn't need to talk about it for hours. Two syllables was enough to convey meaning, and all at once King understood.

No shit.

Meaning, *All we've done for the last twenty years is struggle. We've fought and clawed for our own survival, all for a paycheque. All we know is the eternal fight. So, yes, I struggled. But I didn't let it show. Not to you, not to anyone. Because that's what I've been conditioned to do.*

It wouldn't feel right if they weren't constantly struggling.

Peace was a foreign concept.

King said, 'When are you off on your little vacation?'

Slater twitched, below the surface. That was the reason for his indecision.

He said, 'We fly out tomorrow afternoon.'

'I have no idea how you managed to get away with that.'

'Violetta says we're on good terms with the upper echelon.'

'Wouldn't know,' King said. 'Never met them.'

'But surely you can believe that they're grateful for what we did last time out.'

'There's entire divisions of our government that we'll never lay eyes on,' King said. 'Violetta's above us, and then there's a whole world above her we know nothing about.'

'Why are you telling me this? That's the way it's been our whole lives. Are you expecting it to change?'

'I'm telling you,' King said, 'because I don't think "grateful" exists in their vocabulary. They're the shadow people.'

'You have no idea what their vocabulary is,' Slater said. 'But we saved all of New York from anarchy. You know how close it was. You know we scraped through by a hair's breadth. Sure, they're in the shadows. They're the ones behind the public façade of the President and Congress. They're the ones who don't change when Republicans and Democrats see-saw back and forth in and out of office. But even *if* they're power-hungry sociopaths like you seem to think they are, they'd still be out of a job if New York went dark and the largest city in America plunged into anarchy. So, yes, I think they're grateful. No matter who they are.'

King mulled it over and shrugged. He lifted the beer to his lips and took a swig, then wiped foam off his lip. 'Fair point.'

Slater paused. 'Do you really think that?'

'Think what?'

'That they've got their own best interests in mind.'

'I know what you're thinking,' King said. 'All our operations have been morally straight, so surely they're selfless.'

'Something along those lines.'

'I think they know who we are,' King said. 'We have a track record. If we get dealt a bad hand, we rebel. We've done it multiple times. We don't fall into line just because someone tells us it's patriotic to do so. But the only reason they haven't neutralised us is because we're so damn good at our jobs. That doesn't mean everything they do is pure. It just means they give us the ops they know we won't turn down.'

Slater thought about it.

Didn't answer.

They were good at that. They'd spent so long together that they knew, more often than not, a spiel didn't need a response. Critical objective thinking was the key to their success and longevity. So Slater used it.

He thought more.

Then cocked his head. 'Maybe you're right.'

'I'm just saying the world isn't all sunshine and rainbows.'

Slater tensed his core, felt the faint phantom pain of a hundred battle scars. He looked down and saw his calloused blistered knuckles and the damaged skin along the tops of his hands.

He lifted his eyes to King and said, 'You think I don't know that?'

But he saw the same faint stirring of traumatic memory in King's eyes, and he knew it was a pointless question.

They both knew it.

Maybe better than anyone on the planet.

They'd seen the worst of humanity. They'd been all the way down to the bedrock. And they were still here. Still fighting.

Maybe that said something.

Maybe they knew there was more good in the world than there was bad.

Then a big hand fell on Slater's shoulder, and he looked up into the eyes of a man he hadn't seen in at least a decade. The guy was in his sixties, grizzly, rugged. He still had all his hair, and it was still thick, but it was silver. He'd grown it long and swept it back, tucking strands behind his ears. His face had craters and crevasses and pockmarks — partially from a lifetime of exposure to the sun, but mostly from a lifetime of exposure to pain.

Slater thought the guy was an apparition, a long dormant parcel of his memory now stirred up.

But he was real.

And he was standing over them in a bar in Manhattan.

'Holy shit,' Slater said. 'Jack Coombs.'

3

King wasn't in the know.

He kept silent as Slater leapt up and pulled the grizzled man into a bear hug. They slapped each other on the back hard enough to draw the attention of everyone in the bar, but they seemed to wise up to the commotion they'd caused.

Slater dropped back into the booth and slid across so he was between the old man and King. The guy bent down and dropped into the space Slater had been occupying a minute earlier.

Slater said, 'Jason King, meet Jack Coombs.'

King extended a hand, and Coombs reached out and clasped it. His grip was powerful. Like iron. All three of them were the same. Built with hard corded muscle, but even stronger underneath than they looked on the surface.

Which was considerably impressive, given just how toughened their exteriors were.

King said, 'Guessing you two know each other.'

Coombs smirked. 'Will's an old student of mine.'

'Navy,' Slater said. 'A long, long time ago.'

King said, 'I thought you were Air Force.'

'I did two years there. Then they transferred me, which was a serious abnormality. But they wanted to capitalise on my "genetic gifts."'

Coombs leant forward, dropping both elbows onto the chipped wooden table. 'I was the First Phase Officer in Charge when the boy went through BUD/S.'

Basic Underwater Demolition — SEAL.

The initiation into the Navy SEALs, which included the fabled and feared Hell Week — one hundred and thirty continuous hours of sleep deprivation, physical exhaustion, and mental suffering.

King said, 'How'd he go?'

'That's why I remember him,' Coombs said. 'The kid breezed through it. All the instructors... it mentally fucked us. Even at the end of Hell Week, his body was destroyed, but his eyes were sharp. I'll always remember that. Sharp eyes. Ate the whole thing like a Tic-Tac.'

'Sounds like Will,' King said.

Coombs stared at Slater.

Slater stared back.

Coombs said, 'I can't fuckin' believe it, kid. Here you are.'

'Here I am. How've you been, old man?'

Coombs shook his head. 'This ain't about me. You've got some explaining to do.'

Slater raised an eyebrow. 'Do I?'

'They whisked you outta the Navy real quick, didn't they? You were there, and then you were gone. The rumour mill churned. We all thought you were dead. We thought they got fed up and put a bullet in your head for making the whole thing look too damn easy.'

They all laughed. A mutually genuine, wholehearted

laugh. Not the superficial forced bullshit that usually plagues social interactions.

It was the only kind of laugh King and Slater allowed themselves.

A real one.

Slater said, 'They had other plans for me.'

'Who did? They never told us shit.'

'They didn't tell me shit either. Not until I was already off the books.'

Coombs stared. 'You're kidding.'

Slater jerked a thumb at King. 'He and I. We're cut from the same cloth. We did the same sort of wet work. Spent most of the last fifteen years operating independently. Now we work together.'

Now Coombs stared at King. 'What are you two doing in New York?'

King said, 'We live here.'

'Are you supposed to be telling me this?'

'Hell no.'

'I thought as much.'

Slater said, 'I trust you, and King trusts me. That's all that's needed.'

'You sure? I've only just run into you.'

Slater shrugged. 'It's intuition.'

They regarded each other across the booth. Exchanged glances of mutual respect and understanding.

Whatever's said here does not leave this table.

No matter what.

It didn't need to be vocalised. They were men of discipline. They knew.

Slater said, 'What about yourself, Jack? The hell are you doing here? Retired?'

'From active service,' Coombs said. 'But I'm still working. I'm busier than ever.'

'What does an old dog like yourself do in the civilian world?'

Coombs smirked again. 'You wouldn't approve. Especially if you're still doing wet work.'

'Try me.'

'I'm a leadership advisor,' he said. 'I know — it sounds like I've given myself a fancy title and then jerked myself off. But turns out there's a few tricks this old dog can teach to big businesses. I've crawled my way up to Fortune 500 companies. I give them the time-tested principles that worked so well in the SEALs. Helps that I know them like the back of my hand.'

'You're doing well for yourself?'

'Better than well. Better than I deserve, probably.'

King met the old man's eyes and said, 'We know what you mean.'

Coombs shrugged. 'Turns out it's an untapped market. People are weak. I'm hard. Haven't had a pretty life, but that actually helps in some ways.'

'Of course it does,' Slater said. 'Pretty lives are usually hollow.'

Coombs nodded. Didn't respond. They didn't have to compare past traumatic experiences. It was extraneous.

After a long pause, Coombs finally said, 'I'd say we should go over what we've been doing, but I wouldn't even know where to start. I imagine you're the same.'

Slater gave a nod for both of them.

Coombs said, 'Am I intruding?'

King managed a wry half-smile, but didn't answer.

Slater said, 'Not at all. We just don't usually make

conversation with anyone other than ourselves and our significant others. Takes some warming up.'

Coombs said, 'Can I buy you a beer?'

Now it was Slater's turn to half-smile. 'A couple of months ago I would have jumped at the offer. But not tonight.'

'Tonight in particular?'

'I quit drinking.'

Coombs gave a gruff nod. 'Then you're a braver man than me.'

His eyes turned to King, and King shrugged. 'Braver than the both of us.'

'Can I buy you a beer, then? I respect Will. And he respects you. That's enough for me.'

King said, 'I'd be honoured.'

Coombs got up and drifted to the bar. In other social circumstances, those remaining at the table might have gossiped about the newcomer. But that wasn't King's style, nor Slater's. They sat in comfortable silence. King pondered the directions life could take.

Retirement.

The private sector.

No constant threat of death.

He had to admit, it sounded pretty damn good.

It was a shame he would never know what it was like.

4

Slater thought hard.

He watched King fall into pensive self-analysis, and followed suit.

Coombs had done it. In the Navy, Slater had known him as a hard-charging, take-no-shit drill instructor with zero room for compromise or civility. That was still there, under the surface. But the man had taught himself to suppress it, to only let it show when it was necessary. Perhaps it had allowed him to detach from his old mentality. Allowed himself room to breathe.

Slater had never — not once — given himself room to breathe.

That, potentially, was about to change.

But he hadn't told King.

Before Coombs made it back, King said, 'I might not see you before you leave tomorrow. Make sure you enjoy yourself.'

It seemed like a false sentiment, so Slater didn't respond.

King said, 'I mean it. These opportunities don't come often.'

About that, Slater thought.

But he nodded. 'Thanks, brother. I'll try.'

Coombs returned, and placed a fresh pint in front of King, who accepted it graciously.

Then they talked. Conversation bled on for an hour, then two, and Slater found it easier than usual to compartmentalise. Neither he nor King felt the need to share details of past operations, but they talked about what they did in a broader sense. The training that went into it, the sacrifices they made, the decade-plus of their lives they'd given up. They didn't discuss specific events — not the time they'd spent separately as vigilantes, on the run from their own government, nor the endless man-made disasters they'd prevented by the skin of their teeth, disasters so staggering that their success would have changed the course of history.

Coombs didn't pry.

He knew better.

But as the minutes turned to hours, and the conversation flowed smoother and smoother, the old man got a strange look in his eyes. Slater noticed first, and then he saw King pick up on it. Coombs held eye contact for a little too long, as if the conversation was just surface-level fodder, as if under that surface he was contemplating something drastic. Slater knew Coombs was no threat, but it sure felt that way. It mirrored the instincts he experienced in the field when he sensed the arrival of something unexpected.

What that entailed... he wasn't sure.

The big antique clock on the far wall inched past ten p.m., and Coombs said, 'Well, I best be going, lads.'

Slater figured there was no use continuing to pretend there wasn't something else there.

He said, 'Is there anything you wanted to say, Jack?'

Coombs met his gaze. 'You're a smart fucker, you know that?'

Slater smirked. 'We both know something's up.'

King nodded his agreement.

Coombs said, 'I should have known who I was talking to.'

Slater said, 'We've been reading people for fifteen years.'

'There's something I have in mind,' he said. 'I didn't think about connecting the dots until I was right here in front of you.'

Silence.

Coombs said, 'I have a job opening.'

'We don't deal with the private sector,' King said.

Coombs looked across at him. 'You mentioned before you were independent contractors for the government. How is that exclusive? What's stopping you from doing something for me?'

'*We* are,' Slater said. 'We're stopping ourselves. We're not in that business, Jack.'

'I am,' Coombs said. 'And I've got a gig coming up that I'm all out of options for. It's a simple job. Straightforward. No twists or turns. It's protection detail.'

'And there's a thousand spec-ops washouts who would do protection detail with a lot more enthusiasm than we would.'

Coombs said, 'You shouldn't be so hostile to the possibility. It's a win-win. Easy money. It'd really help me out. I only need you, Will. It's a one-man job.'

'I can't,' Slater said.

'I'm telling you—'

'It's not about the job,' Slater said. 'For one, we'd never be allowed. We're on call twenty-four-seven. If our handler comes to us with an op, we need to act on it within the hour.

We're something of a last resort for the government. We're the guys you call when every option is exhausted and the world's about to go to shit. That's not something we can step away from. And, secondly, I'm unavailable. I'm going on vacation tomorrow.'

Coombs stared. 'You're really going to feed me all that shit about being irreplaceable and then follow it up by saying you're going on holiday?'

'It's a one time thing,' Slater said. 'I used all my favours. I won't get this opportunity again.'

'Wouldn't pick a guy like you to take holidays.'

'Then you have good judgment. This is my first. Ever. I'm putting my foot down, Jack. This is something I need for my own sanity. If you want the truth, I've met someone. She's taking me on holiday, and I don't have the nerve to refuse. Besides King here, she's the only good thing in my life. I'm not about to fuck that up. I've been pretending I'm super-human for too long. I need these next few days.'

It was the longest he'd spoken all evening. Coombs sat there, shifting his weight in the seat. Slater could see the man's distress. He knew, even without Jack telling him, that the job was important. Perhaps crucial for his own reputation. But Slater couldn't budge. This was his life.

Coombs said, 'I don't want to do this.'

'Do what?'

'Do you remember Coronado?'

Slater paused, then said, 'You're right. You don't want to do this.'

'I have to. This is the most important gig of my life, and I need someone who won't fuck it up. You're right — there's a thousand spec-ops washouts I could find. None of them are like you.'

'Don't make me choose between who I owe.'

'You owe *me*,' Coombs said. 'You know you do.'

King said, 'Care to enlighten me?'

Coombs turned. 'It was during BUD/S, at the Naval Special Warfare Command Centre on Coronado Island. I walked in on Will and our best-looking female instructor in a supply closet. It was enough to kick them both out of the military. We barely accepted an angry glance during training. They both would have been out on the street if I did what I was supposed to. But I didn't. Because I saw potential in your friend here. Turns out my judgment was right. But he relied on me, and now I'm relying on him.'

King glanced at Slater, and instantly he knew it was true.

5

Now it was King's turn to think.

In truth, he didn't need long.

As much as he hated to admit it, there was a code. He and Slater had shared it the whole time they'd known each other, and they'd never once broken it. Never even considered it. If you worked in their world, you needed reassurances. You had to know you could rely on your brothers-in-arms.

Loyalty trumped everything else. It cut through every arrangement, every agreement.

You owe someone in their world, you *never* turn it down.

So he knew why Slater was squirming. The man loved Alexis with his whole heart, but this was the brotherhood. Coombs had played his ace, and now there was no going back.

Don't make me choose.

King couldn't let him.

He knew how badly Slater needed time away. He knew how effortlessly the strings of sanity could be cut in their world. King knew he himself was in a good place. He could take the verbal barrage from Violetta he knew would come. He could be the fall guy.

So he said, 'I'll do it.'

Coombs met his gaze. 'No.'

Slater stared at him too, but it was a look of profound and silent appreciation.

King said, 'You said you needed Will. I'm the same thing. Cut from the same cloth. And I'm available.'

Coombs shook his head. 'It's the principle. I wouldn't ask that of you. I don't know you. You owe me nothing.'

King jerked a thumb at Slater. 'I owe him everything.'

Coombs went quiet.

King said, 'It's not just a vacation. For the first time in his life, he's giving his time to someone he cares deeply about. He's never done that before. The job has always come first. Don't rip that away from him.'

Coombs stayed quiet.

King said, 'I'm free. And I'm willing.'

'You'd do that for him?' Coombs said.

'We've done a whole lot more for each other than that.'

Coombs nodded.

King said, 'What's the job?'

'My biggest client,' Coombs said. 'Sam Donati. He needs protection.'

King registered the name. It was familiar. 'Donati Group?'

'Yeah. The king of logistics. You know... transportation and shipping. He's worth a few billion, at least, judging by the size of his empire. I'm on a trial period with him. He's going to Moscow to negotiate a deal with a rival conglomerate. He's paranoid that they'll try to take him out over there. I've had a look over the dossier compiled by his security — leads they fished from the dark web — and I'm convinced it's legit, too. The man's made his fair share of enemies.'

'Is it justified?' King said. 'Is he playing by the rules?'

'As far as I can tell he is. In fact, I think it'd be right up your alley. It seems like he's the only clean fish in a dirty pond. That's why he's being targeted. Because he refuses to follow the trend. You'd think that'd put him out of business, but it hasn't. He's lingering, and he's pissing off his global competitors, and they're a little more... unsavoury. They're willing to do something about it.'

'I'm not a bodyguard,' King said.

'The future of my business rides on this,' Coombs said. 'Donati is the ultimate client. That's why I'm pulling out all the stops. I was going to turn to one of the spec-ops boys you mentioned. But they'd do a subpar job, and you know it. Donati is meticulous. He needs to be impressed. In all likelihood, nothing will happen over there. But I still need to go for broke. I don't think it was a coincidence that I ran into the pair of you at such a pivotal point of my civilian career.'

King went quiet.

Coombs said, 'You're right. You're not a bodyguard. But you're the best. And I need the best.'

'You don't know anything about me,' King said. 'We haven't told you anything at all, if you really think about it.'

'You told me the nature of your line of work. You told me you've been doing it for nearly fifteen years. And you're sitting here in front of me, still breathing.'

Silence.

Coombs said, 'You two are the best.'

King temporarily disregarded the old man. He turned to Slater, made sure he was looking him in the eyes. Slater stared back.

King said, 'Do you owe this man?'

Slater said, 'Yes.'

'Then that's all there is to it.'

'There's something else,' Coombs said.

King raised an eyebrow.

The old man hunched over and leant forward like he was about to share nuclear launch codes and said, 'It's lucrative. I didn't share that at first, because I wanted to make sure you were in it for the right reasons.'

King looked at Slater, and they both smirked.

Coombs sat back, perturbed.

'What?' he said.

King said, 'How lucrative?'

'Donati's offered me a hundred grand for the best,' Coombs said. 'I'm happy to charge full fee, knowing I'm contracting someone like you. I'm willing to give you seventy-five percent.'

Again King looked at Slater.

This time, they laughed.

Again Coombs said, 'What?'

This time with a little more verve.

Now it was King's turn to hunch over and lean forward. He beckoned Coombs closer and lowered his voice and said, 'Keep it.'

Coombs said, 'What?'

Like a broken record, unable to compute.

King said, 'We never needed the money. This was about what Slater, and therefore I, owe you.'

'But... you need to be paid.'

'No,' King said. 'I don't.'

'This doesn't make sense.'

King turned to Slater. 'He doesn't understand.'

Slater knew what needed to be done. He reached out and grabbed Coombs' forearm and turned the old man toward him. He said, 'On average, we were paid seven figures a gig, and between us we completed hundreds of successful gigs. On top of that, two years ago I drained a bank account belonging to a Macau triad. It had a mid-nine-figure balance. Do you understand now?'

Coombs sat there, refusing to outwardly react.

Inwardly, stunned.

Finally, he said, 'Mid-nine-fig— what the fuck? How much money do you two have?'

'Plenty,' King said. 'So keep your hundred grand. When do I get to work?'

6

————

Eighteen hours later, Slater sat on a commercial flight beside the love of his life.

En route to a destination where his only intention was to relax.

He should have been over the moon.

He wasn't.

He had history at Alexis' vacation spot of choice. Sure, he had history all across the globe.

This was different.

His gut churned. The resort they'd be staying in was supposed to be a surprise, but by some cruel twist of fate he thought he knew exactly where they were headed.

Beside him, she was oblivious. He intended to keep it that way.

'Tulum,' he said. 'Mexico. I like it.'

Alexis nestled against his shoulder. When he spoke, she looked up at him and he drank in the warmth of her eyes. Stark green, rimmed by long lashes. She had pale skin, and still wore her straight black hair forward in bangs that stopped just above her eyebrows.

When she looked at him, nothing else mattered.

She said, 'You approve?'

She knew everything. What he did for a living, what he'd done his whole life. Where he'd come from — the broken childhood, the devastation he'd crawled out of, the warrior he'd forged himself into. He'd told her about his most dangerous operations, how close he'd come to death over and over and over again. He'd opened up about how that affected him, how it had shaped him, made him acutely aware of his own mortality.

She knew it all.

Except for one key area.

Ruby Nazarian.

He didn't want to talk about her. Not with Alexis, not with King, not with anyone. She'd died saving San Francisco, just as he'd finally decided he could commit to someone after a lifetime of womanising. It wasn't that he really cared about the number of women he slept with — he'd simply been terrified of anything permanent. His career, and his life, were as abnormal as one could imagine. He'd never wanted to place that burden on anyone. He didn't want to let anyone care about him, because in all likelihood he'd die on the next op.

It was a shadow that had followed him his whole career, always in the background, ever-present. He'd never believed in superstition, but this had been different. He knew, without a doubt, as soon as he opened up to someone, something terrible would happen to either them, or him. So he'd stuck to his guns.

Until Ruby.

She was from his world, a fellow operative, much younger but with a similar level of experience. A protege of the Lynx program, a clandestine government initiative that raised young girls as assassins and unleashed them into the world when they came of age.

She was like a second piece of him.

Two sides of the same coin.

And she'd died. As soon as he'd opened up.

As he'd predicted.

It had taken him months to move on. He still hadn't — not fully. He wasn't sure if he ever would. But Alexis meant just as much to him, if not more. Because she was as strong and as fierce as Ruby Nazarian and simultaneously a civilian. It didn't make sense. She had no combat experience, nothing to do with the world of espionage and murder, but she had an iron-like will. Which somehow made it more impressive. Months ago, during a blackout in New York, Slater had met her through a chance encounter, and since then they'd been inseparable.

But now they were barrelling toward Tulum, toward a small seaside town in Mexico where Slater had reunited with Ruby Nazarian nearly a year ago.

What are the odds?

He promised himself he wouldn't mention it.

She said, 'I still can't believe we're doing this.'

'I pulled some strings. My handler was okay with it.'

Violetta hadn't been.

But Slater was stubborn. And eventually, he'd got his way.

'When you told me about what you did, I thought you'd be away for most of the year. But since New York...'

'That's not what my life is anymore. It was, in the past. Now we're used sparingly. The last resort, so to speak. This,' — he waved a hand around the civilian plane — 'never would have been allowed when I was in Black Force.'

'But now Black Force is gone?'

He nodded. 'It was always flawed. When those flaws were exposed, it imploded.'

'So now you're... what, exactly? I don't think you've ever put a label on it.'

'Independent contractor.'

'Is that what you're calling it?'

He nodded. 'It's the closest I'll get to hitting the nail on the head. Truth is...'

He trailed off.

She put a hand on his forearm.

He'd looked away, but now he returned his gaze. 'I don't know what I am. And...'

He looked away again.

Something had seized in his throat. Hesitation. He knew what he'd been about to say. He didn't dare let it out.

But everything had changed since she'd become a permanent part of his life.

And when she tightened her grip on his forearm, he knew he could never hide the truth from her.

He said, 'I don't know what I want anymore.'

She hesitated.

Like her heart had stopped in her chest.

He looked over. 'What?'

'You mean... with us?'

He took her hand. 'No. You're one of the best things that's ever happened to me.'

'You don't need to say that if it's not—'

'It's true. That's why I'm questioning everything else.'

She froze.

Realising what he meant.

Realising why he'd been so quiet over the last couple of weeks.

She said, 'You want out?'

He tensed up. He didn't mean to, but the words hung in the sterile tube of the plane, and he turned them over and over again in his head. His core tightened, and his fingers came into his palms as he balled his fists. He tried his best to hide it, but she was leaning against him, and she felt it.

He tried to relax.

It took a few seconds.

Eventually, he settled.

But his pulse had sped up. He knew she felt that, too.

He said, 'You know me, maybe better than anyone. What do you think I want?'

She said, 'I think you know. I think you're just terrified to admit it.'

They lapsed into a comfortable silence, and minutes later she dozed off against his shoulder.

He stewed restlessly.

Because he knew she was right.

7

At the same time, back in Manhattan, King faced off with a perplexed receptionist in an impressive yet anonymous building in the Financial District.

His voice seemed to echo off the polished floor beneath him as he said, 'Trust me.'

The guy behind the desk — dressed in a neatly pressed suit with a name badge that read FRANCIS — furrowed his giant eyebrows. He was early thirties, so King understood the hesitation. Francis had probably worked for Donati Group all his twenties, and now he considered himself something of a guardian for the inner circle of the conglomerate's head office. He sat in front of a teak-panelled wall, and had a corded phone in a cradle in front of him with an array of buttons ranging from IT to Accounting.

Francis said, 'Sir, no one has notified me of your arrival, and I assure you it is quite unlike Mr. Donati to not have an appointment scheduled. If you have a complaint, I can be sure to put you in touch with—'

King said, 'Pick up the phone. Call your boss. Tell him I'm here.'

'Sir, I'm afraid—'

King gave thanks for his giant wingspan as he reached over the desk. He took Francis' shoulder in one hand and applied the slightest touch of pressure, which against a pencil-necked civilian was more than enough to keep him glued to his chair. Then he lifted the phone off the receiver with his other hand, and used his index finger to stab the button with DONATI scrawled next to it in freehand on an otherwise blank sticker.

Francis shouted, '*Hey!*'

The line rang twice and was answered.

'What?' a bombastic deep voice snapped.

'Jason King. I'm here to see you. Jack Coombs sent me. Your assistant is being an uncooperative little shit so I had to take matters into my own hands.'

A pause.

Then the booming voice said, 'Be right out. Wait there.'

'Thank you.'

King put the phone back on its cradle and took his hand off Francis' shoulder like nothing had happened at all.

The kid leapt to his feet and snatched the phone up in trembling hands. His voice was shaky as he said, 'Security will be here in a minute. I suggest you leave.'

King sighed, and pressed a finger into each of his closed eyelids.

'Kid,' King said, and he injected the faintest hint of a threat into his voice for the first time.

Francis looked up, and froze.

King said, 'Just sit down. Carry on with your work. Your boss will be right out.'

'You've disrupted his routine,' Francis said. 'That is simply not acceptable, and to make things worse—'

A door flew open down the hall, out of both of their lines of sight.

Francis froze, his face paling.

'Great,' the kid said. 'You probably just got me fired.'

King didn't respond.

Sam Donati materialised in the reception area sixty seconds later. Which meant his office was further away than King had thought, which in turn meant he'd thrown the door open with more verve than normal. King wondered if the man was angry, or if he just approached everything his life with the same rigid intensity.

It turned out to be the latter.

The guy was six-five at least, with an aura like thunder. There was something bristling underneath his exterior, something King didn't often see outside of live combat situations. He guessed that was the intensity needed to survive in the cutthroat world at the top of the corporate hierarchy. This was the realm where men and women worth ten figures searched and probed for any sliver of weakness to be exploited. You had to be uncompromising, but above all you had to be willing to put it all on the line, which had to be approached with the level of focus that existed behind Donati's big brown eyes.

In a roundabout way, King respected that.

Donati sized King up in a single glance, strode forward and offered a huge hand.

King shook it. The billionaire's grip was strong. Nothing King hadn't felt before.

Donati said, 'My assistant wasn't giving you too much hassle, was he?'

Over Donati's shoulder, King saw what little blood was left in Francis' cheeks drain away.

'No,' King said. 'He was more than accommodating.'

That didn't seem to compute. Francis sat rigid and stunned, waiting for the other shoe to drop. But it didn't. King didn't have time for petty squabbles. Life was not about one-upping anyone and everyone. The kid was harmless.

Donati flicked a fat finger in his direction, wheeled around and set off down the hallway. King followed.

They went all the way to a big oak door, which led through to an office with a view that rivalled King's penthouse. He took in the sweeping vision of Central Park, and the hundreds of skyscrapers dotting the perimeter of the gargantuan chunk of greenery. It never got old. No matter how many times he soaked it in.

Donati stared at him, assessing his reaction. He probably found it odd that King didn't seem awed.

He said, 'You like the view?'

King hid a smirk. *I see it every day.*

But there was no justifiable reason to explain that based on the role he was playing, so he said, 'Yeah. It's great.'

The rest of the office was furnished with Scandinavian minimalism. King saw a desk that would have cost six figures, and a chair that would have cost five, and a collection of diverse art pieces that could have cost anywhere from four to nine.

The world of art would always be a puzzle to him.

Donati seemed to notice. The man was perceptive. 'You don't like the paintings?'

King shrugged. 'Art's not my thing.'

'Nor is it mine,' Donati said. 'But there's advantages to it.'

'Advantages?'

Donati didn't seem to care about divulging trade secrets. 'You know why it's so good? Because pieces can be worth whatever the hell you want them to be.'

'I'm not following.'

The big man pointed to a framed piece hanging on the teak-panelled wall next to his desk. It was comprised of a white backdrop with tastefully applied streaks of red. King figured he could have painted the same thing with his eyes closed.

Donati said, 'Let's say I buy that for a million, and then I donate it to a college as an act of charity. A few years later, I can claim it's worth ten. Because, you know, art. That's nine million dollars worth of tax deductions. The college isn't going to say otherwise. I just gave them the painting, after all. What's the IRS going to do? It's bulletproof.'

King didn't say a word.

Donati said, 'You think I'm gross.'

'You're not paying me to think,' King said. 'You're paying me to keep you alive. Right now, that's all I care about.'

Donati smiled. 'Now you're speaking my language. Straight to the point. I like it.'

As the sun set behind them, he pointed to a chair in front of the desk.

He said, 'Let's get down to business.'

8

Slater wasn't used to the civilian world.

He existed in a different sphere of society. His usual life was a carefully constructed system to maximise his time. He didn't cook his own meals. He didn't wait in lines. He didn't unnecessarily complicate his schedule. He trained as hard as humanly possible, then he recovered as efficiently as humanly possible, and between those moments he rested and fuelled his body and strategised.

Then, when he was sent out on operations, he was blessed with the satisfaction that there was nothing else he could have done.

If he failed, it was because the task was insurmountable. Not because he'd slacked off in training. Not because he'd cut corners. He always ensured there were no corners to cut.

So this was odd. Standing in line at Cancun International Airport, waiting to get his false passport stamped, Alexis' fingers intertwined around his. There was no place he'd rather be. All that efficiency, all that prioritisation — it was draining. Sometimes he forgot that life didn't have to be one endless stream of never-ending improvement.

Sometimes you could rest.

Sometimes that's the only place true stillness lay.

Alexis noticed he had withdrawn. 'What?'

He looked over. 'Nothing.'

'You're thinking about something.'

'I'm always thinking about something.'

'Care to share?'

He looked into her eyes. 'There's a lot to it. But I guess, when you break it down... I'm just happy to be here.'

'I don't want you to say that if you don't mean it.'

'Have I ever said anything I didn't mean?'

She touched his lips with hers. 'No. You haven't. That's what I appreciate more than anything. That's not an easy thing to do.'

'I've never seen you do it, either. And trust me — I can tell.'

She said, 'That's deliberate.'

'Is it?'

'You're not a regular catch. I'm taking this seriously.'

He leant closer to her and muttered, 'I couldn't tell.'

He winked.

They fell silent. That was something else he appreciated about their bond — the fact that they didn't need to fill the quiet moments with superficial conversation just for the sake of talking. When they said anything, there was a purpose behind every word.

They made their way past a tired customs officer without incident. Alexis didn't even blink at the name RONALD WOOD on Slater's passport. She knew it came with the territory. The document had been manufactured by an expert counterfeiter discreetly employed by one of the subdivisions Violetta controlled, who'd doctored the serial number without tainting the hologram.

The thought of Violetta, and the world she operated within, churned his insides.

He forced it all aside.

Enjoy this, he thought. *Then figure out your future.*

That thought alone threatened to spiral him into indecision. He'd never even considered getting out. Not when King fled with Klara all those years ago. Not when he found himself excommunicated from the division he'd spent the majority of his adult life working for. Whether he'd been a vigilante or an operative, he'd never wanted to abandon the fight. It was as much a part of him as breathing.

So is that really what this is? Or are you just confused?

He didn't know.

They hired a small nondescript hatchback from a rental car service outside the airport, and Alexis demanded to drive.

Slater protested. 'I've been cooped up in a tube all afternoon. I'm not used to this. Let me do *something.*'

'But when we get there,' she said, 'how will you know where our destination is?'

He shrugged. 'How many resorts can there be in Tulum?'

He knew exactly how many resorts there were in Tulum.

She said, 'There's a few. I've picked a good one. You won't know until we get there.'

I already know, he thought.

He couldn't fight down the sensation that fate would lead him there again.

But he begrudgingly stood down.

Now wasn't the time to tell her.

That he feared they were heading to the exact place he'd reunited with the last woman he loved.

They took Highway 307 south out of Cancun, and the chasm in Slater's gut widened. With increasing disbelief, he realised he hadn't even felt this terrible before his most dangerous operations. He tried to discern why.

Because, he realised, *this means something to you.*

Nothing used to mean anything to you.

He knew it was true. For fifteen years he'd considered his life forfeit. He'd accepted the warrior state of mind, the understanding that death on the battlefield was infinitely preferable to a life lived without taking risks. In the end it was a simple equation, and he'd always broken things down that way. He had talents, and he'd worked impossibly hard to hone those talents, and if he didn't use them he was practically committing a sin.

But when was it enough?

Would he ever be done?

Could he *choose* to be done?

Those thoughts had slowly crept in over the last couple of months, and now he had someone in his life he knew would be devastated if he died.

He'd never had that before.

He shifted in his seat so he could see Alexis. She was fixated on the road ahead, her green eyes quietly determined. There was something fundamentally genuine there. She had planned this trip to the nth degree, all for him. He realised it was a foreign sensation to him. He couldn't remember the last time, outside of King repeatedly saving his life, that someone had done something kind for him. That had never been his world.

He turned back and stared out the window.

Maybe it could be.

9

By the time King and Donati's conversation reached its natural conclusion, it was well and truly dark outside.

They'd gone round in circles for most of it. Donati pried, and King kept his lips firmly sealed.

Now, the billionaire gave it one final attempt. 'I can't pay you if I can't trust you.'

King shrugged. 'Then don't pay me. I'm doing a favour for an old friend.'

'I've spent an hour trying to get your past out of you,' Donati said, as if that meant something monumental.

King didn't bite.

Donati followed it up with, 'Do you know how much an hour of my time is worth?'

'Not as much as mine's worth,' King said. 'Because my time will keep you alive. And that's something you can't buy.'

'I need something. Jack gave you his strongest recommendation, but he wasn't any more cooperative than you're being now. I can't make decisions based on murky implications. That sort of impulsiveness isn't something that carries you to the heights I've reached.'

'Okay,' King said.

'Well?'

King rubbed a hand through his hair, sat forward and placed it firmly on the table. 'Are you not following?'

'I mustn't be.'

'I don't care what you think about me,' King said. 'You need me for Close Personal Protection work. I can tell you I'm probably the most qualified person on the planet for that, but I can't tell you what those qualifications are. You can draw your own conclusions. Truth is, I don't need to be here, and I don't need the money. So either accept me or don't.'

'You have a lot of money,' Donati said. 'You live here in Manhattan, and you weren't impressed in the slightest by the view from this office. You can't talk about the work you've done in the past. So it was lucrative, and it was off the books. Am I understanding what you're getting at?'

'I don't care what you think I'm getting at.'

Donati stared. 'I never get treated like this.'

King said nothing.

Donati said, 'I kind of like it.'

King stayed quiet.

'You're not a pushover.'

'I'm the furthest thing from a pushover. Now am I working for you or not?'

'You are,' Donati said. 'Did Jack fill you in on the details?'

'You're going to Moscow. You're not exactly revered over there. You think your competitors might try removing you from the equation.'

'I don't know how much Jack told you on top of that. But

I'm hated because I'm doing things the right way. I'm not exactly playing by their rules. Because their rules involve media disinformation campaigns and disappeared officials.'

'He mentioned something about that.'

'Do you believe him?'

'I don't believe anything unless I see it for myself.'

'That's the way. Well, I hope I can prove it to you.'

'Sam,' King said, and the bigger man bristled at the use of his first name.

Donati raised an eyebrow.

King said, 'I don't need you to put on a show for me to prove you're the good guy. You could be corrupt a dozen different ways. I don't have the time to investigate. This isn't my usual field. I'm sure you could get more men from a private security firm to guard you, but Jack brought me in because I offer something a little different than your standard protection officer, no?'

Donati nodded.

King said, 'So let's get to specifics. How many men do you have?'

'I've contracted six to come to Moscow.'

'From where?'

'Veloce Security Services.'

King didn't know them, but he imagined they were the usual ex-military crowd looking for a consistent paycheque. He said, 'Do you know them all?'

'Yes.'

'How well?'

Donati said, 'I've been using the same core crew for every overseas trip since I established Donati Group. If you're asking whether I can trust them, the answer is yes.'

'You trust them completely?'

'Yes.'

'Then why am I here?'

'Call me extra paranoid.'

'You don't think they're competent?'

'They're perfectly competent. Jack suggested that you're a different level of competent.'

'If your competitors wanted to get to you,' King said, 'then private security would be their first port of call. Men who are in the trade for profit over decency. The easiest way to get rid of you is to buy off someone close to you. Have any of your men been approached?'

'No.'

'You're sure?'

'They haven't mentioned anything to me.'

'That doesn't mean they haven't been approached.'

'You seem overly suspicious of them.'

'It's my job to keep you alive.'

Donati mulled over that. King looked past him, at the twinkling skyline and the dark void of Central Park. He didn't want to admit it, but without Slater in New York, the city felt empty.

Neither he nor Slater were the sentimental types, but he couldn't deny he'd formed a bond with the man. Everything was habit, and he realised he'd made a habit out of having someone equally talented in his corner. Now, operating on his own didn't have the same ring of freedom to it.

It was hollow.

Dull.

Donati finally said, 'Okay. They'll still come, but you're staying closer to me for the entirety of this trip. I have to warn you—'

King raised an eyebrow.

'—that might rub them the wrong way.'

King didn't answer.

Donati said, 'They're alpha types. They'll see you as an enemy if you one-up them by coming in and taking over their duties.'

King almost laughed, but didn't.

Donati said, 'What?'

'That's the last thing on my mind. You don't have to worry about me.'

He had bigger things on his mind.

Like whether or not Will Slater would come back from Mexico a changed man.

10

They had an extra hour of time difference after flying from New York to Cancun, so they ended up completing the two hour drive to Tulum right as the sun melted below the horizon.

Alexis pulled off the road running parallel to the Tulum Sea, turning onto a giant slab of asphalt resting in front of the entrance to a seaside resort. Past the parking lot, Slater eyed luxurious huts spaced evenly across the white sand. She killed the engine, and he rolled down the window to soak in the atmosphere. It was quieter than the first time he'd been here. Back then the lot had been drenched in sun, beating down on the back of his neck as he sat in an open-topped jeep. He'd driven straight from the Tulum Naval Air Base, having caught a chartered flight on the government's dime.

He'd been here to collect Ruby, then threatened by Chinese *ying pai*.

Last time, he'd pulled into the lot with adrenaline flowing through his system. Now, he was calmer than he'd ever been.

Not on call.

Off the clock.

Free.

He didn't want to admit how good it felt.

Alexis' eyed the huts, and the waves gently lapping at the shore, and the golden sun melting into the horizon, and soaked in the calmness of it all. She turned to him and said, 'What do you think?'

He thought about telling her. About his past here, about he and Ruby's war with cartel *sicarios* through the streets and *cenotes* of Tulum.

But what good would come from that?

What would it achieve?

He let memories of the past fall away. He focused on what was in front of him. What he could control.

Which was all that mattered in the end.

He said, 'I love it.'

She leant across the centre console and kissed him. They didn't rush. They had all the time in the world. There'd be no frantic call from Violetta. It didn't matter if the world was ending. It could all come crashing down around them, and he'd refuse to answer that phone. It had been his only condition for the vacation. Back in Manhattan, he could theoretically take breaks, but there'd always be the tension of impending doom hanging over his head. The constant, permeating threat of the call that said, *We need you. Everything's gone to hell.*

When they parted, she pushed her door open. 'Come on. Let's get inside or we'll be here all night.'

The giddiness of a new relationship usually doesn't take long to fade, but Slater realised it still hadn't. There was an underlying happiness in his chest as he circled round to the trunk and lifted out their bags. He placed them on the ground between his feet, the asphalt still warm to the touch from the day's heat. Now, it was balmy, and he took the time to truly take in the view.

He wasn't here for work. He wasn't here to kill anyone. He was here to stop, and breathe.

It still didn't feel natural.

He wasn't sure if it ever would.

Alexis checked them in and they found their hut right as night fell over the beach, turning the white sand dark. Inside, it was practically a villa, with an enormous four-poster bed and authentic wood-panelled walls and broad windows looking out over the shoreline.

Alexis swung the door shut behind them.

Slater turned and dropped the bags. Looked at her.

She was as stunning as the first time he'd met her.

She noticed him staring, and raised an eyebrow. 'That's the look of someone who doesn't want to unpack first.'

He smiled.

Hours later, deep into the night, they fell apart in a state of mutual bliss. Slater realised he'd never had time disappear like that before. His one-night-stands of the past had been more about the conquest than the actual act itself. Sure, he was good at it, and his partners always showed their gratitude for his talents by returning the favour, but it was always a physical sensation. This was something else. He had a genuine connection with her, something that transcended the simple act of sex, and as they lay there naked, panting, he realised he was thinking about living in a hut like this for the rest of his life.

She ran a hand along his chest and said, 'You seem right at home.'

'I feel it.'

'Is it strange for you?'

He nodded.

There were no lights on in the villa, but outside the moon was silver and full against a cloudless backdrop, and it allowed them to make out the outlines of each others' faces in the semi-darkness. Slater touched a finger to her cheek and stroked it down. Feeling her body against his.

It felt right.

He said, 'Can I ask you something?'

'Of course.'

'This isn't set in stone, but how would you react if, hypo-thetically, I told you I did want out?'

'I'd ask you if it was an impulsive decision or not. What you do is all you've ever known. I don't want you to throw it away for me.'

'It wouldn't be for you,' Slater said. 'It would be for me.'

'That's what it needs to be.'

He said, 'My whole career I'd never even considered it. Because of my skillset, and how many people would die if I stopped using it. But it's strange now. I still understand that theory. But I don't feel compelled to obey it anymore.'

'You still see the point of doing what you do?'

'Yes,' he said. 'But now, when I think about stopping, I don't beat myself up about it. I'm drawn to it, actually.'

'Maybe you've done enough.'

He didn't answer.

In the darkness, he nodded.

She said, 'I'm not from your world. So take everything I say with a grain of salt. But the way I see it, it comes down to how much of yourself you're willing to sacrifice.'

He lay there, waiting for her to continue.

He needed to hear what she had to say.

She said, 'You've told me about the concussions. About the gunshot wounds, the stab wounds, the beatings and broken bones. It happens time after time because they put you in impossible situations. Where's your breaking point?'

'I don't know.'

'Do you want to reach it? You know it's coming. Do you want to hit it and fall apart on the job, or call it a day and tell yourself you've done enough?'

'Do you have an answer?'

'It's not my place to answer for you.'

'But I'm a part of your life. A large part. You should have a say.'

'Not with this,' she said. 'This is you.'

He went quiet.

She said, 'Otherwise you'll second-guess yourself. This needs to come from you and you alone.'

Silence.

She said, 'We have a few days here. Don't decide now.'

The silence drew out, and he sensed her close her eyes and drift away, utterly spent from the evening's activities. He followed suit, but a moment before he went out, he thought, *I've been thinking about this for weeks. I have decided.*

He just didn't know if he wanted to say it out loud.

Because that would make it real.

11

The next morning, King watched grey dawn creep into Manhattan's skyline from the porthole window of Donati's private jet.

It was a Gulfstream G550 with a maximum capacity of nineteen passengers and a price tag of $42 million. Donati Group owned it outright, having purchased it with excess cash three years earlier to outmanoeuvre a tricky year-end tax problem. Even though King had enough money himself for ten lifetimes, this was still a foreign world to him.

But he was barely fixated on the opulence of flying private.

All his situational awareness was on the six Veloce Security Services bodyguards dotting the interior of the jet.

They were taking turns eyeing him off — a foolhardy attempt to establish themselves as the top dogs. King didn't have time for a second of it. He hadn't even bothered to introduce himself. They knew who he was — they hadn't questioned him as he'd pulled up with Donati in the town car.

They'd simply stared, and stewed.

King had no problem with either of those reactions. He was used to getting shot, cut, beaten. As long as they weren't trading blows, he couldn't care less what they thought about him. They were a diverse group — three were white, one was black, and two were Asian. They were equally well-built, and they carried themselves with poise. There wasn't a shred of nerves on any of their features. They were used to keeping their cool in stressful situations. To the ordinary civilian, they were tough, scary men.

To King, they were amateurs.

He put himself in the shoes of an adversary, and brainstormed a million ways he could slip through the security detail to get to Donati. He figured a simple fake-out would do the trick. Approach one of them on the streets of Moscow, feigning ignorance, perhaps hiding behind the language barrier. Take advantage of a second's hesitation to spin the first guy around, use him as a human shield to drop three of them with a semi-automatic pistol, clearing a path to Donati's forehead. Then put a single piece of lead through his skull and worry about the rest of the opposition afterwards.

Simple enough.

All the combat training in the world can be rendered useless by the ability to swiftly generate chaos.

King had been living in chaos his whole career.

Donati lowered his bulk into the seat beside King, which sure didn't help his reputation with the rest of the protection detail. They saw their boss cosying up to the new guy and refused to hide their disgust.

King ignored them.

When the silence of the idling jet gave way to the low rumble of the pilot warming up the engines for take-off, Donati used the opportunity for a discreet conversation.

'Are you wondering why I haven't armed you?' he said.

King looked around. 'No one's armed.'

'We're flying private,' Donati said, 'but that doesn't make me omnipotent.'

'There's still customs to worry about,' King said, stating the obvious.

'Don't worry. We won't be without weapons for long. I have a man on the ground in Moscow.'

King didn't react.

Donati said, 'I'm waiting for your questions.'

'I don't have any.'

'You're not concerned about the legality?'

'Does it look like I'm concerned about the legality?'

'Attaboy.'

'You afraid I'm going to rat you out?'

'I must admit, the thought crossed my mind.'

'Why?'

Donati stared, making a silent judgment call.

Then he made it, and said, 'My man on the ground is a small-time arms dealer. There are warrants out for his arrest. A few years ago, before my first trip to Moscow, I put out feelers on the dark web and got in touch with him. Does that bother you?'

King smirked.

'I asked you a question.'

King turned to look at the big man. 'A small-time arms dealer is the least of my concerns.'

'You mean that?'

'Why would it bother me?'

Donati nodded, satisfied. 'That's what I like to hear.'

King fell quiet. He'd been about to add, *As long as you're doing the right thing.*

But he figured he'd see for himself.

Then he could decide.

The Gulfstream lifted off, and as King's stomach fell he said, 'I need you to know something.'

Donati looked over. 'Yes?'

'I can't go into detail, but this is a side gig for me. I'm usually preoccupied twenty-four-seven with my main job. I was granted leave to do this for you on one condition.'

Donati raised an eyebrow.

King said, 'I'm on call. This whole time. If shit hits the fan back home, I'll bail. I'm warning you in advance.'

Donati stared.

King said, 'Does *that* bother you?'

'Somewhat.'

'I'm sorry to hear that.'

'I'm paying you a lot of money for your undivided attention.'

'Firstly, you're not. My other job pays ten times as much. Secondly, I'm what you might consider a last resort in that job. So if the call comes, you're sure as hell going to want to let me answer it. Because the consequences won't be good if I don't.'

Donati said, 'If you bail, I'll be vulnerable.'

King made a sweeping gesture. 'What do you pay these guys for?'

'They're not you.'

'I'm flattered.'

Conversation petered out, merely because Donati sensed under the surface that King wasn't going to budge. If he needed to leave, that was a talk for another time. Nothing would change now by drawing out the confrontation unnecessarily.

So Donati turned back to the dossier in his lap and continued flicking through it.

King glanced down.

He hesitated.

Donati's finger had come to rest on a surveillance photo of a woman in her early twenties in secretarial garb. Eastern European, naturally beautiful. She was crossing the street, her long blond hair rustled by an invisible breeze, her eyes squinting against the glare of the sun.

Donati was fixated on the photo.

With a strange look on his face.

King said, 'Who's that?'

Donati flinched.

12

S later woke with the rising of the sun.

Alexis was already up, pottering around the open-plan kitchen. Most of the villa consisted of one main space, with a bedroom, kitchen and dining room all rolled into one. She wore nothing but her lingerie from the night before, and instead of getting out of bed he lay back and watched her carry a steaming kettle to the shelf of mugs above the sink, admiring how gracefully she moved. That was new, and strange. There had always been the incessant urge to *act*. Lying around in bed used to be a foreign concept. The old him would have been halfway to the gym by now.

She noticed he had his eyes open, and cocked her head from across the room.

He smiled. 'What?'

'This is a pleasant surprise.'

'What is?' he said, but he knew.

'You're... not doing anything.'

'Maybe I'm tired from last night.'

She narrowed her eyes mockingly.

Again, he said, 'What?'

'We've been together for two months,' she said. 'I know you don't get tired.'

That made him laugh.

She offered a smile. 'Poor me, right?'

He held up his hands like a criminal caught in the act. 'I'm here to please.'

She sauntered back to bed with a mug of brew-filtered coffee in each hand. He watched her plant one toned leg in front of the other in a mesmerising pattern. She passed one of the mugs across, and lingered over him for a second too long. He reached up, placed his palm on the back of her neck, and drew her in.

They kissed, long and slow.

Nowhere to rush to.

Nowhere to be.

He drank in the taste of her, the warmth of her lips on his. Breathed her scent. He was truly comfortable, and he couldn't remember feeling like that around anyone. His time with Ruby had been a whirlwind of foreign sensations. He'd never had the time to get to know her, to learn to co-exist with her in mutual harmony.

With Alexis, he did.

And he couldn't be happier.

She parted first, and tucked her feet underneath her butt, levering herself up into a seated position so she could take a sip of coffee. Now post-dawn, the first rays of sunlight came filtering in through the big windows, drenching every-thing in gold. Slater remained sprawled on his back. The mug insulated the boiling water enough to let him rest it on his chest. He sipped at it, too, and they both embraced the quiet.

In the quiet, Slater could think best.

He could empty his mind only the way a practiced meditator could.

She noticed him withdraw into himself.

She said, 'Are you deciding?'

'No,' he said. 'I'm just... being still.'

'You haven't done that before, have you?'

He said, 'All the time. I've been meditating for over a decade. But... never actually surrounded by stillness.'

She said, 'Go down to the shoreline.'

He hesitated. 'Now?'

'Yes. Go sit out there, on the beach. Find somewhere real quiet. Somewhere you won't be disturbed. Sit there for an hour. Maybe more. I think, when you're that still, and you come out of it... you'll know what you want.'

He took a moment to digest her words.

Then he said, 'I think you know me better than anyone.'

She said, 'I love you. That's why.'

He sat up, drawing closer to her. She placed a hand on his giant shoulder and kissed him, a little softer, a little more gentle.

Then she said, 'Go. Decide.'

He peeled the covers off. Stood up, slipped into a pair of athletic shorts, and went to the front door of the hut, still barefoot, still shirtless. The sun hit him, highlighting every nook and crevasse of his musculature. Highlighting the jagged scars, too.

He turned back. 'I love you, too.'

She nodded slowly.

She knew.

They both did.

He left the sanctuary of the villa and stepped out into the sand. It was fine and white and slipped between his toes. He made his way down to the shoreline, where the golden hue was seemingly stronger, and sat down a few feet from the gently lapping waves. There was no one else on the beach. Not this early. He was alone with his thoughts and the sun and the sand and the quiet breeze.

He shifted to a comfortable position, straightened his back, rested his hands in his lap, and closed his eyes.

Reality fell away.

It wasn't some fantastical sensation, complete with hallucinogenic visions and spiralling thoughts. No, it was just quiet. A total, complete quietness, something that could only be achieved by learning to *not* think. Which was awfully hard to do in the modern world. Thoughts came racing in, seemingly faster and faster with each passing day, and it took serious discipline to force them aside and simply *exist.*

Now, Slater existed.

Eventually his sense of time fell away too. Time is noticeable when you have a reference point. When you can compare what you did ten minutes ago to what you're doing now. Slater couldn't. It was all the same — closed eyes, dark vision, the calming sound of nature all around. There was nothing else.

He didn't think. Didn't feel. Didn't let his mind wander.

Didn't do anything at all.

It could have been an hour, but it might have been two or three. There was no way to know for sure, but he knew to open his eyes. A faint command from an unconscious region of his brain told him to bring his mind back to the present.

So he opened his eyes.

And there, with his mind completely empty and his thoughts completely still, he searched for the first thing to think about.

He found his answer.

It lit up his frontal lobe, bursting forth from his subconscious.

He stood up, slightly unsteady on his feet after what could have been hours of motionlessness. The sun was far higher in the sky. He realised it was close to midday. It somewhat unnerved him. It meant he'd been in a trance-like state for nearly five hours. His stomach grumbled in protest. His limbs felt stiff and heavy.

But his mind was clearer than ever.

He walked back to the hut. Alexis was still there. Fresh ingredients dotted the kitchen countertop. She'd been into town.

She put down the kitchen knife and turned to face him, her expression guarded. He could see how much this meant to her, and he admired the restraint was showing not to voice her own opinion on the matter. She knew he needed to decide for himself, and no one else.

He had.

She said, 'Did you decide?'

He said, 'I've given this everything. I'm done.'

13

Donati said, 'She's nobody.'

King let the silence drag out deliberately. He studied the surveillance photo closer. He guessed the image was taken somewhere in Moscow. King had been to Russia's capital before — the architecture of the shops in the background and the general vibe of the surrounding pedestrians fit the bill. It was certainly somewhere in Eastern Europe. Outside of that he couldn't be certain, but it made sense for it to be Moscow. The dossier appeared to contain information pertaining to the negotiations Donati was set to enter.

So she wasn't nobody.

King said, 'She looks like somebody.'

Donati looked up from the dossier, meeting King's gaze. 'You really don't trust me, do you?'

'I barely know you. I'm impartial toward you.'

'It's none of your business who she is,' Donati said, and then seemed to relent. 'But I respect you, and I want you on my side, so I'll clarify. She really is nobody.'

Donati placed a fat thumb on the top corner of the

image, highlighting one of the pedestrians in the background. The rest of the photo was blurry because of the woman taking up the foreground, but enough details were visible to make out his features. The guy was in his fifties, with a paunchy belly and a grey receding hairline. He wore a grey suit over a white dress shirt that seemed to prop up his sizeable gut. Outside of that, he looked like any ordinary white-collar Russian.

Donati said, '*He's* somebody.'

'Who is he?'

'The Chief Financial Officer for Zima Group.'

King knew almost nothing about Donati's forthcoming negotiations — it wasn't his job, so he simply hadn't worried about it. But he'd overheard snippets of conversation throughout their short time together, and pieced together a framework. Zima Group was Donati's biggest rival, a multi-billion dollar conglomerate that owned and controlled almost all the port facilities in Eastern Europe.

King shivered.

He had bad memories of a port in the Russian Far East.

Years ago, trouble in Vladivostok had brought him out of retirement.

He quashed that down, and focused on what he knew about the future. Donati was en route to Moscow to negotiate with Zima Group about a potential merger.

King said, 'Okay.'

Donati shifted his thumb an inch to the right, so it came to rest on the shopfront directly behind the paunchy man. There was nothing remarkable about the building — low, one-storey, shoddy, rundown. There was no signage visible. It could have been anything.

Donati said, '*That* is the reason I have this photo.'

'What is it?'

'One of Moscow's most notorious fetish clubs.'

'Oh.'

King scrutinised the image. The CFO was most definitely leaving the building in question. The small door behind him was in the process of swinging shut. It was hard to discern features from a CCTV feed across the street, but King thought he could see something close to guilt on the man's face.

King said, 'What goes on in that particular fetish club?'

Donati said, 'You don't want to know. Nothing illegal. Just... perverted.'

'So this is for blackmail?'

Donati said, 'Do you have a problem with that?'

'You seem to think I have a problem with everything.'

'You seem cautious. And wary.'

'Guilty. I like to know things. Doesn't mean I disapprove.'

'He's a piece of shit,' Donati said. 'I'm going to use this to get a better deal. They're all corrupt over here. It's a prerequisite for being an oligarch. I refuse to play by their rules, but if they're doing some shady stuff in their personal lives, I'm not above using it.'

'Trust me,' King said. 'I know what oligarchs are like.'

He refrained from adding, *I suspect you're the same, deep down.*

Because he didn't know for sure.

And until he had actual confirmation, everything else was irrelevant.

Donati said, 'Do me a favour.'

King raised an eyebrow.

Donati said, 'I get your shtick. You're morally righteous. You're inquisitive. But this is a murky world. I made a compromise with that information I just gave you, but when we touch down I can't waste time explaining every little thing you're suspicious of. I'm paying you to keep me alive. Is that clear?'

It was the first time the man had been firm with King.

King was unperturbed.

He said, 'That's fine.'

'We land in Moscow in eight hours. At Sheremetyevo. It'll be ten-thirty p.m. over there because of the time difference. I have town cars waiting to take us to our hotel. We're staying in the penthouse suite of the Zvezda. They've ensured we'll have total privacy — part of the asking price. Once we touch down, I'll alert our arms dealer, and he'll meet us at our suite with the weapons we ordered.'

'What did you get?'

'Glock 17s,' Donati said. 'And a few MP5s, just in case shit hits the fan.'

King nodded. 'Works for me.'

'Anything else you need to know?'

'There's two days of meetings, right?'

Donati nodded. 'We'll get a few hours of sleep tonight, then it's straight into business. My biggest fear is travelling to and from Zima's HQ. As far as I can tell, that'll be the opportune time to take me out and make it look like a regular road accident. And, let's face it, things will escalate when I reveal I have this photo.'

'How did you get it?'

'I have hundreds of people working directly for me,' Donati said.

He seemingly didn't feel the need to elaborate further.

King nodded.

Donati said, 'What else do you need from me?'

King shook his head. 'Nothing.'

'Did you want to run me through your procedures—?'

King gave the man a withering look, silencing him.

King said, 'You asked me to stop concerning myself with your business. I'll ask you to stop concerning yourself with mine.'

He could have elaborated. He could have said, *All it really comes down to is reaction speed. There's only so much tactical surveillance you can do before you've covered all your bases. If someone gets through the outer perimeter, all that matters is winning the game of instincts. That means being on guard, and I don't need your input for that.*

But Donati didn't need to know any of that.

The billionaire had his own problems to worry about.

King settled back into his seat.

Truth was, he didn't trust anyone.

Not Donati. Not his men. Not Zima Group.

He was here because Slater owed Coombs, and that was it.

14

Slater had reached his decision, but it didn't feel real.

Sure, he'd spent months considering it. Weeks seesawing back and forth, refusing to continue lying to himself. Now he'd meditated for close to five hours to confirm it.

But it was still all he'd known for fifteen years.

There was still so much to unpack.

He decided to cleanse himself the only other way he knew how. He'd heard rumours of a unique Tulum gym along the beach, but he'd never seen it in the flesh. He told Alexis he needed more time to think, and that he'd be back in a few hours. She didn't seem fazed. Neither of them were needy. Back home, she was a busy professional, and so was he. Different sorts of professionals, sure, but mutually busy. There wasn't an enormous chunk of time across their schedules to coordinate, so they had to cherish what time they *did* spend with each other. Now, in each other's company for days straight with nothing on their calendars, their time seemed endless.

Being apart for a few hours at a time was the least of their concerns.

He found the destination on his smartphone and strolled for the better part of half an hour along the shoreline, welcoming the harsh heat of the day. Perspiration broke out along the back of his neck and in his armpits, but it barely fazed him. Discomfort was second nature. He felt right at home at the height of it. He ended up encouraging the sweating by breaking into a comfortable jog, his bare feet sinking an inch or so into the damp sand with each footfall.

He pulled up to the Tulum Jungle Gym with a thin coating of sweat covering his entire body.

He paid the exorbitant daily fee at the reception desk, but he figured the price was justified. Half the outdoor gym rested on the beach itself, and the rest was composed of a collection of cabañas with traditional thatched roofs. The receptionist informed him that all the equipment had bamboo and wooden exteriors, with stone filling the inside to add weight. Slater took in the old-school setup and smiled.

It was primitive, primal, animalistic.

A throwback to simpler times.

Just what he preferred.

He found his tunnel vision, and tuned everything else out, and pushed his body to its physical limits. He lifted wooden, stone-filled barbells until his heart rate skyrocketed, then pushed harder by heaving sizeable boulders off the sand and hurling them over his shoulder. He repeated the process, sweating and panting, his muscles burning, his lungs screaming for mercy.

Everything else fell away, giving him time to think about what made him happy.

This did.

Life, as far as he was concerned, was simple. The rapid advancement of modernity across the first world had created swathes of unhappy, unfulfilled, unsatisfied people. He saw it every day back in Manhattan, every time he stepped out onto the street. He watched men and women in formal attire rush to their cubicles, their minds clouded by uncertainty, unsure of what they really wanted from life.

Slater didn't blame them. He'd grappled with the same issues for most of his career.

At first, he thought it was money he wanted. Black Force paid handsomely, but it only took a few months of financial freedom to realise he needed a better reason to throw his life on the line over and over again. Then, he pivoted into genuinely wanting to help people. But that too could only last so long. You couldn't ignore your selfish impulses forever. Sure, he wanted to do good, but it couldn't be his only reason for embracing a life filled with such an ungodly amount of suffering.

Eventually he had to learn to find joy in the suffering.

And he had.

So wanting out didn't mean abandoning what made him happy. Pushing himself, testing his limits, seeing what could be accomplished with his physical vessel — that gave him contentment. And as much as he didn't want to admit it, so did righting wrongs.

He decided it wouldn't be retirement.

Not completely.

But he had to step away from Violetta and her shadowy subdivision and the rest of the government.

He had to be free.

Maxing his heart rate, pouring sweat, he finished his

final boulder throw and dropped into the sand beside the giant rock.

It only took a few minutes to catch his breath, no thanks to unparalleled cardiovascular conditioning. He could recover from physical exertion like a world-class endurance athlete. By the time he sat up, head clear, mind sharp, his heart rate had plummeted.

He saw a future laid out before him.

He walked back to the villa. The afternoon sun was no less intense. Halfway back, he dove into the ocean to shed the salt caked to his skin from the workout. Enclosed by the coolness of the sea, stillness flooded him.

When he resurfaced, he opened his eyes to a new world.

A world without unending self-expectation. A world where he wasn't going to mentally beat himself up for slacking off. He'd given fifteen years to unconditional self-improvement, and he'd done everything for his country. He'd saved thousands of people. Millions, if you factored in the disasters he'd prevented.

He found an ultimatum, and etched it into his mind.

Alexis was waiting for him in the villa, her head buried in a faded paperback. She'd draped herself across one of the decorative reclining chairs to catch the rays of sun filtering in over the windowsill, and when he stepped inside she lifted her gaze to meet his. Her eyes glowed green in the sunlight.

Just like Ruby's had glowed.

She said, 'You okay?'

'Yeah.'

'You want to talk?'

'Maybe later.'

She nodded. 'There's no rush.'

Then he reconsidered. 'There's one thing I'm set on.'

She didn't pry. She waited for him to gather his thoughts.

He said, 'If I see someone in trouble, I'll help them. I can't turn away. That reflex... it's part of me by now. But I can't do it officially anymore.'

'Aren't you already unofficial?' she said, but she knew what he meant.

'No more employment,' he said. 'No more contracts. No more structure. It's like I've been weaponised my whole life. That's what I'm sick of. When I was a vigilante, I was happy.'

She said, 'Is that what you're going to be?'

'I can figure that out later. But now I know one thing.'

She nodded.

She knew.

But he said it anyway. He needed to say it out loud.

He needed to know he meant it.

He said, 'I'm done with the government.'

15

W hen they landed in Moscow, they waited aboard the jet for customs officials to conduct a sweep for any smuggled goods.

The plane was clean.

They handed over passports, including King's false documentation, and the Russians ushered them through without incident. Town cars took them to the luxurious Zvezda Hotel within the Garden Ring, and an hour after they'd settled in King heard Donati order a woman's death.

The necessary steps unfolded.

He moved from the antechamber to the office.

They made eye contact.

They had their confrontation.

It played out exactly how King thought it would.

He was ready.

As Donati roared, '*Help!*' he was already halfway rotated toward the closed door. He initiated a timer in his head, counting the seconds since Donati had screamed for help. He swept through a mental checklist of the six men working for Veloce Security Services. He ascertained who seemed to have their wits together the most, and settled on the African-American man with short close-cropped hair and intense eyes. That guy had sat deathly still the whole flight over, and the rest had fidgeted. He was ready to protect his boss at a moment's notice. And he was more athletic than the rest of his colleagues.

He'd come in first.

How tall was he?

King guessed six three, and planned accordingly.

When the door burst open, a body on the other side hastily smashing against it, King closed the gap and opened his hips and lashed out with a body kick before he'd even laid eyes on his target.

Sure enough, it was the dark-skinned guy.

And he was six foot three, as predicted.

He took one step inside the room and King's shinbone hit him in the liver like a steel bat. The sheer intensity of the pain he felt shut his body down, killing his ability to defend himself, and he sunk to his knees with a slack-jawed expression on his face. King didn't follow up with a knockout blow. That'd be extraneous, and he couldn't waste movement.

Instead, he waited for the inevitable logjam.

Sure enough, all six of them were in a simultaneous frenzy to get inside. When the first guy went down on his knees the two behind him switched gears and tried to skid to a halt, but that's almost impossible in a congested hallway with three more testosterone-fuelled bodyguards taking up the rear. One of them literally went head over heels as he caught his feet on the first man, and King locked in on his jaw with laser focus as he tumbled and kicked like he was punting a football. The toe of his boot connected and the guy suffered a broken jaw and went unconscious in unison.

King sidestepped the body as it face-planted the carpet

of the office and lunged forward, tying up the third guy in the doorway. This man had managed to come to a halt fairly smoothly, but King got a giant palm on the side of his head and smashed his skull into the door frame. It didn't put him all the way out, but the second time it did.

A member of the trio taking up the rear came barrelling forward, intent on catching King out of position.

King dropped the unconscious third man on top of the stunned first man and lunged backward, crossing the threshold again.

Creating the first lull in the action.

Which was intentional. Six on one was a serious problem, and required a degree of recklessness to even the odds. Three on one was manageable. King could now back off with the berserker-style offence and select his shots a little more comfortably.

Not that there was anything comfortable about fighting for his life.

Thankfully, he had a touch of experience in this realm.

The three remaining bodyguards clambered over their trio of fallen comrades. They shot a couple of curious glances at the first guy, who definitely wasn't unconscious, but definitely wasn't moving, either. The guy was still on his knees, his face contorted in a mask of agony, literally incapable of moving as his seizing liver turned his limbs to stone.

King backed off another step.

Pointed to the first guy while staring at the remaining three.

He said, 'You want what he got?'

No one answered. It was an unnecessary question in hindsight. To most people — even seasoned ex-military bodyguards — a fight is something rare. When a brawl breaks out, it's brutal and ruthless and often one-sided. On the street, whoever lands the first decent blow usually gets the upper hand. There isn't a whole lot of back-and-forth when you can break bones and tear muscle with a single well-placed punch or kick.

There isn't usually time to chat.

So the three remaining men had one mode: Attack. Their brains were flooded with unfamiliar stress chemicals, screaming, *Kill this motherfucker.*

There was no processing space to think, *Maybe he's right. Maybe he can do to me what he did to the first guy.*

They really should have considered it.

King faked an all-out charge at the first of the three and then pulled up short. It made the guy flinch, rooting him in place for the couple of seconds King needed to focus on the other two. He leapt forward, sensing a window of opportunity, and stomped down with the sole of his boot on the outside of the second guy's knee. With two hundred plus pounds of bodyweight behind the stomp, and the awkward angle with which he'd skewered it into the ligaments, the results weren't pretty. His whole leg contorted inward and he went down on it, adding more weight to the injury.

In the same smooth-flowing motion, King ducked into a crouch and pivoted at the waist and cocked his left hand and curled a fist and threw it with every ounce of kinetic energy he had to give.

Right into the unprotected liver of the third guy.

Who doubled over and hit the floor like he'd been disembowelled.

King straightened up, and saw the final man charging at him, but now it was one on one.

The guy threw a right hook, and it was pretty respectable. It actually came close. King used a dash of head movement to slip to the side — boxing 101 — and then the guy was right there, inches away, vulnerable and exposed. He'd overcommitted with the right hand and now he was stretched out like an amateur, about to stumble past King.

King didn't let him.

He smashed his calloused elbow into the centre of the guy's forehead and smacked his brain around in his skull. The guy didn't go out cold, which was also pretty respectable. But he sure as hell didn't play it off like it was nothing. He stumbled a couple of steps in a semi-conscious state, his equilibrium gone, his balance non-existent, his gait that of a baby deer learning how to walk.

He actually reached the desk, and planted his palms down on its oak surface, and made a second of woozy eye contact with Donati.

Then, in his clouded state, he seemed to remember that he was in a fight.

He turned around.

King struck him in the face with an open palm, adding insult to injury. He only put as much weight into the palm strike as he knew he needed. It flipped the switch inside the guy's brain, capping off the performance, and he went limp and collapsed at the foot of the desk.

It was a gesture designed to intimidate.

King had taken care of Donati's last man by practically swatting him aside.

King paused to give Donati time to process what had happened.

Four men out cold. Two shut down by liver strikes. No one around to put up anymore of a fight.

Donati tried to keep his composure, but his throat turned redder, and sweat broke out across his upper lip.

King said, 'Pick up the phone. Call off the hit.'

16

Donati didn't exactly burst into motion.

So King switched gears.

He backed up a couple of steps and came to a halt beside the guy he'd hit with the clean liver kick. The man still sported the same mask of agony, the same twisted features and inhuman grimace and general air of surrender. King put a hand on the back of his neck and tilted him back a few inches so the downlighting in the office caught his features.

Presenting him to Donati as an example.

King said, 'I can very easily do this to you.'

Donati didn't respond.

King said, 'These six men are the only help you have in-country. Besides me, of course. I could keep you in this penthouse for as long as I like. I could make things very painful. I don't think you're even remotely prepared to deal with it.'

Donati said nothing.

King said, 'Think about your options.'

In his head, the clock ticked. It had been just over sixty

seconds since Donati had got off the call. King had spent the first thirty stepping into the office and talking to the man, and the other thirty taking out his entire entourage.

King said, 'I won't give you any more time.'

Donati reached for the phone on the desk.

He picked it up, thumbed a button, and pressed it to his ear.

'Speaker,' King said.

Before it had finished ringing, Donati lowered it and thumbed the touchscreen. The ringing erupted from the phone's tinny speakers, filling the silence in the office.

It connected.

A low voice said, 'Yes?'

'There's been a development,' Donati said. 'You haven't moved in yet, have you?'

'We're seconds out.'

'Call it off.'

'Why?'

'Do I pay you to question me?'

A pause.

Not a long one.

Then the voice said, 'Okay. There'd better be a damn good reason for this. This took some serious prep.'

The call disconnected.

King breathed out.

Donati gently placed the phone back down and surveyed the scene of destruction all around him. He grimaced. He said, 'What happens now?'

'Now we talk.'

'I don't want to talk. I did what you wanted. What is this? You going to rat me out now?'

'We're going to talk,' King said. 'You're not in a position to say no.'

'You're doing your job terribly,' Donati noted.

'I think I'm doing my job just fine.'

'What is it you want to know, exactly?'

'The supposed CFO of Zima Group,' King said. 'The guy in the background of the surveillance photo. That was bullshit.'

Donati hesitated, as if ashamed to admit he'd been ousted.

Then, begrudgingly, he nodded.

King said, 'It was always the girl, wasn't it?'

Another long pause.

Then a shrug.

Donati said, 'Yeah. I came up with the other thing on the fly. You bought it.'

'You're a good liar,' King said. 'Explains why you're a billionaire.'

Silence.

He hadn't asked a question, so Donati hadn't entertained him with a response.

King said, 'So what exactly did I just prevent?'

'Does it matter? You're just going to kill me anyway.'

'That's not set in stone.'

'Isn't it?'

Donati injected skepticism into his tone, but King saw through the veil. He'd generated hope in the big man. A faint possibility that this might actually be reversible. That his career, reputation and life were all still salvageable.

King said, 'Give me the truth, and I might let you live.'

Donati thought about it.

Behind King, someone stirred.

He turned to see the recipient of the second liver shot clambering to his feet. His face was pale, and his eyes were wide, but he had his wits about him. The other five were nowhere near coherent. King stepped in, steadied the guy by putting a hand on one of his shoulders, and then used his other fist to thunder an uppercut into the man's gut.

He went straight back down, whimpering in pain.

King turned back.

Message received.

'Okay,' Donati said. 'Fine. I used the CFO of Zima Group as a cover story because it was front and centre in my mind.'

'Why?'

'He's not in the photo. The guy in the background is just a civilian. There's no fetish club. But that girl...'

He trailed off.

His cheeks flushed.

It can be shameful to say out loud what you were going to do behind closed doors.

King said, 'Say it.'

Donati said, 'The CFO's the one ultimately calling the shots in the forthcoming negotiations. And there's a deadline. No matter the personal troubles, Donati Group and Zima Group need to leave these meetings with an inked agreement. It's written into the contracts. So, I figured, if his daughter had an accident...'

King said, 'Christ.'

'Then he'd be pliable. The boardroom would be the last thing on his mind. We could have acquired the terms we wanted without difficulty. He would have signed anything.'

'You honestly think that's the way to go about it?'

'You didn't ask me for an apology,' Donati said. 'You asked me for an explanation.'

'Jack said you were one of the good guys.'

'Jack's naive, then.'

'Why are you being so upfront? You've got to know I'd never take your side on this.'

'I respect you enough to not waste your time,' Donati said. 'That's what happened. I'm not proud of it. Big business is something incomprehensible to most. It's a whole different ball game up here.'

'It doesn't have to be like that.'

'It does. That's the way the game is played. That's the level I have to stoop to.'

'No,' King said. 'It's not.'

He didn't waste words. A lecture would prove pointless. Donati thought it was justified, and that was that. No amount of convincing would change his mind. And, frankly, King was sick of the endless loop he found himself stuck in. Thinking, *Maybe this time they're doing the right thing.*

And then getting let down, time after time.

He was sick of it all.

Donati said, 'Are you sure we can't reach a compromise? My previous offer is still on the table.'

King stared. 'Yeah, Sam. I'm sure.'

Silence.

'Tell me one thing,' King said.

'Yeah?'

'What do you mean by "accident?"'

Quiet.

King said, 'I'll know if you're lying. Trust me.'

Donati said, 'One of my independent contractors in-country was going to run her over.'

'With what?'

'A truck.'

'How fast?'

'Fast enough.'

'Survivable?'

Donati hesitated, but that said it all. He seemed to realise it, too, and the realisation sank home that King could see through to his soul, so he shrugged and said, 'Most likely not.'

King said, 'Then you get the same odds.'

He clenched his fists and rounded the desk.

17

There hours later, an ordinary civilian flight prepared for takeoff at Sheremetyevo International Airport.

King sat in a quiet corner of the boarding gate, a baseball cap pulled down over his features. He'd changed out of the formal attire suitable for someone carrying out Close Personal Protection work, switching to ordinary civilian garb. He'd purchased a size up in both the shirt and pants to mask his abnormal physique. At an initial glance he seemed shapeless, perhaps overweight, but definitely not packed with muscle from head to toe.

One false passport had been switched for another. He'd brought a spare for exactly these sorts of circumstances. Customs hadn't found it upon entry to Moscow, and Donati hadn't bothered to frisk him for his own personal reassurance.

Now King was Richard Baker, a self-employed investigative journalist returning home from Moscow after location scout work for an upcoming piece.

Boarding was estimated to begin in fifteen minutes.

That was enough time.

King slipped his personal iPhone from his pocket, giving silent thanks for the encryption procedures installed within the device. The phone had been modified free of charge by Violetta's tech team, which made its security practically indestructible. He thumbed a familiar contact name and pressed it to his ear.

She answered almost immediately.

She still wasn't happy.

'What?' she snapped.

'I thought we already settled this,' King said. 'Why are you still angry?'

'You told me exactly what you were going to do, and I didn't have a say in the matter. You left me to explain to my superiors that out of the two experts they rely on to respond to critical incidents, one is running off to Mexico for a holiday and the other has started taking civilian gigs despite the fact he's on call twenty-four-seven.'

'And I remember telling you this was a once-off. Abnormal circumstances. I owe my life to Slater, and he owed a personal favour to an old military contact. Besides, I'm an independent contractor. There's no exclusivity. There's nothing in writing that says I can't do my own thing every now and then.'

'There's nothing that says you can, either.'

'There's *nothing* in writing,' King said. 'Full stop. Realistically, I can do whatever I please. But I gave you due notice, and now I'm coming back. So relax.'

'Wait, what?'

'That's why I'm calling.'

'You've been in country for less than five hours.'

'Things went south.'

'Oh, Jesus. Are you okay?'

'Yes.'

'Do you need extraction?'

'No.'

'Where are you?'

'Sheremetyevo. I'm using the spare passport.'

'If the authorities...'

'My problem isn't with the authorities. I'm unknown to them.'

She paused to compute. 'Donati?'

'Yeah.'

'How'd it fall apart? Is he hunting you?'

'He's dead.'

A pause.

Violetta said, 'Please tell me there's a justifiable reason.'

'Have I ever done anything without a justifiable reason?'

'Was it self-defence?'

'Not quite.'

Silence.

King said, 'More like an eye for an eye.'

'What do you mean?'

'He came here to discuss a potential merger with one of his competitors, Zima Group. He wanted their Chief Financial Officer to be compliant. So he tried to hit the man's daughter with a truck.'

There was no *"Oh my god,"* or *"No way,"* or *"That can't be true."*

Violetta operated in the shadow world. She knew exactly what powerful people were willing to do to maintain their power. She understood the mentality of those who would do anything to avoid regression. That was half the reason King loved her. She was harsh and uncompromising within her role as handler, because she had to be. She'd be chewed up and spat out in an instant if she became a pushover. But underneath that, she understood King's world, and she understood *him*. She cared for him regardless. That didn't come around often.

It was the same reason why King knew Slater loved Alexis so deeply.

She and Violetta understood men who, every now and then, were forced to become monsters.

Now, after a moment of silence, Violetta said, 'Wouldn't that have ruined negotiations? The guy would have been distraught...'

'There was some sort of time constraint in place. Written into the contract, apparently. The deal needed to be done in the next few days, personal issues notwithstanding. That's why Donati needed me — that's why he felt so threatened. And that's why he decided to play offence instead of defence. Because, no matter what happened outside of that boardroom, someone needed to walk out with the better deal. And when you lose a child in a freak accident, that clouds your decision-making skills.'

'Scum.'

'Not anymore.'

'What about his security?'

'They've all got headaches,' King said. 'But they're licking their wounds in the hotel suite. I couldn't justify a massacre.'

'I'm glad.'

King didn't say anything.

She said, 'What do they know about you?'

'Only what I look like,' King said. 'No personal details. Nothing on record. Donati recruited me off the books. There's no trace I was ever there.'

'This is going to make international headlines,' Violetta said. 'The whole conglomerate will be thrown into disarray.

It's named after him, for Chrissakes. When did this happen *exactly?'*

'A few hours ago. I'm getting on a plane in ten minutes. I erased all trace of myself from the scene. And I'd wager all six of his security have concussions. There's going to be a lot of confusion. They're in a foreign country. They're not clued in on their boss's contacts. They're rank amateurs, really. They're going to sit around for a while and debate their next move. There's a dead guy in their hotel suite, after all.'

'So we have time?'

'Not much. But some.'

'You're sure you're not in danger?'

'Positive.'

'Then we can rendezvous when you get back.'

'I need something from you while I'm in the air.'

'Okay.'

King half-smiled. No questions. No half measures.

Total cooperation, because he needed it.

'Escalate this,' he said. 'Get the necessary agencies to dig deep on Donati Group. They'll have an excuse in the aftermath of the CEO's death. I doubt I coincidentally was with him the first time he did something truly evil. There's got to be a web of darkness to uncover. But that's not my job.'

'It's technically not mine, either,' Violetta said. 'This is your personal gig. We have our own priorities—'

'And what decides your priorities?' King said. 'I thought you were in the business of stopping bad shit from happening.'

'We are.'

'Then this is no longer my personal gig. I can testify about what I saw, if you want to get official, but we both know that's not how our world operates. You need to trust my judgment.'

'I do.'

'Then dig,' King said. 'If not you and your department, then someone else. You'll find proof of something, at least. And you might be able to prevent someone else getting hit by a truck.'

She said, 'I'll do what I can.'

'That's all I'm asking.'

'Are you okay?'

He said, 'Professionally or personally?'

'*You,*' she said. 'Forget about work.'

'We agreed not to talk about—'

'How many times have we broken that agreement?' she said. 'What's the use in even trying to maintain it?'

A part of him wanted to remain steadfast.

He ignored that part.

He said, 'I'm okay. I'm just glad I overheard him ordering the hit. If I didn't interfere, she'd be broken and twisted on the sidewalk. Probably dead.'

She said, 'Get back here. I miss you.'

'I know you probably took the blame for this gig.'

'I did.'

'Thank you.'

'It's nothing.'

'They yelled at you?'

'Yes. And they're not the sort of people I want yelling at me.'

'When?'

'When you came to me after you met Coombs in the bar and told me what you were going to do. I went straight to my superiors. They practically screamed at me.'

'You didn't mention anything about that before I left.'

'I can take a grilling,' she said. 'And I knew you had to do it. I could see it in your eyes. You needed to go. You didn't need to worry about me.'

'Thank you,' he said. 'For understanding. You didn't have to say yes.'

'I did,' she said. 'We're in this together, remember?'

King settled back into his seat, allowing himself a brief moment of gratitude. 'Only thing that keeps me sane.'

'Me too.'

'I'll see you when I'm back.'

'Stay safe.'

'Always.'

King ended the call, and as if on cue a tinny announcement resonated through the lounge.

Boarding had commenced.

He stood up, and halfway to the gate he realised he'd forgotten to ask her the one question that had plagued him for hours.

Have you heard from Will?

18

They lay side-by-side in the sand, clad in nothing but their swimsuits, their bodies still damp from the morning swim.

The sky was cloudless, and the sun beat down.

Alexis rolled onto her side, and draped a hand across Slater's chest.

He opened his eyes, stirring from a half-sleep. It was their second full day in Tulum, and it was also the first time he'd dropped his guard in what felt like years. It wasn't smart. Wanting out didn't make his enemies vanish. He'd killed and maimed all across the globe, and there were still hundreds if not thousands of adversaries left behind who'd want nothing more than to make him suffer for what he'd done to them. Realistically, he should keep his back to a wall at all times, and survey every face for anything that might constitute a threat.

Something had changed within him. He didn't much care for paranoia anymore. If they came, they came. It would be what it would be.

Right now, he wanted nothing more than to enjoy the

moment. Which made sense. He'd been practicing meditation for a decade, teaching himself to silence his thoughts
on command, but he'd never used it to live in the present.
That was the whole point of meditation.

Now, he did.

He didn't worry about the future, or stress over the past.

It felt good.

She said, 'Tell me what you're thinking.'

He shifted his weight, rolling onto his own side so he
could look at her. He'd never get sick of looking at her. 'You
might not like it.'

'Share.'

'I think we need to go back today.'

She didn't outwardly react. But he knew the proposition
didn't thrill her.

He could see her letting the initial emotions fade,
replacing them quickly with logic.

He loved that about her.

She said, 'What you went through to get time off...'

He said, 'That's why I need to go back, as soon as possible. I've made my decision. I need to tell them. There's no
point leaving them in the dark.'

She went quiet.

He put a hand on her shoulder. 'Think about it.'

She looked at him.

He said, 'I tell them. They have a tantrum about it. I hold
steady. They begrudgingly accept. Then we get the hell out
of Manhattan forever. We can live anywhere. Do anything.'

She smiled. 'Go back now, and then you won't need to
ask for time off ever again.'

'There's a lot to think about. We can stay in the city
while we decide on—'

'No,' she said.

Her tone was firm.

'Your job,' he said. 'Your apartment. Your life.'

'Inconsequential,' she said. 'I'm looking at the bigger picture.'

He didn't respond.

He let her think about it.

But she didn't need to.

She said, 'When I'm lying on my deathbed, you think I'll be happy I stayed in the city for a job where I'm treated like shit instead of having an actual life with the only person in New York I care about?'

That made him smile.

He couldn't help it.

She said, 'I'll pack my things. Let's get the hell out of here.'

'You read my mind.'

He started to lever himself up into a seated position, but she put a hand on his chest, keeping him in place. He cocked his head to the side.

She said, 'Just one thing.'

He kept his head cocked.

She stared at him with her full green eyes. 'You said they'll have a tantrum.'

'They might.'

'Who's "they?"'

Realisation dawned on him. He said, 'You want the truth? I have no idea.'

'Is that how it works? I guess we've never discussed... specifics.'

'You know King? My coworker?'

'The one I've met?'

Briefly, Slater thought. He'd been walking her down to

the lobby one morning after she'd stayed over at his place and ran into King in the hallway, coming out of his adjacent penthouse. Recognition had flared in his eyes, and Alexis had noticed. She was highly perceptive.

She'd said, '*Is this the guy you've told me so much about?*'

King hadn't reacted, but she knew the truth all the same.

They'd exchanged pleasantries. King hadn't denied anything, which practically confirmed his secret to an ordinary civilian, even though it broke every rule in the book.

Neither he nor Slater had ever been very good at following rules.

Now, Slater said, 'King's partner, Violetta, is our handler. She's the front of house. She's all we've ever seen. We don't know how deep the web goes. It's all a mystery. Really, none of it matters to us. Because we're operatives, not bureaucrats. So I'll tell Violetta, and she'll pass it up the chain of command.'

'What if they say no?'

'I'm not going to ask them. I'm going to tell them.'

Alexis paused, screwing up her face, contemplating something. She said, 'How does that work? King and Violetta... as a couple?'

'I don't know how they do it. I'd never be able to separate the work from the personal life like that.'

'You do it with me. You never give me the details of what happens at work.'

'You don't send me into war zones. Makes it a little easier to trust you.'

Alexis smiled.

Then her face fell.

He said, 'What?'

'You and King are close, right?'

Slater nodded. 'Closer than you could imagine.'

'But his partner works for the government you're about to displease.'

Slater said nothing.

She said, 'What if he's forced to choose?'

19

King unlocked the front door and stepped inside, dropping the duffel bag filled with meagre supplies between his feet as he entered.

His penthouse reflected his life. Every piece of its contents had a use, a purpose. Nothing was wasted. The atmosphere was cold and modern thanks to the polished floors, the staggeringly high ceilings, and the minimalistic art dotting the walls, but the furniture and decorations had been arranged with the help of an expert interior designer, so some subtle aspects made the apartment seem warm and inviting at the same time. King liked it. It made him appear human, even though in reality every inch of the space was sparse and utilitarian.

It was a flawless, impeccably designed apartment made to appear imperfect.

Just like in the field, every time he had to assume an identity that wasn't his own.

He wasn't tired. He'd slept on the flight. It made him briefly ponder the ludicrousness of his life. He'd killed the infinitely powerful head of a global conglomerate in a foreign country, beat the man's entire security cohort sense-less, and yet it still paled in comparison to a usual operation. He felt surprisingly safe considering the circumstances, cocooned in anonymity.

There was only one person who might publicly connect him to the debacle.

King had elected to tie up that loose end as soon as possible.

He hit a touch pad on the wall just inside the entranceway with an open palm, and a series of ambient lights lit up the penthouse's central space. The deep yellow glow deliberately fell short of glaring against the floor-to-ceiling window panes running the length of the far wall, so he still had an uncompromising view of the Manhattan skyline at dawn.

He'd left Moscow at two in the morning, flown direct for ten hours, and then commuted an hour from JFK International Airport back to the Upper East Side of Manhattan. But the clock had wound back seven hours due to time zones, so now it was six a.m. in New York. The rapid time zone changes had thrown his body clock all the way off, and now he existed in a strange fugue state, somehow simultaneously dead tired and wide awake.

Only two minutes after arriving home, someone knocked at the door.

It could only be one guest, because King had only approved one guest. Slater was still in Mexico, and he was the only resident with keycard access to the top residential floor, so it had to be that sole guest. After two separate inci-dents within the tower over the last year, Violetta had turned the building into an invisible fortress. King knew that government operatives specialising in wet work were there in the shadows, twenty-four hours a day, seven days a week, protecting two of the secret world's most valuable assets in King and Slater. They would never let anyone reach this floor that didn't have permission.

He left his bag where it was, went to the door, and opened it.

Jack Coombs stood there, just as grizzled and serious as when King had first met him in the bar.

On top of that, the military vet looked disgruntled as hell.

King said, 'Are you happy to see me?'

Coombs shot him a withering death stare and stormed inside without invitation. He tried to bump King on the shoulder as he brushed past, but King slid effortlessly aside, a few inches out of range, making the older man look like a fool.

Coombs spun, rattled.

King killed the niceties and said, 'Let's cut the shit. You're not happy, but don't get petty. Voice your concerns man to man. Posturing is ugly.'

Coombs digested this, then swept through into the penthouse's main space. He surveyed the designer furniture, the multi-million dollar view, the marble countertop of the kitchen island, the invisible stench of wealth.

He grunted, 'You weren't kidding about the money.'

King said, 'Do I look like a liar?'

Coombs turned to face him. 'I don't know what the hell you look like, kid.'

They stood there, facing off across the giant space that now seemed hollow, permeated by tension.

King said, 'Let's get one thing straight.'

Coombs raised an eyebrow.

King said, 'You're here because I allowed you to be here.

You shouldn't know about this world. Really, you shouldn't know Slater or I exist. After what happened in Moscow I could have vanished off the face of the earth. You'd never have been able to locate me, let alone berate me. But I felt I owed you an explanation.'

'You're damn right you owe me an explanation.'

'Your client was a pathetic low-life criminal.'

'Do you have proof?'

'I'm not supposed to tell you a goddamn thing about what happened over there. In fact, that's what my handler explicitly ordered.'

Coombs fell quiet.

He didn't plead. He didn't get angry, either. He just lapsed into silence.

King respected it.

So he said, 'I'll share. Because I don't think you have bad intentions.'

'I don't,' Coombs said. 'I just want to know why my entire career's about to go to shit.'

'Can't you try damage control?'

'That only works with public information,' Coombs growled. 'But this is all private. *Behind* the scenes, everyone in the know is aware that I vouched for the man that went rogue and wreaked havoc.'

'If you're going to be investigated, we can quash that.'

Coombs shook his head. 'These people aren't the type to investigate. But word will spread. I'll never be used again.'

'I didn't have a choice.'

'You did.'

'Sam Donati ordered the death of an innocent woman. All to get a few percentage points inked into his contract.'

'You're sure?'

'I heard it.'

'So you killed him and assaulted his security?'

'Assault implies there was no self-defence. It was seven on one.'

'That's your story?'

'I have no story,' King said. 'I don't exist.'

Coombs stared. He reached up and tucked a strand of thick grey hair behind his ear.

King said, 'I'm not going to apologise.'

'My career is over.'

'You made hay while the sun shone,' King said. 'And then you slipped up. You didn't do your due diligence. You sent me into a situation where I had to act. If I did nothing, I'd be corrupt through to the core. That's on you. I'd do the same thing a thousand times over, if I had the choice.'

'There were other ways to handle it.'

'Not in my book.'

'You could have let the law sort it out.'

'An endless trial. A small army of the world's best lawyers against me. All based on conjecture. All based on what I heard. I don't think so.'

'That's why laws exist.'

'They're rigid. And they take too long. That's why people like me exist.'

Coombs frowned. 'I thought you didn't.'

'You're right. I don't. Is there anything else you want to say to me?'

A vein pulsated on the side of Coombs' throat. His neck had the texture of sandpaper.

King said, 'You want to kill me, don't you?'

'No,' Coombs admitted. 'I'm just angry.'

'Which is understandable.'

'I have money,' Coombs said. 'I'll be fine. But the bulk of

my work is over. No more high-roller clients. All thanks to you.'

King said nothing.

There was nothing left to say.

He decided to let the old man vent.

'Did he try to bribe you?' Coombs said.

'Of course.'

'How do I know you didn't take it?'

'Because he's dead in a hotel suite.'

'You could have double-crossed him.'

'I didn't take your money,' King said. 'Which was perfectly legit. Why would I take his?'

A pause.

Then a shrug of acceptance.

Coombs walked back to the door.

King followed.

When the old man placed his palm on the handle, he looked back over his shoulder. 'You know ... deep down ... maybe I'm wishing I had your integrity.'

A rare moment of honesty.

Then he stepped out, and was gone.

Exiting King's life as quickly as he'd entered.

King savoured the newfound quiet, and methodically removed any feelings of irritation or resentment from his mind. Coombs was no longer a subject of concern, so there was no point wasting time wondering what the man's future might entail. King had approached life that way for as long as he could remember. It was no business of his what other people thought about him. He simply tried to contribute to the common good. The incident in Moscow had required swift retribution, and that's what he'd delivered. Sure, there'd be consequences, but what he'd done in the moment had done the most overall good, so he didn't much care what resulted from it.

He took a deep breath in, closed his eyes, and let it out.

He opened them again and went to the fridge to get a beer.

S later stepped out of the civilian plane and onto the jet bridge, Alexis by his side.

As soon as he was free from the aluminium tube and found a couple of bars of reception, he dialled Violetta's number.

When it connected, he said, 'I'm back.'

A pause.

She said, 'What?'

'I'm in New York.'

'What happened? Relationship troubles?'

Slater almost smirked. 'Far from it.'

'We argued for weeks about you taking this goddamn holiday. What made you give it up?'

'I need to talk to you.'

'So talk.'

'Not over the phone.'

A pause.

She said, 'Is everything okay?'

'Never better.'

'Will,' she said. 'You need to give me more than this.'

He thought about it.

And came to a conclusion moments later.

He said, 'Actually, Violetta, I don't owe you anything. I'm asking to meet. Are you in town?'

'Yes.'

'With your team?'

'Most of them. I'm back at the same setup you saw, working with Alonzo.'

Slater had caught a peek behind the curtain a few months ago, right here in Manhattan. Due to unusual circumstances, Violetta had been forced to bring them to one of the temporary black-ops HQs that the government ordinarily went to great lengths to hide them from. An enormous space within a rundown tenement building, hidden in plain sight, populated by dozens of software engineering geniuses sitting in front of computers, dressed in casual clothing, sifting through and analysing data at an incomprehensible rate. It hadn't exactly lined up with his expectations, but it made sense in hindsight.

As the world became more modern and unfixed, there was little need for the attention-grabbing enormity of massive campuses and headquarters' like the Pentagon. All that created was an unnecessary target. Now, staggering processing power existed within a single computer tower, which you could slot neatly under a desk. So the big data that Violetta and her team used to determine which situations required a response from last-resort operatives like King and Slater could be analysed from anywhere. It made perfect sense to decentralise, to erect dozens of temporary set-ups across the continental United States and move the whole roaming circus between discreet locations. That way, there was little risk of being targeted by enemies of the state. Not even the government's own operatives knew where their shadowy secret HQs were located.

Alonzo was one of Violetta's best tech prodigies, capable of translating mountains of data into something halfway understandable.

Slater said, 'Am I needed?'

'Not right now.'

'Okay. That's all I wanted to know. If you're in town, I assume you'll come to me?'

'I'm rendezvousing with King in the morning. I'll come to you afterwards.'

Slater paused. 'What? He's back?'

'You two haven't spoken?'

'No.'

'You're both back early. But it sounds like his mini-vacation ended a whole lot worse than yours.'

'What happened?'

'Donati wasn't the man King thought he was.'

Slater wasn't exactly surprised. He couldn't think of a more obvious twist than a billionaire known for hoarding wealth and capital turning out to be corrupt.

He said, 'Is he in one piece?'

'I believe so. He didn't tell me about any injuries. We haven't spoken much.'

'How bad is it?'

'Donati's dead.'

By that point, he and Alexis were out of the jet bridge, flowing with the masses of passengers in the giant terminal. He spied a bank of televisions along the far wall, above the conveyor belt. Several of them displayed separate twenty-four hour news stations. He scanned the headlines with a practiced eye, and came away with nothing of note. The death — a grisly one, if Slater knew King at all — of an

American billionaire in Moscow would be plastered across every screen if it was public information.

He said, 'Word isn't out yet?'

'Apparently not. We're monitoring traffic.'

'You speak to him first,' Slater said. 'I'm sure he'll need to debrief you, and whoever else you're working alongside.'

'You know how it works,' she said. 'He tells me everything. I relay it up the chain. If there's any discrepancies, then we get other parties involved. But it's always something we liked to avoid.'

'He killed an important person on the economic hierarchy,' Slater said. 'There's no way he's not in trouble.'

'He had his reasons.'

'Of course he did. When don't we?'

With a snap of clarity, Slater realised he didn't much care about the inner workings of black operations anymore.

He said, 'Let me get some sleep. Then we'll talk.'

'Eleven a.m.,' Violetta said. 'How's that work?'

Slater checked the Hublot on his wrist. It was a hair after two in the morning.

He said, 'Works just fine.'

'Can you give me a heads up?'

'About what?'

She paused.

She said, 'Is it something serious?'

'You said it yourself. I fought for weeks for that vacation. And now I'm back on day two.'

Silence.

He said, 'You figure it out.'

He hung up.

They strolled in the general direction of international arrivals, and Alexis said, 'She's not going to be happy, is she?'

She hadn't heard the call from Violetta's side, but she'd put two and two together from what Slater had said on his end.

He said, 'It's just bad timing. That's all.'

Alexis took his hand. 'Why?'

'I really shouldn't tell you. You need plausible deniability.'

'Don't worry,' she said. 'You don't have to.'

'It's King. He could be in deep water.'

He said it because he had to vocalise it. Otherwise the thought would bounce around his head until it drove him mad. There was something bristling inside him, something he didn't want to address.

A toxic concoction.

Guilt, shame, unease.

Bad timing for King.

And bad timing for him.

She sensed his turmoil. She was better at that than anyone he knew. She stepped in and said, 'Your whole lives have been in deep water. If he stays in, he's always going to be in it. That's something you have to be okay with. If you leave, he's on his own.'

Slater turned inward. Went quiet. The swarming passengers all around him seemed a world away. He was detached from civilian life, disassociated, depersonalised.

He'd always known that would be the case.

But had he *really* considered it?

He said, 'I know. I understand.'

But he didn't think he did.

21

King topped up with two brief hours of sleep to compensate for the sporadic rest he'd managed on the plane, then began the day like any other.

A clueless onlooker would never know he'd beat up six trained combatants and killed a well-known billionaire on another continent the day before.

He rolled out of bed, padded straight to the fridge, and drank half a gallon of water mixed with electrolytes and... something that wouldn't pass Olympic drug testing. He and Slater had labelled the drink "Recovery Concoction" for a reason. There was no use breaking down their bodies in training if they didn't take advantage of rapid advancements in performance-enhancers. Their schedules and mutual workload all but required it to keep them in one piece with the aid of "special" supplementation.

Hydrated and invigorated by the power nap, he sweated off the jetlag by burning a thousand calories with a routine run-of-the-mill workout. He figured he'd been pushing his body so consistently for so long that he knew how to work with discomfort better than anyone on the planet bar Slater.

Maintaining an elevated heart rate came as naturally as breathing, and he alternated between high-intensity intervals on the assault bike in his workout room and five-minute rounds on the heavy bag, launching punches and kicks and elbows into the thick leather with relentlessness.

The whole time, a simple electronic band on his wrist tracked his performance. He'd been working with fitness trackers for the better part of two years now, and they'd accelerated his progress over the long term. It had taken him far too long to realise that maxing out your system each and every day didn't get optimal results. Rest and recovery were just as important as the work itself, and by tracking his heart rate variability, resting heart rate, and sleep cycles, the band let him know when his body was ready to push, and when it was time to pump the brakes and recharge.

Of course, in a live operation, he had to go all out regardless of how ready he was, but during periods of downtime he could use the data to hone himself into as devastating a weapon as possible.

Truth was, whether it was civilians awed by their impressive physiques on the street, or mercenaries and terrorists awed by how effortlessly King and Slater could beat them to a pulp, everyone assumed it came naturally to them. Their genetic gifts were real — ungodly reaction speeds that had placed them at the forefront of government black operations — but everything else came from consistent, unwavering hard work.

And slowly, over the course of decades, King had learned that hard work and smart work were one and the same. In his twenties, he could have slaved away at a back-breaking construction job and made decent coin instead of joining the military. He damn well had the physique and the grit for it. The work no doubt would have been as equally hard physically as even the most gruelling training regime. But it took just as much tenacity to use his brain, to recognise fields in which he was particularly talented and then focus rigidly on improving himself in those fields. Discipline to stick to the right areas of expertise was hard work in and of itself. It was the invisible work, the work that gave a small percentage of the population obscene riches and resources, and kept the rest in poverty. King had been conscious of it for as long as he could remember. Fixating on the things in his life that reaped maximum rewards, honing them over and over again, and completely ignoring the rest.

It had gotten him here.

Dripping with sweat in a fifteen-million dollar Manhattan penthouse, in possession of one of the most devastating skillsets on the planet.

He'd modified his fitness band to suit his needs, so as soon as he hit a thousand calories, a small green light on the device came to life. He registered the illumination, then ended his workout with a final teep kick into the heavy bag.

A cold shower and a change of clothes freshened him up, and he began preparing breakfast to replenish when a knock came at the door.

A lighter, gentler knock than the one that had come earlier that morning, before dawn had broken over the city.

He went to the door, opened it, and pulled Violetta in close.

They breathed each other's scent before they kissed, and when their lips touched all the treachery and tension and deceit that existed in their professional lives disappeared. He'd never lived in the present before he'd met her. Not truly. She crossed the threshold blind, eyes closed, face pressed to his. He swung the door shut behind her with a practiced push, sealing them in.

She pulled herself away, then placed a hand on his chest.

He raised an eyebrow.

'I told you not to go,' she muttered.

He half-smiled. 'Because you thought I might be needed here. Not because you thought I'd get myself killed over there.'

'You vouched for Donati.'

'Because Coombs vouched for him. And Slater trusted Coombs. That was all I needed.'

'Bad call.'

He nodded.

She said, 'At least you're back in one piece.'

He glanced down at the athletic garments draped over his frame. Then he looked back up. 'You don't know that. You should probably make sure. Conduct a thorough search.'

She smiled.

He said, 'Do we need to debrief right now?'

'Let's pretend I arrive an hour from now.'

'I like the sound of that.'

He put his hands on her waist and she wrapped her legs around him.

He carried her to the bedroom.

22

Slater and Alexis stepped into his penthouse right on three in the morning and each managed a replenishing five hours of sleep.

Slater stirred first, and hit a button on the nightstand that controlled the blackout blinds. They rose with a barely audible whir, exposing Manhattan and Central Park. Alexis grumbled beside him, and he rolled to his side so he could whisper in her ear.

'You should go home,' he said.

She sat up, her eyes half-closed, her hair tousled. She said, 'Seriously?'

'What?'

'Feels like I've just had a one night stand.'

He smiled, then it faded. 'It's for the best.'

She took a moment to compose herself. Reached up and wiped her eyes, then drank half a glass of water from her own nightstand. It seemed to clear her head.

She said, 'You don't think your news is going to go down well?'

'It might not,' Slater said. 'I want you well and truly back home when I hand in my resignation.'

She scoffed. 'Hand it in? You've got a letter?'

'That was metaphorical.'

'What *actually* happens?' she said. 'What's it going to involve?'

Slater paused. 'I don't know. I've never retired before.'

'You said in the past you were a vigilante.'

'Those were different circumstances,' Slater said. 'Back then, I was an enemy of the state. I abandoned my position. So did King.'

'So if it all goes to hell, you could do the same here?'

Slater shook his head. 'That was different. It was all or nothing. If I'm doing things the right way here, then I need to stick to the rules. No matter what.'

'But there are no rules,' she said. 'You work off the record.'

'I know. But I can't repeat the past. It's too dangerous.'

'For you? Or for me?'

'I've made an enemy of the entire government before,' he said. 'It's not good for anyone.'

She didn't respond.

He said, 'I don't want to be looking over my shoulder my whole life. We both deserve better than that.'

She said, 'What if they don't accept?'

He lapsed into silence.

Thought hard about it.

He said, 'I'm not going to ask them. I'm going to tell them. They can do what they want with the information.'

'And if they decide they don't like your ultimatum?'

'I'll burn that bridge when I get to it.'

'You're not afraid of that?'

'I won't have a choice. It's what I'll have to do. Fear's never really played a part in anything I've done.'

'So you *do* get scared?'

'Of course. All the time.'

'But you do it anyway?'

'Yes.'

She paused. 'I guess that's the definition of bravery, when you think about it. Doing things despite fear.'

'Maybe. I don't think much. I just do.'

She slipped out of bed and put on one of the spare sets of clothes she kept in his walk-in wardrobe. He lay there, savouring the view, wondering if he would be forced to leave the penthouse behind because of its proximity to what would come to be known as his past life. Because of its proximity to Jason King, who would still be a live operative.

That was the whole other side of the coin.

Slater had spent most of his career blissfully unaware of King's existence, but the moment they'd been introduced he knew they'd be inseparable. They were one and the same, cut from the same cloth, forged in the same fire. They'd hunted each other for a brief spell on the Mediterranean island of Corsica before uniting to take down a soulless smuggler. That seemed like it had happened decades ago. So much had unfolded since then. So much war, so much death.

He was tired to his core of it all.

But he didn't know how King would take it.

Slater wondered if King and Violetta were in their own penthouse suite, debating his hasty return, ruminating on what it might mean. He didn't want to face King until he'd spoken to Violetta.

Alexis came to the bedside, recognising that he was deep in thought. She bent over him and kissed him on the forehead.

He looked up at her. 'I'll make it quick. I don't want to

hang around any longer than I need to.'

'I hope it goes well.'

'If it does,' he said. 'I'll be free.'

'*We'll* be free.'

'You're free now. You could leave me if it all goes to hell. Start fresh.'

'No,' she said. 'I couldn't.'

He threw the covers off and walked her to the front door. An ominous heaviness stewed his gut as he twisted the handle and pulled it open, but all it revealed was an empty hallway outside. For some reason he'd anticipated Violetta standing there, watching like a hawk, waiting to pounce.

Something told him she'd be expecting what he had to say.

He didn't think he'd played his hand early. Hell, he hadn't even made a final decision until he'd opened his eyes on the beach in Tulum. But maybe King knew. The man was perceptive. Maybe he'd told her.

Alexis kissed him. 'Good luck.'

She went to the elevators, and he closed the front door. He would usually dive straight into a carefully calculated morning routine that he followed without fail every time he slept in his own bed, but now he abandoned it. He didn't need to be perfect anymore. He could still train. He could still fight. He could still improve. But he didn't have to optimise it.

There could be downtime.

He dropped into an armchair, closed his eyes, and focused on the breath. Emptying his mind of unnecessary thoughts. There was no use overthinking, overanalysing. All it would do was allow him to seesaw back and forth. He'd made his decision. He was going to stick to it.

He waited calmly for Violetta to arrive.

23

King lay on his side, propped up on one elbow so he could face her.

Violetta finished redressing and assumed a seated position on the mattress, feet crossed, back perfectly straight. A few locks of blond hair fell over her face, and she tucked them firmly behind her ear. Her cheeks were still flushed from the morning's activities. He was shirtless — besides a lengthy visit to a Gracie jiu-jitsu gym later in the evening, he had no commitments for the rest of the day. He was supposed to still be in Moscow, so his ordinary schedule had been cleared. He'd resume his training, maybe call in K-1 kickboxing legend Rory Barker for some pad work, but outside of that there was nothing urgent that needed addressing.

For most, a physically exhausting, mentally gruelling regime.

For King, far slower than usual.

He said, 'Did Slater give anything away?'

Violetta shook her head. Her blue eyes flared with curiosity, and he knew she was personally invested in what awaited. It wasn't just for the job. She'd come to know Slater closer than almost anyone else in his life save Alexis and King. They had their professional disagreements, but that wasn't out of the ordinary. Slater disagreed with almost everyone. Overall, King knew he respected her. He trusted her deeply, too. Which was why he'd gone to her first.

She said, 'How do you feel about this?'

He cocked his head.

'He hasn't spoken to you about it, has he?'

King shrugged. 'We just work together.'

'It's more than that. When you got back from Nepal, he said you were brothers.'

'Yeah,' King said. 'We are.'

'So why weren't you his first port of call?'

'Because this probably has nothing to do with me.'

'It's work-related,' Violetta said. 'Otherwise I wouldn't be involved. So, by extension, it involves you.'

'Are you concerned?'

'You know how badly he needed time off,' she said. 'Have you ever seen him like that before?'

King didn't immediately answer.

He took a moment to ponder it.

She was right.

'No,' he said. 'I used to think he was incapable of burnout. But maybe he hit a wall. Maybe he depleted his reserves.'

She said nothing.

He looked up. 'What?'

'Maybe he depleted them for good.'

King hesitated. 'He would have said something to me, first.'

'That's why I was concerned.'

'You really think he might be done?'

'I don't know,' she said. 'Maybe.'

He went quiet.

She said, 'What if he is? Hypothetically. How would you react?'

'I don't know.'

'I need you to prepare yourself. Because that might be the way this goes.'

King shook his head. 'He would have told me. I would have picked up on it.'

'You did pick up on it. Subconsciously. You accepted a dangerous job in his place, a job you didn't need to accept. Which means you knew how fragile he was. He needed time off. And when you have a foot out the door in this business...'

King's stomach churned.

Truth was, for the last few days, Slater had been out of sight, out of mind.

The prospect that his mindset had changed so drastically in that time...

Then King reconsidered. It would have been a gradual process. A slow realisation that the world was changing, and his spirit wasn't keeping up. When you knew you could no longer put your life on the line, there was no way to continue doing what they did.

King said, 'Go find out.'

She nodded, and went to the bathroom to freshen up.

He sat on the bed, stared out the window, and went into his own head.

He thought about what a future without Slater might look like.

He didn't like what he saw.

24

Three light knocks at the door.

Slater opened his eyes.

He stood up, went to the entranceway, and glanced through the peephole. An automatic precautionary measure. Violetta was there in the fish-eye lens, her long blond hair tied back, her expression severe.

Work mode.

Slater opened the door, so they could see each other face to face.

Neither said a word.

Then he said, 'Can I ask you something?'

'Of course.'

'Can we ... not treat this like work?'

She faintly tilted her head to one side. 'But this is work.'

'I know, but...'

He trailed off.

He'd never voiced this before.

He said, 'You're just about the only person I trust in this world outside of King and Alexis. And I'd never admit this to anyone I didn't trust. I'm at a particularly vulnerable time in my life.'

She practically stopped dead in her tracks. She'd been in motion, about to step past him into the entranceway, but now she froze in a double-take. She tried to analyse his face, but he kept his features expressionless. His eyes were stone.

She said, 'Are you okay?'

'Yeah,' he said. 'But I don't know how this is going to go.'

'You want out?'

Now it was his turn to freeze. He tried his best not to, but it was inevitable. She would have seen the jolt in his eyes, the *Oh shit* expression, the understanding that she'd been suspecting this all along.

He said, 'You'd better come inside.'

He ushered her through to the main space, which was practically a carbon copy of King's residence. There was a shade more exercise equipment, and a little less tasteful decoration, but for the most part the penthouses were identical. Which made sense, considering how similar the men who owned them were.

He dropped onto the sofa and said, 'I was going to be all stoic about this, but outside of all this, I consider you a friend. So I'll say it like it is.'

She sat down in the armchair opposite, crossed one leg over the other, and placed both her hands on her top knee. Her face gave nothing away.

Slater said, 'Is this going to be a problem?'

'I'm going to need more from you than just a simple "I want out."'

'Why?' he said. 'What does the reason matter?'

'Because you didn't want this to be a work conversation,' she said. 'And I consider you a friend, too. So — as a friend — why?'

'I've done enough,' he said simply.

She nodded. 'I get it.'

'You do?'

'Of course. Who wouldn't? What you do on a daily basis ... the stress that would bear down on you at all times...'

He said, 'It's not so much the stress.'

She looked at him, waiting for him to elaborate.

Patient, as always.

He said, 'It's you.'

'Oh?'

'You, meaning the government, in a broader sense. I know nothing about what goes on behind the scenes. And I'm getting older. I'm not the young bullheaded wrecking ball I used to be. Sure, I can still tap into that when I need to, but it's not who I am. Deep down. And now I'm starting to realise how much of a pawn I really am.'

'You're an operative,' she said. 'You carry out tasks for us. There's entire departments that analyse data to work out which tasks are best for you to carry out. It's best, for deniability, that—'

'I know,' he said, holding up a hand to cut her off. 'Trust me, I understand the reasoning. It doesn't change how I feel.'

She nodded.

He said, 'I don't want to be sent to places anymore. I don't want to be on call. Stress is fine. I've been swimming in it my whole life. I don't know anything else. But I want a shot at freedom for once.'

'You had it,' she said. 'You were out. And you came back.'

'When I was out, I was still using myself as a battering ram. I had nothing in my personal life. I'd just barrel toward danger, over and over again. I never tried anything normal.'

'You want to give that a shot?'

'I'd like to try.'

'No more fighting?'

He shrugged. 'It depends. If I see someone in trouble, I'll help. But I won't go looking for it.'

She said, 'Have you thought about this? I mean, *really* thought about it?'

'Yes.'

'Has this been brewing for some time?'

'Yes.'

'Then why haven't you told King?'

Silence.

Slater felt King's own question in her words. It cut through to his core.

He clammed up.

She said, 'When *are* you going to tell him?'

'Soon.'

'You don't think he'll like what he hears?'

'I think he'll understand what's best for me. He tried the same thing, after all.'

'He did,' she said. 'And it didn't go well.'

'So I shouldn't be allowed to try? Because he failed?'

'I didn't say that.'

Slater went quiet.

She stood up. 'I'll do everything I can to make this go smoothly. But at the end of the day, it's not up to me.'

He hesitated. 'What?'

She looked at him. 'We're talking as friends now, right? Not professionals.'

'Yeah.'

'Then let me tell you something,' she said, unintentionally lowering her voice. 'I'm just as much a pawn in this game as you are.'

Silence.

She said, 'I can vouch for you. I can take your side. But I'm not the one who makes the call to let you out.'

'I didn't think I was trapped.'

'You are. We all are.'

Before he could respond, she turned and made for the door. He leapt off the couch, striding hard, so he came to the entranceway in unison with her. She reached out to grip the handle and he slammed a palm on the door, trapping her inside.

She turned to face him. 'Not the right move, Will.'

'I want answers.'

'You won't get them. I wasn't supposed to tell you any of that. If you want me on your side for this, take your hand off the door.'

'What side?' he said. 'I told you I'm done. That's final. That's all there is to it.'

She smiled a sad smile. 'That's not how it works.'

'I'm saying it is.'

'You know things. About how this country is actually run. About what goes on behind closed doors.'

He didn't respond.

She said, 'They might not want you running around with those secrets in your head.'

'Who's "they?"'

The sad smile fell away.

She recognised that he'd taken pressure off the door, and swung it open. She stepped outside, and he saw the deep exhale catch in her throat. It struck him that she feared him. She feared what he could do to her.

Maybe that's a good thing.

Maybe I need to use fear to get out of this in one piece.

She said, 'Trust me. I'll do what I can. I'm sorry I can't be any more help. I want the best for you.'

'Then sort this out.'

The sad smile returned.

She said, 'It's not up to me.'

Then she turned and walked away.

He let the door swing shut on its own, whining softly along its trajectory. The lock fell into place, and it clicked closed.

He stood alone.

Understanding, for the first time, that where he fit in the puzzle of the shadow world would only be revealed when he tried to escape from its tendrils.

He looked toward an uncertain future. He couldn't shake the feeling that he'd just upset the status quo. Stirred the invisible pot.

The way he saw it, their talk couldn't have gone any worse.

25

L oitering in his own entrance way, King heard the faintest sound outside.

Slater's door, opening and closing.

He paused a beat, then quietly opened his own door, but instead of seeing Violetta standing there, he caught a flash of blond hair disappearing into the waiting elevator down the hall.

And then she was gone.

It mustn't have gone well, but that wasn't what unsettled him the most. It was that she hadn't confided in him. Whatever they'd discussed, it had been between the two of them, and whatever conclusions had been reached had caused Violetta to flee the building. Which meant panic. She hadn't even taken the time to give him a heads up.

Like, *Hey, that really didn't go well, and I need to regroup with my team to discuss it.*

He lingered in his own doorway for a few seconds, then made to take a step back, sealing himself back in his domain. But he couldn't do it. His foot froze in mid-air, and before he knew it he'd stepped outside. His door swung shut behind him. It made a soft *thud* as it clicked into place, which seemed to seal his decision.

He made straight for Slater's door.

Stepped up to it, raised a fist to knock against the wood.

Before he could make contact, the door swung open in his face.

Slater stood at his full height, shoulders back, chin raised. If he was intimidated by his talk with Violetta, he sure as hell wasn't showing it. But that had never been his style. King knew the man could very well be crumbling internally, and he wouldn't display a shred of it.

Slater said, 'I knew you'd come. Let's talk inside.'

King still had his fist raised like a caricature frozen in ice. He lowered it, then gave a curt nod and stepped into Slater's apartment.

They didn't speak. It didn't feel right, not within the claustrophobic confines of the hallway. Of course, it was an enormous entranceway in comparison to any other apartment in Manhattan, but they were accustomed to the staggering view further within their dwellings. So King followed his closest friend through to the main space. Slater walked right up to the floor-to-ceiling windows and crossed his arms over his chest. He looked out over the city.

Silent.

Pondering.

King pulled to a halt beside the kitchen island and circled behind it, putting a physical barrier between the two of them. He dropped his elbows on the marble and leant his weight on them. He stared at the back of Slater's neck, as if he could read the man's mind.

Slater didn't move. Didn't so much as budge.

King said, 'Are you thinking about what you told her?'

Slater didn't turn around. He said, 'Did she tell you?'

'No. But she guessed beforehand. And I think she was right.'

Now, Slater did turn. But he stayed where he was, across the penthouse. Physically distanced from King.

Slater said, 'What did she guess?'

'That you wanted out.'

'Then she *was* right.'

'How long ago did you decide?'

'In Mexico. On the beach.'

'Don't you think you're rushing it?'

Slater hesitated. 'That's when I *decided*. I'd been building up to that decision for months.'

'Since the blackout?'

Slater shook his head. 'Since before that. I just didn't know how to interpret it back then. Because I'd never felt like that before.'

'Is it because of Alexis?'

Another head shake. 'She's someone I can see a life with, after all this ... madness. But if I decided for her, it wouldn't last.'

King put more weight on his elbows. Tried to see through Slater's eyes, into his soul, but it was like trying to stare through a brick wall.

Slater said, 'I wasn't suggesting...'

'Whether you were or you weren't, it's true,' he said. 'When I met Klara, nothing else mattered. I lay low on Koh Tao because of her. Even if that's not what she would have wanted, it's why I did it. I didn't fully do it for me.'

'And that's why you came back when she died.'

King nodded. 'If I was out for good, nothing would have brought me back. Definitely not revenge.'

'But you were avoiding the fight on Koh Tao,' Slater said. 'You were hiding from it. That's not what this is for me.'

King said, 'It's the government, then?'

A nod.

Slater said, 'I can't keep doing it like this.'

'Why not?'

'I just can't.'

'I need more than that.'

'Not really,' Slater said. 'You should respect my decision.'

'We did this together,' King said, a touch of irritation creeping into his tone. 'We bought these apartments together. We moved to this city together. It was an agreement. We'd keep each other in the loop.'

Slater didn't answer.

King said, 'You go, and I'm on my own. I'm back to solo ops. I'm sure as hell not working with anyone else.'

Slater shrugged. 'Okay.'

'That's it?'

'I can't make decisions like this based on your feelings. I've been destroying my body for other people my whole life. Sooner or later, I have to take my own needs into consideration.'

'Of course,' King said. 'I'm not going to stop you.'

'You might have to.'

'What?'

'You might have to stop me. You might have to choose.'

King opted for silence, aware that it'd draw an elaboration out of Slater eventually.

Slater said, 'Violetta practically shit herself when I told her. Then she told me she's not really in control of anything. None of this is up to her. This is bigger than just the three of us. She's our handler, but she's a pawn. So someone else is going to decide whether I'm allowed out or not.'

King could respond a dozen different ways to that. He said, 'Surely you're allowed out whenever you want.'

'That's what I thought. Apparently not.'

King went quiet.

Slater said, 'I'm out. Regardless. No matter what they decide. You think Violetta's going to side with me if I go rogue again?'

Silence.

Slater said, 'You might have to pick a side.'

'Don't make me do that.'

Slater shrugged. 'You won't have a choice. Especially considering what you now know.'

'And what's that?'

'That if *you* want out,' Slater said. 'You might not be allowed.'

King didn't respond.

Because he'd never thought about it.

Now, though...

Now, he sure as hell would think about it.

Slater said, 'I need some time. You know, to myself. Can we talk this evening?'

King nodded. 'Sure. What did Violetta tell you?'

'That she'd vouch for me. But she didn't promise anything. She couldn't.'

'What sort of timeframe are you looking at?'

'She didn't say. A couple of days would be my guess. It should be a straightforward yes or no answer.'

'And then what?'

'And then I either walk away quietly, or disappear.'

'Leaving me here.'

Slater stared. 'It's your choice to be here. There's nothing that's keeping you chained.'

'Yes,' King said. 'There is.'

His home.

His partner.

His whole life.

He registered Slater's withdrawal from the conversation, and made for the door with a nod of farewell.

They both needed time apart.

To think.

To digest.

To ponder.

He reached the door, stepped out, and shut it behind him.

26

Slater had never wanted a drink so badly in his life.

The urge rose up out of nowhere, as soon as King left him alone. It gnawed at him, and he couldn't escape it. No amount of pacing around his apartment could shed the cloud hanging over him. It was the last thing he'd been anticipating. He could barely focus on forming a plan for going rogue, if that's what was required. All he could think about was racing to the nearest bar, ordering a double shot of whiskey, and throwing it back.

Instead, he called Alexis.

She answered fast and said, 'Is everything okay?'

'I don't know.'

'How did it go?'

'Hard to say.'

'So not great.'

'Not terrible, either. Violetta's on my side.'

'That implies there's someone who isn't.'

'She's not the one who calls the shots.'

'Did you know that already?'

'I guess I had a suspicion. But she'd never confirmed it.'

'Who does?'

'I don't know.'

'They're the ones that grant final approval?'

'Yes.'

'Powerful people.'

She wasn't asking. She was stating. It was implied.

Because King and Slater had considerable power on their own — devastating skillsets, infinite resources, the ability to get almost anything they wanted through sheer application of force — and in turn Violetta existed above them. She was their handler, with access to resources they couldn't fathom, with control over departments that could wipe them out with the best weaponised tech DARPA had to offer. Then, above her, there were the shadow people. The ones who controlled it all, who remained in power as public political parties came and went, who shaped the future of the country as they saw fit. It simply didn't make sense to give control of all the unofficial off-the-books programs to elected officials who may very well be out within four years, and certainly would be out within eight.

Let the façade go on as they pulled the strings that mattered.

Alexis didn't know any of this, but she could sense the implication. Because in her view, Slater was a battering ram, an unstoppable force of nature when he needed to be. She'd witnessed it first hand when they'd met during the blackout in New York. So if there were people with more influence than him, and then people with more influence on top of that...

Well, they *had* to mean business.

Slater said, 'Can I come over tonight?'

'Is that a good idea?'

'They're not going to execute me. Not yet. But if they

deliver the wrong verdict, I'm out anyway. We need to discuss exactly what that's going to involve.'

'I told you I'm on board with anything that—'

'You did,' Slater said. 'But there's a difference between saying it and doing it.'

'Not to me.'

He believed her. She'd never uttered a lie the whole time he'd known her, not even a tiny white one. It was one of her most redeeming qualities, as far as he was concerned. He'd seen the slippery slope in the real world. It was how bad men became truly evil. Tell one lie, then a handful, and before you know it you're doing anything to justify the exploitation of others. There was no better example of it than the cartels. They wrote fabled *narcocorridos* about the heroism of their *patróns,* lauding over the construction of churches and the donations to rural villages and the gifts to the needy, but they swept the torture and murder and mass beheadings and vicarious killings of thousands of junkies under the rug.

Those who told the truth never held the spotlight, but they were responsible for most of the good in the world.

Because sometimes telling the truth is a nightmare.

Like right now.

Slater said, 'You might be in danger. If I was to make the right decision for you, I'd stay in. That way, we could have a good life together. But if I go rogue again...'

He trailed off, but she didn't fill the silence.

Eventually he picked back up.

'We'll always be running. Always be hiding. It won't be the stress-free life we imagined.'

'It doesn't matter,' she said. 'Because it's the right thing to do.'

He smiled, and she seemed to sense it through the phone.

She said, 'I'm with you. No matter what.'

'So can I come? We still need to talk in person.'

'Of course. Have you spoken to King?'

'Yeah.'

'How'd *that* go?'

'We didn't get very far. I think I made him realise his place in all this.'

'As in — he ever wants out, then he's in trouble too?'

'Exactly.'

The line was silent.

Slater said, 'You there?'

'Yeah. Just thinking.'

'About...?'

'What if he gets rebellious thoughts too?'

Slater went quiet.

Alexis said, 'What if you've started a revolution?'

27

A t an esteemed Brazilian jiu-jitsu gym in an enormous underground basement in Manhattan, King fought off a third degree black belt who'd swiftly attached himself to his back.

Both donning traditional *gis,* they wrestled in a mutual pool of sweat. King cursed his complacency and distracted-ness. It had allowed his opponent, Maurice, to take his back with one smooth change of direction, switching position on the mats so he could wrap both legs around King's waist and set up the inevitable choke.

But King wasn't going to let him have it.

At this level of the practice, there was no use being bull-headed. Maurice had his back with both hooks in, and his dominant arm (the right one) looped around King's chin, compressing his jaw. Maurice was holding back — in competition, he would have initiated a neck crank and got the tap nine times out of ten. But he wanted the choke across the throat, so it was a clean undebatable victory, and King didn't want him to have it with equal verve.

He simply wasn't in the mood to lose.

Both of them were coated in perspiration. With slick technique, Maurice inched his corded forearm down toward King's exposed throat.

King flipped a switch.

He never ordinarily utilised it, but now he visualised Maurice as an enemy on a live operation. The dynamic changed. Instead of simple drilling, this was now a life-or-death altercation. King kept it within the rules of jiu-jitsu, refraining from launching into strikes or eye gouges or groin shots, but he bucked up and down with a single testosterone-fuelled jerk of the hips. Maurice thudded into the mats, not hard enough to draw attention, but hard enough to drive the breath from his lungs. King's level of intensity, previously unseen, shocked him.

Like a shark with a taste of blood, King twisted viciously out of the grip, shedding Maurice's arm like it weighed nothing, and then launched himself at the slightly smaller man. Maurice rolled, sensing an incoming submission attempt, but it did nothing to deter King. King latched onto Maurice's back in turn and got his giant arm around the man's throat. Maurice did all the right things, forcing a hand between King's forearm and his own unprotected throat, but King simply caught Maurice's hand in the choke itself and used brute force to crank it tight.

Maurice tapped.

Either to stop himself going unconscious, or to prevent his hand from breaking.

King rolled off, panting.

Maurice said, 'What the fuck, man?'

King stared at his feet.

Maurice said, 'What was that?'

'I won.'

'We were rolling,' Maurice said. 'You've been coming

here for years. You're a black belt, for Chrissakes. You *know* what rolling is. You almost broke my ribs with that nonsense.'

'What nonsense?'

The older man scoffed and levered up to his feet with the dexterity of a cat. 'When you leave today, sort your head out. And don't come back until you do.'

King made to retort, but cut himself off immediately as a spear of rationality lit him up from the inside. Maurice had considerable influence in the gym's operations. He wasn't asking a question, or offering a suggestion. It was a demand. And King would do well not to get himself kicked out of a gym like this.

Objectivity had always been his greatest strength. He used it now.

You're impulsive. You're angry about Slater. Don't let it bleed over into the rest of your life.

He said, 'You're right. I'm sorry.'

Maurice paused a beat, thrown off by the sudden change in demeanour. Then he nodded, and walked away with his injured hand held close to his chest.

Guilt stabbed at King.

He headed for the showers, rinsed himself off, changed back into casual clothing and threw his sweaty possessions into the duffel bag he'd carted over from his penthouse. He raised the bag vertically and slipped it onto his back with the help of the attached shoulder straps.

Then he left.

There was half an hour of the session left.

But he was compromised. And he knew it.

It was a cool afternoon when he resurfaced at street level — the late morning had bled away underground, time passing amidst a montage of sweat and blood. Jiu-jitsu involved no striking, but at King's level the stakes were higher. The flabby hesitance of white and blue belts was a world away, replaced by competitors who were made of hard sinewy muscle, who could use their hands and fingers like weapons, who could crank chokes impossibly tight in milliseconds. He was bruised and battered and sore and depleted, but that was normal.

He shrugged a jacket over his broad shoulders and blended into the masses of pedestrians on the sidewalk for the trek back to the Upper East Side.

Objectivity.

Now was the time to use it.

He pulled his phone out and dialled the number he knew he needed to dial.

Slater said, 'Yeah?'

'Fuck our feelings. We need to talk properly about this.'

'I was going to say the same.'

'Change of heart?'

'I didn't need to be alone for long. I just needed time to digest. Where are you?'

'I was rolling.'

'How'd it go?'

'Average. I'm a little distracted.'

'I'm at home.'

'Where else would you be? I'll be there soon.'

He ended the call before Slater had the chance to misinterpret the rhetorical question. He'd meant, *You're effectively on house arrest until the government decides your fate, so where else would you be?* Not, *You're a loser with no hobbies besides training, and everything you need to train is in your penthouse, so where else would you be?*

He wasn't sure which way Slater had taken it.

He set off for the Upper East Side, and on the way home

he realised what drew him to New York City: it had the highest population of a major metropolitan area in the U.S., all condensed into a small collection of boroughs. There were over eight million people here. No matter how infamous he became, it would still be close to impossible to identify him in such giant crowds. It was the reassurance of anonymity.

In a world where he'd made hundreds if not thousands of enemies, that was something at least.

But now he would have to either side with Slater, or not.

And if he did, he'd make a whole new class of enemy.

Again.

Then not even New York would be safe for him.

He crossed the street with his shoulders slumped and his insides constricted.

28

Slater had been alone for several hours.

Ordinarily, that would be nothing out of the ordinary.

He'd spent most of his life alone — self-reliant, self-driven, self-motivated.

Now he hated it.

He worked out, because that's all there was to do. Sure, there were probably more poignant ways to master his current mindset, but right now meditation was about as appealing as going rogue. So he switched to athletic-wear and hammered punches and kicks into the heavy bag suspended from the ceiling of the spare room until he'd seemingly sweat out half his bodyweight and depleted his energy reserves. It's hard for uncertainty and unease to survive that amount of physical exertion. Sure, it was the equivalent of telling a clinically depressed person to "just go for a run," but in his case it worked.

Maybe because he'd spent a decade inching further along the spectrum of self-torture, increasing what his body was capable of tolerating, so that now what he classed as a "decent workout" was probably the equivalent of a civilian running a marathon with no training.

Exhausted, he showered and changed back only minutes before there was a knock at the door.

He let King in without checking.

It wouldn't be Violetta — not this soon — and he'd firmly warned Alexis to stay away from his building. He still planned to spend the night at her loft in the Bowery, but he'd make sure to get there discreetly, employing a lifetime of espionage training to make sure there wasn't a soul alive that knew his location.

As King entered, he said, 'You're making me paranoid. You know that?'

Slater sipped from a gallon jug containing a mixture of chilled water and electrolyte powder. 'Why?'

'Suggesting that the government is going to force my hand. I spent half the walk back from the BJJ gym looking over my shoulder.'

'I'm the one who should be paranoid,' Slater said. 'And I'm not. So cool it.'

'Neither of us are addressing the elephant in the room.'

'Which is?'

'You haven't asked me what I'd do if they told me to choose.'

'Because that's your decision to make,' Slater said. 'Not mine.'

'You seem indifferent.'

Slater narrowed his eyes. 'Really? One option leaves me fighting — and probably losing to — someone I considered a brother, and the other lets me escape to a new life with that brotherhood intact? You honestly think I'm indifferent?'

'Nonplussed, then. You're hiding it well.'

'Compartmentalising. It's what we're best at.'

'Why aren't you trying to sway me?'

'Because I respect you too much for that,' Slater said. 'You care about Violetta just like I care about Alexis. I'm not about to tear your life apart to save my own skin.'

King didn't respond. He sauntered over to the kitchen island and pulled out one of the stools. He sat, and drummed his fingers against the countertop.

Slater said, 'If it comes to it, just decide. I'll deal with the fallout.'

'What if they task me with neutralising you?'

'You and I both know there's not a chance in hell you'd do that.'

He could see King pondering whether to bluff or not, simply to be hypothetical. But the man gave that up straight away. He knew Slater was right.

Slater said, 'That's not even the biggest elephant in the room.'

King raised an eyebrow.

Slater said, 'This will affect both of us if it goes that way. If they decide that I know too much to be allowed to run around out there in the big wide world on my own, then what does that mean for you?'

King said, 'But I don't want out.'

'You will. Eventually. You don't want to do this until your body crumbles. Or your brain. That was never on the cards. There had to be an expiration date. Even if it was just to keep you sane.'

King lapsed into silence.

Slater said, 'What are you going to do if I have to go rogue and you're left here on your own? How long is it going to take you to start doubting everything?'

'Explain.'

'There's been an endgame scenario in both our heads

this whole time. The knowledge that, if things get too intense, we can pull the plug and get out. We're independent contractors, after all. So, what if you see me going rogue, and realise that quietly retiring was never an option? That'll pull the rug out from under you.'

'What are you suggesting?'

'Nothing.'

'Yes, you are.'

'I'm just asking you to think,' Slater said. 'It might affect who you're likely to side with.'

'I *thought* that's what this was.'

'I need to keep my own best interests in mind,' Slater said. 'But that doesn't mean I want you to get fucked over in the process.'

'What if I don't want out?' King said. 'I mean, ever. You said yourself that you're not going to stop helping people. I'm the same. It's in our DNA. So why would I ever want to do it outside of this structure? Think about it. We have our country on our side. We're given tasks that do the most overall good. We get compensated handsomely. It's beneficial all round.'

'But we're not free,' Slater said. 'We always thought we were. And now Violetta is probably going to come back and say, "Sorry, no deal." What then? You're just going to be blissfully oblivious? You're going to pretend you're not trapped in a cage you can't escape?'

'It's not a cage.'

'Stockholm syndrome.'

'Cut the shit,' King said. 'I—'

Slater said, 'Have you and Violetta ever spoken about who she works for?'

'The upper—'

'The upper echelon,' Slater said. 'I know. That's what I

was told too. But that tells us absolutely nothing. Has she ever elaborated?'

'It's off-limits,' King said. 'And it benefits no one for me to know. We talk about work. But not about that.'

'You should have seen what she was like in here. She smiled the saddest smile when I said I wanted out. None of this is up to her.'

King didn't say a word.

Slater said, 'She's trapped. Just as much as we are.'

'This whole thing is overblown. In all likelihood she'll come back here and give you the all-clear.'

'And if she doesn't?'

King stood up. 'Then we'll talk.'

He made for the door. Slater could see, below the always-calm exterior, the man was rattled. Because Slater had gone for the jugular, and King hadn't masked the doubt with anger. He'd stayed calm, subdued, processing it instead of allowing himself to react immaturely.

Which meant he was taking it seriously.

Slater said, 'Where are you going?'

King froze with a palm on the door handle.

He turned back.

He said, 'Now I need time alone.'

Then he left.

29

Some time later, afternoon transitioned to dusk, and Slater flicked a handful of light switches the moment the sun dropped below the horizon.

The last thing he wanted was to spend any time in the shadows.

Not right now.

Somewhat unnerved, he dialled Violetta.

It rang, on and on and on. The faint ringtone emanating from the tiny phone speakers was the only sound in the penthouse.

She didn't pick up.

He tried again.

Same result.

'Fuck this,' he muttered.

He snatched up a coat to combat the evening chill and left the apartment. The hallway was dead quiet, but that was to be expected. Soundproofing and competent insulation were the foundation of any expensive piece of Manhattan real estate. Paper-thin walls weren't a problem. Hell, both he and King had fired unsuppressed gunshots at assailants on this very floor. They still passed other residents in the lobby without incident. There was no suspicion of illicit activity whatsoever, despite waging war two separate times since they'd moved in.

He made it to the lobby and exchanged a passive nod with the concierge, a polite man in his forties named Sebastian. Slater had spoken to him a handful of times, but not for long. He still remembered the last concierge, caught in the crossfire when mercenaries targeted Slater and King during a city-wide blackout.

Now he refrained from getting too close to any of the staff.

The last thing he wanted was for his goodwill to cost them their lives.

Which concerned him, the more he thought about it. He knew, deep down, that anyone he got close to was in danger. So if he truly cared about Alexis, then by extension he should cut her off.

For her own good.

But not even someone of Slater's mental toughness could dip to that level of self-torture.

He made a beeline for the Bowery, despite what was smart.

No one's perfect, after all.

He traced the same route that he and King had followed on that fateful night months earlier, when the lights had gone out and they'd prevented the city being plunged into anarchy by a hair's breadth. It still lingered in the back of his mind. It always would. Each past operation was the same. It existed as a fragmented memory, a cut-together rapid-fire blur of sight and sensation. Most of it violent. Most of it agonising.

All of it unpleasant.

He had memories like that everywhere. All across the globe. If location alone triggered the post-traumatic recollections, then he'd never be able to step foot outside his apartment. Thankfully, he could force it aside when he needed to. He could work on his harrowing past when he deemed it necessary — it didn't roar into his prefrontal cortex at random, debilitating him on the spot.

He knew there were many, many men and women who'd seen combat who weren't so lucky.

He took random lefts and rights throughout the trip, zigzagging down side alleys, loitering sporadically at random intervals, never adopting a pattern, never making things predictable. There wasn't a chance a sentry trying to keep track of him could do so without being spotted. They'd get caught up in trying to guess his movements and eventually run into him. But no one did. He was confident there was no one following him.

Evidently, Violetta and her superiors weren't that paranoid yet.

He made it to a familiar intersection in the Bowery, and saw the giant bank building across the street, still cordoned off with police tape. There was little commotion around it, but for a few weeks after the blackout it had been constantly swarmed by nosy civilians and rabid journalists alike. There'd been dozens of eyewitness reports of a brutal shootout on this very intersection.

The NYPD realised the speculation wouldn't fade on its own, and immediately issued a press release, claiming that a gang shootout exacerbated by the tension of the blackout had spilled out onto the streets. Several officers had fallen in the line of fire, and their heroism would be honoured with a state funeral.

There'd been no mention of two vigilantes storming the

building, tearing it apart from the inside, putting a stop to something far more sinister than anyone thought possible.

Slater didn't care.

Being the subject of headlines would only make things a hundred times worse.

Opposite the bank building was the same residential complex he'd sought refuge in on that fateful night. The complex where he'd met the woman he now loved.

So was it fate? Did you need to suffer that night, to find someone you shared a connection with? Would your bond be as strong if you hadn't met at such a turbulent time?

He didn't like to think about any of that.

It went down dark, dead-end roads.

There wasn't much good in his world. When it came, he liked to make it uncomplicated, so he could appreciate it all the more.

He entered the lobby of Alexis' building, and this concierge recognised him too. He nodded to her, then strode fast and hard for the stairwell instead of the elevator. He stepped inside the cold concrete cylinder and moved to the side as soon as the door swung closed.

There, he waited.

For a truly unnecessary length of time.

No one followed. No one came creeping in, not ten minutes after he entered, not fifteen, not twenty. He didn't allow himself to get distracted, which was simple enough. Doing absolutely nothing was effortless. He'd emptied his mind before he stepped out of his penthouse, maximally focused on not getting tailed.

When he stepped back into the lobby, it was empty save for a couple of residents. They didn't throw a second glance his way.

The concierge did.

She said, 'Forgot something?'

He crossed to the elevators and stabbed the UP button with his thumb. 'I was just getting some exercise in the stair-well. Missed my workout today.'

She laughed, unsure whether he was serious, opting to interpret it as a joke regardless.

Exactly what he wanted.

He stepped into the elevator when it arrived and it whisked him upwards, leaving her awfully confused.

lexis answered the door with her familiar smile, and Slater found himself spontaneously struck by insidious thoughts.

Not toward her.

Toward the rest of his life.

She could tell. 'What's up? Do you have your answer?'

Slater said, 'No.'

He stood there, thinking.

She let him.

Finally he said, 'Do I *need* an answer?'

She didn't respond. She knew what he meant. She clearly didn't like it.

He kissed her and stepped into her loft. He'd grown to love her space — his own home was cold and empty in comparison. Here he appreciated the exposed wooden beams along the ceiling, the staggering array of greenery from a nearby nursery, the tastefully arranged furniture. It was all less expensive than the contents of his penthouse, but he'd come to learn that money didn't mean a thing if you didn't know what to do with it. The priciest furniture in the world was still ugly if your home didn't feel like a home.

Slater's home felt like a training compound.

Which wasn't a bad thing, given his occupation. It was better to expunge feelings and hone your skills if your life depended on it.

But he didn't want that anymore.

Alexis followed him inside and said, 'What are you saying?'

He turned to her. 'I'm saying why am I waiting for permission?'

'Aren't there logistical problems?' she said. 'Don't they control your fortune?'

'No. I've always made sure my accounts are untraceable. I set it up that way when I was a vigilante, scattering my wealth through Grand Cayman. I didn't hand over control when I came back to work for the government. I just gave them an account for one of my shell corporations, to deposit the money into. From there, I send the funds straight into the labyrinth. They might be able to trace it to one or two other entities, but never all of them. They'll never be able to hit me where it hurts.'

She processed this.

He said, 'So let's go. Right now.'

'Have you spoken to King?'

'Yes.'

'You've said your goodbyes?'

Slater paused. 'I'll see him again. Eventually.'

'Is that smart?'

'It's the way it has to be. He means too much to me. It's hard to explain.'

'I get it,' she said. 'I've never seen combat, but... I get it.'

'You can't really explain the bond.'

She nodded.

Then she said, 'They might be expecting you to run.'

He shook his head. 'There's a chance they saw me leaving my building. But not arriving here. And I didn't step out with a single possession. Not even a bag.'

She looked him up and down. 'Do you need anything?'

'No.'

'Clothes? Personal stuff?'

He stared, unresponsive.

She said, 'You don't have personal stuff, do you?'

'I have you,' he said. 'That's about the extent of my life outside of work.'

'We need to work on that.'

'We will. We have the chance, now.'

A smile came over her, despite the circumstances. She stepped forward, closing the gap, killing the separation between them. He reached out for her, and pulled her in, and kissed her.

When they parted, he said, 'What do you say?'

'If you were going to wait around for the answer, what do you think it would be?'

'I don't think they're going to let me walk away.'

'So no matter what, we need to run?'

He took his time to nod. He didn't want to admit the truth. But he nodded all the same, because he'd been taught to only deal with the truth, no matter how painful it might be.

She said, 'I'll pack.'

His heart thudded. Packing meant cutting off everything they had here in the city. It meant fleeing with new identities, new lives. It meant tipping their whole world on its head.

And for Slater, perhaps most importantly it meant walking away from Jason King.

She made for the bedroom, where the closet contained the suitcases she needed to fill with all her worldly possessions, and he stayed behind in the living room.

He reached for his phone out of impulse.

To find the contact KING and dial.

But when he pulled it out he stopped his thumb in its tracks, refusing to swipe across the screen and unlock it.

He couldn't half-commit.

He couldn't seesaw back and forth.

Calling to say, *'Sorry, I didn't get to say goodbye.'*

Full measures only.

It was the only way.

So he inched his phone back toward his jeans.

Then it rang.

He looked at the screen.

VIOLETTA.

His heart thudded again.

Time to decide.

He answered and lifted it to his ear and said, 'Hey.'

She didn't talk for a beat.

Long enough for him to ponder whether she was even on the other end of the line or not.

But she was.

She said, 'Don't even think about it.'

31

He didn't skip a beat.

Hesitation kills.

He said, 'What are you talking about?'

'You know exactly what I'm talking about.'

'Feel free to enlighten me.'

'Where are you?'

'Not home.'

'I know that. You shook off the tail.'

Slater bristled at the confirmation. It proved he was dealing with people who knew what they were doing. It would have taken an expert to recognise the right time to back off and avoid getting caught in the traps he'd set. In the past he'd ensnared many experienced trackers with the same movements.

He said, 'Cut the bullshit. You know me. You know where I am.'

'Jiu-jitsu at the Gracie gym, or practice at the shooting range, or running in Central Park, or rendezvousing with Alexis. Those seem to be the only things you do.'

'The latter.'

'Why are you telling me? I didn't expect you to.'

'Because you're out of position, and if I wanted to leave right now, I could. You'd never find me.'

'Want to bet?'

'Obviously. It's the ultimate bet, isn't it? Life or death.'

'I'm not going to kill you.'

'I know. *You* couldn't. But you might task a team to try.'

'You got resources? As far as I can tell, you're dead in the water.'

'Yes,' Slater said. 'I have resources.'

'We know all your passports.'

'You think I only have the ones you gave me? You think I couldn't get more? What do you think I did when I was a wanted man?'

She said, 'I could send your picture to every airport in the country within minutes.'

'Then I'll go for a long drive. It'll take me about two days to change my appearance enough to breeze through.'

'Your girlfriend's identity will be burned.'

'I've already got her a new one.'

'But that doesn't erase the past,' Violetta said. 'Her parents are in the UK, but they're still traceable.'

Slater went so quiet he couldn't even hear himself breathe.

Violetta noticed.

She said, 'Will?'

'I was playing your little game,' he said. 'But if you even think about touching her family, I'll fucking destroy you. You know I will.'

He'd never used that tone with her.

It rendered her speechless.

In the loft, Slater heard the creak of floorboards. He looked up to see Alexis staring at him, shock on her face.

She'd never heard it either. The tone of a cold-blooded killer.

The tone of a savage.

The tone of someone speaking the absolute truth.

'Now what do you want?' he growled.

'Get back here. Let's not resort to anything irrational.'

'You'd better give me a reason.'

'The reason is that I've accepted your retirement, and I want to discuss the terms with you. Is that good enough for you?'

He paused. 'What terms?'

'That's not something I'm at liberty to discuss over the phone.'

'You'd better.'

'Or what? You'll run? Even after what I just told you? That would be an incredibly stupid decision.'

He made to respond, but she cut him off.

'That's it,' she said. 'There's nothing left to discuss. Get back here. It's in your best interests.'

The line went dead.

Slater kept the phone pressed to his ear. Indecision plagued him.

You'll run?

That would be an incredibly stupid decision.

She was right.

He looked up at Alexis. 'I need to go back.'

'It might be a trap.'

'Maybe. But Violetta still reached out. That's all I was looking for. A swift answer. It seems like I've got it.'

'What did she say?'

'That she's accepted my retirement.'

'Those exact words?'

'Yes.'

'Then it's a trap.'

'Why?'

'Because it's not up to her.'

'They know I'm here,' Slater said.

'Because you told them.'

'No point hiding it. Where else would I be?'

Alexis lapsed into silence. 'Maybe me being the only personal thing in your life wasn't for the best. It made you predictable.'

Slater nodded.

He said, 'I have no choice.'

'What if they kill you?'

'You're safe,' he said. 'No matter what happens to me. But they won't kill me. I promise.'

She descended the stairs two at a time and came to him. He held her, and she buried her head against his shoulder. He thought he heard her stifle a sob. She wouldn't let it show. She had the heart of a lioness.

She said, 'How can you be sure?'

'Because I wouldn't sit back and let them do it. I'd put up a fight, and they don't want that in the heart of Manhattan. Because I'd tear this city to the ground to defend myself. That's why.'

She wasn't one to let emotions overwhelm her, but when she stepped away from him she was pale. She wasn't blinking. Her eyes were wide.

He reached out and touched her cheek. 'I'll be fine.'

'Caring about you is so fucking stressful,' she bemoaned.

He smirked. 'Now imagine *being* me.'

Before she could highlight the ridiculousness of cracking jokes, he went to the door and opened it.

He looked back.

'I'll be okay. Trust me. I'm not going to roll over. Do you still have your taser?'

'Yes.'

He said, 'Anyone comes through this door that isn't me ... use it.'

She bit her lower lip and nodded.

Holding back tears with every ounce of willpower she had.

He closed the door behind him, and he knew, in the isolation of the empty loft, she would finally be letting them out.

32

After such a mentally exhausting day, King was satisfied with the training he'd put in, so he rid himself of guilt as he poured a couple of fingers of whiskey into a crystal tumbler.

There was no changing the past. Tomorrow, he'd go and apologise to Maurice. He'd admit his wrongdoing. There was no point posturing. Winning a pointless victory by arguing his case achieved nothing. There were endless excuses he could provide. His head wasn't in the right place, there was too much stress at work, his closest friend might be running away for good...

All beside the point.

He'd been rash and reckless and impulsive within the walls of an esteemed jiu-jitsu gym, and that was all there was to it. The reasons why were beside the point. All he could do was ask himself, *Where should I go from here?*

It took a weight off his shoulders. It would be easy to find another gym, but there was more to it than that. Brazilian jiu-jitsu was a martial art founded on the principles of respect and humility. He'd do good to be humble, and it gave him peace.

Then Violetta unlocked his front door and appeared in the hallway.

He cradled the tumbler, raised it to his lips, and took a sip as he looked her up and down. She was dishevelled, her blonde hair frazzled, her eyes hollow with stress. She'd applied a touch of eyeliner half-heartedly, and then seemingly given up on the rest of her usual makeup routine.

No matter how draining his day had been, in a single glance he knew hers had been worse.

They kept looking at each other.

King said, 'Do you want to talk about it?'

Her lower lip quivered.

She said, 'I need to speak to Will.'

'I know.'

'He's not back yet. Can I wait here?'

'Of course. You know this is just as much your home as it is mine... why are you even asking?'

Her gaze lingered on his. 'Because I'm not giving Slater good news.'

'How is that my problem?'

She let his question hang in the air, highlighting its ridiculousness.

Of course it's my problem, King thought. *We're a duo. A unit. We work together. We live side by side.*

We're brothers.

She said, 'You don't really mean that.'

'He's his own man. He makes his own decisions. If he wants to run, then that's a burden he's going to have to bear.'

'It sounds like you're just trying to convince yourself.'

'Maybe I am.'

She didn't take her eyes off him. 'You know what this means, right?'

He raised an eyebrow.

She said, 'What if you ever want out? What if *I* do?'

'Then we won't go about it as haphazardly as Slater.'

'*How,* exactly?' she said. 'He came. He asked. I passed it up the chain. I got a firm answer. How can we make it any less haphazard than that?'

King said, 'You need to think things through. I don't like what you're suggesting here.'

She shook her head. 'I'm not suggesting anything. I just ... need to talk to Will.'

'He'll come back.'

'Did you know he was gone? He and Alexis ... they were going to run. Tonight.'

King shrugged. 'But you told him to come back. And he respects you. So he will.'

The faintest echo of a noise came from the hallway.

Violetta put her hands on her hips and sighed. 'I hope this goes alright.'

'What are you going to tell him?'

'I said yes. My superiors didn't.' She paused — not to intentionally dramatise, but it had the effect regardless. 'They want to meet with him.'

King froze with the tumbler in his hand.

He said, 'They've never done that before. For either of us.'

'There's a first time for everything.'

'That doesn't sound promising.'

'It's not,' she said. 'It's bad.'

Her eyes stayed unblinking.

She said, 'They've never got involved before. I...'

She trailed off.

He said, 'Tell me.'

'I don't even know them. I have a contact, like a middle-man. He passes information back and forth.'

'That sounds awfully complicated.'

'It's the deniability system for an entire country's black ops.'

King paused, then shrugged. 'You're right. I guess it needs to be complicated.'

They both went quiet, listening for the sound of Slater at his front door.

They heard nothing.

Violetta waited a few beats, then suspicion clouded her features. She turned and threw the door open and took a long look in either direction. She looked back over her shoulder, evidently having come up empty-handed. 'You heard the elevator, too, right?'

King nodded.

She said, 'He changed his mind, then. He's gone.'

A reflexive twitch hammered home.

King said, 'Or it wasn't him.'

He crossed to the kitchen island, ripped a Sig Sauer handgun from an unremarkable drawer previously locked with a fingerprint scanner, and stormed straight past her.

'Jason,' she said.

He barrelled out into the hallway, opting for offence over defence, and there he froze.

Gun raised.

Mind sharp.

The seconds ticked by.

They turned to minutes.

Nothing.

Then something buzzed in Violetta's pocket, back inside the penthouse.

King turned back to her, lowering his guard, and saw her staring guardedly at the illuminated screen of her phone.

She looked up.

'It's him,' she said.

t street level, concealed amidst the pedestrians on the sidewalk outside his tower, Slater pressed the phone to his ear.

Violetta answered and said, 'Got cold feet?'

'How do I know you're not going to put a bullet in my head when I step through the doorway?'

'There's no one here. It's just me. And King.'

'That's what I'm worried about.'

'He's not a threat to you.'

Slater turned his emotions to steel. 'I know that. That's not my worry. I've fought him twice. I won both times. But I don't want him as my enemy. Neither of us deserve to be enemies.'

'You're paranoid,' Violetta said. 'He doesn't even know what I'm going to tell you.'

'Come downstairs.'

'You need to come back here eventually. Why bother drawing this out?'

'I sure don't.'

'You didn't leave with a bag. Earlier tonight.'

'I don't need a bag.'

He thought he heard her give a soft grunt of understanding. 'You've never needed anything but the clothes on your back, right?'

'Right.'

'It's impressive,' she said. 'But we need to talk upstairs. Trust me.'

'Don't take it personally if I don't trust you right now.'

She said, 'So it's a stalemate, then?'

'Staten Island,' he said. 'The St. George neighbourhood. I'll meet you there.'

She made to respond, as if she was going to say, *No way.* Then she paused, and instead said, 'Why there?'

'Because it's dodgy as hell, and you don't know your way around it, so anyone you scramble to send will stand out like they've got a flashing light above their head.'

She drew in air, a sharp inhalation. 'Will, I can't.'

'I'm telling you to. Or I'm gone.'

She fell quiet for a solid ten seconds. He didn't fill the silence with unnecessary chatter. He let her think.

Then she said, 'Alright. Fine. You've forced my hand.'

'And what hand might that be?'

'I called you up here to do you a favour and give you an explanation. But, frankly, there's no time left.'

He tensed up.

She said, 'So I'm going to have to tell you over the phone. Because I just got word that they're here.'

'Who's here?'

'My employers.'

'Who are they?'

'I don't know,' she said. 'That's the honest truth. But they're not happy.'

'I didn't expect them to be.'

'They want to speak to you.'

'So give them my number.'

'No,' she said. 'Not like that.'

Slater sensed foreign movement behind him, and whirled out of instinct, hand flying to the concealed Glock at his waist. Ready to rip the gun free and engage in a shootout in the middle of civilised Manhattan, if that's what it came to.

But the reality wasn't as immediately threatening. An unmarked black Navigator — a big no-nonsense SUV — had whispered to the kerb out the front of his building.

The rear door swung open from the inside.

Exposing a dark, gaping hole.

Through the phone, Violetta said, 'Get in.'

'And if I don't?'

'Then it's out of my hands.'

He stood motionless, the phone pressed to his ear. Civilians flowed past, oblivious to the standoff unfolding nearby.

She said, 'I'm trying to help you, Will. I told you to trust me. But don't trust them. Not for a moment.'

He said, 'Am I going to make it out of this alive?'

'Yes,' she said. 'They only want to talk.'

'Is that what they told you?'

She went quiet.

He said, 'You said it yourself. You don't know who they are.'

He stared into the shadows of the Navigator's interior.

He said, 'So really, you have no idea what they'll do.'

She said, 'Go with them, Will.'

'Do I have another choice?'

'Not anymore.'

His insides crumbled.

She said, 'They have eyes on you now. You're in their crosshairs. Get in the car.'

He hung up.

She couldn't help him anymore.

The dark rear seats beckoned.

He could run left or right. But they'd hit him. No question.

And, realistically, he'd only endanger innocent lives.

Checkmate.

He stepped down off the sidewalk and got in the car.

34

King said, 'They won't kill him.'

Violetta had lowered the phone seconds earlier, distraught. She seemed genuinely affected by Slater's predicament. He could tell she wanted the best for him.

She said, 'How can you know that?'

'Because if they do, I'll be angry,' he said. 'Beyond angry. And they know how close we are. It won't be worth felling us both.'

'They couldn't fell you both if they tried.'

'Exactly.'

Violetta paused, looking past him, out the window. Ruminating.

She said, 'You'd do that for him?'

'Why wouldn't I?'

'You two aren't happy with each other. I can tell.'

'Which is nonsense, in the big picture. He's my closest ally. We're going to disagree. In fact, we do it all the time. But what we have runs beneath that. That's why I went to Moscow. That's why I went alone. For him.'

Her face fell.

Out of nowhere.

Like she'd just realised something else.

'What?' he said.

'There's something else I came to talk about. It's urgent.'

'As urgent as this?'

She nodded.

He sighed. 'If it has to do with work…'

'It does.'

'Violetta,' he said. 'Slater's life is hanging in the balance. You think I care about—?'

'You should,' she said. 'Slater should be a separate issue entirely. Especially seeing what I'm about to tell you came from your own tip.'

'*My* tip?'

'Donati Group,' she said. 'What you told us to investigate. We investigated. We found something.'

He froze. 'Really? I thought that'd be the last thing on your mind.'

'The world doesn't stop because Will Slater has a midlife crisis.'

'I know,' he said. 'But I thought you might have been preoccupied.'

'This has nothing to do with me,' she said. 'I'm only in this state because I care about Will.'

'So what did your people find?' King said. 'With Donati?'

'It's early stages,' she said. 'But there's something happening in California.'

'What?'

'We came across what we believe to be a live criminal operation. There were … how do I put this? There were discrepancies in some of the files we dug up in the wake of Donati's death.'

'I told you there would be.'

'But as this unfolds...'

She trailed off.

He said, 'Just tell it like it is.'

'This is horrible timing.'

'I know. But the timing's never right, is it?'

She said, 'We might need you.'

He massaged his temple with two fingers spaced wide.

She said, 'There's a unique opening. Alonzo found it. Before I tell you more ... I need to know whether you're in or not.'

'What if Slater needs me?'

'That's the problem.'

'How urgent is it?'

'You don't have to accept,' she said. 'But...'

But.

It said everything.

But this is still your job.

But innocent people are in danger.

But bad people will get away if we don't act now.

The same old story.

This time, a little different.

But ultimately the same.

King said, 'What are his chances?'

'Slater's?'

He nodded.

She tightened her mouth, but her eyes remained kind. The age-old *"your guess is as good as mine"* expression.

He tried to weigh it all up, analyse it logically, come up with the most optimal solution. Just as he'd done his whole life. It only took him a couple of seconds to realise it wouldn't work here. There were too many variables. Too much pressure. He'd simply have to decide, and commit to his decision.

He looked at her.

He thought about Slater.

But Slater wasn't standing here. The man had made his own choices. He'd put himself in a volatile situation. Violetta was still here, doing her job, persevering in the face of hardship. He respected both choices, for different reasons.

He said, 'I'm in.'

'Are you sure?'

He nodded. 'Let me guess. It's a one man job?'

She nodded back. 'There's only a window for one opera-tive. You just came back from Moscow. Ordinarily, if these were normal circumstances, I'd ask Slater. So you two were even. But...'

But.

As always.

He said, 'California, you said?'

She gave a barely perceptible nod.

He said, 'So, if I get killed in California, it's Slater's fault?'

She didn't answer.

Just stared at him.

Then said, 'You know, maybe you're not in the right state of mind for this gig.'

'You got anyone else?'

'Of course.'

'You got anyone else like me or Slater?'

'No,' she said. '*That* I don't have.'

'There's got to be dozens of SF boys with the same reac-tion speed as me,' he said. 'You've had over a decade to screen for it. I pioneered the division, but surely I'm a relic of the past.'

'Not yet. There are younger men with the same reflexes as you. But they don't have the experience. They don't have the cool-headedness. You've been on hundreds of solo operations and you're still alive. That's the real unicorn.'

He said, 'You honestly need me?'

She said, 'Yes.'

He said, 'Then it doesn't matter what my state of mind is, does it?'

She said, 'That's the answer I wanted.'

'I'm tired. I want to go to bed. Can we turn work mode off?'

'Not yet. We need to wait.'

'For what?'

Her silence answered the question.

He said, 'How do you think he's doing?'

After a long pause, she said, 'I don't know.'

35

The Navigator's driver was the only occupant.

Slater got in diagonally behind him, sliding into the rear passenger seat. He sized the man up, which revealed nothing. The guy was almost deliberately ordinary — shapeless, flabby, and white, with thin sandy hair and a pair of faded spectacles resting on the bridge of his nose.

Slater said, 'Are you my boss?'

Keeping both hands on the wheel, the driver looked over his shoulder. Behind the spectacles, his pale eyes were ice. 'What?'

'I was making a joke.'

'Okay.'

The guy turned back to the road, put his blinker on, and carved the Navigator away from Slater's tower.

It was late enough that they made good time. Good for Manhattan, at least. They took FDR Drive north until it became Harlem River Drive, and then crossed the Hudson River via George Washington Bridge. The late evening traffic receded, and then the driver wordlessly got on the

Palisades Interstate Parkway. It ran parallel to the Hudson for eight miles and then weaved north-west, crossing the New Jersey/New York border. They were heading toward Bear Mountain. Slater had done the occasional hike up there.

Quiet country.

Backwoods.

His stomach twisted.

The view out the window of estates and industrial zones dissipated in density as they moved through Mt Ivy, and then the darkness became all-encompassing as they plunged into the woods of Bear Mountain State Park.

They hadn't been on the road for any longer than an hour, but to Slater it had been an eternity. He ran a finger restlessly over the cool metal of the Glock, feeling it there in its holster. The driver hadn't confiscated it, or even demanded to frisk him.

Which meant they didn't care that he was armed.

They were either so far ahead that any resistance he attempted would prove futile, or they simply wanted to talk.

He had never been the optimistic type.

Dark tree trunks flashed by, framing the Navigator, threatening to swallow it whole.

Halfway through the state park, Slater said, 'Just where the hell are we going?'

'You can't honestly expect me to tell you that.'

'What if I put a gun to the back of your head and asked politely?'

The driver didn't turn around, or even register the threat.

His dark silhouette remained fixed in place.

Quietly, he said, 'Then they'll know you did, and when we get there, they'll bury you.'

Above the low hum of the motor and the *whoosh* of tree trunks flashing past, the silence was deafening.

Slater took his finger off the Glock.

Killing the temptation.

He sat a little straighter, and breathed a little deeper, and hoped like hell he'd live to see the sunrise.

They burst free from the woods and crossed back over the Hudson at Purple Heart Memorial Bridge. From there they drove up through Garrison, then Cold Spring, until finally they were racing further north with the dark, silent river on their left. Ten minutes later the driver veered inland, putting a natural barrier of trees between the Navigator and the river.

Finally he eased off the accelerator.

The SUV crawled to a halt on the side of the road, its wheels rumbling against the gravel.

Then it stopped.

Slater sat motionless in the back. He didn't go for his gun, but he didn't play along, either.

The driver said, 'This is you.'

Slater looked outside. Saw the outlines of trees, black against the blacker backdrop. He thought he could make out the moonlight glinting off the Hudson, deep in the background, but he couldn't be sure.

He said, 'What is this, exactly?'

'There's a dinghy waiting for you on the riverbank,' the driver said. 'Use it to get yourself over to Pollepel Island.'

'What?'

The driver spun in his seat, mildly irritated. 'There's an island out there in the middle of the Hudson, maybe a thousand feet from shore. It'll be a quick trip. You can steer a dinghy, can't you?'

'Yes,' Slater said. 'I can steer a dinghy.'

'Go to the island. You'll see Bannerman Castle. Go there. They'll find you.'

Slater said, 'Are you fucking with me?'

'I assure you I'm not.'

'Will I find a magic scroll there? Maybe a lost civilisation? The long-buried tomb of an emperor?'

'It's not a castle anymore,' the driver said. 'It's a pile of abandoned ruins. My employers are cautious. That's where they want to meet you.'

'A great place to bury a body, no doubt.'

'Yeah,' the driver said, unapologetic. 'Probably. That's none of my business though.'

'And if I decide to take the dinghy elsewhere?'

'They'll know. If I had to guess, that's why they wanted me to bring you all the way out here. Because you have a gun, and I'm sure you have wilderness survival training, but that won't be enough. You won't make it back to the safety of the city in time.'

Slater stewed restlessly.

The driver shrugged. 'You came. You dug your own grave. But maybe they don't want to kill you.'

'Do you know what they want?'

The man smiled wryly. 'I don't even know who they are.'

Slater fidgeted.

The man said, 'Good luck.'

Slater took that as his cue. He nodded, found the handle, popped the door, and stepped out of the Navigator. The temperature had plummeted. His phone told him it was a shade after nine p.m. He exhaled softly, and a cloud of breath whispered out and dissipated.

He closed the door behind him, and the car pulled away. It looped a U-turn and then rumbled off back the way it had come. When it was out of earshot, Slater tasted the silence.

It didn't offer him comfort.

But if darkness and treachery and uncertainty deterred him, he wouldn't have made it a week in his profession.

So he turned and made straight for the tree line and the uncertain fate beyond.

36

The dinghy was small and metal and rusting.

Slater guessed it could only fit three or four people without capsizing, but that wasn't something he needed to worry about. It was abandoned on the shore, half in the water, half on the wet dirt.

He pushed it into the river, held it in place by putting a palm on the outboard motor, and used his other hand to yank the ripcord three times in a row. It sputtered to life, and he pushed off the bank and leapt in. He kept the Glock in its holster. The driver was right. Resistance was futile. He knew there'd be a minimum of three snipers with night optics trained on his head from separate vantage points.

You can't kill what you can't see.

All his surroundings were pitch black, but even still he could make out Bannerman Castle. He'd thought it odd that the driver hadn't given specific directions, but now he realised there was no need. The ruins loomed on the eastern side of the island. Even the silhouette was foreboding. If they were truly abandoned, then they'd normally be festering with junkies, vandals and the homeless, but Slater had no doubt any witnesses had been driven out long before this meeting.

He steered toward the castle.

The outboard motor ruptured the night with its throaty chugging. It was practically deafening on the quiet lake, but it didn't perturb him. They knew he was coming regardless, and even if he was quiet as a mouse they'd still have eyes on him.

He figured he might as well announce his arrival as bombastically as possible.

Get this over and done with.

He pulled up to the eastern shore of the island, largely unfazed. If they thought shadows and old ruins and a permanent sense of foreboding would rattle him, then they hadn't even bothered to have a glance at his case files.

He drove the dinghy straight onto the dirt bank, where it ground to a halt. He used the momentum of the boat slowing to vault off the damp wooden bench within and leap out over the hull. He landed in the dirt, and in one motion drew the Glock from its holster and stuffed it in the pocket of his leather jacket.

He kept both hands in his jacket pockets, to throw up a decoy smokescreen.

Then he advanced toward Bannerman Castle, trudging through overgrown weeds and scores of bushes.

It was dead quiet. Now that he could see the looming ruins up close, he thought he recalled a faint echo of information about the castle from his military days. He'd heard it mentioned before. It used to be an old military surplus storage facility, or something of the sort. Now it was only a tourist attraction from a distance, visible along the Amtrak route.

Out of curiosity, Slater touched two fingers to his neck, measuring his pulse.

Perfectly normal.

You're going to need to do better than that, gents.

Dealing with fear was his greatest strength.

Only a couple of dozen feet from the castle, a handful of key features became visible. One wall had collapsed entirely, and modern steel supports propped up what was left of the edifice. A moss-covered set of concrete steps, framed by uneven brick banisters, led to a regal archway.

Darkness loomed beyond.

Slater mounted the steps without hesitation. There was no one visibly waiting for him. Not even a temporary lighting setup. He reached the archway and stepped through, into the ruins' interior.

Which turned out to be nonexistent. What remained of the castle acted as a U-shaped perimeter for an uneven patch of hillside exposed to the stars.

There was no roof over his head, and his eyes were adjusting to the lack of light, so when he came to rest between a couple of small boulders he made out the four silhouettes immediately.

They were there, motionless, waiting for him in the centre of the ruins.

Four old men in suits.

Apart from that, their features were indiscernible.

Slater exaggerated a shiver, making sure they knew he was mocking them. 'Scary stuff.'

No one offered a response.

They all stared.

Like rock golems, frozen in time.

Now, Slater had to stifle an actual shiver.

The old man on the far left said, 'It's discreet.'

His voice was low, and commanding, and utterly confident. Every syllable had a purpose. He didn't waste words.

Slater said, 'An apartment in Manhattan is discreet. This is unnecessary.'

'We think it's perfectly necessary.'

'Because you have multiple vantage points?' Slater said. 'So your men can draw a bead on me? You're a suit. You don't spend time in the field. So you didn't think about the fact that,' — Slater's Glock materialised in his hand in a half-second, its barrel aimed rigidly at the old man's forehead — 'I'm a hell of a lot faster than your men. And now you're fucked. It's a standoff. Your man shoots me, and you die. You're not ready to die.'

'I am,' the old man said, supremely confident.

Slater didn't blink.

The man continued. 'If you pull that trigger we'll have Alexis Diaz cut up into little pieces while she's still alive.'

Slater's stomach knotted. He didn't budge.

He said, 'You wanted me here to talk. So talk.'

'Not before you put that gun at your feet and kick it over.'

'Not a chance in hell.'

The man on the right, in a husky, gravelly voice, said, 'Then your girlfriend is already dead.'

Like they'd synchronised their speech beforehand, the man on the left continued, 'We don't even have to give the command. It's my men who are watching who will. Maybe they already have. You're acting awfully threatening. One of my best men is probably strangling the life out of her as we speak. Every second you keep that gun aimed at my head is another second she can't breathe.'

Slater put the gun down.

He kicked it over.

He said, 'Talk.'

Even in the darkness, he saw them all smile.

Wicked smiles.

They'd tasted victory.

His heart skipped a beat.

37

Slater had the humility to realise all his skepticism about the dramatic nature of the location had been posturing.

Really, deep down, he knew he was fucked.

The men in front of him had full control. They had the resources of a global superpower at their fingertips. They could do whatever they wanted with total anonymity. They could snap their fingers and have both him and Alexis wiped out in seconds. There'd be men watching her apartment, lying in wait for her to try and make a run for it. They'd snatch her. It wouldn't be hard.

He quickly realised the only option he had was to play along.

No matter what they wanted.

The man on the left said, 'We understand you are no longer satisfied with your career.'

'That's right.'

Choose your words carefully.

Don't overcommit.

The old man said, 'May I ask why?'

'I've given my life and my health to my country,' Slater said. 'My brain will be mush twenty years from now. I probably won't live to see old age, even if I don't take another scratch. Because of accumulative damage. I want to enjoy what little time I have left on this planet. Is that good enough?'

'You're a useful asset,' the man said. 'So is King.'

'King isn't leaving.'

'You don't know that. The two of you are inseparable. Perhaps he promised to stay, but that's probably a false platitude. He's probably going to reconsider less than a week after you leave.'

'Is that what this is about?'

'We've got hotheaded operatives with similar physical gifts,' the old man said. 'What we don't have are the pair of you. You're not easily replicable. Maybe we could forge a couple of killers into what the two of you are, but it'd take us years. We're in the process. But we're not there yet.'

'So...?'

'So you're not out. We need more notice. You can't up and leave. You will leave behind positions that require filling, and we don't have the necessary candidates to fill them. Yet.'

'What happened to Black Force? What happened to all those men?'

'They were good,' the old man said. 'But they weren't you.'

'I won't be useful anymore,' Slater said. 'My heart isn't in this world. That's most of the reason King and I are in the position we're in. Because this is our whole lives, and we dedicated everything to it. I can't do that anymore.'

'You must.'

Slater opened his mouth, but the words caught in his

throat. He realised they were useless. He wouldn't convince these four of anything. They were miles above him on the hierarchy. He had individual talent, but they wielded entire departments and divisions.

Big, big difference.

He said, 'Whatever I can do, King can do. And he won't leave.'

The four silhouettes lingered, silent, watchful.

Slater said, 'What?'

One of the men in the middle — Slater couldn't be sure which — said, 'I'd wager we understand human motivation a little better than you do. We've been pulling strings for decades. King will go if you do.'

'What if I can guarantee he won't?'

'You haven't confirmed that with him.'

'How do you know?'

'Because I can read it all over your face, and all I have is the moonlight. You're throwing shit at the wall to see what sticks. You're a bad liar.'

'This is what he does,' Slater said. 'This is his life.'

'Same goes for you.'

'Not anymore.'

'Too bad,' the old man said. 'We have a couple of operations in the pipeline that we may need you both for. Are you really going to let innocent people die?'

'I've given it my all.'

'You haven't. Not yet.'

'I don't have a choice?'

'You don't.'

'You really want an operative in the field who doesn't want to be there?'

'You may not want to do the job,' the old man said. 'But

you want to survive. If we drop you in a war zone, you're going to fight your way out regardless.'

'I didn't sign up to this to be a slave.'

'But you signed up. So now you're ours.'

'Is this a concrete decision?'

The man stared. 'What part of what we said made you think it wasn't?'

'I thought you might like to think about it. Reconsider.'

'Your girlfriend,' the old man said. 'Alexis Diaz. She's a civilian. She knows what you do. She knows ... the truth about how this country gets things done.'

Slater didn't try to bluff his way out of it. He figured they deserved some level of respect.

He nodded.

The old man said, 'The only reason you are alive is because you're of use to us. Serve your country, complete the tasks we need you for, and then we might reconsider neutralising you for treason. That's the best you're going to get.'

Inside, Slater raged.

Outwardly, he said, 'Yes, sir.'

'Do we have an understanding?'

'We do.'

'Don't try anything brash,' he said. 'We'll be watching.'

'Wouldn't dream of it.'

'You would,' the old man said. 'You'll think about it day and night. But you won't do it. Because you know what we're capable of.'

Slater went quiet.

The same man bent down, picked up Slater's Glock, and tossed it back. 'Your driver will meet you at the same place he dropped you off.'

Slater caught the gun and returned it to its holster.

Addressing all four of them, he said, 'Are you going to tell me who you are?'

The man on the far right said, 'No.'

Slater half-nodded.

He sensed his cue.

He turned on his heel and strode out of the ruins.

Back to the boat.

38

As the time inched past midnight, Slater stepped out of the Navigator for the final time.

The return journey had mirrored the trip there — he'd motored the dinghy back to the banks of the Hudson, clambered into the back of the SUV, and sat silent for the whole ride.

There'd been much more to think about this time round.

He and the driver didn't offer each other a gesture of farewell. There was little point. They would never see each other again. Slater got out and went into his lobby, fully aware that he was probably in someone's crosshairs.

He found it hard to care.

Nihilism plagued him.

Am I destined to do this forever?

Back and forth, back and forth, back and forth. Like a pendulum.

An enemy of his country, then a loyal warrior for it.

An endless cycle.

Unless he killed the cycle.

Unless he got out, and stayed out.

He rode the elevator up, wondering what he'd find. Wondering where the allegiances of his closest colleagues lay. King first, then Violetta a distant second. Outside of that, he had no work relations.

He felt utterly alone.

He reached his floor, and made straight for King's apartment. He knew they'd be in there. There was nothing in his own dwelling except himself and his thoughts, and he wanted to spend as little time in his own head as possible.

For now, at least.

He only knocked once before the door swung open in his face.

It wasn't King.

It was Violetta.

She was genuinely concerned, her features marred by stress and guilt and fear. She said, 'Did they hurt you?'

He looked himself over, as if it wasn't obvious that he was untouched. 'Yeah, they shot me five times. Can't you tell?'

She said, 'Sorry. I'm just worried.'

'Don't be,' he said.

He brushed past her and made for the living room.

King was sprawled across an armchair, lazily squeezing a metal grip trainer between his fingers. It was an unconscious pastime Slater had seen him steadily become addicted to over the course of the last year. He sat still, absent-mindedly staring into space, his giant forearms rippling with veins as he compressed and released the handles. There was no way you'd be able to tell he was crushing two hundred pounds of resistance in his grip.

He looked up as Slater entered. 'How'd that go?'

Slater paused. 'Not great. You don't look so good either.'

'Poor timing all round,' King muttered.

'What are you talking about?'

He sensed Violetta materialise behind him, catching up after he'd brushed past her. 'King has a job.'

Slater wheeled on the spot. 'Are you serious?'

'It has nothing to do with you.'

'Sounds like it does,' Slater said. 'A convenient solo op. You're getting him out of here so he can't talk to me?'

'What are *you* talking about?' King said. 'That's a bullshit conspiracy.'

'I'm sure you know all about how that meeting went,' Slater said. 'Did Violetta bring you up to speed before she said you need to get out of the city?'

Violetta said, 'He doesn't know how it went. I don't either. We don't even know who you met.'

Slater looked at her and rolled his eyes.

She said, 'I'm serious. You think you two are the only ones they're keeping in the dark?'

'So you report to...?'

'A middleman.'

Slater went quiet. Frankly, he didn't have any evidence she was lying — they'd be going round in circles if he remained steadfast in his disbelief. So he backed off. 'Okay. Fair enough.'

'How'd it go?'

'They said no.'

The atmosphere tightened.

No one spoke.

King said, 'What does that mean?'

Slater turned to face him. They stared each other dead in the eyes, which said a whole lot more than words could. All the nuances, all the uncertainty, all the determination — Slater knew King could see it.

King said, 'You're thinking about running. But for now,

you're still employed. So why don't you take this solo op, if you really think it's a conspiracy to whisk me away?'

'I know nothing about it.'

'Neither do I,' King said. 'That's the way this job works. Or have you forgotten that already?'

You could cut the air with a knife.

Violetta said, 'I'm going to leave you two to talk it over. Jason — pass on what you know. There's a ticket booked for California tomorrow morning. One of you needs to get on that plane. And I need to know tonight. Alonzo needs a final decision, so he can create a fake identity.'

Slater said, 'California?'

She said, 'That's right.'

Then she left.

Nodded to both of them, made for the door, and disappeared through it before either of them could utter a word of protest.

Leaving them to discuss a volatile future.

39

King sized up Slater as soon as Violetta walked out.

The man was visibly rattled. Whatever he'd seen had spooked him, as much as he might like to pretend it hadn't. Which made conversation unnecessary. Slater would lie, putting on a brave face, and King would know better. So he didn't bother prying.

Instead, he said, 'You think this is all a scheme. So take the gig. Prove it's not.'

'My heart isn't in this,' Slater said. 'That's not going to change. I'm not foolish enough to half-commit to a line of work this serious.'

'So... what?' King said. 'Where does that leave you? You've been forced to continue working, and now you're refusing to work.'

'You were asked first,' Slater said. 'You fucking do it.'

'I just came from a solo gig.'

'Which had nothing to do with the government.'

'You never would have said that before. You never would

have nitpicked. That's not what we do. We help each other, and we split the workload — whatever that entails.'

'What are you trying to prove? I told you I've changed.'

'You've made a decision. It doesn't mean you're any different to the person you were a week ago.'

'I'm not going to California.'

'If I do,' King said, 'and you stay here...'

'Say it.'

'I doubt you'll be here when I get back.'

'You think I'd be that stupid? To disobey the government?'

A rhetorical question if King had ever heard one.

'Yes,' King said. 'I think you're exactly that stupid.'

Slater eyed him.

King said, 'Because I am too.'

Slater gave a half-nod. King watched his guarded expression lift. Ever so slightly. Anyone else wouldn't have noticed it.

Slater said, 'If I asked you to stay, would you?'

King thought about it.

Then he said, 'No.'

'No?'

'You want out. I don't. Not yet. I've got a good thing going. And as long as I'm still working, then I can't turn down a job.'

'You can. There's dozens of other operatives who can do it. I'm telling you I need you here. Because I'm objective enough to recognise that I might make a reckless decision in the next few days. I need you to be the voice of reason.'

'You'll have to be your own voice of reason,' King said. 'I'm going to California.'

Slater steered away from his own problems. 'What's the job?'

'The paper trail left behind in the wake of Donati's death,' King said. 'Violetta had her people look into it discreetly. They found a discrepancy with cargo en route to the Port of Los Angeles. A colossal cover-up. Something fishy is arriving in the next few days. The evidence would usually be swept under the rug, but now it's exposed because the head honcho is dead.'

'Why do they need you?'

'Over ten million shipping containers pass through Long Beach every year. There isn't a chance in hell they can narrow down which one they're looking for. But Alonzo found a way in. He came across a discreet ad on the deep web for a manual labour job. Apparently a bunch of rich gangsters with a condo in Emerald Bay are looking for someone to stay with them for a few days and help move "illegitimate cargo" on the exact day Donati's paper trail says the container is arriving. It's too coincidental. It means they're the muscle on the ground in Cali. Alonzo can forge any document on the planet, so he's going to put one of us in as a crook with a mile-long criminal record. That way the gangsters think we're legit, and think we have something to lose.'

'Surely the container is listed in the paper trail?'

'It's redacted. Donati had covered that much before I killed him.'

Slater said, 'You have to admit it's suspicious timing. This came out of nowhere.'

'Because I only got back from Moscow yesterday,' King said. 'They've barely had twenty-four hours to dig. It's unfolding in real time.'

Slater shook his head. 'There's no breaks in this life, is there?'

'There is if you run,' King said. 'If that's what you want to do, I won't stop you.'

'You couldn't stop me if you tried.'

'Maybe. Maybe not.'

'So you're going to Cali?'

'I don't have a choice.'

'You do.'

'As soon as you start thinking that there's a dozen other people who could do the gig you've been tasked with, you need to get out. There's no room for doubt in what we do.'

'I'm doubting everything,' Slater said. 'So, based on your diagnosis, I need to get out.'

King stood up for the first time since Slater had walked into the apartment. He drew to his full height — three inches taller than Slater — and faced the man across the room.

He said, 'Neither of us is doing what the other is asking. That's never happened before. You know what it means.'

Slater slowly nodded. 'Is this it?'

'It has to be.'

'I didn't think this would happen so ... fast.'

'Life is fast.'

Slater took a step forward. 'We're done?'

'You're out. I'm in. So we're done.'

Now King stepped forward. They were six feet apart.

He said, 'Will I see you again?'

Slater said, 'Maybe.'

'Will you be here when I get back?'

'No.'

'I assume you don't want me to pass this information onto Violetta.'

'I'd appreciate it if you didn't.'

'I can do that much, at least.'

'Thank you. But it doesn't much matter, does it? This place is probably bugged.'

King shook his head. 'Not a chance. I sweep it regularly.'

'If it was bugged, you wouldn't tell me. You'd lie.'

'I've never lied to you. I'm not about to start.'

Slater offered a hand. 'Good luck, brother.'

King's blood went cold, but he accepted the handshake regardless.

Sometimes in this field you have to do things you don't want to do, but you know are for the best.

He said, 'Enjoy retirement.'

'I'll try.'

'Do it better than I did.'

Slater repeated, 'I'll try.'

King could see the man holding back. Neither of them felt the need to dive into lengthy speeches reminiscing on their shared adventures. They both knew what they'd been through with each other. Repeating it was useless.

Slater nodded.

King nodded back.

He watched his closest friend, his brother-in-arms, his comrade, walk out of his life forever.

40

Slater stepped outside.

Violetta was standing by the elevators with her back to the wall. Waiting for him. She eyed him off down the corridor and said, 'Are you going to California?'

He shook his head.

She said, 'So you'll stay here. King will go.'

A nod.

She said, 'You'll run.'

He looked at her.

Thought about lying.

But she'd know better. So he didn't lie, but he didn't tell the truth either. He simply let his stare turn icy, and he didn't blink, and he hoped she understood.

She did.

She said, 'I won't report this.'

He'd been about to walk back to his own apartment, but he froze.

He said, 'Don't lie to me.'

She said, 'I'm not.'

'They'll kill you if they find out you knew in advance.'

'They won't find out. Here's what you need to know. There's an off-the-books tier-one crew watching Alexis. There's a separate, equally talented crew watching this building. If you can slip past both groups, you'll be away, and you'll be a step ahead, but that's a tall task. These are legit special mission units who aren't publicly disclosed. And if you get out from underneath them, they'll never stop hunting you.'

'Special operators whisked out of the usual elite units?' Slater said, seeking confirmation. 'Delta, DEVGRU, 24 STS?'

Violetta nodded. 'Serious players. They're special sanction tactical teams.'

'Tell me where the crew watching this building is set up,' he said. 'That's all I need.'

She said, 'I can't do that. I'd be contributing to their deaths.'

'You have my word I won't kill any of them.'

'You'll have to. If that's what it comes to.'

Slater shook his head. 'They might have been assigned to keep tabs on me and neutralise me if necessary, but that doesn't make them bad men. They could have been told anything about me. They don't deserve to die.'

Violetta stared at him from down the hall. 'But if you're both aiming at each other, and it's you or them…'

Slater said, 'I won't kill them. If I say it, I mean it.'

She bit her lower lip.

Indecision seared her from the inside. He could see it weighing her down, drenching her in misery.

Finally, she said, 'They're in the building. Seventh floor. Room 732.'

'How are they watching it at street level?'

'Cameras, obviously. Human sentries are a thing of the past.'

'Are they expecting me?'

'Hell no.'

'Is the room fortified?'

'Yes.'

'How many?'

'I'm not sure. I think there's five of them.'

'They're all inside?'

'I have no idea. Don't move now. They could very well be scattered all over the place. When King leaves tomorrow morning, then you do it. Because they'll be expecting you to make a run for it, so they'll be bunkered down watching every camera. That's when you'll catch them.'

Slater said, 'If the upper echelon finds out you told me this...'

'I can't get any more dead, can I?'

'Why are you doing this for me?'

She said, 'Because you deserve a life.'

Then she turned and thumbed the elevator panel. Instantly, the nearest doors whispered open, and she stepped in. She didn't turn back to look at him. She let the doors close on her hunched frame, whisking her out of sight.

She'd just put her life on the line for him.

Slightly unstable, he went to his door and unlocked it. An observer wouldn't be able to tell, but he felt the slightest hint of a tremor in his fingers.

Tomorrow, it'd all blow up.

The stage was set.

There was nothing left to do but execute.

41

King's alarm sounded at five a.m.

The plane to California, for which he had a one-way ticket, was due for takeoff at nine.

One way, because there was no knowing the extent of the job until he was in the thick of it.

He clambered out of bed with the knowledge that Violetta and her entire team had pulled an all-nighter. They'd told him as much the previous evening, working until the early hours of the morning to get all the documentation and a bulletproof cover story in place. He knew if they'd pulled it off in time, a foot soldier would have slipped the fresh passport and briefing dossier under his door sometime during the night. Violetta would have provided him with access to King and Slater's level of the tower.

With a slight sense of foreboding, he padded barefoot through the main space and into the entranceway.

A passport and a manila folder rested on the tiles, a foot from the locked front door.

King sighed.

Game time.

He picked up the passport first, and committed the details to memory. Now he was Liam Kingsley — thirty-eight years old, born in Dallas. Generic details. He knew the dossier would contain the juicier information.

He went through his predictable morning routine, including the workout, but he halved the intensity. He needed plenty of gas left in the tank when he made it to Los Angeles. The operation had been sprung on him out of nowhere, but that didn't mean it was any less dangerous. In the field, the slightest mishap could leave you with a bullet in the back of the head, so he held off on scrutinising the dossier until his head was clear. He showered, packed several changes of clothes and an assortment of toiletries, shoved a decoy laptop into his backpack that Violetta had hand-delivered the previous evening, and then went straight to the door.

She'd arranged transportation to the airport, too.

Everything was being arranged on the fly, so when he made it downstairs and slipped into the rear seat of the waiting town car, he savoured the quiet. He exchanged a brief nod of greeting with the chauffeur, and then pointed to the roof above his head. The driver understood. Wordlessly, the guy thumbed a button on the console and the privacy screen — made of thick tinted glass — slid up, putting him out of earshot.

King pulled out his phone and called Violetta.

'Hey,' she grumbled.

'Are you going to sleep soon?'

'I'll try. But I'm stressed about Will.'

'Let's run through this,' he said. 'Just to be sure I have all the details. Pull me up if I'm wrong about anything.'

'Go for it.'

He started flicking through the dossier, narrating as he went.

'I'm a civilian. Liam Kingsley. Alonzo's planted surface-level evidence that I was involved in several outlaw motorcycle gangs up and down the East Coast. I'm tech-savvy from dealing small arms and drugs in New York over the dark web, which is how I found the ad in the first place. It lined up with a trip I wanted to take to California, and I conveniently meet every requirement. Alonzo submitted all of this to the posters of the ad, who are suspected to be a collection of low-profile gangsters who live in a giant condo in Emerald Bay.

'You and your team believe the ringleader is—' King flicked a page '—Ryan Duke, a successful entrepreneur in Laguna Beach who intelligence agencies have long suspected of leading a life of crime. He's meticulous, so you've never been able to pin anything on him, but it's believed that he operates in human trafficking and other illicit activities in and around the Port of Los Angeles. You suspect he launders his money through his legitimate companies, which he does with the help of financial gurus and a few morally bankrupt accountants.

'As for the container in question, what you have to work with is—' another page flick '—an informal list of shipping logs left behind on Donati's personal computer in the wake of his death. You used the NSA's services to take a peek at its contents before his helpers could destroy any trace of the hidden files. You didn't do this before, because ... well, you didn't know where to look. You found evidence of a shipment due to arrive at the Port of Los Angeles late tomorrow night. It aroused suspicion because it's only one container buried in an entire ship's worth of goods, but for some reason Donati had its arrival time noted down on his personal computer. The serial number of the TEU in question is redacted, but you're certain that Ryan Duke and his merry band of degenerates will lead you to it. You believe that Donati Group has hired Duke because he's meticulous, and he can be trusted to handle delivery. He knows the port, and he's been conducting his own business in and around it for years.'

Violetta said, 'So answer this — why is Duke posting an ad for manual labour on the dark web?'

'Because he was looking for someone like me,' King said. 'Liam Kingsley, that is. This is a new age, and you don't need to source local help anymore. You can put the feelers out across the country to find the right man for the job, no matter how seemingly insignificant it is. Duke is meticulous, so that's what he does. He wanted someone with something to lose, and he found it. He knows he can trust me to keep this silent, because Alonzo planted several pieces of compromising information on me that Duke now has in his possession. He'll threaten to ruin my life if I talk about what I'm handling at the port. Now *that's* leverage.'

'Good,' Violetta said. 'You have it all covered.'

'So,' King said. 'I show up, I meet Ryan Duke and his boys, I stay with them for a night, and then tomorrow we go to the port and they lead me straight to the container in question. Seems fairly straightforward.'

'You've got it.'

'Why don't you just tail Duke and then send in an army of SWAT as soon as he leads you to the container?'

'I don't think you understand the definition of "meticulous" in this case. There's a reason he hasn't been caught yet.

He'd smell something fishy, and he'd disappear. It's easy to vanish these days if you know what you're doing.'

Something twitched faintly in King's subconscious.

Easy to vanish if you know what you're doing.

Slater knows what he's doing.

He said, 'But he won't catch a whiff of the same scent on me? How good is Alonzo's cover story?'

'The absolute best,' Violetta said. 'You've seen Alonzo in action before. Without him, New York might still be dark. He can find information, and he can plant it, too. It helps that he has unlimited resources to work with.'

King sifted through the dossier one final time, scanning the pages, giving them a once-over.

He said, 'I think that's it. Over to me?'

'Over to you.'

'What do you think it might be?' he said. 'In the container.'

'I don't know,' Violetta said. 'But I'm sure it's not the first. It seems like an established pipeline. If you hadn't taken Coombs' gig, they would have got away with it scot-free.'

'They still might.'

'Do your thing,' she said. 'And then get back here. Slater needs you.'

King went quiet.

He knew she was making the call from one of the temporary black-ops HQs. Which meant it was being recorded — noted and filed for future reference if it was necessary. It'd make sense for her employers to discreetly keep track of all official conversation passing between handlers and operatives. But it also meant they both had to pretend like they didn't know Slater was going to run. Neither had discussed it with the other — not even in private.

They both just knew.

He said, 'Slater will be fine.'

He hung up.

Clenched the phone tight and glared out the window, unblinking.

42

Slater had his own alarm set for five, too.

He used a burner phone — untraceable, unconnected to his work — to call Alexis and run through a handful of details. He spoke slow and quiet, making sure she understood what the next few days were going to entail. She didn't ask questions. She didn't protest. She listened. At the end of the call, he asked her if she was still willing to do this. If she'd really thought about it.

'Yes,' she said.

'Your family.'

'Overseas. I haven't seen them since I came to the States. I have nothing worth staying for. And I understood what I was getting into when I first agreed to see you. I'm not naive.'

He said, 'I love you.'

'You, too.'

'See you soon.'

He lowered the phone to the bedside table, showered, dressed, and then went to the entranceway. There'd be a considerable waiting period, but purposeful observation was second nature to him. He'd packed the night before — a false passport he'd acquired in his own time (of which the government was unaware) and a credit card for an account owned by a shell company the government had no idea about.

That was it.

One might assume his life was hollow and empty if that was all he needed to start fresh, but he considered it freeing that he didn't have attachment to material possessions. His old phone, his old clothes, old mementos he used for decoration in this penthouse — none of it was necessary, and all of it was traceable, so it stayed behind. Everything he needed to access his hidden fortune — account numbers, passwords — were all in his head. From there he could build out a new life once he and Alexis bunkered down somewhere off the grid.

The penthouse meant nothing to him.

All he regretted leaving behind was the burden King would have to bear as a solo operative.

The waiting ended when he heard King's door opening, so faint and imperceptible he almost missed it. He wanted desperately to step outside and get one final look at his closest friend, but they'd said their goodbyes last night, and there was no point being extraneous. If he was to survive the day, there'd need to be no wasted movement.

He counted out long seconds, giving King time to step into the elevator, and when he was sure the coast was clear he patted himself down.

Passport.

Credit card.

Compact Glock 19 in a polymer appendix holster with an attached suppressor.

Four spare fifteen-round magazines, and a full one already loaded into the gun.

That now constituted all his worldly possessions.

He threw the door open and strode hard for the elevators, refusing to even give his penthouse a final glance. He made it to the panel, hit the DOWN symbol, stepped inside when the doors whisked open, and hit GROUND. Then he backtracked, leaving the metal box before it could seal him in, and made for the stairwell. Just in case the tactical team in room 732 were tracking the elevator's motion. He and King's twin penthouses were the only residential dwellings on this floor of the building, so the crew would know it was Slater on the move after observing King leaving the tower minutes earlier.

They'd be fixated on the lobby cameras for the next few minutes.

The stairwell was too bare and alien to hide security cameras. Everything was cold and concrete, with sharp corners and no shadows. Slater knew the coast was clear, but he remained diligent anyway. He leapt down three stairs at a time, absorbing each impact in stride, covering most of the eighty floors in what had to be record time. He reached the seventh floor fast, and entered it fast, because through the glass of the stairwell door he spotted a Hispanic maid wheeling a servicing cart.

Of course.

These floors are for hotel rooms.

So the crew hadn't set up shop in an empty apartment. They would have rented a room under a false name. Room 732 was a suite.

As Slater stepped out of the stairwell, he improvised. The maid hadn't noticed his presence yet, so he tapped into his mind muscle connection and deliberately constricted his throat. He held his breath and strained with all his might until his eyes bulged, turning bloodshot with each passing second.

Blood rushed to his face.

With one explosive breath, he gasped for air.

The maid wheeled around, startled. She was short and plump with a motherly demeanour. He snatched at his throat as he locked eyes with her, wheezing and spluttering and clawing for air.

'What wrong?' she said loudly, her accent thick, her English rudimentary.

'A-asthma,' he gasped. 'Asthma attack. Can't breathe. Oh...'

'Where is room, sir?'

He forced tears out, letting them stream down his face. He stumbled past her, only a couple of steps, making sure his voice didn't carry. She put a hand on his elbow to steady him, and he wheezed harder, but quieter. There was a method to the madness. Direct what little noise he made in the direction of the maid, but otherwise rely on bombastic visual gestures. That way, there was little sound to float under closed doors...

He stopped in front of the door numbered 732, and went completely silent, pretending his airways had closed.

He patted his pockets frantically. Then he widened his eyes even more. The widest they could go. He injected mortal fear into his features and then spun to face the maid.

'Key,' he gasped, his voice no louder than a whisper. 'Oh my god. My puffer. Inside. Key... *no.*'

It worked.

No time to ask for proof that it was his room. No time to do anything but frantically react. And she did, because she was a kind, caring soul that he felt terrible for taking advantage of. He hoped there were no cameras in the hallway. He hoped this didn't get her fired. Because she lunged for her cart and fished through a small plastic tub of keys and came out with the right one and bounded forward to force it into the lock.

Slater stepped back, and as soon as he was out of her peripheral vision he breathed normally.

Settled back into kill mode.

Then a dark thought struck him.

He kept retreating, putting his back against the far wall, keeping every nearby doorway in his peripheral vision.

The maid kept wriggling the key in the lock, too panicked to make it smooth.

Finally, the door clicked.

It swung open.

An empty room.

Which she thought was normal.

Slater had expected the reveal with seconds to spare, so when the door to room 730 burst open, a couple of feet to his left, he was already pivoting toward it. A big guy in a chunky tactical vest came out with a Beretta handgun raised, moving so fast that the maid still hadn't registered what was happening, but as soon as he crossed the threshold Slater was on him.

Smashed the butt of his Glock into the bridge of the guy's nose, with a single train of thought racing through his head.

Violetta doesn't make mistakes.

She knew.

She set you up.

43

Alonzo had passed Liam Kingsley's number onto the California muscle at some point during their encrypted email chain, so King landed at John Wayne Airport to a text message.

It came from an unknown number and arrived on his new burner phone.

I'm at the arrivals pickup area. Curbside.

King fired a text back.

Just landed. See you in 20.

He went through baggage claim, collected the small duffel that had been a hair too large for carry-on, and made his way out of the terminal. It was a warm day, far warmer than New York at this time of year. As soon as he stepped outside he upturned his face to a cloudless sky, drinking in the sun the same way a guy who'd spent most of his life on the East Coast would. He kept his face raised in full view of the arrivals pickup area. Carefree. Unfazed.

When he lowered his face and opened his eyes, a guy was standing in front of him.

Blond dreadlocked hair tied back in a thick ponytail. A

tall thin frame, deeply bronzed skin. Just enough wiry muscle to look athletic. He wore a sleeveless shirt and cargo shorts, with Doc Martens on his feet. A strange combo, but he pulled it off with natural charisma. He had intensely blue eyes, and right now they were scrutinising King.

'You know what they say,' the guy said. 'West is best.'

'Are you Ryan?'

'The one and only. Liam?'

King extended a hand, and Duke shook it.

King said, 'I thought you would have sent one of your boys.'

'You're new,' Duke said. 'And I'm careful, brother. You never know — there might be something kinda shifty about you that one of my boys would be too stupid to pick up on. Pays to be careful.'

He winked.

'Sure does,' King said. 'I can attest to that.'

Duke jerked a thumb over his shoulder. 'Car's this way.'

They set off, weaving through freshly arrived passengers hunched over phones or scouring their surroundings for rental car hire signs.

Duke said, 'Thanks for coming all this way.'

King had studied the email chain meticulously, so he knew exactly what Alonzo had and hadn't communicated to Duke.

'It's no problem,' he said. 'You know I was planning a trip to Cali anyway.'

'Bet it can't hurt to make some extra cash while you're here.'

King nodded. 'Cash never hurt. Any way I can get it.'

'You're speaking my language.'

Duke led him through the car park to an open-topped khaki Jeep Wrangler with modified suspension and oversized tyres. The epitome of California cool. Duke rounded the hood and got behind the wheel, and King threw his duffel in the rear seats and got in the passenger seat. Duke was tapping away at his phone, firing off a couple of messages, but as soon as King closed his door the man fired the 4x4 to life.

King said, 'Emerald Bay, right? That's where you live?'

'Yeah,' Duke said. 'Job's tomorrow night, in case you forgot. You can crash with us for a night. We've got room.'

'I Googled the suburb,' King said. 'Some of the houses I saw ... figured you'd have room.'

'I do alright.'

'Am I ever gonna find out what the job is?' King said, playing it off with a wry smile. 'You know ... what we're moving.'

Duke stared for an uncomfortable amount of time. King faked squirming. It served him better for Duke to think he was the one in charge, that he controlled the narrative. Really, King could deal with awkward silences like clockwork, but a careless arms dealer from New York might not be so socially competent, so he fidgeted in his seat.

Duke said, 'In due time. What's the rush?'

King shrugged. 'Couldn't care less. Just thought it might be important.'

'Not yet.'

Conversation petered out. Duke had yet to drive out of the parking spot. One hand was on the wheel, and his other elbow rested on the centre console. He'd twisted to face King, to size him up.

Duke reached for the keys in the ignition and twisted them back to their original position.

Killing the engine.

The silence got uncomfortable.

Duke said, 'You're in good shape, yeah? Hit the gym a bit? That's not gonna cut it out here. Alright?'

King kept fake-squirming. 'What's the deal, man? I thought we were cool.'

'We're very cool,' Duke said. 'But I went through the dark web to find a helper for a reason, brother. I need someone I can trust absolutely.'

'You can trust me absolutely. Swear.'

'I know I can,' Duke said. 'Because if I think you're getting untrustworthy, I might give One Police Plaza in New York an anonymous tip about a certain apartment you're leasing on Staten Island under a false name. An apartment you're using to stockpile guns with no serial numbers.'

King clammed up.

He used the mind body connection he'd honed in his early Black Force days to drain the colour from his face.

Duke nodded and said, 'Yeah.'

'How the fuck do you know that?'

Because you took Alonzo's bait.

That's why.

Duke said, 'I'm good at research. That's why you're here, buddy. Because I have leverage on you. I don't want there to be any misunderstanding.'

'Right,' King said.

'So what I'm getting at is,' Duke said, firing the car to life again, 'I'll tell you what I want to tell you, when I want to tell you it. Don't ask for more than you need to know.'

'Got it,' King said. 'I'm sorry, Duke.'

'Play by the rules, and keep your mouth shut, and you'll get paid. No problems.'

King nodded, staring at his feet.

'And I pay handsomely,' Duke said.

He craned his neck to reverse out of the spot, and then

floored it for the parking lot's exit. As they picked up speed, and the wind lashed his dreadlocks, he said, 'That's what you gotta learn, brother. All about what happens up here.' He tapped a long spindly finger to the side of his head. 'All that muscle you got — it's just for show.'

King nodded again, this time even more sheepishly.

Duke seemed to get off on the power trip. It made him comfortable. Out of nowhere, he said, 'You heard of Donati Group?'

'Yeah,' King said. 'I have.'

Hook.

Line.

Sinker.

44

Slater's first strike — with the butt of the Glock — broke the guy's nose.

For a couple of seconds after that, it doesn't matter if you're a tier-one soldier. You might as well be a common civilian.

Because your septum swells and your face puffs up and involuntary tears make your eyes water and your vision blurry. Not to mention the disorientation of the pain. Slater had broken his nose a few times in the field. It never gets easier. You never get used to it.

He smacked the Beretta out of the guy's hands and grabbed his skull in one palm and smashed the side of his head into the door frame. Which put him damn close to unconsciousness, and Slater used the hesitation to spin him around and use him as a human shield. He stormed into room 730 with the Glock pressed to the side of the guy's head, and he kicked the door shut behind him, sealing the petrified maid outside, out of harm's way.

Slater faced the room.

He said, 'Guns down. Right now.'

At least the rest of Violetta's intel had been truthful. There *were* five of them. The guy with the broken nose who'd stepped out first, and four other men spread across hastily erected folding tables around the beds, hunched over laptops, seated in front of an assortment of guns — some disassembled, some not. Two had been watching the screens when Slater stepped in. The other two had picked up weapons of their own, a fast response to the noise of the maid fiddling with the door to 732.

Too fast.

They'd been warned in advance.

Slater's blood ran cold, and the last shreds of trust he'd formed now fell away. Cynicism washed over him, and truthfully he liked it. He hadn't been built to rely on others, and now it felt damn good to sever all allegiances. Now, he cared about no one but himself and Alexis.

Violetta could burn, as far as he was concerned.

Right now there was a more imminent problem on his hands.

Namely, two more Berettas aimed in his direction.

Slater said, 'Don't be fucking stupid, boys.'

'There's backup on the way,' one of the men said.

'No,' Slater said. 'There isn't.'

They didn't answer.

Slater said, 'I can wait here all day. And all night. And all the next day. I won't budge an inch. Not even a hair.'

They stared at him, gazes furious, but the atmosphere in the room was ice. All six occupants — Slater included — were the elite of the elite. They lived and breathed combat. But there were levels.

Slater said, 'One of you is going to make the first mistake. I guarantee it. Anyone reaches for a phone, or looks like they're going to pull a trigger, I'll pull this one. Your buddy will be dead. You want to live with that?'

'You're dead if you do that.'

'Maybe,' Slater said. 'Maybe you don't hit me with the first shot. Maybe you hit him. I've got a shield and you two don't. I can have a bullet in each of your skulls in a second flat. You want to play that game? You think it's worth the risk?'

'We put our guns down,' the same guy said, 'and we're all dead.'

'You have my word I'll let you live.'

'Why would you do that?'

'Because I don't feel like killing you. You're not bad people and neither am I. But I've got the jump on you here, so that's just the way it has to go.'

'You won't make it out of the city.'

'I think I will.'

They kept staring.

'Guns down,' Slater said. 'Now.'

They thought about it for a beat. Slater tightened his forearm around the human shield's throat. The guy grunted in pain. It helped expedite the process.

The two men with Berettas put them down.

Slater said, 'All of you lie flat on your stomachs.'

No one moved.

Slater cocked his head. 'I really don't have time for this.'

They complied.

Slid off their chairs. Slow and methodical, to show they weren't going to lunge for a weapon. They knew better. Slater had no doubt they'd been provided with his case files. They knew of his genetic abnormality. It was probably the main reason they'd shied away from a Wild West shootout in the confines of the hotel room.

Because, even though it was five on one, he would have killed at least three of them before they had the chance to put him away for good.

And deep down in their cores, they believed him.

He wasn't a monster.

Nor were they.

They flattened themselves to the scratchy carpet and pressed their foreheads to the floor. Slater let go of the human shield, and trained the Glock on him, and the man sunk down to his knees without any further prompting. His nose had already swollen, inflaming his face beyond recognition. He pressed his forehead to the floor, too.

Slater moved with purpose.

He stepped forward, took careful aim, and pumped the trigger five times.

Sending a suppressed round through the sole of each man's left foot.

The group writhed and moaned in unison, but they'd all live. Blood flowed, and the pain and nature of the wounds would render them unable to walk for the foreseeable future, but all five of them were trained operators, and they'd know to stem the bleeding and maintain pressure until emergency services arrived.

Above the chorus of protests from the tactical team, Slater said, 'Sorry.'

'Fuck you,' one of them muttered through gritted teeth.

'So you wouldn't have followed me if I left you here alive?'

'You ... could have ... restrained us.'

'I did,' Slater said. 'The most effective sort of restraint. One you can't slip out of. One that needs time to heal.'

They fell begrudgingly silent.

He said, 'Consider yourselves lucky.'

He returned the Glock to its polymer holster, turned and left the room before anyone in the group had the time to process that he was on the move.

By the time they snatched their Berettas back up, Slater was a ghost in the wind.

45

D uke thrashed the jeep to its limits as they merged onto California State Route 73.

Toward Laguna Beach and the small alcove of Emerald Bay, home to some of the most impressive real estate on the West Coast.

King watched the man get cocky in real time. Duke had revealed the dirt he had on Liam Kingsley, and now he was über-confident. It made King wonder — *is this all it takes?* But when he looked at it objectively, it made sense.

Few had the bombastic bravery to go straight into the field at a moment's notice with little information or resources besides what resided in their own head. He'd done so, and, backed up by a flawless cover story from Alonzo, was now integrated with Duke and his crew. Now the fake Kingsley had just as much to lose as the West Coast gangsters he was helping.

It takes serious effort to convince a seasoned criminal they've got all the leverage in the world, but when they're convinced of it, lips loosen and compromising information starts to flow.

Duke said, 'An anonymous source reached out to me and my boys last week. It took some serious demanding to get them to reveal who they were representing, but I'm persuasive, so eventually they told me they're from a hidden department within Donati Group.'

King nodded. It made sense. It was the same principle.

Donati Group wouldn't have got in touch with Duke unless they knew he had something to lose, also.

If either of them went to the cops, it was mutually assured destruction.

So secrets were kept.

Duke said, 'There's a certain container showing up tomorrow night that's worth its weight in gold. They know I know my way around the port, and they don't have people they can trust with illicit activity in Cali, so they figured I was the man for the job.'

'Are they okay with me being here?'

'They don't know,' Duke said. 'It doesn't concern them. My usual crew is seven, and I've worked with seven the whole time I've been doing this. I don't like to change what isn't broken. Roman got spooked two weeks ago and did a runner. Fucking scumbag.'

'How'd Donati Group know you were dirty in the first place?'

'There's rumours,' Duke said. 'In the intelligence community. I've bought off the right people, so I hear the rumours before the law does. They're not unsubstantiated. But there's no way they can prove any of it. Donati Group, however, knew the rumours were probably true.'

'And what are those rumours?'

'That my businesses are fronts for the profits I make from distributing illegal goods out of the port. You know —

drugs and guns and girls. I'm the middleman. I make sure things get where they're supposed to go.'

'You confessing to me?'

Duke rolled his eyes, and raised his voice above the wind whipping through the exposed cabin. 'Why the fuck did you think I brought you here, brother?'

'Because you were feeling generous?' King said, deliberately sarcastic.

Duke grinned. 'Nah. Cause I know I can tell you whatever I want, and you can't do shit with it. Or you go down, too.'

'You *are* careful.'

'Only way to be. Only way you can thrive.'

King nodded.

'God bless the Internet, hey?' Duke said. 'Gives me a way to screen hired help before I bring them in.'

Gives you a way to get fed bullshit, too.

King elected not to divulge that train of thought.

Duke veered onto the Pacific Coast Highway, with the ocean on their right and trees and bushes on their left. The sun beat down on the back of King's neck, and he took a brief moment to be present. The weather was good, and the wind on his face made him feel alive.

He knew he wouldn't get another opportunity to savour California.

As soon as they arrived, he'd get to work. That never involved peace. Then he'd jump on a plane straight back to New York and do his best to sort out the Slater situation.

And think about your own future.

His life had never been more turbulent.

Then the jeep flew through Crystal Cove and hit Emerald Bay, and any extraneous thoughts fell away.

Duke pulled into the long curved driveway of a multi-million dollar house. Three storeys, a big balcony with a metal railing running the entire length of the second level, the whole thing propped up on the edge of a rise in the land. Prime real estate. Incredible value. The weather made it look like something out of a fantasy — gorgeous sparkling water, cloudless sky, hot sun, acres of land. Landscapers had installed a stand of tall palm trees in the dirt at the foot of the hill, with the fronds falling just shy of the house's elevated foundations. The trees put the cherry on top of the idyllic setting.

Duke parked next to a jet-black Maybach, both vehicles resting in front of a dormant fountain, and said, 'What do you think?'

King stared up at the house in false awe, even though his real abode back in New York cost four times as much. 'I need to do crime on your level, brother.'

'You'll get there,' Duke said. 'You're still young and foolish.'

'Foolish?'

'Look how easily I got dirt on you.'

King shrugged. 'Maybe I don't care about that.'

'You should.'

'I trust you.'

Duke looked over. 'I appreciate that, brother. But don't let anyone get the jump on you. No matter how much you trust them. I've got power over you now, you see? I can get you to do whatever you want for me, and if you refuse, I'll feed the evidence I found to the cops. You ain't got shit on me. Nothing you can prove, anyway. You see now? I don't even have to pay you.'

King fell quiet.

Duke said, 'You're lucky I'm a stand-up guy.'

'Appreciate it, my man.'

'Come on,' Duke said, opening the door. 'Let's go in and meet the boys.'

King got out, keeping what Duke had said before locked in his mind.

Drugs and guns and girls.

Probably fentanyl from China for thousands of kids to overdose on, and rifles with no serial numbers for the cartels and gangs to shoot up innocents with, and sex slaves for the rich and powerful to use and discard.

Ryan Duke facilitated all of it.

With steely resolve settling over him, King followed Duke to the mansion. As he walked, he opted to make this as quick and brutal as possible.

He didn't have time for scum.

46

Slater handed over a fifty-dollar note, and Manuel palmed it.

The chef ushered him through the kitchen of the ground floor restaurant.

Slater strode past smoking grills laden with prime rib-eyes and bubbling vats of oil filled with fries, then dipped into the storage room out back and exited his building discreetly. He came out in a quiet narrow alleyway with minimal vantage points — just what he needed to avoid the snipers he knew would be trained on the lobby's entrance. Dawn had broken, crisp and cool and grey. He had no bag, no possessions besides the passport, credit card, and gun. Despite all that, he was oddly free.

He'd stepped out of his tower for the last time — now, technically homeless — and he didn't care in the slightest.

He took a deep breath.

Disregard the past.

Focus only on what's ahead.

Advice he'd do well to keep in mind for the next few days, if not weeks and months.

He gazed down the length of the alley, and waited for an opportunity. Exactly eight minutes later, a plain white van with GUTIÉRREZ KITCHEN SUPPLIES turned into the mouth. Slater had always known it would happen eventually. His tower was comprised of eighty floors and multiple restaurants and bars, all of which needed regular servicing.

Slater put on his game face, projected an air of authority, and strode to intercept the van.

It slowed, and the Latino driver wound down the window. 'Where do you need it?'

Referencing the cargo.

Slater mumbled something.

The guy leant further out the window, squinting.

Slater circled around the hood and get in the passenger seat. The driver looked across, perplexed.

Slater took the Glock out of its holster and angled it up at the man's face.

The blood drained from the driver's cheeks.

Slater said, 'You're going to drive me to the Bowery.'

'Okay. Anything you need.'

They took FDR Drive without incident. Traffic was congested, which aided Slater's need for invisibility. It would be impossible to monitor the entire Upper East Side for sightings. They'd need to stick to a certain radius. Besides, they'd still be watching the lobby. The bumper-to-bumper traffic created a hundred thousand potential targets. Safety in numbers. Manhattan was a nightmare for surveillance.

They inched through the morning rush as the sun trickled above the horizon, intermittent shafts of light breaking free from the thick cloud cover. He hoped Alexis had rehearsed his instructions a thousand times in her head, so that when she executed them it would be as comfortable as breathing.

He'd certainly rehearsed his own movements.

Over and over and over again in his head.

He withdrew his burner phone, opened his messages, and texted: *Now.*

Drawing on schematics of the building he'd fished from public record the night before, he waited for the driver to turn left onto Second Avenue and then directed him to the outer edge of Alexis' residential complex, to another indiscriminate laneway reserved almost exclusively for deliveries. The intersection was crammed with vehicles at this hour, so there was plenty of time for observers to see the delivery truck turning in, but they wouldn't think anything of it.

Slater told him to pull up at an emergency exit door skewered into the side of the complex. There was only a couple of feet of space on each side of the van.

Slater said, 'I'm getting out for a minute. If you don't run, I'll give you a thousand dollars cash.'

The driver didn't visibly react.

But he didn't seem flustered, either.

Slater swung the door open and dropped out of the passenger seat to the damp concrete.

The emergency exit door burst open in his face.

Alexis hurried out, walking as fast as she could manage, and moved straight past him, chin tucked, eyes wide, a hood drawn over her hair.

Two burly men in civilian garb followed her out, hasty to corner her in the quiet of the laneway. Slater had told Alexis to deliberately get herself spotted in the lobby, and keep a measured pace as she exited through the kitchen so they had all the time in the world to follow closely.

They ran right into Slater.

One of them looked dead ahead and kept walking, intent on brushing past the newcomer to get to the girl, witnesses be damned. The other guy took a longer look, and realisation dawned.

Slater smashed him unconscious first, elbowing him square in the forehead and then head-butting him in the jaw. He crumpled, and Slater stepped over him and kicked the second guy in the groin, doubling him over, which allowed Slater to drop an elbow on the back of his neck, sending him face-first to the laneway floor. His unprotected face ricocheted off the concrete and he lay still.

He kicked them once each in the head, making sure they sported concussions to go along with their temporary sensory deprivation, and then turned back to the van.

Alexis stared in horror.

She'd probably never seen violence like that in the flesh — at least, nothing as ruthless and unrelenting as the punishment Slater could dish out.

Especially not from the man she loved.

He said, 'This is what I do.'

She nodded, biting her lower lip.

He said, 'You still want to come with me?'

'Of course,' she said.

'Get in the back.'

She threw open the rear doors, and he skirted back to the passenger's seat. The driver hadn't budged. He was staring rigidly forward. Out of sight, out of mind.

There was no privacy wall separating the back of the van from the cabin. Slater could pivot and talk directly to Alexis, who'd dropped into a crouch between two pallets of supplies so she could see through the gap between the seats.

He said, 'Have you got the money?'

She passed over a tightly bound bundle of hundred-dollar bills.

Slater gave it to the driver. 'That's two grand. Take us to Bay Ridge, Brooklyn.'

He stared down at the money. Probably more than he'd make this month.

He said, 'Okay.'

Slater simply nodded.

Compliance was easy if you knew the right pressure points.

The van set off for the other end of the laneway.

Tier-one crews had all the expertise in the world, but nothing could stop calculated momentum. Slater had learned that long ago. He'd barely stopped to breathe ever since he stepped out of his building, and now Alexis' complex melted into the background along with the rest of the Bowery.

They came out on East Houston Street and vanished into the stream of traffic.

47

King met the crew.

They were all in the kitchen, the atmosphere of which closely resembled a frat house. It was an odd dynamic. Duke had five "boys" — close friends turned illegal business partners. Which made sense, if you gave it a moment's thought. It was an effective cover story — they'd grown up together, they'd gone to the same high school, they'd hung in the same cliques, they'd started failed businesses together. So if Duke succeeded, why wouldn't he lift up his entourage as well? There was no reason they wouldn't live together, especially somewhere as beautiful as Emerald Bay.

King met Cal, Aaron, Quinn, Kurt, and Vince.

He didn't bother with last names.

Not that he wouldn't have remembered them. He'd honed his memory that much, at least. It was simply unnecessary information. He didn't need all their details to know they were all pieces of shit who deserved what they had coming to them.

'So you're the new Roman,' Cal said.

He was in his late twenties, with the same thin athletic frame as Duke, but much shorter. Five-eight, tops. His height didn't seem to faze him — he still had personality in spades. Cocky tone, passionate eyes, an aura of charm. He might have made something of himself if he hadn't strayed off the path. King was almost disappointed.

Wasted potential.

King said, 'That's me.'

Duke wagged a finger. 'Not quite. This is a once-off.'

'What if I impress?' King said. 'Sounds like you'll need to keep bringing in randoms if seven is the magic number and Roman ran off.'

Duke eyed him. 'Maybe. Who knows? I don't trust you yet.'

Which put a dampener on the wisecracking, jovial atmosphere in the kitchen.

'You got a beer?' King said. 'That's the fast-track to trust, ain't it?'

Most of Duke's boys beamed.

'Speaking our fucking language!' Quinn shouted, then leapt off his stool and went to the fridge.

Quinn was average height, average build, slightly flabby. It seemed like he compensated for his overall plainness with a loud mouth. He jerked the fridge door open, worked a Corona free, and held it by the neck as he offered it over.

King took it, fetched a bottle opener from the marble countertop, cracked it open, and took a swig.

This part didn't require an act.

Enjoying a beer was well within his skillset.

Kurt said, 'East Coast, huh?'

He was tall — as tall as Duke — and big. Thick frame, head shaved bald, fat lips, pale skin. It didn't gel with the

California stereotype, but he seemed comfortable in the heat regardless.

King nodded. 'My whole life.'

'Maybe staying with us will convince you to embrace the good life. It's better on this side.'

'Maybe,' King said, and toasted the offer with his Corona. Condensation glistened on the glass.

The two who hadn't spoken — Aaron and Vince — remained silent. King had them as the quiet ones. Aaron was tanned, blonde, blue-eyed. Looked like a surfer. Almost certainly *was* a surfer. Vince was the Asian equivalent. Just as tanned, with black hair and black eyes, but sported the surfer vibe with the same amount of Laguna cool.

King looked past them, through the floor-to-ceiling windows, tinted a few shades darker than usual for privacy. But the tint didn't hinder the view — cliffs, turquoise water, Santa Catalina Island in the distance.

He said, 'I could get used to this.'

'Don't get used to it,' Duke said. 'There's no free ride. We worked to earn this.'

'I don't doubt it, brother.'

Duke nodded, accepting the compliment.

King said, 'But what if this goes smoothly? What if the seven of us work like a well-oiled machine? Donati Group will like that. And they're *big*. Bigger than anything I've dealt with, that's for sure. And — no offence — bigger than your current clients, without a doubt. Sure, this place is worth a few mil, but Donati is much more than that, boys.'

The perfect amount of passion, optimism, and positivity.

He knew they wouldn't outwardly react, but they'd start dreaming.

That's all he needed.

If they believed in the possibility, that's all it would take.

All he needed was for Duke's paranoia to wear off for a few minutes.

It'd create an opening like nothing else.

As he suspected, no one responded to his rant. But they cracked more beers and went out onto the balcony and shot the shit for a couple of hours, complete with King fabricating tales of adventure and excitement as a small-time crook on the East Coast. Quinn dropped his guard first, opening up with a couple of key details that a newcomer normally wouldn't be privy to.

'The key,' he said when King pressed him, 'is to be generous with the bribes. You know how much port security makes? Scraps. We donate to their rainy day fund, they let us straight through. Aaron and Vince and — well, you — play lookout down the delivery corridor, and the rest of us find the right container and load it up.'

'Quinn,' Duke said. 'Shut the fuck up. He doesn't need to know.'

King drained his third beer. 'Why not? You said it yourself. I talk, and you bust my safe house. Then I go down in flames.'

'We have more to lose than you do. And the more you know, the more likely you can bring us down.'

'Am I helping you with this job or not?'

'Probably,' Duke said. 'All in due time...'

'You really haven't decided?'

Quinn stepped forward and draped an arm over King's shoulder. 'Oh, come on, Duke. Give him a break. He's a good lad.'

'Get him proper drunk,' Cal said. 'Then interrogate him. Hard to lie well when you're plastered.'

They all laughed it off, but King sensed an undercurrent of truth in the suggestion.

He said, 'What's the plan for tonight?'

'Dinner at Laguna Beach,' Duke said. 'All on us. A gift for putting up with our bullshit.'

It seemed Quinn and Cal's interference had softened him a bit.

That's your cue, King thought.

Dinner sounded nice. He had no doubt they'd order platters of the most expensive stuff, accompanied by unlimited drinks, with an unimpeded view of the Pacific and a golden sunset, but then he remembered he'd be in the company of scumbags and the simple truth was he could expedite this process right here and now.

He said, 'You got a bathroom?'

'Yeah,' Quinn said. 'I'll show you.'

48

The delivery driver dropped them at the edge of John Paul Jones Park in Bay Ridge.

They pulled up in the lee of the enormous Verrazzano-Narrows Bridge.

When they got out, Slater nodded to Alexis, and she handed over another bundle of notes. She'd withdrawn both sets the previous day at Slater's request — if he'd left his tower to go to a bank, Violetta and her people would have known he was planning something. Now, he handed the thick wad of hundred-dollar bills to the driver.

'That's another two grand,' he said. 'I haven't hurt you. In fact, I haven't laid a finger on you. You can go report this to the police, and they'd arrest me, but then I'd tell them about the bribe I paid you, and you'd have to cough it up. Better for everyone if you keep quiet.'

'Yes,' the driver said, nodding vigorously.

Four grand would change his life.

He wouldn't say a word.

Foolproof.

The van peeled away, leaving them standing there on

the sidewalk, with the two enormous suspension towers of the bridge behind them, like massive beacons in front of the Manhattan skyline. They'd slipped off the island practically effortlessly. Beside them, the park stretched out in its carefully tended pleasantry. The atmosphere was calm, quiet, serene. It didn't gel with the ordinary chaos of New York.

Alexis took his hands in hers and looked him in the eyes. 'What happens now?'

'I sorted accommodation online,' he said.

'What?'

'I booked an Airbnb, right here next to the park, under a false name. It's ours for a month, with the option to extend. We can order meal delivery and get them to leave it on the doorstep. No one is going to see us for as long as we don't want them to. If you know what you're doing in today's society, it's easy.'

She said, 'We're staying here?'

'They'll expect us to run,' he said. 'And I need to see what they do. Worst case, they put our photos out for the mainstream media to run with. It won't be hard. Enemies of the state, delusional, psychotic, likely to rant about secret government black divisions. That sort of thing. But I have a hunch they don't want this in the public eye. It's too volatile. I know too much. In all likelihood they'll use all their resources to try and track us down discreetly, but they'll cast the net wide, expecting us to be on the move with each passing day. Patience is the key. If we hole up, they'll never find us.'

She bit her lip and nodded. 'A month?'

'At least,' he said. 'And I go dark. No contact with King, no contact with Violetta...'

He trailed off, the name triggering a wave of anger that he immediately quashed.

Silent, he pulled out his burner phone.

'What are you doing?' she said.

'Sending a final message. This call is encrypted. They'll never track it.'

He dialled a familiar number.

It rang.

He wasn't sure if she would answer.

She did. Silently.

He said, 'You bitch.'

Alongside him Alexis froze, unaware of Violetta's betrayal.

Violetta said, 'I'm sorry.'

'Oh, I'm sure.'

'I had no choice.'

'Of course you didn't.'

'The crew in your building was assaulted. So were two of the tactical team at Alexis' building. There's no sign of either of you.'

'It wasn't hard,' he said. 'There's eight million people in New York. Good luck trying to track us through that maze.'

'This isn't the way it should have gone.'

'You really left me with a range of choices.'

'You shouldn't have run. You shouldn't have asked me. I never could have been honest.'

'They would have killed me,' Slater said. 'If I wasn't fast enough. If I actually stepped into 732 and got bottlenecked, like you wanted.'

She didn't answer.

'At least you're not trying to pretend it was an honest mistake,' he said.

'No,' she said. 'No point lying anymore.'

He said, 'You're never going to see me again. You're never going to hear from me again. And you'd best be watching over your shoulder, because when all this dies down...'

He trailed off.

She said, 'What?'

'I'm coming.'

He ended the call, snapped the smartphone in half, and skewered it into the nearest public bin, burying it under the top layer of greasy rubbish. Then he wiped his palm on his jeans and took Alexis' hand with his clean one.

'She betrayed you?' Alexis said.

'She did.'

'I'm sorry.'

'Don't be,' he said. 'I was done with that world regardless.'

'Will you really go back for her?' Alexis said.

He knew what she was really asking.

Did I agree to run away with a monster?

'No,' he said. 'But she deserves to be worried about it, at the very least.'

Alexis nodded. She couldn't hide her relief.

Slater said, 'Come on. It's this building here.'

He led her across the wide road to an orange brick building facing the park. It was three-storey, old-school, built like a motel with landings out the front of the apartments, all three walkways connected by thin metal staircases.

There were no witnesses in sight as they sauntered up to the second level. Slater put his hands on the railing and looked out at the park, the bridge, and the skyline. The clouds had receded, and the sun was out, and the view was beautiful. Birds chirped in the trees. He savoured it, knowing full well he probably wouldn't step outside for quite some time.

She stood alongside him, doing the same.

Subconsciously, she knew too.

Then he turned to face room 204, fished the key out of the pot plant by the welcome mat (as per the Airbnb instructions), unlocked the door, and stepped inside.

The modern equivalent of going dark.

49

King thought about waiting.

It made sense for so many different reasons, the first of which was ordinary common sense.

He'd been at their Emerald Bay compound for less than a half-day, and knew nothing about the layout of the house. He had a handful of rudimentary details about the operation itself. There was also much to gain by cosying up to Duke and his crew at dinner, and then the subsequent morning. Maybe they'd go for a surf at Laguna Beach, or play volleyball at the nets on Main Beach, or down a couple of pre-game beers at one of the hotel bars before the big job tomorrow night.

But, really, all of that was unnecessary. Truth was, King had sized them all up, and despite his unpreparedness he wasn't worried about going for it.

There were bigger things on his mind than a ragtag gang of crooks who thought they were geniuses because they could launder their dirty money.

Quinn led him through the open-plan kitchen and living room, and now that King didn't have to focus on introducing himself to five different people he could take in the towering ceilings and stark white walls and columns scattered throughout. There'd been no corners cut on construction of the house — everything was expensive, and everything was high quality.

King said, 'You like it here?'

Quinn looked over his shoulder. 'Of course, bro.'

King nodded. 'Thought as much. I'd love to live in a place like this.'

It subconsciously put him below Quinn on the dominance hierarchy. He wanted to appear like he was looking up to the crew, wondering how they were living such an incredible life, fantasising about one day maybe joining them. It said, *I'm not as good as you,* without explicitly stating it.

It disarmed Quinn.

He shrugged, almost sheepishly. 'One day, man. Never say never.'

They went down the big central hallway branching off from the kitchen, leading into a number of bedrooms with en-suite bathrooms. King knew this because some of the doors lay ajar, offering views of big rooms with unmade king-sized beds and messy clothes strewn across floors. It seemed all of Duke's crew were similarly unruly, adding to the frat-house feel. He spotted a couple of surfboards propped against walls, a few wall-mounted TVs facing the beds, and state-of-the-art laptops and MacBooks thrown around the floors at random.

Young, dumb and rich.

That's what they were.

Then, en route to the communal bathroom at the end of the hall, King glanced into the last bedroom and spotted a sleek grey SIG Sauer P226 handgun resting on one corner of the mattress. There was no magazine inserted, but he saw a couple of full mags on the desk opposite the bed. He estimated that the gun and the ammunition were ten feet apart.

He veered left and stepped into the room.

Quinn said, 'Whoa. What are you doing?'

King pointed to the abstract hand-painted art piece mounted to the wall above the headboard. 'That's fucking awesome. Is that an original?'

He took another step forward.

Quinn was oblivious. He lingered in the doorway. 'Yeah, man. Cal likes art.'

'What's that bit on the corner?' King said.

'Huh?'

'On the corner of the piece. Right there.'

He pointed.

Quinn stepped into the room, squinting.

King picked up the SIG and pivoted and thrust the barrel into Quinn's trachea. The metal smashed against his windpipe and choked him up, and he doubled over, his face turning the same shade as a beetroot. Veins protruded from his forehead, and his hands flew to his throat, and by the time he'd recovered enough to eke out a cry of protest King had crossed to the desk and chambered a magazine of Parabellum rounds.

He had the loaded gun aimed squarely at Quinn's forehead before the guy could open his mouth and shout.

Quinn froze, face paling.

King kept his voice even, maintaining the exact same tone as before, so anyone within earshot would hear identical murmurings with no change in intensity.

He said, 'You ever had a gun aimed at you before, Quinn?'

Quinn's mouth said yes.

His eyes said, *Fuck no.*

King said, 'You're not ready to die.'

Quinn tried to maintain a brave face. It was respectable. He gave it all he had. But his hands began to tremble involuntarily. Staying calm whilst staring death in the face is one of the hardest things you'll ever do.

King said, 'Do you know how to get into Duke's computer, or are you useless to me?'

Quinn's pupils flared as he spiked with adrenalin.

He knew what being useless would mean.

He said, 'I'm—'

'Voice down,' King said.

Quinn composed himself. 'I'm the tech guy. Of course I have access. I'm the one who does all the dark web stuff through Tor browsers. Duke doesn't have a clue. He delegates.'

'Good,' King said. 'Then you're useful. Congratulations.'

'What do you want from me?'

'Bring up the dialogue with Donati Group. I need to know which container you're picking up.'

'The computer's in the den.'

'Where's the den?'

'Back the way we came.'

'Then that's where we're going,' King said. 'You'll walk first. If you even think about alerting one of the others I'll put two rounds through the back of your head. *Pop pop.* Got it?'

'Got it.'

'You're not going to fuck me over, are you?'

'No,' Quinn said.

'Say it. I want to hear it from you.'

'I'm not going to fuck you over.'

King nodded. 'Excellent. After you, then.'

Quinn tried to relax his shaking hands, but couldn't. Eventually he gave up, took a deep breath, and spun to leave Cal's bedroom. King tucked the SIG under his shirt, then spotted something hanging on a desk chair in the corner of the room.

'Wait,' he said. 'Wait right there.'

Quinn froze.

King said, 'Don't move. Don't turn around.'

He busied himself with the object. He was familiar with it, so it only took half a minute to achieve what he needed. When he was done, he said, 'Okay. Go.'

Quinn set off, and King maintained a respectable distance, only a couple of steps behind.

Quinn stepped out.

King followed.

Cal was right there in their faces, a questioning look on his face.

Like, *What are you doing in my room?*

He looked at Quinn. Who was pale, and still shaking, and wide-eyed, despite his best efforts to mask it. Then Cal's gaze switched to King.

Who had a distinct bulge at the front of his shirt, with one hand underneath it, too.

Cal knew what his own gun looked like.

And he was a lean, wiry ball of aggression.

He didn't shout for help. He didn't turn and run.

He lunged forward with venom in his eyes.

50

King sized up trajectories and angles.

His brain became a supercomputer, calculating a precise algorithm.

And it found a solution.

Cal came in fast and determined, his chin raised and his right arm in the process of cocking back to deliver a colossal hook to King's jaw. An observer would have seen only a flash of rapid violent movement, but King saw every muscular twitch, every intention in the kid's eyes, every inch of his footwork. It wasn't slow motion, per se — just a fundamental understanding of how the human body operated in motion. It allowed him to predict where Cal was going to be a second from now, and therefore avoid it, setting up an elbow of his own.

It broke Cal's face.

The kid didn't cry or gasp or yell — he couldn't. Pain like that is so overwhelming you can't do anything but silently collapse. He hit the tiles on his stomach, and his chest and face followed suit, aggravating all the injuries King had just created. King dropped to one knee, right beside Cal's head, and grabbed his skull with an open palm — like cradling a bowling ball — and drove it downward.

Bounced it right off the tiles.

Putting him out cold.

He didn't bother with restraints. The moment he'd picked up the SIG he'd created an invisible countdown timer, inching steadily down to an inevitable explosion. There was no way to cover this up, so the key was rapid movement. The sooner he extracted the information he needed, the sooner he could get the hell out of here before he had to deal with four more angry criminals.

King stood up over the unconscious body and saw Quinn staring, slack-jawed.

The man had never seen anything like that.

Never seen anyone move like that.

'What have I got myself into?' he bemoaned.

Cal looked dead, but King knew he wasn't. The man would wake up in a couple of minutes with an unstoppable headache and fuzzy short-term memory. He'd sit there on the tiles, feeling cold and confused for a few minutes more, before stumbling back to Duke and the rest of the crew. He might throw up. They'd think he'd fainted. On the off chance he remembered exactly what had happened to him, he'd still have trouble forming coherent sentences for at least half an hour. It'd take an impressive effort on Duke's part to get the necessary information in time.

So King forgot about him, and turned back to Quinn, and said, 'The den. Now.'

Quinn didn't need further prompting. He'd just witnessed this volatile madman break his friend's face by using his elbow as a whip. He led King straight down the hallway and into a sizeable den, complete with an iMac Pro desktop set up on a huge oak desk facing the driveway and courtyard. King looked down through the big windows at the jeep, the Maybach, and the Rolls Royce Phantom. Three tiers of wealth, all of which were affordable to Ryan Duke.

He gave the rest of the room a quick once-over. Beside a broad bookshelf covering one wall was a whiteboard with various indecipherable business dealings scrawled across it. King recognised at least one word — a formula written on the top left of the board.

DONATI = 1R.

Payment instructions, maybe.

King grabbed Quinn by the back of the collar and dumped him down in the desk chair. 'Work your magic.'

Quinn nodded, still trembling.

'I'm watching closely,' King said. 'You do anything you're not supposed to, and...'

He took the SIG out and rested the barrel against the back of Quinn's head.

The trembling got worse.

Quinn tapped in the password. He navigated to an internet browser application that King didn't recognise, but figured was something related to the dark web. What had Duke mentioned before? *Tor browser?*

Quinn dived into a complicated web of folders that King guessed were uploaded to a cloud buried in the deep web, so they could be accessed from anywhere with total privacy. He found a subfolder labelled DONATI and opened it up. It contained a single file.

'There,' he said. 'That's what you need.'

King hunched forward and scrutinised the information.

From what he could gather, the payload in question was a refrigerated container (a typical twenty-foot TEU) connected to one of eighteen hundred plugs at the Pier 400 Container Terminal. That terminal rested between berths

401 and 406 in the port. The plug served to keep the container at a certain temperature in storage until it was collected.

It had already arrived. It was scheduled for collection tomorrow evening.

King didn't want to wait that long.

He memorised the plug number and the details of the Pier 400 Container Terminal, and then said, 'Okay — thanks for that.'

'What now?'

'Now I have a talk to you and your friends.'

'A talk?'

'If I'm going to be honest, I'm a little pressed for time. This isn't how I wanted this to go. I need to deter the lot of you from a life of crime. Ready?'

Quinn's hands shook.

'Come on,' King said. 'Get up.'

Quinn stayed where he was.

King said, '*Up.*'

Quinn got up.

King grabbed him, spun him around, and jammed the barrel into the small of his back. He led him like that across the den, and told Quinn to open the door, slowly and carefully.

Quinn opened the door, slowly and carefully.

He froze in place.

King poised behind him, calculating.

A voice said, 'Jesus Christ, Quinn. You see what happened here? Cal fuckin' fainted...'

Quinn stayed where he was, his frame filling the doorway, blocking King's line of sight. King could hear the man flapping his lips, unsure how to respond.

'Quinn?' the other voice said.

Harmless. Non-threatening.

King recognised his cue.

He shoved past Quinn, keeping the SIG behind his back. Vince was there, crouched over Cal. Cal was semiconscious, his eyes glassy and unfocused, no threat whatsoever. His skin was still pale and clammy. The elbow and subsequent impact with the floor had mangled his nose beyond recognition. Vince was cradling Cal's head in his hands, propping him up, his own face wracked with confusion and shock.

King widened his eyes in mock surprise. 'That's gnarly.'

Vince barely even looked at King. He kept his eyes down, focused on Cal. 'I know, man. I just found him here like this. What—'

King stepped forward and punted Vince square in the jaw.

51

It was a clean connection.

Lights out.

Vince flailed back, spread-eagling across the tiles like a starfish, his face now in a similar condition to Cal's.

King wheeled to face Quinn, bringing the SIG up to make sure he didn't get any rebellious ideas. 'For a bunch of traffickers, you're all terrible at being cautious.'

Quinn didn't answer. He gulped. There'd been hope before. Sure, King had neutralised Cal without blinking, but everyone gets lucky occasionally.

Now, King had casually smashed Vince's face in with a well-placed boot.

Things weren't looking too hot.

King grabbed Quinn by the collar again and threw him in the direction of the open-plan area. Quinn stumbled out into the kitchen, heading for the floor-to-ceiling windows and second-storey balcony opposite.

Aaron and Kurt were furthest away, holding half-finished Coronas, seated on bar stools, confused as to Quinn's behaviour.

Duke was closer.

Standing on this side of the kitchen island. One palm on the countertop. The other empty. His eyes cunning, calculating. He'd figured it all out in a heartbeat. Saw Quinn stumble into view, pale and sweaty and wide-eyed, and knew what was happening before King followed a second later.

When King stepped into view with his SIG raised, Duke looked like he'd been expecting it.

'You fucking idiot, Quinn,' Duke said, more disappointed than fearful.

King hesitated.

Quinn said, 'I'm sorry. He got the jump on me.'

'That's not what I mean,' Duke said. 'Watch this.'

He jerked hard in King's direction.

Moved like a whip.

King reacted instinctively to the sudden threat. Turned and lined up his aim and pumped the trigger once without a shred of hesitation or remorse. That was the way it had to go, especially in this world. Anything else would get you killed.

But nothing happened.

The trigger clicked uselessly.

The confusion took milliseconds to recover from, milliseconds King didn't have. Because his only chance was to make a last-ditch, leaping lunge of his own. He didn't commit to it, opting instead to beat down the three remaining men with his bare hands, but he didn't get the chance.

Duke smacked the big coffee machine aside with an open palm and snatched up the identical SIG Sauer P226 resting behind it.

Loaded with a full magazine, already cocked.

No obstacles between Duke's finger and the trigger.

He had *that* weapon aimed between King's eyes before King could blink.

King lowered his own useless gun.

Now his pulse rose.

Duke's bright eyes flared, and he flashed a glance at Quinn. 'You don't remember what Cal did to his gun?'

'Oh,' Quinn said, taking a step back, away from King. 'You're right. I *am* a fucking idiot.'

'When am I wrong?'

King glanced down at the SIG in his palm. 'Fingerprint sensitive?'

Duke nodded. 'Cal's a little bit mechanic, a little bit electrical engineer. And a whole lot bored.'

Aaron and Kurt shot to their feet, as if on a live-action tape delay. They'd seemingly just figured out that Duke had regained control of the situation. Aaron kept his cool, but Kurt grinned broadly, spreading his big lips in a lurid smile. He towered over everyone.

King went into survival mode. There was no other choice. He could very well die here.

In fact, it was more likely than not.

'Shoot him,' Quinn said. 'You should see what he did to Cal and Vince.'

Duke's eyes lit up with the slightest flicker of anger. 'Are they dead?'

'No.'

Duke breathed out.

Quinn said, 'But he messed them up. He's some elite soldier or something.'

'*Is* he?'

'I'm right here,' King said. 'Ask me.'

Duke said, 'Okay. You some elite soldier or something?'

'Go fuck yourself.'

Duke bristled. 'You think I'm going to make a mistake. Get angry.'

'*Shoot* him,' Quinn said. 'Did you not hear a word I said?'

'I want to know what he knows,' Duke said. 'He sure breezed his way in here, didn't he? I don't trust anyone, but I dropped my guard around him. *That* takes something special.'

'Shoot him, you moron,' Quinn said.

'He won't,' King said. 'He didn't get this house by being too cautious. And he's right. This was easy for me. My name isn't Liam Kingsley. There *is* no apartment in Brooklyn. There's no leverage. If I'd gotten away, all his leads wouldn't have turned up a damn thing. I'm a ghost.'

The speech was carefully spoken. Every word had intent.

King could see they worked.

They made Duke think, *Could it be true?*

Because it *was* true, and on top of that it was feasible. And that threw him off. Now he was thinking, *If this mother-fucker can do that, who else could?*

It was the equivalent of calling your enemy's phone and hearing it ring right behind you.

It had well and truly spooked him.

He'd let an imposter into the house, allowed him access to his private space, made himself vulnerable.

Duke didn't let the SIG waver an inch.

He said, 'Kurt. Tie him up.'

King stiffened.

He knew if he let that happen, he was as good as dead.

But from here, he couldn't spot any feasible escape plan.

He'd been stumped by a goddamn fingerprint sensor.

As Kurt rummaged around in one of the kitchen island drawers for something to restrain their prisoner with, King vowed that if he made it out of Emerald Bay alive, he would never allow a mistake like that to happen again.

52

Dead quiet.

Kurt lifted a couple of rolls of duct tape out of the drawer and held them up for all to see. Duke flicked his gaze sideways, took in the sight, and nodded once. Supremely cautious. Barely allowing a half-second without his eyes fixed on King.

King could see Quinn in his peripheral vision. The guy had his shoulders hunched, and his whole body was wound up, tight with stress. Unease rippled off him like he was radioactive with the stuff. The only other person in the room — Aaron — was an enigma. He shifted his weight from foot to foot, his movements lazy. King figured that unless the surfer lifestyle had made him inhumanly calm, then Aaron was probably high as a kite.

Which would make him useless in a fistfight, if that's what it came to.

King's heart thudded. He could feel it pounding in the left side of his chest, creeping up to his throat, where a vein in his neck pulsed at a hundred and twenty beats per minute. He actually hoped Duke noticed, because it was deceptive. Hopefully Duke took it as a sign of weakness. It didn't mean he was afraid. The physical stress response is inevitable in a situation like this.

You're going to be on edge regardless.

What you do with it is the key.

King stayed deathly still, ratcheting the intensity of the atmosphere up a few notches. If he had any hope of surviving...

Kurt approached.

Duke tightened his grip on the SIG.

'Drop your gun,' Duke said. 'You don't need it. And you need your hands freed up.'

King dropped the gun.

He tried to raise his heart rate even further.

It worked.

The vein in his neck pulsated, a little harder, a little faster.

Duke noticed.

A half-smile crept into the corners of his mouth. He said, 'Afraid?'

'A little.'

'You should be.'

Kurt kept coming forward.

Quinn backed off a step.

Aaron seemed to sense something. Out of the corner of his eye, King saw the surfer tense up. Anticipating...

Maybe it was good weed. Maybe he was so high he'd become prescient.

Because he sure as shit should be anticipating something.

If that duct tape went around King's wrists, he was rendered useless.

He was at the mercy of Ryan Duke.

Which simply couldn't be allowed to happen.

He'd rather die.

King put his wrists together, making no sudden movements. He offered the pair out to Kurt.

Who smirked and reached forward with the duct tape.

Then King made a sudden movement.

He interlocked his fingers, forming a two-handed club, and swung it up toward the ceiling with all the strength his shoulders could muster.

He could muster a goddamn tank's worth of strength.

He'd picked the right trajectory. There was a key obstacle between his fists and the top of their arc.

Kurt's chin.

He shattered half the teeth in the big man's mouth with the uppercut. The exact same physical reaction played out. No matter how tough you think you are, that sort of abhorrent discomfort isn't something you can train for. You can pump yourself up all day and inflate your ego with tales of how you'll push through pain and overcome adversity, but until you experience both rows of teeth being smashed together and half of them breaking, you really have no idea how you'll react.

Kurt leapt backward like he'd been electrocuted.

But King had been expecting that.

He leapt with him.

Duke panicked and fired and hit Kurt in the small of his back. The gunshot roared. No matter how high the ceilings were or how big the space was, it was still a gunshot. It blared, and Quinn practically shit his pants, ducking for cover. King lost sight of Aaron but it didn't matter because all his attention was focused on keeping Kurt in front of him. The big man roared in turn, hand flying to where he'd been struck, and King knew the guy's concentration was now ruined.

He skewered himself into the ground with one foot and used the other to front-kick Kurt in the stomach.

Perfect placement.

Smooth technique.

Inhuman strength.

Accurate trajectory.

Check, check, check, check.

Kurt careened backward, completely off-balance, and crashed into Duke. King sprinted after them and hurled Kurt aside and found Duke's aim was now off by a few inches.

Not much. Any sane person would have panicked and tried to run, because all Duke needed to do was swing the barrel around and pull the trigger and King would die in grisly fashion. That was enough to deter almost anyone.

Not King.

He realised if he kept his momentum the bullet would miss. So he threw caution aside and threw himself forward and crash-tackled Duke to the floor. The SIG went off, but the bullet went wide. King had no idea how close it had come — all he knew was that it didn't hit him.

He landed on top of Duke, and instead of throwing a strike he pivoted on top of the guy and snatched at his gun hand.

He got both hands on Duke's wrist.

Then it was simple physics.

He smashed the wrist into the floor, maybe breaking it, definitely bruising it. Duke still had his finger inside the trigger guard and he pumped it with all the desperation he had left. He fired four shots at random, none of them coming close to hitting the adversary on top of him. King slammed the guy's wrist into the floor again, this time definitely breaking it.

Duke gasped and let go of the SIG. King snatched it up and shot to his feet and planted the sole of his boot into Duke's throat, crushing his windpipe, pinning him to the floor.

He surveyed the scene.

Not pretty.

Kurt was facedown on the tiles, a rapidly expanding pool of arterial blood forming around his head. One of Duke's stray shots had hit him in the face or neck. King took in the information, filed it, and promptly forgot all about Kurt.

He wheeled, searching for Aaron.

He found the surfer in the far corner of the living area, in newfound possession of another SIG Sauer P226. Their weapon of choice, apparently. Duke must've received a case of them, which King figured were scattered all over the house, considering Aaron had found one in seconds.

The surfer locked his aim onto King's centre mass like he'd been exclusively practicing that motion his whole goddamn life.

King panicked.

He hadn't been anticipating the accuracy, or the reaction speed. He'd underestimated the kid, writing him off as too high to function, when maybe it was a particularly effective strain of weed that had made him scarily sharp. Whatever the case, Aaron raised and aimed and fired a tight cluster of shots that went high. They would have drilled through King's brain and pulverised his head if he hadn't dropped behind the kitchen island milliseconds before the rounds burst forth from the chamber.

He flattened himself down, and the bullets whisked overhead, tearing the opposite cupboards to pieces.

He took a deep breath.

Worked his way back to a crouch, pressing his upper back to the drawers, affording him a good look at Ryan Duke a few feet away.

The man's wrist was mangled, and the skin on his neck was bright red with King's boot imprint. He'd managed a crouch of his own, but he was clutching his bad arm with his good one, rendering him useless, and his face was creased with unfamiliar pain and shock.

King looked him in the eye and shook his head.

Don't move.

Or I'll have to kill you.

Duke stared back, and King knew he understood.

Whether he would listen was another matter entirely.

Technically, he obeyed.

He didn't move.

He said, 'Aaron, now.'

53

King steeled himself and ran through a number of ways the firefight could unfold.

He was halfway through that list, dissecting tactics and possible manoeuvres, when he heard a rapid chain of footsteps from the other side of the island.

Close.

Way too close.

He realised what was happening, and knew he needed to forget about Duke entirely.

There was a far more imminent threat.

He looked up and braced himself and raised the SIG to a vertical trajectory, just in time to see Aaron's wiry frame slide over the lip of the countertop above him.

That's the worst thing about madness. It's unpredictable, and it throws off even the most tactically sound plans. Of all the possibilities King had contemplated, he'd never expected the kid to dive head-first onto the countertop and use its smooth surface to slide all the way across, coming down in a heap of limbs on top of him. Of course it was suicide. Of course it wouldn't work. But it didn't need to be foolproof. It just had to buy Ryan Duke some time. And clearly his "boys" were more than old buddies. Clearly they were willing to die for this man who had given them everything.

It changed the whole dynamic instantly.

King fired three times, given the fact that he'd miraculously predicted the move and had the SIG aimed in the right direction.

All three bullets slammed home in Aaron's torso — two in the chest, one in the stomach.

Suicide, as predicted.

But his body came down directly on top of King's head, the deadweight nearly snapping King's neck. A few inches to the right and it might have. But King rolled out from under the bleeding body and rescued his grip on his own SIG and searched rabidly for Duke.

He found him.

Duke was six feet away.

On his feet.

He'd snatched up the gun Aaron had dropped in his death throes.

Duke angled the SIG diagonally downward and fired three shots into King's chest at close to point-blank range.

The right move.

Go for the largest target.

Minimise your chance of missing entirely.

Duke had combat training.

The bullets struck hard, knocking King backward, throwing him off his feet.

He sprawled to the tiles, all the breath pounded out of his lungs...

...but with no other significant injuries.

Duke hesitated.

Confused.

King shot him between the teeth. The bullet went through the back of his mouth and came out the rear of his skull in a grisly exit spray. Duke's lifeless body twisted and fell and the gun clattered out of his limp hand.

'That's what you should have done,' King muttered.

He gave himself the once-over before he got to his feet, but none of his ribs were cracked. He breathed a sigh of relief, because he *could* breathe. He'd broken ribs before. It was abhorrent how useless it rendered you. He stood up, wincing at the bruising he knew would already be forming across his chest and stomach, but bruising paled in comparison to what might have been.

Before he checked the full extent of the damage, he swept the rest of the space.

Quinn was still alive.

Cowering in the corner behind an authentic Eames chair.

The other three were dead.

Kurt.

Aaron.

Ryan Duke.

All corpses.

King said, 'Get up, Quinn.'

Quinn rose shakily, hands raised above his shoulders, fingers spread wide, a ridiculous demonstration of the fact he was unarmed.

King said, 'Put your hands down. I know you don't have a gun.'

Quinn nodded, practically blinking back tears, and lowered his hands inch by inch, until they were out of sight behind the chair.

King froze, watching closely.

Then he shook his head in disbelief.

Quinn said, 'What?'

'You're a terrible actor,' King said. 'Two choices. Either you put a finger on either side of the chair back, and spin it slowly around to show me the gun that's taped there, or you try to pry that gun free and use it to kill me, in which case you're dead.'

Quinn didn't move.

King said, 'It's a simple decision, Quinn.'

Quinn's hands came back up.

There was nothing in them.

He extended a finger on each hand, put them both on top of the chair back, well out of harm's way, and swivelled the whole thing around.

Exposing another SIG Sauer P226 resting in a polymer holster glued to the wood.

King said, 'Duke thinks of everything, doesn't he?'

'I wasn't going to use it, man.'

'That's why you went and hid behind the Eames chair. So you could *not* use the hidden gun attached to it.'

'I swear,' Quinn said.

'I don't care that you wanted to protect yourself, Quinn,' King said. 'I *do* care if you lie to me.'

A long, uneasy pause.

Then Quinn said, 'I'm sorry.'

King shrugged. 'I'm not the one who needs your apology.'

'Who does?'

King looked around. 'Whoever you're going to have to explain this to.'

'Fuck,' Quinn said, putting his face in his hands. 'Oh, God, man. I...'

'You didn't know it would be this way?'

Quinn lifted his gaze. 'Yeah. I guess.'

'I've heard that before. Let me guess: Duke roped you into all of this, it was his idea, you only saw dollar signs, you didn't think about the consequences of your actions, you didn't think about the cargo you were transporting, or where it was going, or whose hands it would end up in. You didn't think. Blah, blah, blah.'

Quinn bowed his head again.

King said, 'Am I on the right track?'

Quinn shrugged.

Speechless.

King said, 'Do one thing for me.'

Quinn's eyes flared with hope, despite the fact he could see three of his closest friends' brains splattered across the mansion's walls.

King said, 'I'm going to leave now. There's nothing stopping you finding a phone and alerting whoever you know at the port about an incoming unwanted visitor. They could probably assemble some manpower and pull the container off its plug before I make it there. They could feasibly hide it.'

Quinn stared, sheepish, clearly disappointed King hadn't let him off the hook.

King said, 'If that container isn't there, I'll come back and murder you. Even if you're in custody, I'll find you there, too. Actually, you know what ... I won't kill you straight away. You'll wish you were dead.'

King finished his spiel and stared at a broken man. Quinn was pale, shellshocked, hunched over, remorseful, guilty, terrified — every negative adjective, really.

He wouldn't be speaking to anyone.

'Okay,' the man said, still struggling to put a sentence together. 'So what *do* I do?'

'You take care of Cal and Vince. I'd wager they're heavily concussed. You make sure they don't drop dead before the cops or the ambulances get here.'

'Isn't that... your job?'

King raised an eyebrow. 'Because I'm a cop?'

'Yeah.'

'Not quite.'

'Then who are you?'

'You'll have plenty of time to come up with theories in prison.'

King turned, satisfied, figured he'd leave it there.

Then he reconsidered.

The path of least resistance was a bad rule to follow in day-to-day life, because it led to trading short-term comforts for long-term unhappiness, but on a mission it was best to make things as effortless as possible. There was no point passing up an opportunity staring him right in the face.

So he turned back and said, 'Actually, I've changed my mind. You're coming with me.'

54

King led Quinn downstairs at gunpoint.

The guy had zero combat experience, and was scared out of his mind, but King remained diligent regardless. Sometimes, stupidity results in the most brazen actions.

Take Aaron, for example.

As they descended the giant staircase, King said, 'What the hell was that, anyway?'

'What?'

'Aaron got himself killed to give Duke a slightly higher chance of survival. That's some serious selflessness.'

'Aaron ... wasn't ... all there,' Quinn said. 'You know, mentally.'

He took giant pauses between words, as if he still couldn't comprehend what had happened. It had to be a fever dream. There was no way a hired helper had revealed himself as an elite combatant, killed half of Quinn's friends, and left the other two potentially brain-damaged.

King said, 'He looked high.'

'He was high,' Quinn said. 'Every hour of every day. First

thing he did when he woke up every morning. For him it kept ... the demons at bay.'

King waited for Quinn to elaborate, letting the silence draw out. He knew Quinn would cave first.

Quinn said, 'He was schizophrenic. He was like a ... Rain Man type. You saw how good of a shot he was. He gets, you know, obsessed with things. Sort of hyper-focused. But he was irrational. Duke made him do all the risky shit, because he'd do it every time, no questions asked.'

'Sounds like Duke was a real stand-up guy.'

Quinn shrugged. 'He hurt some people. Helped some others.'

'You're saying he was Robin Hood?' King said. 'Take from the rich, give to the poor?'

Quinn tried to ignore the opulence all around them, but couldn't. 'Not exactly.'

'Yeah,' King said. 'You're damn right "not exactly."'

'What about you?' Quinn said. 'What the hell are you made out of?'

'Huh?'

'Duke shot you three times. You barely flinched.'

King undid the top two buttons of his shirt and parted the material to the side, allowing Quinn to look over his shoulder and see the armoured plating underneath. It was a Modular Body Armor Vest, utilised by a wide range of Special Forces operators due to its mobility and light weight.

Quinn couldn't believe it.

'How the fuck did you get that through airport security?' he said.

'I didn't,' King said. 'It's Cal's. It was hanging on his desk chair. Remember I told you not to turn around.'

'Oh,' Quinn said.

King shoved him out the entrance archway and steered him toward the jeep.

'You drive,' he said.

Quinn got behind the wheel and King got in the passenger seat, keeping the barrel angled at the man's face at all times. Quinn reached out and took the wheel in both hands.

They trembled.

King said, 'I'm not going to kill you.'

'You are,' Quinn said. 'Or you would have left me back there.'

Fear swirled in his eyes.

King slapped him across the face, and then used the same hand to tilt Quinn's chin toward him. Turning his face to the sun, which made him squint and drew beads of sweat from the corners of his forehead. Disorienting him, and making him even more uncomfortable.

Good.

King needed him vulnerable.

He said, 'You're in deep shit, Quinn. But you can come out of this alive if you get me to that container.'

Quinn squinted harder, confused.

King said, 'You know people at the port, right? That's how all this works.'

'Yes. But they won't let me in if they see you with me. They don't know you.'

'Then they won't see me.'

'I don't remember the details.'

'I do. Drive.'

They took the Pacific Coast Highway north, passing designer coffee joints packed with hipsters and surfers and rich white-collar workers staying at their holiday homes. Then they saw those holiday homes themselves — the exclusive real estate between Laguna Beach and Newport Beach with staggering ocean views and permanent sunshine. Then came Huntington Beach, followed swiftly by Long Beach, and after that King knew they'd be approaching Terminal Island.

He said, 'Okay, Quinn. Pep talk.'

Still pale despite the sun beating down on him, Quinn nodded his understanding.

King said, 'I'm going to get out of sight. I want you to be as charming as you can. If they suspect something's wrong, I'll kill you. If you point out that there's a person in the back who's currently holding you hostage, I'll kill you. If you drive straight to any other criminal buddies you have and try to pump me full of lead before I can retaliate, it won't work ... and then I'll kill you.'

Quinn nodded again.

'Any questions?'

Quinn shook his head.

'I'd like to remind you what happened to your buddies.'

'I know what happened to them,' Quinn said, like he was trying to hold back tears.

King said, 'They were prepared. Duke had the jump on me. It was six on one. You all still failed.'

Silence.

King said, 'Whatever you're thinking about trying, it won't work.'

'I know.'

Resignation.

Acceptance.

Defeat.

King said, 'Good man. I'm putting my head down now. If I see *anything* other than Container 55D when I look back up, you're dead.'

'What's the rest of the information?'

King fed it to him, verbatim, reading it off the page he'd memorised.

As Quinn sped along the Seaside Freeway, King turned and put a foot up on the passenger seat and vaulted over into the rear seats. He grabbed the removable soft top usually reserved for draping over the jeep's frame when it rained once a year in California. He skewered himself down into the footwell, and draped the soft top over his own frame instead.

Darkness.

55

Bumps.
    Jolts.
    Rattles.
Muted conversation.

More bumps.

More jolts.

More muted conversation.

King listened harder.

He thought he caught snippets of jovial banter — perhaps a half-hearted verbal jab from someone outside the vehicle. Then something very similar to a nervous laugh emanating from the driver's seat.

He tensed up.

If port security smelled something fishy on Quinn's end, they might overreact.

Especially if they were on the payroll. Because that made them morally bankrupt, and morally bankrupt people were capable of plenty of unsavoury things.

King imagined the conversation.

Where's the rest of the boys?

They sent me ahead, to ready the container.

You drew the short straw, hey?

Something like that.

Have a good one, buddy.

You, too.

That was the best case scenario.

That's not what happened.

The second muted conversation lasted a whole lot longer than the first. The weight of the soft top pressed down on King, stifling his breathing, absorbing the heat of the sun, cooking him in the footwell. He started perspiring freely — his armpits soaked, his face flushed, his grip on the SIG ever so slightly compromised. If they threw the soft top away and tried to shoot him where he lay, that'd be an issue.

He tried his best to control his breathing, fighting off the tendrils of claustrophobia.

Outside the jeep, he thought he heard someone say, '*How long do you think you'll be?*'

More questions.

Not good.

King tightened his grip. Tried to wipe his palm on his pants, but he couldn't. The angle wasn't right. He lay deathly still, not daring to move a muscle. Another voice — a new voice — emanated from the passenger side.

A second port official.

Were they surrounding the car?

He weighed his options. He could sit up, throw the soft top aside, draw a bead on whoever was closest, threaten them until they let him through. It'd work. He doubted port security had the firepower and reflexes to rival his own.

But as soon as Quinn rolled the jeep through, they'd raise the alarm. King might make it to the container in time, but then he'd have the entire port descending on him. If the cargo was something sinister, and required immediate action on King's end … well, that'd complicate things. It'd be hard to smuggle a nuclear bomb off Terminal Island with alarms blaring and security in hot pursuit.

He stayed put.

It was mightily uncomfortable, but in his profession, what the hell wasn't?

The voice on the driver's side moved closer to King. He realised, two feet above him, the official was looking down at the soft top. Scrutinising. Giving the rear seats a once-over.

He held his breath, which wasn't necessary — it caught in his throat anyway.

Silence.

Then a grunted affirmation, and Quinn threw the jeep into gear, and it rolled off the mark.

King let the breath out. It was masked by the rumbling of the engine. He gave it a full minute, counting out the seconds from one to sixty, until Quinn had accelerated to a respectable speed. Then he sat up and heaved the soft top aside.

Quinn looked twice as nervous as when King had burrowed out of sight.

King said, 'How'd that go?'

Quinn shook his head, scared shitless. 'That was close.'

'Why?'

'Duke hadn't called ahead. He always calls ahead.'

'But they let you through anyway?'

'We pay them more than enough to allow exceptions.'

King vaulted back into the passenger seat and soaked in the scenery. They were barreling down a giant concrete multi-purpose dock. On either side he eyed a cluster of administrative buildings, a couple of giant warehouse facilities that he guessed were for maintenance, and at least a dozen cranes all around them. In the distance, the rest of the terminals on the island spread out facing the harbour, making up a single conglomeration of industrial sprawl.

The sky was still cloudless.

The sun still beat down.

King used his sleeve to wipe sweat off his face.

He said, 'Any idea what I should be expecting?'

'The cargo?'

'Yeah.'

'You're not going to believe me,' Quinn said, 'but I honestly have no idea. If anyone knows in advance, it's Duke. And usually he doesn't, either. Discretion is key for the clients we work with.'

'Ignorance is bliss, right?'

'I know you hate me.'

'I don't feel anything towards you.'

'That's good, at least.'

'It doesn't mean I won't kill you if I need to.'

Quinn shivered. 'I know.'

They took a left into a cargo zone filled with stacks and stacks of TEUs. The towers speared into the sky, practically blocking out the sunlight. Quinn navigated down a couple of shadowy laneways, steering with practiced familiarity. He'd done this before.

'55D, right?' Quinn said.

King said, 'Right.'

Quinn slammed on the brakes.

For a moment King thought the ferocity of the action was a ploy to throw him against the glove compartment and try to enact a getaway. Then he would have to shoot Quinn, which ruined his chances of streamlining this.

But it turned out that Quinn was simply desperate to

impress. He'd do anything not to overshoot the container, which was right alongside them.

The jeep skidded to a standstill.

King looked over at the row of refrigerated containers. There were no plugs in sight — they must have all been hooked up at the back. They were all big and ridged and metal and orange. They sat in their places, dormant.

Quinn said, 'You know how it works, right?'

King nodded. 'Oh, yeah. I know how it works.'

He was intimately familiar with Twenty-foot Equivalent Units. A lifetime ago at the tender age of twenty-two, on his second official operation as a Black Force operative, he'd been introduced to the dark secrets of the international shipping industry in Somalia of all places. He knew hundreds of thousands of containers containing illegal items passed through borders globally each and every day, whether that be guns, drugs, trafficked humans, or simply undeclared goods. None of them were searched. It was impossible. Every year, hundreds of billions of dollars worth of goods passed through the Port of Los Angeles alone. The manpower didn't exist to screen even five percent of what came through.

It left all sorts of openings for officials to be bribed, and it was an easy frame of mind to slip into. A lone port worker would think, *What's the point of staying out of the action? The cargo comes through anyway, no matter what I do. Why should I stop something I can't control?*

So, yeah, King understood how it worked. And he knew how to work a TEU.

Quinn said, 'Here's the key.'

Handed over a single silver key.

King said, 'Where'd you get it?'

'Someone from Donati Group express shipped it to us. I don't know all the details. Duke handled it.'

King nodded. 'Keep your hands on the wheel. If I hear you move, it's game over.'

He got out and approached the giant cargo-door lock of Container 55D. There were big leverage handles, easily identifiable, and as soon as he'd figured out the lock he seized hold of them and swung them out. Something clanked and thudded on the left-hand side, then on the right. The lock rods.

It was open.

King listened hard, letting his heartbeat settle, letting the sound of the idling engine recede. Kept quiet, until there was just the hot wind blowing through the corridors and the gentle creaking of towers of metal.

He raised the SIG in a familiar motion, and put his other hand on the edge of the huge door frame.

He swung the right-hand door steadily outward, moving the barrel along the same trajectory, clearing the space inch by tense inch.

When he swung the door all the way out, he stopped in his tracks.

The container was completely empty.

56

King didn't move for a long ten count.

He sensed Quinn behind him in the driver's seat, staring in horror.

King turned around.

Quinn's expression was a man looking death right in the eyes.

He started babbling.

'No, no, wait,' he said. 'I didn't talk to anyone, man. I swear. Please don't kill me. Oh, God, I don't want to die here. Please, man, please, you have to understand—'

King held up a palm.

Quinn stopped mid-sentence. His eyes were wider than saucers. His face was pale and oily.

King said, 'I know you didn't talk to anyone. I've been with you this whole time, remember?'

Pure relief washed over Quinn. 'I thought you might have thought, you know...'

'What?'

'Thought I talked to those guards.'

'Unless they're superhuman, and could locate and

empty this entire container before we got here, then, no, you're in the clear.'

Quinn nodded. 'I'm just scared, man.'

King's mind fired. He couldn't quiet it down. He was connecting dots, harbouring suspicions, drawing unwanted conclusions.

He said, 'Quinn.'

'Yeah?'

'Answer me one question.'

'Anything.'

'How do you know this job came from Donati Group?'

Quinn paused, thinking. 'Because, you know, they came to us. To do it discreetly. Off their books.'

'But what proves it was *actually* them?'

Quinn hesitated again. 'We have paperwork. We have payments.'

'How easily could they be forged?'

'I ... I don't know.'

'Think.'

'I don't fucking know, man. I don't know who you are. I don't know what you want. I don't know what's going on. Help me. Throw me a bone.'

'How easily could it be forged?' King repeated. 'Think.'

Quinn went silent. Stared at the steering wheel, as if it could give him the answers he needed. But King knew he was racking his memory, ticking off pieces of evidence, trying to find anything that didn't mesh with King's newfound opinion.

He couldn't.

He said, 'I guess there's nothing we saw that couldn't be forged. We've spoken to people, but I guess we don't have documented video proof that those calls came from bent Donati Group employees. So, yeah, maybe. It could all be a ruse. But who would want to frame Donati Group?'

'Nobody,' King said, his blood beginning to boil.

'Who, then?'

'The real question is — who wanted me out of New York?'

'What? I don't understand.'

King turned and thundered a kick into the side of the empty shipping container. The metal groaned and rattled and the reverberation echoed within, bouncing off the walls, resonating through the bare space. When he composed himself, he turned back round.

Quinn said, 'Just because it *could* be forged, doesn't mean it *is*. It'd take an army of experts. Based on the documents I saw.'

King nodded. 'I agree.'

He knew exactly who had access to an army of experts.

His blood boiled harder.

He said, 'Sit there and don't say a word.'

He pulled out his phone and dialled a number he didn't want to dial.

He wasn't sure whether she'd answer.

Whether she suspected anything.

But she did.

Violetta picked up and said, 'Hey. All good?'

'All good,' King said, staring at the sole member of Duke's crew still functioning.

She said, 'I take it you've found a secure location.'

'Why else would I be calling?'

'Relax,' she said. 'I'm just making sure.'

'I'm perfectly relaxed.'

'Any issues integrating?'

'None,' King said. 'I'm in the bathroom at the Coyote

Grill. In South Laguna Beach. We're having a late lunch. This place overlooks the water — it's beautiful.'

'Sounds like you're living it up. Now I'm worried you might not come back.'

He forced himself to laugh.

He said, 'Oh, I'll come back, alright.'

She said, 'Good. I miss you.'

He couldn't bring himself to say, *I miss you too.*

She filled the silence by saying, 'Is everything still on schedule?'

He grunted an affirmation. 'We're scheduled to pick up the container tomorrow night.'

'Do you think you'll be able to get a look inside?'

'Hard to say. It won't be easy. There's six of them, and they've got a man watching me at all times, apart from when I need to piss. Like right now.'

'You don't need to look inside,' she said. 'Alonzo dug up some more information.'

'Did he?' King said. 'That's interesting.'

'Yeah,' she said. 'It's fentanyl. From China. The cartel sent it to Russia first to throw us off the scent, and packaged it properly over there. Then they used Donati Group to ship it to California. Duke and his crew — you included — are going to deliver it to the Baja cartel. Alonzo pieced it all together.'

'Wow,' King said, staring at the inside of the empty container. 'I'll be damned.'

'So we know what's in it,' Violetta said. 'And we can track it. All you need to do is help them deliver it to wherever it needs to go, and we'll handle it from there.'

'Will you?'

'Are you deliberately being sarcastic?'

'No,' King said. 'I'm just surprised you came up with all that so quickly.'

'What can I say?' Violetta said. 'Alonzo's a genius.'

King kept the phone pressed to his ear, and sealed his mouth into a hard line. A particularly hot gust of wind blew down the corridor, exacerbating how alone he suddenly felt.

She said, 'Everything okay?'

'Yeah,' he said. 'Undercover work is just taxing. I'll be fine.'

'I know you will,' she said.

'Any update on Slater?'

She said, 'Not yet. He's still in his apartment.'

King checked his watch.

Not a fucking chance he's still in his apartment.

So she was lying about that, too.

He said, 'Okay.'

'Anything you need from me?'

'No,' he said. 'I'm good.'

'I love you.'

He ended the call. He couldn't say it back.

If this was all a huge misunderstanding, then he'd blame it on bad reception.

But he knew it wasn't.

He put the phone back in his pocket.

Still motionless in the driver's seat, Quinn said, 'What happens now?'

'Now you drop me at the airport.'

'What about me?'

'What about you?'

'Aren't you going to call the cops on us?'

King thought of the price they'd paid. Duke, Aaron, and Kurt — all dead. Cal and Vince — badly concussed. Is that penance enough? He tried to think, but couldn't tear his mind away from the phone conversation.

A small voice told him, *They're still traffickers. They're still terrible people. They deserved it.*

But Violetta used them.

And he knew without Duke they were nothing.

He didn't have the processing power to figure out how to handle the rest of it. So he said, 'You figure it out. Just get me to the airport.'

Quinn hesitated. 'Why? What's changed?'

'I think I have to kidnap my girlfriend.'

This time, the hesitation was even longer. 'What are you on about?'

King rounded to the passenger side, slipped in, and half-heartedly angled the SIG at Quinn. 'Just drive.'

'You're a weird dude.'

Quinn put the jeep into gear and pulled a U-turn, leaving Container 55D wide open, exposing the empty cavern within.

57

D arkness fell over Brooklyn.

John Paul Jones Park quietened.

Within the small walk-up apartment, Slater sat in front of a fresh MacBook Pro he'd ordered two days previously, with express shipping guaranteeing delivery for today. The courier had left it on the welcome mat out front with Slater's online permission, and at midday he'd discreetly opened the door and picked it up. Zero potential witnesses. Then he'd set to work installing various dark web services, including a private browser several levels beyond Tor. By the time he'd finished, the computer was impenetrable — at least for the purposes he wished to use it for.

Namely, accessing the accounts scattered across Switzerland and Grand Cayman containing the bulk of his fortune.

He'd already briefly scanned the accounts the government knew about, and sure enough his legitimate funds had vanished. They'd drained all the money he'd made over the last couple of years in service of Uncle Sam, perhaps thinking that might impede his mobility. It was a cute move. He wouldn't miss the money.

What really mattered was the nine-figure sum he had accruing interest in numbered accounts, of which the government knew nothing about.

Confident that the device was now secure, he hunched a little further over the screen, basking in the artificial glare. Alexis was out cold in the bedroom, napping after the stresses of the day. He didn't blame her. If constant discomfort and uncertainty didn't encompass the entirety of his waking experience, it might have affected him, too.

He logged in through the dark web, making sure all trace of his presence was invisible, and found the principal account, containing most of what he'd stolen from a triad in Macau.

$421,555,908.03.

An incomprehensible sum. Sitting there on the screen in one giant lump, but in reality diversified across a portfolio of investments. Mostly liquid, all executed by a trusted advisor in a shadowy corner of a bank in Zurich.

Slater simply didn't have time to watch his money.

He delegated accordingly.

Now he navigated to the cash account and found a far smaller sum than the total assets, which was to be expected.

What wasn't expected was the figure itself.

$31,500,000.00.

He hadn't done that deliberately, and the last time he'd checked his cash account, it had been a random blur of different digits. Definitely below the $31,500,000 mark, but not by much. Which meant someone had made deposits to round the account up — to make the sum noticeable, to make it stand out.

To catch Slater's attention.

His advisor?

He didn't think so.

That wasn't part of the drill.

With a sinking feeling in his stomach, he navigated to the list of account transactions and pulled the most recent transactions up on the screen.

All deposits from an unspecified account.

All with accompanying descriptions — an ordinary transfer procedure with a low character limit.

$107.80 — RETURN.

$76.00 — IMMEDIATELY.

$50.55 — OR.

$69.09 — THE.

$45.00 — GIRL'S.

$101.00 — FAMILY.

$456.00 — DIES.

The sinking feeling turned to freefall.

He sat motionless, nihilistic, suddenly plagued by a foreign sensation he couldn't place. It didn't take him long to figure out what it was.

Despair.

He'd always thought Violetta could maintain control. She could rant and rave all day about her lack of ability to interfere, but when it came to crunch time, she could surely prevent Alexis' family from being touched.

He now realised why he'd been so foolish.

He'd met the four old men at Bannerman Castle, and fully believed their threats, but ultimately he thought he worked for a fundamentally good institution. A group of shadow people who broke rules regularly, just as Slater did, but had the greater good in mind.

He'd miscalculated horribly.

Maybe this *was* their idea of the greater good. What did it matter if an elderly couple in the UK had to perish under suspicious circumstances? If that was what it took to draw a rogue operative out of hiding, then so be it. Slater jeopardised their ability to remain in the shadows, and their existence in that darkness allowed them to accomplish missions and tasks they formally weren't allowed to do.

So it made sense.

But he'd never considered it reality until now.

He put his face in his hands and warped his features, crushing his lips and spreading his eyes apart, becoming the personification of the despair he felt. He allowed himself that reprieve, if only for a moment.

Then he sat up, shook it off, and set to work attempting to salvage it all.

Because what the hell else was he to do?

He could control his own actions — not others'. That's how people crumbled. That's how hope was lost. He could give up in the face of bad odds, but that would be conducive to submitting to external circumstances. It was no secret that terrible things would happen — to himself and those he loved — and there was nothing he could do about it except his best. So his best was what he did now. Even if it would cost him everything.

His accounts weren't secure, but he believed the brand new laptop still was. There was simply no way they could trace it back to this apartment — not with the procedures he was using. He knew there were countless ways they could have gained access to his fortune. He'd physically visited his advisor in Zurich a couple of times. A long time ago, but he'd done it regardless. If he'd been caught on CCTV footage, it'd be a simple process. The upper echelon wanted him badly enough to waive morality, so they could just threaten to execute each and every member of his advisor's family unless he passed over Slater's account numbers.

That was all they needed.

Not the passwords.

Just enough detail to make deposits and send a message.

But they probably had the passwords, too. He thought about changing them, but realised how futile it would be. So eventually he reached a decision that he thought was inevitable, and he went to the website tab used to make internal transfers and sent himself three separate sums from a smaller cash account.

$1.00 — IF I DO

$1.00 — WILL YOU LEAVE

$1.00 — HER OUT OF IT?

A shiver crept up his spine as he sat back away from the screen. His hidden advantage was now laid bare, exposed, available to the people hunting him. If it all vanished — all the accounts, all the dollars, all the investments — what then?

He'd make do. He knew he would.

Money wasn't the problem.

Freedom was.

He masked all the uncertainty rippling through him, stood up, and walked to the bedroom.

Steadily realising that to keep Alexis safe, he might need to turn himself in.

Abandoning her forever.

He didn't see it, but on the screen behind him, the banking paged automatically refreshed. Revealing a new transfer from an anonymous account, freshly deposited.

$1.00 — YES.

58

When Quinn pulled up at the drop-off point outside John Wayne Airport, King ejected the magazine from the SIG and handed the empty gun over.

Quinn took it in a shaking hand, his face paler than ever, luminescent under the terminal's exterior lighting.

'You'll be alright,' King said. 'Move on from all this chaos. Forget it happened. Get an honest job. Distance yourself from what happened in Emerald Bay.'

'You killed my friends.'

'They weren't your friends. Duke was an opportunist. If you didn't provide value, he'd have cast you out and brought in someone else.'

'You don't know that.'

'I know people,' King said. 'I knew everything about Ryan Duke the moment I met him.'

'What else do you know?'

'Whoever Roman was,' King said, 'I doubt he ran away.'

Quinn stared.

King said, 'You always had your suspicions, didn't you?'

'He wasn't the type to run. That's what I always thought.'

'He probably didn't. He's probably six feet under the yard.'

'Duke wouldn't do that.'

'You sure?'

Quinn hesitated. Then shook his head.

King said, 'I thought so.'

'How do I extricate myself from this? You didn't kill everyone. I can't just walk away.'

'Sure you can. Vince and Cal are badly concussed. They won't remember details. They didn't see what happened. For all they know, I killed you and buried you way out near the Cajon Pass. Under a big rock, maybe. Definitely somewhere in the desert.'

Quinn shook his head. 'I'd have to leave them to fend for themselves. They'd be the only ones to take the blame for the massacre.'

King made to respond, then realised he didn't care what happened to Quinn. He was being generous enough by not putting one through his skull. He said, 'Whatever. Go back, don't go back. You figure it out.'

Quinn stared vacantly at the middle of the steering wheel.

King said, 'Look at me.'

The guy looked over, sporting the same ghost white pallor.

King said, 'Whatever you do ... whatever happens ... I wasn't here. You'd better make sure you stick to that. Even if you turn yourself in. Or I'll come for you.'

Quinn half-nodded, but not all the way.

King said, 'You think I won't?'

'I know you will.'

King closed the passenger door, fetched his bag out of the rear seats, and slapped the door twice. 'Get going.'

The jeep rolled away, and King entered the terminal.

He knew his anonymity was secure — he used a second passport for the flight back to New York that neither Violetta nor the government had any knowledge of. He'd planned in advance, even slipping brown contacts into his eyes that he'd fished from a tiny case of solution. The passport photo was *just* similar enough to give him no issues on the way through, but different enough to avoid triggering any alerts if his picture was being circulated through the system.

It was all precautionary, anyway. Violetta trusted him. She wouldn't be looking for him. Not yet.

The night was still young.

At the gate, before boarding the red eye, he called her.

She picked up. 'All good?'

'Yeah,' he said. 'I'm out front, out of earshot. They're all inside, all drunk. They trust me completely.'

'That's good,' she said, sounding genuinely relieved. 'You've always been world-class at undercover work.'

'Shower me in compliments, why don't you?'

She laughed. 'Only one more day.'

'Feels like forever,' he said. 'I miss you.'

He felt horrible.

Not because she didn't deserve to be manipulated, but because he'd never stooped to this level before. Their sacred bond was desecrated. It left him empty and hollow, but he knew there was no alternative.

She said, 'I miss you, too.'

'Where are you?' he said.

'Why?'

'I've just been thinking,' he said, putting a slur into his

voice, as if he was feeling the effects of keeping up with the rest of the crew, beer for beer. 'If Slater decided to … you know…'

'That's not my problem,' she said. 'There's a whole world above me that is handling that problem. I'm at home.'

'He doesn't know where you live, does he?'

'No,' she said. 'Only you.'

Only me.

Unfortunate for you.

He said, 'Stay frosty. You never know what he'll do. What he's capable of.'

She hesitated. 'Do you know something we don't?'

I know he's the most loyal person I've ever met, King thought. *I know you're hunting him as we speak. I know you're counting on me being in California for another twenty-four hours at the very minimum. So you can deal with this before I get back.*

He said, 'No. I'm just worried, that's all.'

'There's security measures in place,' she said. 'You don't have to worry about me.'

Yes, he thought. *I certainly do.*

He said, 'What security measures?'

'My bosses sent out a tier-one crew to establish a perimeter around my place. I think it's unnecessary, but…'

'They wouldn't have done that unless there was a serious threat.'

'They're being paranoid. Trust me, it's fine.'

He said, 'How good's the perimeter?'

'Why does it matter?'

'Humour me this much, at least.'

'You haven't heard from Will, have you?'

'No,' King said. 'Why? Has he threatened you?'

'No,' Violetta said after a half-second's hesitation that said everything. 'Of course not. Look, I get you're concerned.

But trust me — this is legit. I've met the tactical team myself. There's four guys — two in the walk-up opposite my place, one in the apartment next to mine, one staying in my spare room.'

'That's some serious muscle.'

'My employers spare no expense. You know that. And it's only temporary. Until this all dies down.'

He said, 'Stay safe.'

'Always. Good luck tomorrow.'

'Thanks,' he said as the boarding announcement resonated through the gate. 'I'll need it.'

He hung up and went to queue for the plane.

59

Dawn broke over the park, and in the dinghy little flat, Slater hit "Enter" on a brand new transfer.

As it went through, he masked a sigh.

$1.00 — WHERE?

It had been a restless night.

He couldn't help mentally torturing himself. He'd been naive, he knew, but if he never made a mistake in his life then he was nothing more than an automaton. Mistakes make you human. He'd placed too much faith in the general decency of the shadow world. He'd figured, because Alexis was a civilian, it would be a stretch to harm her at all, let alone track down her distant innocent family members in another continent and threaten to execute them. There was no feasible way he could have sent her entire extended family into hiding before they ran, so it was a chance he knew he would have to take if he wanted a life with her.

Sometimes love makes you blind.

She'd noticed something was up, but hadn't commented on it. Now, she sauntered out of the bedroom, wearing one of his shirts and her own underwear. The top was enormous on her, almost reaching her knees.

She said, 'Is everything okay?'

He wiped his face with one hand, blinked hard, and rested the side of his head on his palm as he looked at her. 'Yeah. Just stressed, you know.'

'I know,' she said. 'But we did it, right? We got away with it?'

'For now.'

Every word felt hollow, every syllable faked.

She wandered over and stood behind him, putting her hands on his shoulders. He gently tapped the MacBook's touchpad, discreetly switching tabs. Hiding the list of transfers.

'What was that?' she said.

'Hidden accounts,' he said. 'I'm working on the money situation.'

'You don't have to hide it from me.'

'I just don't want you to know too much,' he said. 'For your own safety. If this all goes bad. Maybe you could claim obliviousness if they take us in, you know?'

'How could it go bad?' she asked. 'We just stick to your strategy. Order meal delivery and get them to leave it at the door each time. Order new clothes online. Order everything online. No one will see our face for as long as we need. You explained all this to me already. How the way society is set up nowadays makes it *easier* to vanish. Which is, you know, paradoxical, because of surveillance.'

She was saying too much — they both knew it.

The more silence she could fill, the longer it'd be until she had to ask, *Why are you so concerned? What went wrong?*

Notifications chimed from the other browser tab — five separate *ping*s, only a couple of seconds apart.

Slater knew he couldn't hide it from her any longer.

He tapped back across.

$1.00 — Where you were

$1.00 — Dropped

$1.00 — The first time

$1.00 — We met.

$1.00 — Three hours.

She read the descriptions.

She went silent.

Thinking.

After a spell she said, 'These are your private accounts. The ones the government don't have access to.'

Slater nodded. 'That's what I thought.'

She read the words, over and over again. 'You don't have to obey them.'

'Yes,' he said. 'I'm afraid I do.'

60

Dawn also broke over the neighbourhood of Great Kills in Staten Island.

It was a glorious morning — cool and crisp and sunny — and the boats were out in the harbour. Small hobbyist yachts began drifting away from their moorings as the sun came up, filling a cloudless sky. Four blocks in from the shore, a leafy residential street home to several swanky apartment buildings bristled with life. White-collar workers stepped outside and sauntered down to ground level, steaming thermoses of coffee in their hands. Middle-class mothers wheeled prams down the wide sidewalks, and elderly residents led their dogs to Great Kills Park or trotted them toward the various marinas dotting the harbour for their morning sun and maybe a swim.

When the initial rush of activity faded to a slow crawl, a plain black sedan pulled up against the kerb below one of the apartment buildings. Its windows were tinted, but the driver's window rolled down a crack, providing whoever was inside with a clear view across the street. There the car waited, its driver clearly surveilling the opposite apartment complex, keeping his gaze firmly fixed on the terraced balconies and the lobby entranceway.

Biding his time.

Watching.

Waiting.

Patient.

It took three minutes for two men to step out of the narrow laneway on the sedan's side of the street. They'd come from the building the sedan was resting beside. They wore expensive black windbreakers and khaki pants and their hair was buzzed all the way down to the scalp. They didn't gel with the quiet suburbia of Great Kills, but they didn't need to. They were spending most of the time behind closed doors, out of sight and out of mind.

Now they moved with practiced efficiency. If they had to be seen in public, they wished to be seen for as little time as possible. Best to use their training to get this over and done with in seconds, whether it was hostile or not. They both kept a hand under their windbreakers, and there was no mistaking what they were clutching. They swarmed the sedan with deceptive speed, one man rounding to the driver's side, the other darting to the rear passenger seat, affording him a potential angle on anyone in the rear seats as well as a clean line of sight diagonally across to the driver.

Excellent execution.

The man by the driver's side pulled his Sig Sauer automatic handgun and tapped the barrel twice on the driver's window.

It came down instantly.

There wasn't a moment's hesitation by either man. They were both in operational mode, supremely focused on neutralising the threat, ready to do whatever it took.

The driver was a plain pudgy guy in his middle-fifties

with a horrific comb-over and a pair of ridiculous sunglasses covering his eyes. There was no one else in the car — at least, not in the passenger or rear seats.

The driver mumbled something.

The guy by the driver's side ducked down, folding at the waist. Maybe to say, *Sir, please leave the area. Don't loiter here.*

He didn't get the chance.

King came sprinting out of the same laneway the two tier-one boys had come from, a two-hundred and twenty pound freight train of momentum, and he was on them before either had the chance to realise what was happening. They were expertly trained, but they weren't inhuman. They could only focus on one thing at a time, no matter how sharp that focus was. The driver was an unknown threat, in the process of mumbling something that may or may not relate to the job they were on, so the guy on the driver's side had his line of sight ruined as he leant in through the open window to hear the man better.

King barrelled straight for the guy on the rear passenger side and grabbed him by the back of his head with a giant palm and threw it forward into the tinted window hard enough to splinter a spider-web of cracks across the glass. It would have broken his nose and knocked him clean out simultaneously, so King disregarded a follow-up shot and took advantage of the fact that he hadn't slowed down one bit. The sedan was low to the ground and King was six-foot-three and incredibly athletic, so all he had to do was leap off both feet and momentum did the rest. He slid along the roof on his hip and when the same momentum launched him off the other side he came down on top of the guy still leaning through the driver's window.

Which made the guy crumple, because he hadn't been bracing for a two hundred plus pound weight slamming down onto the small of his back. He was leaning *just* far enough into the car for his throat to smash against the sill, which eliminated any chance of offering resistance, because you can't aim a gun when you're gasping for air and paralysed by the pain. He fell away from the sedan in literal agony, hands flying to his throat, convinced his airways were restricted and he was on the verge of death. King had landed alongside him, and opted to take the man's terror away by pivoting onto his side and slamming an elbow down against the guy's forehead. It was a move he'd practically perfected, and it turned the lights out like clockwork.

King scrabbled to his feet, threw open the rear driver's-side door of the rented sedan, and hauled the unconscious man to his feet. He threw him over one shoulder, stepped forward, and dropped him across the rear seats, where he splayed with all four limbs going in separate directions. It was crude but efficient.

King rounded the hood, repeated the over-the-shoulder manoeuvre with the other guy, and dropped him on top of his friend, both of them mutually disoriented. You don't stay unconscious for long, so they were both coming too, but they were concussed. They were fundamentally useless.

King collected their weapons and threw them through the now-open passenger window.

The driver was already out of the sedan. He levered to his feet in the middle of the street, took off his sunglasses, and placed them on the driver's seat. He was short, fat, and older than he looked.

King said, 'Thank you. If you want to keep that money, then you never saw me.'

'Saw who?' the old guy said with a reassuring wink.

He swaggered away from the scene, and didn't look back once.

King had found him on the street and offered him five grand to drive up, sit there, and act confused.

Money well spent.

He got behind the wheel, reversed a few dozen feet, and turned the nose of the rental car into the laneway beside the apartment complex. As soon as the sedan was off the street, he pulled into the shadows under the lee of the awnings and stamped on the brakes. The glove compartment popped open all on its own, and King reached across the centre console and fetched the four rolls of duct tape he'd picked up from a hardware store.

He'd yet to find a more efficient way to restrain a resisting foe.

He got out and set to work tying up his two hostages.

Two down.

Two to go.

61

S later was dead inside.

There was no other way to put it.

He thought he'd felt dread before. He thought he knew what it meant to be totally, overwhelmingly crushed. Now he realised he'd never come close. He'd never reached the bottom of the barrel. He'd been down in the depths, but there was a world of difference between what he'd experienced in the past and what he experienced now. It was worse than learning of Ruby's death. It was worse than anything.

Because Alexis was here, in front of him, her face open, her eyes trusting.

And he was going to have to ruin her life.

He stood up. She backed off a step, confused by his brashness, and then she saw his eyes. They were wet, but he hadn't teared up with sadness.

It was rage.

She said, 'What is it?'

His face softened. He said, 'I'm so sorry.'

She stared at him, uncomprehending.

He said, 'This was all a mistake.'

Silence.

He said, 'I need to go back.'

It didn't compute. 'What?'

He pointed to the laptop. 'All this was futile. The accounts were just the beginning. They'll have us surrounded within days. They run the country, Alexis. They're all-seeing, all-knowing.'

She took a shaky step to the nearest armchair and put her hand on top of it to steady herself. The blood drained from her face. 'Will...'

'I communicated with them,' he said. 'They said, if I came back, they wouldn't touch you. You can go back to your old life. You can pretend none of this ever happened. You can still ... have a life. I can't.'

He refused to reveal the truth.

If she knew her family's lives hung in the balance, she would carry that paranoia forever. She didn't deserve the burden.

He would shoulder it.

All of it.

He always had.

Her face had collapsed, but she was still able to bottle her emotions. She said, 'What about everything we talked about? What about us?'

He said, 'I'm sorry.'

'*Will.*'

He took a step backwards. Away from her. Getting closer to the door.

She said, 'No.'

It'd make it a thousand times harder if he left her with a good impression. Internally he was broken, destroyed, torn to pieces. He couldn't let it show. If she had fond memories of him, she'd be more likely to try and throw herself back into his world — whether she was looking for him, or information in the wake of his death. It was the hardest decision of his life. He could see the love in her eyes, and below that, the horrors of betrayal.

She said, 'Please, Will. There's a way through this. You know there is. Don't give up. Please.'

He tried to respond, but couldn't.

He took another step back.

Her face contorted, and her shoulders slumped, and she had to put both hands on the chair back to stop herself from crumbling.

He said, 'I'm sorry. There's no other choice. There's no point us both dying.'

She couldn't answer.

He said, 'If you love me...'

She looked up.

'...live a good life. Do the things you want to do. Make it worth it.'

'Where has this *come from?!*'

She screamed the last two words.

He shut himself off. Emotionally, mentally, spiritually. The more he tried to explain, the more it would hurt.

What could he say?

If we keep this up, your family will die. Innocent people will be butchered. People who have nothing to do with this. And then they'll probably get us, too, to top things off.

If he told her the truth, he was effectively ruining her life. Because she'd blame herself for it all, and there was no way in hell he was letting that happen.

He said, 'I'm sorry. I hope you understand.'

His leather jacket and his Glock were on the table by the door. He slipped the jacket on, picked up the Glock within its polymer holster, and attached it to his waist. He draped the jacket over it. His actions were hollow, empty. Just like he was.

When he was ready, he looked up at her one last time.

She was so beautiful. So strong.

The best thing that had ever happened to him.

She deserved more than him.

She deserved more than chaos, suffering and death.

He forced back the tears with every ounce of his willpower, turned, and walked out.

on't waste time.

King armed himself with one of the Sig Sauers — a P226 with a black suppressor attached — and hid it under his jacket. He cast one last look at the two operators practically cocooned in duct tape, sandwiched into the rear footwell with only enough space around their heads to breathe.

They weren't going anywhere.

He left the sedan draped in shadow and threw the keys away. It wasn't so out of sight that the pair would die of thirst before they were discovered. But it would take at least a couple of hours for a passerby to summon the nerve to check on the car. By which point King would be a world away.

He knew exactly where Violetta's apartment was, as well as the layout of her building. He recalled what she'd told him about the perimeter. There was another operator in the apartment beside her, and a man staying in her spare room. She was in there, no doubt. Kept on lockdown until the Slater issue was cleared.

The key point being neither her apartment or the one next to her faced the street.

So if there was a sniper's nest, it was now empty, populated by the two men in the sedan from the opposite building. King shivered as he crossed the street, terrified that his analysis was inaccurate, expecting his head to burst apart at any moment. Seconds later he reached Violetta's lobby without incident, proving himself correct.

Don't waste time.

The mantra of the hour.

Every second that went by only threatened to amplify the resistance. He had surprise on his side, and little else.

He caught a twenty-something woman coming out of the lobby, and intercepted her perhaps a dozen feet from the entranceway. He tapped into every sliver of his charm and displayed it across his face, accentuating his physique, flashing a broad grin. It was no secret he was a handsome man. And rugged and built on top of that, which only added to it. He could use it when necessary. She was tall and long-limbed, wearing a blouse tucked into tight blue jeans.

He said, 'You're going to think I'm a moron.'

She stopped in her tracks, and gave him the brief once-over that everyone gives a stranger. She clearly liked what she saw. She said, 'What?'

But there was no irritation in her tone.

It was playful.

He said, 'It's petty. But you look like fun. Humour me for a second or two.'

She said, 'I'm listening.'

He said, 'Look over my shoulder. You see those balconies across the street?'

She nodded.

He said, 'My ex-girlfriend lives in one of those apartments. We broke up yesterday. She's genuinely psycho. She cheated on me, and to make things worse she's refusing to let me see the dog.'

The woman pouted. 'What kind of dog?'

'Golden retriever. His name's Zeus.'

'I'm sorry. You deserve better.'

An overt hint.

'She's watching us right now,' King said. 'I don't know if you can see. Don't look too hard.'

Discreetly, the woman scouted the balconies. She said, 'No. Can't see her. But I didn't look too hard.'

'If you take my hand right now and smile and take me into your lobby, she'll get so mad she might pass out.'

A devilish smile crept over the woman's face before she could suppress it.

She said, 'Oh, really?'

'Depends how good of a job you do.'

'I'm a theatre major.'

'Let's go, then.'

He reached out and offered his hand and she took it and cosied up to his arm like they were in the honeymoon stage of a new relationship. He muttered some small talk in her ear and she giggled at it as she turned and retraced her steps. When they stepped into the lobby, they kept their faces turned to each other. She was a good eight inches shorter than him, so it was perfectly natural for him to look down at her, keeping his features masked from any surveillance cameras. They made it all the way across the lobby hand in hand, and King had confidence that his presence would have been automatically discarded by any prying eyes fixed to the CCTV footage. Sure, the physical features matched, but he wasn't the only big guy on Staten Island. They hadn't seen his face, and if he was hand in hand with a resident they could assume he hadn't kidnapped or blackmailed her.

He stopped by the elevators, let go of her hand, and said, 'Thanks. She'll be traumatised.'

'Glad I could be of service.'

He loitered, waiting for her to leave.

She looked him up and down. 'Want my number?'

He half-smiled. 'No. It's for your own good. I'm trouble.'

He got into a waiting cable car and smacked the button for the eighth floor.

The doors whispered closed in her face.

63

K ing stepped out into a quaint hallway made silent by thick carpet that silenced his footfalls.

Good.

He had reasonable expectations that no one knew he was here, so he made straight for Violetta's apartment, recalling the words that had come through the phone at John Wayne Airport.

One in the apartment next to mine.

If he'd asked her to clarify whether that was left or right, it would have triggered all kinds of suspicion.

So he simply walked up to the apartment to the left of hers, knocked sharply three times — *rap-rap-rap* — and stepped to the side, out of sight if anyone looked through the peephole.

He waited fifteen long seconds.

Nothing happened.

He thought about moving on.

Then the door opened.

An elderly woman stood there, hunched over a walking frame, shorter than five feet. She was frail and confused. She craned her neck to look up at him, and it didn't seem comfortable.

He said, 'Sorry, ma'am. Wrong apartment.'

'Oh,' she said, and left it at that.

She closed the door in his face.

He walked straight past Violetta's apartment, to the door to the right of hers. He repeated the process — knocked three times and stepped aside.

This time he only had to wait six seconds. The door opened halfway between the sixth and seventh second, revealing a huge man who looked like he'd spent most of the last few years of his life on the frontlines. He had a pock-marked, weathered face, with deep lines of stress etched into his forehead, and red ruddy cheeks. Iraq, maybe. He was serious business, and he had one hand behind his back, which no doubt clutched a handgun, but that didn't matter because King was already pivoting as soon as he glimpsed the guy's frame. After a ton of wind-up he ordinarily couldn't afford, he slammed a perfectly placed right hook square into the centre of the guy's face, causing a plethora of damage as it simultaneously sparked him out cold. Breaking his nose, maybe fracturing an orbital bone, maybe shattering one completely.

Serious, serious damage.

The clean punch would have shattered every bone in King's hand if he was a novice combatant, but in much the same way Muay Thai fighters harden their shins by kicking poles, he'd hardened bone and tissue in his hands over a lifetime of use.

Unhurt, he stepped over the threshold and shut the door behind him.

Three minutes later he stepped back out, an entire roll of duct tape lighter.

He went one apartment over, and knocked on Violetta's door. Repeating the same process. An icy impenetrable calm had settled over him, before he'd even stepped foot in the building. He thought nothing of what he was about to do — the bridge he was about to cross. There was no point second-guessing. He'd made up his mind. This was his decision. He'd have to live with it for the rest of his life.

She opened the door — probably because no one in the tier-one crew had alerted the guy in her apartment to any danger — and before recognition and confusion spread across her face he made sure to memorise every part of her features.

The straight blonde hair, the kind blue eyes, the pale skin, the flawless complexion.

She was beautiful, and he realised it might be the last time she'd look at him without hate in her eyes.

As if on cue, recognition and confusion seized her.

She managed a single, 'What the—?' before he filled the doorway with the Glock raised, sweeping the space over her shoulder.

The final operator was there — a tall wiry athletic guy with sharp features and a pronounced jawline. He'd come out of the spare room, and he'd come prepared. In the snapshot King caught he saw a flustered man, probably aggravated by Violetta abandoning protocol. He must have demanded he be the one to answer the door each and every time. She likely considered it ridiculous, especially if there was a sniper's nest across the street and a guy next door watching all the CCTV feeds in the building. So he was pissed at her disobedience, which meant he'd reacted fast. He had a Beretta in his hands and those hands were on an upward trajectory, and now there was primal recognition in his eyes as he acknowledged King's presence.

Suddenly King saw it all laid out before him.

He saw it from the operator's perspective.

A rogue enemy of the state standing across the threshold. A handler between them, but not an important one. If it came to letting King escape with their country's darkest secrets or taking out Violetta as unfortunate collateral, he'd go for the latter.

He would have been given those instructions, too.

Explicitly.

Do not, under any circumstances, let King get his hands on her. If he shows up in New York, then he's allied with Slater.

Neutralise him.

Whatever the cost.

For milliseconds, King considered the possibility of a non-lethal response, then realised it was never going to work. He couldn't be pure in this world if he wanted to exist in it.

He forced Violetta aside and shot the operator in the forehead before the guy could get off a shot of his own.

When he saw the trajectory of the operator's barrel, and the closeness of the guy's finger to the trigger, he knew the first shot would have blown through the back of Violetta's head.

The body fell back against the plasterboard, and its neck bent in a way necks shouldn't bend, and it collapsed to the floor.

She turned and stared at the corpse.

She didn't speak.

A million questions played on her lips, but she settled on, 'What did you do?'

'Saved your life.'

She turned back, her pale face paler than usual. 'What is this?'

He was still frozen in place, Glock raised to head-height, aimed at the bloody patch of wall down the corridor, showered by the residue of the exit wound.

Now, he drifted the barrel over and aimed it at the love of his life.

He watched her finally realise, with a gut shot of clarity, what was happening.

'No,' she said, her face falling.

'Come with me,' he said. 'And don't say another word until I ask you to.'

Fear and sadness rippled behind her eyes.

He said, 'And get your story straight. Because I need answers.'

64

S later didn't hail a cab right away.

He walked, with his head down and his hands in his pockets. The sun was gone, replaced by thick cloud. Just for once he'd hoped for a few minutes of good weather — not that it would have achieved anything — but it seemed even that had been stripped from him. The sweatshirt under his leather jacket had a hood, and he pulled it up. The last thing he wanted was to get recognised as a person of interest, for the red-and-blue flashes of police lights and the wailing of sirens to ruin his last miserable moments of freedom.

He wanted desperately to have an outburst, but didn't allow himself to. Nor did he let himself curse his fate, or curse what was probably the abhorrent ending to his career and life. He walked past a park bench and planted himself down at it, staring at the pavement, wracking his brain for any potential solution to his woes.

As he suspected, there was nothing.

There were a million solutions if he was on his own, which was the reason he'd spent most of his life in solitude.

No collateral, no responsibilities, no bait to dangle over his head. When he wanted to disappear, he disappeared. He'd thrown that all aside by introducing Alexis, and he should have known better. There was no fairytale ending. His skillset was useless if he was facing off against the entire shadow world, and there wasn't a thing he could do to protect her entire extended family.

There was no way around it.

He had lost.

He could run now. He could let them butcher everyone Alexis knew and loved in their desperation to get to him. Then they'd probably kill her, too, for her awareness of state secrets. Other than her, he had nothing, so vanishing would be effortless. He had as much freedom as he wanted, as long as he was comfortable taking the nightmares and shoving them deep in a vault inside his head.

So that was that.

Live as a monster.

Or die with his soul intact.

He already knew there was no reality where he'd ever choose the former. You could strip him of all his training, all his experience with pain, all the limits he'd forged simply by enduring longer than anyone else thought possible ... you could get rid of everything, and he'd be the same man underneath. He'd have the same principles. He figured he was born with them.

And he'd die with them.

He stood up, probing his mental map for the closest busy street in Brooklyn. Wherever he could most easily hail a cab. Strangely, he felt nothing now. Maybe he'd experienced everything. Maybe by abandoning Alexis, by making the love of his life hate him, he'd ticked that final box on the checklist of the human emotional spectrum. Maybe, with that all wrapped up, all he was left with was emptiness.

He spotted a cab, across the street in the distance, maybe a couple of hundred feet away.

It was idle.

If he got in, it would take him to the gravel hard shoulder off the bank of the Hudson River. He'd get out. He'd watch it drive away. As soon as there were no witnesses, a sniper would put a round through his skull.

There weren't any other options.

That was his fate.

So he made for the cab, but it was a two-minute walk, so before he threw his burner phone away forever he figured he'd make one final call. Perhaps she'd listen to him now. Now that she knew he was a dead man walking. Perhaps he could make her understand what she'd done to him.

He pulled out the phone and dialled a number he knew off by heart.

He didn't expect her to answer.

She did.

She didn't say anything.

'Violetta,' he said. 'It's me.'

Silence.

He said, 'This is the endgame. You win. Will you listen to me now? Before I go.'

'Don't do anything stupid,' a male voice said. 'Just tell me where you are.'

A voice he knew.

Slater froze.

Literally stopped dead in his tracks, in the lee of a rundown tenement building. Somehow, the sky turned greyer. Uncertainty swelled. And his heart sank.

He said, 'You never went to California, did you?'

Silence.

Slater said, 'That was all bullshit, wasn't it? You've been working with her this whole time.'

King said, 'I went to California, alright. Now I'm back.'

'I'm sure you did.'

'She set me up, too.'

Now it was Slater's turn to fall silent.

King said, 'Yeah.'

'How do you have her phone?' He paused. 'Did you kill her?'

'No. She's with me.'

'How can you trust her?'

'I can't,' King said. 'Which is why she's not here with me voluntarily.'

'Christ,' Slater said, turning in a half-circle. 'This is a mess.'

'Tell me about it.'

'You're burning bridges.'

'Only the ones you've already burnt.'

Slater went quiet.

King said, 'You think I'd just give up on you?'

'What happened in California?'

'It was a dummy lead. It led to nothing. They fed a bunch of small-time crooks some false information that'd keep me busy until tomorrow night.'

'I'd be dead by then.'

'Sounds like you would have been dead within the hour.'

'Yeah. Probably.'

'Don't do anything stupid,' King reiterated. 'I'm here. We're going to fight this.'

'How can we?'

'We'll figure it out.'

'What's she told you?'

'Nothing yet. She's here beside me. I've instructed her not to speak. I want us to talk to her together.'

'I'm going to kill her.'

King went quiet.

Slater said, 'Is that going to be a problem?'

'We'll see. Depends what we hear.'

'Does she know I just threatened her life?'

'No. I'm not on speaker.'

Slater fed King the name of the street he was looking at, upon which rested the cab that would have sealed his fate.

'Brooklyn?' King said.

'Yeah.'

'Sit tight.'

King hung up.

Slater kept the silent phone pressed against his ear.

65

After the throaty cough of the suppressed gunshot had well and truly faded, King took Violetta by the arm and led her out of her apartment.

They went downstairs and covered the length of the lobby. He held her hand like they were an ordinary couple, and kept the Glock under his jacket, angled at her stomach. No one gave them so much as a second look. They stepped outside under an overcast sky and crossed the street, silent, looking straight ahead. King walked her a couple of hundred feet away from her building, and on the sidewalk he took her wrist in a firm grip to make sure she didn't make a break for it.

A shiny Land Rover was the first civilian car to materialise. It turned into the leafy street they were in and came trawling slowly toward them. King stepped out into the middle of the street, putting a frantic look on his face. The car slowed.

He pulled the Glock and rounded to the driver's side, pulling Violetta behind him.

He tapped the window with the barrel.

It came down, revealing a middle-aged woman with dyed blonde bangs and too much concealer makeup. She was scared out of her mind.

He said, 'Get out.'

She nearly had a panic attack fumbling with her seat-belt. But she managed, and threw the door open, and stepped out of the car.

'Thanks,' King said. 'You got insurance?'

She nodded, clearly unsure if she was dreaming or not.

He said, 'You'll be okay, then. Thanks again.'

He guided Violetta into the driver's seat, and then rounded the hood and slipped into the passenger's.

Leaning across the centre console, he said, 'Apologies.'

The woman said nothing.

He nodded to Violetta. She drove off.

Five seconds later, her phone rang.

She instinctively reached for it, withdrawing it from her pocket.

King saw the contact name: WILL SLATER.

He took it off her hands, and answered with silence.

Five minutes later, after a revelatory conversation, he hung up and put the phone in his lap.

She said, 'Can I talk now?'

He said, 'Not until we pick up Will.'

'I can explain.'

'Did you hear me?'

'Shoot me,' she said. 'I know you won't. You wouldn't dare. You're a good man.'

'I'm a morally rigid man — that's what I am. If I'm convinced you've betrayed me and tried to aid the capture and execution of my best friend, I won't hesitate to kill you. No matter how much you mean to me.'

She didn't respond.

He said, 'If you want to test that theory, by all means start talking.'

She didn't.

She knew him.

She knew it'd tear him apart, but that didn't mean he wouldn't do it. She knew, perhaps better than anyone, how he was willing to ruin his own life to preserve his integrity. He did it every operation, for Chrissakes. Got cut and shot and beaten to a pulp to protect others.

He fed the address Slater had given him into the Land Rover's GPS unit and told Violetta to follow it.

He kept the Glock's barrel aimed at her the whole time.

He settled back and considered the timing. He figured he had at least a few hours before everything went ballistic. The tactical team would miss their next check-in, but that wasn't automatically the end of the world. It'd take some time for reinforcements to be called out. The three operators still alive were trapped in their tape cocoons. It didn't matter how strong or tough they were — they weren't getting out of their restraints.

So a few hours, at best.

After that, he stopped thinking entirely. He found it best in times of maximal stress. His whole world had collapsed, he might have to kill the woman he loved, he and Slater had ostracised themselves once again. It was chaos. It'd tear him apart at the seams if he dwelled on it.

He focused on the breath. In and out, in and out. That was all.

Twenty minutes and one bridge crossing later, Violetta pulled up in a quiet, grungy section of Brooklyn. There were twenty-four hour pizza joints and diners and laundromats and pharmacies and bottle shops.

She sat patiently, both hands on the wheel, unnaturally calm.

She'd composed herself on the drive.

Compartmentalising just as well as he could.

Thirty seconds later, a man in a hooded sweatshirt and a leather jacket stepped out of a nearby alleyway.

King had never seen a colder expression on Will Slater's face. His eyes were ice. His mouth was a hard line. He made straight for the Land Rover, threw the rear driver's door open, and got in behind Violetta so King could look back at him diagonally.

King said, 'Rough day?'

Slater eyed the Glock in King's lap, angled up at Violetta. 'For us both.'

Violetta said, 'Can I speak now?'

King saw something dark flash in Slater's eyes.

Slater said, 'The first thing out of your mouth better be a promise to call off the threats on Alexis' family.'

'I'll do you one better than that,' she said. 'I'll make a different kind of promise.'

'I don't want a different kind of promise.'

Violetta looked across, staring deep into King's eyes. He felt he could see through to her soul. She was laying it all bare. She wasn't lying.

She said, 'Yes he does. Convince him to listen.'

King looked over his shoulder. 'Listen. Even if it leads nowhere. It's worth listening.'

He could see Slater using every ounce of forged willpower to stay motionless.

King turned back to her. 'Better be good.'

'It's good,' she said. She twisted round in her seat, so she could look straight at Slater. 'I got Alonzo to falsify official documents that I fed to my superiors. The address they have for Alexis' parents leads to an abandoned warehouse in an industrial estate in Bradford. Every trace of their official records has been buried. You've seen Alonzo in action. He's the best. They're safe.'

Slater stayed motionless.

Violetta said, 'So let's go get her.'

66

S later refused to let relief wash over him.

He wasn't about to lower his guard until all was well, and all was *certainly* not well yet. But at least the pure despair receded. It wasn't a desperate ploy on Violetta's behalf to save her own life. She knew he was technologically savvy. He could gain access to public records, corroborate her story, figure out whether she was bullshitting or not. She wouldn't have lied to him. There was no point buying herself more time if all roads led to the same destination.

He said, 'Give me your phone.'

She handed it over. He dialled Alexis's number from memory. He wasn't sure if she'd answer an unknown number.

She did.

Her voice was tentative, and behind it he could tell she was crushed. 'Hello?'

'It's me,' Slater said. 'Where are you?'

She didn't answer.

He said, 'Alexis. I love you. Where are you?'

'Still at the Airbnb. I was just about to leave...'

'Stay there.'

'What are you doing, Will?'

He bit his lower lip.

She said, 'What is this?'

'I'll explain,' he said. 'Trust me, I swear to God, I'll explain. Just stay there. I'll be there in five minutes.'

'What if I don't want you to be?'

He didn't answer that.

She said, 'You can't do this. You can't throw my life into turmoil like this. You just abandoned me.'

'I told you I'd explain.'

'That's it?'

'That's it. I need you to trust me.'

She sighed. 'Okay. I'll stay.'

'Thank you.'

'There'd better be a damn good explanation for this.'

'There is. See you soon.'

He ended the call, brought the phone away from his ear and pressed the top of the device to his forehead. He closed his eyes and exhaled.

King said, 'All good?'

'All good. Let's go get her.'

They both stared at Violetta as she drove, unsure what the hell was going on, unsure where allegiances lay.

King looked at Slater and said, 'I'll ask it if you won't.'

Slater shrugged. 'Be my guest.'

King looked at Violetta. 'Why would you do that?'

'I've spent this whole time wanting to explain,' she said. 'Are you finally going to let me?'

'Sure.'

'I've been forced to do certain things,' she said. 'Things I'm not proud of. Yes, I sent you to California for little reason. Yes, I did it so you wouldn't be here when Slater went rogue, as everyone knew he would. But they weren't my ideas, and I had no choice.'

'You always have a choice.'

'I didn't,' she said. 'It's all well and good being morally righteous, but not when there's a gun to the head of someone you care deeply for. So I had to comply, but I did everything I could to buy time. I made sure Alexis's family wouldn't be touched, which risked everything. I fought for them not to blow Slater's head off with a long-range weapon. I bought him a day or so. But the pressure was too much. They wouldn't budge. And they could tell I was stalling. The tactical team they surrounded my apartment with was just as much to keep me prisoner as it was to protect me.'

King stared at her. 'There was never a gun to my head.'

She said, 'I'm not talking about you.'

He sat still.

She said, 'There's things you don't know.'

'Care to explain?'

'Is this the place?' she said, craning her neck to look out the windshield as she pulled up out the front of the three-storey walk-up.

Slater nodded. He tapped the same number on the contact screen of Violetta's phone. When it was answered, he said, 'Come down. We're here.'

She appeared on the second-storey landing moments later, a small backpack slung over her shoulder. Slater knew it would contain the laptop, along with a handful of smaller possessions. He'd never met a more alert and intuitive civilian — it was as if she had combat experience hardwired into her system from birth — so she would have known to remove every trace of evidence from the small apartment, no matter the circumstances.

She spotted the Land Rover, and the outline of his face through the tinted glass of the rear windows, and descended the stairwell.

He couldn't wait.

He got out and crossed to her. She was holding herself together, but not by much. He outstretched his arms, and she fell into them.

'Why?' she whispered.

He told her the truth. Kept it straightforward, kept it objective, kept it unbiased. She deserved that much. Deserved to know what might have been.

When she stepped away as he finished, her green eyes blazed. Her skin had paled.

She said, 'You were going to die for me. For my parents.'

He nodded.

He said, 'They're safe. No one will touch them. Violetta's computer guy draped a veil over them. They can carry on living their lives, but as far as the U.S. government is concerned, they no longer exist.'

She doubled over and put her hands on her knees.

Trying not to hyperventilate.

When she stood up, she said, 'Don't ever do that to me again. Just give me it straight from the get-go. I'm a big girl. I can handle it.'

He said, 'I promise.'

'Christ,' she said, rubbing her eyes. 'Okay. Let's go.'

He led her to the car, and they got in the rear seats.

Tense introductions were made all round, which wasn't helped by the fact that as King introduced his girlfriend he kept his gun pointed at her stomach.

Alexis said, 'This is weird.'

'Yeah,' Violetta said. 'It's weird.'

Slater said, 'What the hell happens now?'

'We have a few hours before they find out King's gone rogue too,' Violetta said. 'When the tactical team is discovered, and they find me missing, it'll be absolute carnage.'

'So what should we hope to achieve before then?'

'I have access to safe houses across the city, but then so does everyone I work with.'

'No need,' Slater said, jerking a thumb at the landing above their heads. 'I have a safe house of my own we can use temporarily.'

Violetta looked at King.

He nodded.

They all piled out.

67

There's things you don't know.

King needed to know.

They scaled the flight of stairs as discreetly as they could, each shooting paranoid glances out over John Paul Jones Park, but it was largely unpopulated. Alexis unlocked the door, and they all spilled through, and King saw the knowing glance Slater and Alexis exchanged as they entered the cramped space.

We need to talk.

Slater looked at King, who nodded his understanding. *Go.*

They moved to the corner of the room, out of earshot, and sat down on the sofa. Hushed words were exchanged almost immediately — apology, acceptance, forgiveness, trust.

King turned away from them, allowing them their privacy, and sat down with Violetta at the kitchen table.

She eyed the Glock in his hand.

He looked at it.

Looked at her.

Then put it down on the countertop between them, and spun the barrel away.

She reached out and put a hand on his knee, then leant forward and kissed him briefly on the lips. It conveyed everything they both wanted to say but couldn't.

This world is madness. Let's not make this personal.

He said, 'Can you tell me?'

She cocked her head.

'What they threatened you with.'

She sighed.

She said, 'If I do, it means that I lied to you. Back when we first met.'

He nodded.

She said, 'How will you take that?'

'Depends,' he said. 'I'm sure you did it for the right reasons.'

'I did.'

'Then let's hear them.'

'Do you remember when we discussed losing the people we've loved?'

King nodded. 'Our exes. Klara for me. Beckham for you.'

'Do you remember what I said happened to him?'

'First you said he was mugged. I saw right through it, so you revealed he was tortured and murdered by the cartels in Guadalajara. He was over there working on a story, right? An investigative journalist. He must have done his job too well.'

'That's all true,' she said. 'But they didn't kill him.'

King didn't respond. He let her compose her thoughts, so she could communicate them the right way.

She said, '*Plato o plomo.* Silver or lead. That was true. They offered him a bribe to stand down, and he refused. But they didn't force him into a car, and his body didn't turn up three days later. They shot him like a dog in the street. Four times. Walked right up to him on the sidewalk and pumped him full of lead. One of the bullets hit his spine. He survived, but it paralysed him from the neck down. He's a quadriplegic.'

King said, 'Christ.'

'He hated me for it,' she said. 'He blamed me. I remember telling you he had the mentality of a junkyard dog. If he found something worth investigating, he'd sink his teeth into it and wouldn't let go, no matter the consequences. That's ... partially true. He didn't start out that way. I shaped him into it. I kept pushing, because he wanted to do stellar work as an investigative journalist, but he was too hesitant, too shy. I was deep in my own government work at that point, and I was stubborn. Foolhardy. I told him, *If you want to do something big, go after the cartels. Don't bow down to them.* I poked and prodded until he agreed. Then it took on a life of its own, and it consumed him, but I was the spark that started the flame.'

'That's not your fault,' King said. 'We make our own choices.'

'I don't blame myself,' she said. 'But I understand why he does. He broke up with me, and cut off all contact. I didn't care about the injury. I loved him. I still do, in a way. But he wanted nothing to do with me.'

'Why didn't you tell me?'

She sighed. 'It's emotionally complicated. I don't even feel comfortable talking about it now. I beat myself up about it all the time. It's not ... something I wanted to unload on a man I'd just met, a man I really liked. And then ... well, it never came up again after that. Until now.'

'Where is he now?'

'The cartels caught wind that he'd survived. They

started pulling out all the stops to finish him off. Paying off whoever they could get their hands on. It didn't take long for them to make real progress. That's when I offered to step in.'

'WITSEC?'

Violetta nodded. 'I knew he despised me. I didn't blame him for it. I figured it was a way for both of us to move on. I used the connections I had to get him straight into the program, and they set him up with a whole new identity, a whole new life. Found him a top-of-the-line disability home that catered to his every need. They didn't tell me where it was. He vanished, and I went all-in on my career. The more I worked, the less time I had to think about what he might be thinking of me. That's how I got to the heights I did. Because I slept, I ate, and I worked. Until you came along.'

'They threatened to kill him if you didn't comply?'

Violetta nodded. 'They knew where he was. I didn't. Eventually I got Alonzo to find out, but it didn't do any good. Any government resources I marshalled to rescue him would be known to my superiors. They had him in the palm of their hand, and they could crush him anytime they wanted.'

King said, 'This is a lot to process.'

Violetta said, 'You know what? Now that I'm vocalising it ... maybe I do blame myself. Maybe that's why I obeyed. Because I feel like I owe him everything.'

'You admire him. You loved him.'

'Yes.'

'Then it's not that you *owe* him,' King said. 'It's that you'd do anything for him, voluntarily.'

She looked at him. 'Just like you do. For all the people you save. The people you protect.'

'That's what I try to do,' he said, then looked down at the

Glock he'd been aiming at her all morning. 'I'm far from perfect.'

'You are to me.'

'I just kidnapped you.'

'You had your reasons.'

He reached down and took her hand in his. It was tiny in comparison — her fingers small and gentle, his massive and coarse.

He heard movement behind him, and turned to see Slater getting to his feet.

He turned back to Violetta. 'He needs to hear this.'

68

S later sat and listened.

All throughout, he realised Alexis was his rock. Now he could see everything with clarity. He could methodologically determine what was right, and what wasn't. Back in the Land Rover, he'd been ready to kill Violetta without listening, and now he understood it was because he'd been plunged back into isolation again. He'd lost the person he cared about most.

Now Alexis was back.

Now he could relax.

Now he could forgive.

As Violetta finished up, she added, 'There was no win-win. I had to conspire against you, Will, or they'd kill Beckham, they'd kill Jason, and they'd probably kill me too. I had to be objective, even though it was the last thing I wanted. And every step of the way I fought for you. I protected Alexis. But if you want total honesty from me, then so be it. If I had to choose the only two men I've ever loved, as well as the lives of a civilian and her family, over you, I'd do it. I'd do it every time. Ask yourself what decision you'd make if you were in my shoes.'

Slater sat, brooding.

She said, 'If you want to kill me, kill me. I had no choice. I can't go rogue like you two can. I can't drop everything. The government had me in their grip, and they wouldn't let go. They dangled Beckham over my head. They were saying, *You're responsible for his condition. Don't be responsible for his death, too.*'

Slater held up a hand.

She stopped talking.

He said, 'I'd have done the same.'

She froze.

She said, 'We're good?'

He nodded. 'We're good. You did the right thing.'

'I like to think so.'

Now, he felt relief. Like nothing he'd ever felt before. Out there, in the big wide world, everyone was now their enemy. The whole country, the secret world, everything that existed in the shadows. But here in this room, the four of them were united for the first time since all this shit had unfolded.

Across from Slater, King said to Violetta, 'Answer me one thing.'

'Sure,' she said.

'Why didn't you at least fill the container with something?'

She cocked her head again. Confused. 'What?'

'The container from Donati Group. The payload you faked. You could have at least put guns in it, or packages of fake fentanyl. You must have known I might have been able to sneak a look inside at some point.'

She stared. 'You saw *inside*?'

'Yesterday afternoon,' he said. 'I handled Ryan Duke and

his crew, and then went straight to the port. It was empty. That's when I called you.'

She stared harder.

Her face paling.

He said, 'What?'

'The fentanyl thing was bullshit,' she said. 'I said that just in case you were thinking about leaving. To make it seem more important. But the actual container wasn't fake.'

Again, he said, 'What?'

'Hold on,' she said. 'Something's not right here.'

'No shit.'

'Jason, that was a genuine op. It wasn't as important as we thought it would be, but we didn't plant that container. We *actually* got it from Donati Group's paperwork. It can't have been empty.'

'It was empty. I saw it with my own eyes.'

'That can't be. Why would Donati go through all that trouble to ship a decoy container?'

King put his head in his hands.

Slater observed all this from a distance. He didn't interfere, and he didn't ask questions, but he could imagine King's short-term memory flaring. The man was running through a categorised replay of his time spent in Los Angeles.

When he looked up, he said, 'Oh, fuck.'

Slater said, 'What?'

'There was a whiteboard. In Duke's office. It had dozens of formulas and business calculations scrawled on it. One stood out to me. DONATI = 1R.'

Slater didn't need to respond, but he thought he'd facilitate King's train of thought. 'What does that mean?'

Violetta said, 'One to the right.'

King said, 'A physical equation, never entered into any

computer, only passed from man to man via encrypted calls. To protect them from a software breach. Or to protect them from an idiot like me who took their house by force and then demanded to see the paperwork. Because an idiot like me would take one look at "Container 55D" in the Pier 400 Container Terminal and leave satisfied. Not realising 55E was the golden goose.'

Slater threw his hands up in the air.

King turned to him.

Slater said, 'Really? This is what we're focusing on? You know how much illegal stuff goes through ports? You're stressing over one container you missed? Fine, you screwed up. The Baja cartel gets a few more guns. If you busted that shipment, they would have simply ordered another. It's inconsequential. We've got bigger things to worry about.'

Violetta chewed her bottom lip and said, 'Unless it's human cargo.'

Slater saw King rewinding the tape in his head, scanning through the last few days.

Then the man seemed to stop on a certain memory.

His face fell.

He said, 'It *is* human cargo.'

69

K ing saw it all laid out before him.

Crystal clear, now that he'd pieced it together.

He remembered stepping into Donati's office, and the conversation that had ensued about the girl in the surveillance photo. Donati had already lied to him once. Claiming she was nobody, claiming the real target was the guy in the background. *She's nobody. He's the CFO for Zima Group.*

Then, in his office, Donati had supposedly admitted the truth. *Fine. You got me. She's not nobody. She's the daughter of the* actual *CFO. The guy in the background has nothing to do with it.*

But King still hadn't fully believed it, and he'd never been sure why.

Now he knew.

He'd promised that he might spare Donati if Donati gave him the truth, so the billionaire had crafted another lie. Because a quick, painless murder — getting hit by a truck —

sounded a whole lot better than what was actually supposed to happen to the girl.

For the first time, King realised he'd never actually heard Donati order a *hit.*

He'd just assumed.

The entirety of what Donati had said:

'You're sure she's alone?'

'Okay. Do it. Make it quick.'

'I don't care. You know what this is worth. Be discreet. Get it done.'

That didn't mean "kill her."

It meant "take her."

Now, King said, 'Sam Donati ran a human trafficking operation through his conglomerate. He takes girls in Eastern Europe and ships them around the world. That's why the containers in question were refrigerated. Temperature control, for live cargo. What I thought was an execution over there was really a kidnap. Which is worse, considering she's going to suffer for the rest of her life in captivity. That's why he lied.'

Slater said, 'I'm not following.'

Violetta said, 'I am.'

King looked exclusively at her. 'You know I can't let this go.'

'Jason...'

'I'm perfectly happy to walk away from the government,' he said. 'So is Slater. What we're *not* willing to do is watch people suffer just because it's inconvenient for us.'

Slater nodded. 'That's always how it was going to work.'

She said, 'This makes things a hundred times more complicated. You don't think the shadow world is going to be eyeing the operation you left behind? You go there to salvage it, and they'll spring a trap.'

King shrugged. 'I don't much care.'

'Jason.'

'I left three of them alive,' King said. 'I didn't turn them in, because I didn't understand what I was dealing with. Now I find out the one who took me to the port — Quinn — knew he was leading me to the wrong container the whole time.'

'That doesn't matter.'

'Yes,' King said. 'It does.'

She fell silent.

He said, 'I see a problem, I fix it.'

'You won't just be fighting those Cali gangsters,' she said. 'You'll be fighting legitimate tier-one operatives from our own military. They'll be lying in wait — you know they will be.'

'Didn't seem to be a problem in Great Kills.'

'Why keep throwing yourself in danger like this?'

'Because that's the story of my life.'

Slater said, 'You're not going to change his mind.'

She held her tongue instead of retorting. She rose, crossed to the window, and looked out through the see-through curtains. 'I know.'

'I'm going,' King said. 'I'll finish it.'

She turned. 'We still have time until they realise I'm not being held against my will. I'm in the system. I have access to my team. I can get us the resources we need.'

He said, 'You'll come?'

'What else am I going to do?'

Slater sat forward. 'Where is Beckham?'

She froze in place. King saw the pain and tension on her face. It was probably the first time someone else had muttered the man's name since the falling out. Her dark secret, out there for all to see.

She said, 'Why?'

'Because you have time,' Slater said. 'But not much of it.'

She looked at him.

He said, 'You told us you found out the address of his disability home, but you said it wouldn't do you any good. Because you can't rescue him if the whole shadow world's coming to neutralise him. Because you're not a wrecking ball with a death wish.'

Silence.

He said, 'I am.'

She said, 'No.'

'Eventually they'll find out you left voluntarily. You think they won't follow through on their promise to execute him when you blatantly betrayed them?'

Her eyes rapidly calculated possibilities, landing on the conclusion he'd reached five minutes earlier.

Slater said, 'Sounds like you and King have business in California. So let me get Beckham. Let me protect him.'

'Why would you do that for me?' she said.

'Because you care about him,' he said. 'And I care about you.'

'I was complicit in an attempt on your life.'

'Water under the bridge.'

'How do you do this?' she said, putting her hands on her hips. Then she turned from Slater to King. 'How do either of you do this?'

'We've seen it all,' Slater said.

Which said enough.

She said, 'I'm not comfortable with it. You don't owe me anything.'

'You're right,' he said. 'I don't. Now where's Beckham?'

She thought about it.

But not for long.

Time was of the essence.

'Richmond, Virginia,' she said. 'Five hour drive. The place is the Hooper Quadriplegic Centre. It's a state-owned facility that permanently houses its residents. Beckham's name there is Jonathan Powell. You know, WITSEC...'

Slater nodded slowly.

She said, 'It's being watched. Twenty-four-seven. You don't have a hope in hell of getting him out of there without a war.'

Slater said, 'Then it's a good thing I'm an expert on war.'

70

After that, the next steps were straightforward.

Dangerous. Possibly fatal. But straightforward.

Violetta got on the phone to Alonzo, and laid out what she needed, and he set to work implementing it. At the end of the conversation, Slater overheard her explicitly tell the tech guru not to pass this information up the chain. He heard Alonzo ask, '*Why?*' through the tinny handheld speaker.

Violetta said, 'Because I'm asking. Please.'

'*Okay.*'

That was all it took.

There was little more to be said. A flight awaited. Violetta and King nodded to Slater and Alexis in turn, who both nodded back. Then they were gone, Violetta leading the way, slipping out of the tiny apartment.

Leaving Slater and Alexis alone to deal with the chaos of the last twenty-four hours.

She turned to him, pierced him with her green eyes. 'I can't believe you offered to do that for her.'

'Are you mad at me?'

'No,' she said. 'Quite the contrary.'

'I'm putting myself in danger again.'

'If I was mad at that, I never would have agreed to a first date.'

'You knew what I was,' he said. 'The first time we met, you knew.'

'Not *what* you are,' she said. '*Who* you are. You're not a monster.'

'Sometimes I don't know where the line is.'

'That's bullshit,' she said. 'You've never even eased a toe over that line. You were going to die this morning to protect my family. People you've never met.'

He didn't respond.

She said, 'I've never met anyone who had more of an understanding of where the line is.'

'That means more than you know.'

She hugged him, looping her arms over his shoulders, drawing him in. He savoured the warm embrace for a few seconds, and then methodically flipped a switch in his brain. When he stepped back, he was imperturbable.

He said, 'Let's go.'

Everything was already crammed into Alexis's backpack — they'd used the room as a meeting place, nothing more. All that was left to do was step out and move forward. So they did. They left the room behind, what was supposed to be their sanctuary for weeks or months of quiet, peaceful existence. And now he was thrust straight back into a hostile world.

Really, he felt ridiculous for assuming he could stay away for any considerable length of time.

They hovered on the landing for a beat, staring down at

the lot below. The Land Rover was gone — King and Violetta had commandeered it.

Alexis said, 'So we steal a car?'

Slater shook his head. 'I have identities the shadow world still doesn't know about. We use one of those to rent a car. If we steal a ride, it'll be reported before we make it to Richmond. We need to be discreet.'

She put her hands on his shoulders and turned him to face her. 'And then what?'

'What do you mean?'

'We rescue Beckham, rendezvous with King and Violetta — provided they're not dead — and ... what?'

He said, 'I don't know if you realised this, but I don't plan my life very far in advance.'

'You do, though,' she said. 'I've seen what you put your body and mind through. I've glimpsed your training. It's regimented. It's disciplined. That takes planning.'

'But that's all preparation,' he said. 'I never know what I'm preparing for. I just know the value of preparing.'

She nodded.

He said, 'When we get to Richmond, you might not like what happens.'

'What do you mean?'

'I might have to become someone you haven't seen before,' he said. 'If the place is protected. If Beckham's not already dead.'

'I know what you do.'

'But you haven't seen it,' he said. 'Not in person. It's different.'

She kissed him. 'I'll be fine.'

'I hope so.'

Any words after that were meaningless, and they both knew it. They held hands and Slater pulled his hood up to disguise his features, and they set off for what the web told them was the closest rental car spot. A smiling staff member took his fake identification without a moment's suspicion, and thirty minutes and three signatures later they sat in a blue Hyundai i30 that reeked of air freshener.

Slater gripped the wheel and ran his hands over the material. He savoured the moment of stillness. One might think he was hesitant to put the car into gear, hesitant to take the first step. Hesitant to barrel toward a confrontation with the government he'd worked for a week ago.

At least, that's how Alexis interpreted it.

She said, 'We don't have to do this.'

He said, 'Yes, we do.'

He set the GPS for Richmond, Virginia.

A five and a half hour drive.

They'd reach the Hooper Quadriplegic Centre late in the afternoon. That left all night for a siege, if it was necessary. Slater figured he had one night at the very least. It would take time to determine that Violetta was not a hostage, that she was simultaneously missing and utilising government resources. They'd piece it together eventually, but that didn't mean their first knee-jerk response would be to execute Beckham.

Or maybe that was all bullshit, and right now they were planning to neutralise him.

He got rid of the stillness, put the Hyundai into "Drive," and accelerated toward Virginia.

71

Eight hours later...

Joshua Banks had no idea what he was doing in California.

He'd been pulled straight from a hostage rescue drill and shipped out here to watch a goddamn civilian mansion for an unspecified length of time. The lack of information threatened to drive him mental. As an assaulter in Blue Squadron of DEVGRU, he was a world above this bullshit. This was a stakeout, and there was no room in his world for a stakeout.

He'd been briefed on the potential existence of a unicorn — black-ops assaulter Jason King, an enigma in the shadow world who'd maybe gone rogue — but from what little intelligence he'd pored over, it hadn't been hard to determine that King was nowhere to be seen.

There was a flabby-looking thirty-something guy with a receding hairline who came and went at random, and the most notable part of the whole endeavour was the guy coming back an hour ago at the wheel of a tractor-trailer truck. Then the gates had sealed him in, and now Banks was waiting again.

He'd follow the truck when it left again — that was no problem.

The problem was the futility of this entire job.

He didn't like being alone either.

His superiors had preached the benefits to him, of course — discretion, ability to blend in with other civilians, the fact that a lone wolf was far more unsuspecting than an entire squadron, especially in a laidback coastal town like Emerald Bay. He'd nodded and nodded and nodded, but now he was here — clad in a ghillie suit, buried in the undergrowth and shrubbery across the street from the mansion's walled perimeter. He was as much a part of the landscape as the bushes around him, and his skillset was worthless. There was nothing worth watching — even if the tractor-trailer truck contained dark secrets, that was not the responsibility of a DEVGRU member to handle.

Banks was about ready to make a call highlighting the ridiculousness of the operation when someone lay down in the dirt right beside him.

Whoever it was, they'd approached without making the slightest hint of noise. Banks' resting heart rate was in the forties, and despite being disgruntled he'd still been approaching the task with all the professionalism it required — meaning unflappable situational awareness. He'd been attuned to every discrepancy, every whisper of hostility, so whoever was now alongside him had trumped the tactical skillset of a Blue Squadron member.

Not feasible.

Banks rolled, dropping the night-vision optics, reaching for the knife strapped to his chest, favouring it over the Beretta at his waist.

The man who'd dropped to the ground beside him caught his knife hand and pinned it to his chest.

The assailant's grip was rigid steel.

To keep Banks from retaliating took inhuman strength. The silhouette had it.

The man said, 'Relax. Let's talk.'

Banks didn't say a word. The moment the hold on his wrist relaxed, he'd wrench his hand free, pull his combat knife and shove it through the guy's face, just for having the nerve to approach like this.

Then a sliver of moonlight struck the silhouette's face, illuminating important features.

Banks recognised him. 'They warned me about you.'

'You know who I am?'

'Jason King.'

'Then you know we're on the same team.'

'I don't think so.'

'Not based on the intel,' King said. 'I meant based on the fact you're not dead.'

'So I'm supposed to side with you?' Banks said. 'A rogue operative? All because you didn't put a bullet in me.'

'No,' King said. 'I don't want your undying allegiance. Just your help tonight.'

Banks said, 'Think logically, brother. I have my orders. Orders aren't something I can pick and choose at random. If I want this gig, I execute them. What do you think my orders are regarding you?'

'To shoot me on sight, I'm sure.'

'So let's not kid ourselves,' Banks said. 'You know how this goes. Pretend you're a saint all you want, but if you really want to spare me, then run. I'll give you ten seconds from when you let go of my wrist. Otherwise, put a bullet in me like you were supposed to. There's not a chance in hell I'm even going to hear you out.'

'You'll hear me out,' King said. 'You don't have a choice.'

The man was right. Banks saw the Glock glinting in King's other hand, aimed up at his throat.

Banks said, 'You really want to go that route? Battle of reflexes with someone like me?'

'Every word you just said could have come out of my own mouth.'

Banks went quiet.

Mulling over it.

Then said, 'Okay. Talk. If you think it'll do you any good.'

'Why'd you join the military?'

'To serve my country.'

'You don't get to the level you're at through patriotism alone. There's got to be something else there.'

'To contribute. To help.'

'Did you see a truck drive in earlier tonight?'

'To where?'

'Cut the bullshit,' King said. 'I know what house you're watching. I was there yesterday.'

'Yeah,' Banks said. 'I saw it.'

'The crew who own the house are smugglers who work the port. Half of them are dead. That was my doing. The trailer you saw attached to the truck has a container in it. Girls from Eastern Europe. Hand-picked, kidnapped, trafficked. The three men I left alive are going to deliver that container to the Baja cartel for an enormous handling fee. They take the risk of bribing port officials, they reap the benefits. I want to deal with them, and then follow the container to its final destination, and then deal with whoever's there. But I knew someone like you would be watching.

And despite the light I've been painted in, I'm not the enemy. So I'm not willing to kill you on sight.'

Banks said, 'What exactly do you want from me?'

'Let me do what I came here to do,' King said. 'You don't have to involve yourself. You don't even have to watch. Blissful ignorance, or whatever. But deep down I think you joined the military for the right reasons, and those same reasons won't let you kill me when I'm trying to eradicate a little bit of evil in the world.'

Banks said, 'Why should I believe you?'

'Because there's no point lying about any of this when I had the jump on you from the start,' King said. 'Why the fuck would I make this up if I had ulterior motives? You wouldn't be around to hear me out.'

Banks thought about it.

And, as much as he hated to admit it, he couldn't find a hole in the story.

He said, 'After this, you disappear?'

King said, 'Of course.'

They hadn't agreed on anything, but King let go of Banks's wrist. He settled back in the dirt, still flat on his stomach, now a few feet away. No longer uncomfortably close.

If Banks wanted to, he could kill the man right then and there.

It was an overwhelming display of trust.

Banks moved his knife hand, and watched King bristle. But instead of clasping at the hilt, he tilted the top of his wrist toward his own face and checked his digital watch.

'Clock's ticking,' he said. 'Get to work.'

72

Under a dark sky, Slater conducted surveillance of his own.

He didn't face a mansion in Emerald Bay. He faced the Hooper Quadriplegic Centre, which resided in the leafy suburb of Stratford Hills to the west of the city, just over the James River. It was ordinary suburbia — brick houses with wide lots on either side, broad sidewalks, an aura of stillness. The nine-to-fivers had come home from their jobs to lounge in front of the television, and the elderly were in bed. The children were too, only involuntarily. No one was out at nine in the evening. The city centre would be busier.

Here, you could hear a pin drop.

He watched the big government building from a distance, statuesque behind the wheel of the Hyundai, parked across the street. A handful of visitors came and went over the course of the evening, but little else happened. There was no real way to conduct illicit proceedings — the building sat in the middle of an enormous lot with a neatly manicured lawn. There was no secret way in.

No tunnels underground. If the shadow world had come for Beckham, they wouldn't need to send an army. They'd send a lone man or woman with a syringe or a knife. No need for a gun — that'd be loud and messy.

The more Slater thought about it, the more he figured a needle would be the way to go. Quiet, discreet, no blood — and if the stuff inside the barrel of the syringe was advanced enough, it'd look like natural causes.

He knew, without a doubt, the government had access to those sorts of concoctions.

The question was: Did they know about Violetta?

Slater wasn't about to wait around to find out.

He turned to Alexis in the passenger seat. 'I'm going to do this quickly. In and out.'

'What if there's eyes on us right now?'

'I have no feasible way of knowing that,' he said. 'But why would there be forces here in advance? To make sure he doesn't escape? He's a quadriplegic.'

'If they know Violetta's gone rogue, they'll send men straight here.'

'But they wouldn't have pieced that together until a couple of hours ago at the very earliest. You think they have shadow forces right here in the city they can trust? You think they have a whole army on standby willing to execute a helpless quadriplegic in his disability home?'

'I don't know,' Alexis said. 'I don't know anything about this world.'

Slater looked pensively out the window. 'Nor do I.'

She didn't respond.

He said, 'But what's waiting around going to accomplish?'

She shrugged.

He handed her the spare Glock and said, 'Remember what I told you.'

She said, 'I won't hesitate.'

He knew.

He'd found two potential rapists in her bathroom the night he'd met her. She'd tased and subdued them both in the midst of a New York blackout.

He kissed her on the lips, then stepped out of the car and reflexively touched his own Glock in its appendix holster. He adjusted his leather jacket over the concealed weapon, shot a final look up and down the street, and then strode into the shadows, aiming for the weak entranceway light of the building.

No one followed.

There was no explosive reaction from hidden vantage points.

Just the quiet of a residential suburb.

He stepped up onto the concrete patio and stopped in front of the sliding glass doors. A sensor light blinked in recognition above his head, but the doors didn't part. Common enough procedure. He'd need to be buzzed in after hours. He wiped all trace of hostility or tension from his face, slumped his shoulders as if in embarrassment, and rapped his knuckles lightly on the glass. A startled receptionist's head popped up from behind the desk on the left of the sparsely furnished lobby. She was mid-fifties, slightly overweight, with deep stress lines etched into her face.

Slater offered a smile of apology.

She shook her head, but only half-heartedly.

He injected something vague into his eyes, and stared right at her.

Sadness. Urgency. Uncertainty.

This is important.

I need to see a loved one.

She buzzed him in, and the doors slid open.

He made straight for the desk. 'I'm so sorry about the timing. I've driven all day.'

'Who are you here to see?'

'Jonathan Powell.'

'Are you a relative?'

'I'm from the brotherhood.'

She looked at him.

He said, 'We were in the military together.'

Her expression softened. She said, 'He never mentioned he was in the military.'

'That's something we have in common,' he said. 'We're private men. Listen, I have news he needs to hear. Something personal. I'd prefer to catch him awake.'

She nodded. 'Of course.'

She glanced at the visitor log book in front of her, contemplating whether to make him fill it out. Then she shrugged and waved him through. 'Go on. Get to it. You look like you need rest, darling.'

'It's been a long day.'

'For you and me both.'

'What's his room number?'

'52,' she said. 'Just down the hall and to the left. You'll see the signs.'

'Thank you.'

'My pleasure.'

He set off at a brisk but unsuspicious pace. As if he truly did have news for the man, instead of the revelation that he was here to effectively kidnap him. He went to the end of the hall and turned left, exactly as she'd instructed, and found a door labelled "52" after a couple of minutes following signs through sterilised carpeted corridors. It was thick and pale cream in colour, also surrounded by pale cream walls. The place felt like a hospital wing.

Slater knocked three times, waited a few beats out of courtesy, and then opened the door and stepped into the room.

73

Quinn Chapman didn't lead a good life, and he'd finally made the admission that it was his own doing.

It was a weight off his shoulders. In fact, it was the first time he'd truly been objective since he'd moved into Duke's multi-million dollar shack. It also didn't mean he was going to stop. Recognising you were scum and taking steps to change your ways were two very different things.

He was willing to do one, but not the other.

The money was just too damn good.

He killed the majority of overhead lights in the mansion with an app on his phone, and then finally let himself breathe out. Standing on the enormous front porch, draped in shadow, he was safe, enclosed, protected by the darkness. It was a second home to him. It had afforded him the resolve to bury Duke, Kurt and Aaron in the Cajon Pass, just as the mysterious assassin had suggested. They were now packed into a shallow grave in the lee of a boulder at the bottom of a steep slope, and no one was going to find them for months at the very least. Cops might swing by asking questions, but it'd be easy to act oblivious for a couple of days. He didn't need to worry about who would inherit the house or its contents or Duke's vast fortune.

As soon as he delivered Container 55E and its contents to its rightful owners, he'd be the one to receive the cash for it.

Now, there was no boss to cart the profits back to.

Just Quinn.

Cal and Vince were still badly concussed. They'd spent the whole day in their beds, tossing and turning, groaning in pain, sensitive to light. They wouldn't be functional for days. Days was more than enough time for Quinn to disappear with a cool five hundred k in cash. That'd last him years on the road living a simple life. A decade, if he was lucky. He was on the precipice of living a simple carefree life for the rest of his existence, and all he needed to do was be blissfully oblivious for another hour, tops.

Pretend you don't know what's in that container.

Deliver it.

Collect the payment.

Dust your hands off, and move on.

The container in question rested within the trailer Duke owned, pulled by the tractor unit Duke owned, all resting in the driveway Duke owned. It didn't seem out of place against the backdrop of the enormous house. An unmarked delivery truck, probably dropping off designer furniture or a hundred-inch television — at least, that's what any nosy neighbours would assume if they peered through the gate.

Hiding in plain sight.

Quinn locked up, making sure the giant double doors were secure, and then trotted down the front steps. He liked the dark. There was room for all sorts of flexibility in the dark. For reasons he'd never know, the mystery assassin had spared him. The guy actually thought he'd turn and run, even though the real payload was still there, and all that separated Quinn from five hundred thousand was satisfactory delivery.

He could do that on his own, that's for damn sure.

He made for the tractor unit, made to get behind the wheel.

Halfway across the driveway — firmly in no man's land — he froze in his tracks.

The driver's side of the tractor unit was blocked by a large silhouette.

Quinn pulled his weapon.

A shot blared, and he felt the surreal numbing sensation of a bullet passing straight through his forearm. He found himself oddly detached from the pain. All he experienced was a series of still images.

Lying on his back on the gravel, unsure when he'd fallen.

His gun kicked away, frozen in mid-air, punted by a giant boot.

Then hands on his collar, and suddenly he was off the ground, back on his feet.

He stood there, pale and bleeding and shocked.

The mystery man stood across from him.

'What's this truck doing here, Quinn?' the man asked.

Looming over him.

Quinn spluttered, 'I—'

'You don't know?'

'Yeah, man,' Quinn said. 'I don't know. I think ... maybe Cal and Vince got it. They're feeling much better, you know. I think they snuck out. Maybe they knew about another container or something. I sure didn't.'

'Cal and Vince are tucked up in bed.'

'No they ain't.'

'They sure are. They'll be there until someone finds their bodies.'

Quinn shivered. 'Christ, man. What did they do to you?'

'To me? Nothing.'

Quinn stared up at the silhouette. 'You know, don't you?'

The silhouette said, 'Of course I know.'

'How'd you find out?'

'You had it written on the whiteboard.'

'I thought you didn't see that.'

'I did.'

Quinn bowed his head.

The silhouette said, 'All you had to do was show me the right container. The result would have been the same.'

'You would have killed me.'

'Probably not.'

Quinn shivered.

The silhouette said, 'But now it's a certainty.'

'This was all Duke, man,' Quinn said. 'Not me.'

'You picked it up all on your own. You're taking it somewhere all on your own.'

Quinn tried to find the words for an explanation, but those words didn't exist.

The silhouette said, 'If you tell me where you're taking them, I'll let you live. I'll let you walk out of here a free man.'

'You promise?'

'You have my word.'

Quinn gave the address — a ranch-style compound way out in the desert, with gates and walls and *sicarios* patrolling the perimeter. He'd been there three times previously, for three separate deliveries. But the silhouette didn't need to know that. Quinn masked his smugness, because it wouldn't do him any good to reveal it. Inwardly, he couldn't believe the guy had bought his shtick for a second time.

The mystery man repeated the address back to Quinn.

Quinn nodded.

'Thanks,' the silhouette said, and brought its Glock up.

Quinn's face collapsed. 'You promised.'

'Just like the human cargo gets promised a safe and harmless journey?'

Silence.

The silhouette said, 'No one keeps promises in your world, Quinn.'

A trigger was pulled.

It was the last thing Quinn Chapman ever saw.

Beckham Lang was mentally indestructible.

Slater knew that the moment he met the man's gaze.

There wasn't an ounce of self-pity in his eyes. His stare was uncompromising, and he didn't blink or waver, not even when he failed to recognise the bulky stranger who'd stepped into his room. He was across the space, sitting upright in a modified wheelchair, his thin pale arms resting on supports. His body had clearly been unresponsive for years, and most of his muscle mass had wasted away entirely, but his face was tanned from sun exposure, and he held his chin high, and his hair had been cut recently. It was brown and thick and swept back stylishly off his forehead. What little he could control he paid careful attention to, refusing to allow himself the leniency he probably deserved.

Slater admired it. This was not a man who accepted compromise. He recognised his condition, but didn't wallow in it.

When Slater stepped through the doorway and closed the door behind him, Beckham said, 'Who are you?'

'Someone you need to trust.'

'Oh, great,' Beckham said. 'That wasn't cryptic at all. Are you going to give me a riddle next?'

Slater paused, allowing himself a half-smile despite the circumstances.

Then he remembered why he was here, and the smile vanished.

Beckham said, 'Are you here to hurt me?'

Slater stared. 'No. What makes you think that?'

'There's a look in your eye,' Beckham said. 'I've seen the same look before. A long time ago. On the face of the man who did this to me.'

'Aggressive?'

'Volatile. Unhinged.'

'I'm here to help. But you're in danger. That's why you see that look on my face. Because if anyone else comes in that you don't know, I'll hurt them.'

'What sort of danger?'

'Threats have been made on your life.'

'Why? I'm nobody.'

'Violetta LaFleur.'

Beckham's face became steel.

Slater said, 'Now's not the time for grudges.'

'"Grudge" is putting it lightly.'

'Drop the tough guy act,' Slater said. 'It doesn't suit you.'

'You don't know a thing about me.'

'No,' Slater said. 'You're right. But I know Violetta. She's a work colleague. You know what that means. You know what she was doing when you two parted ways. She's still doing it, only at a higher level. Which means higher stakes, too.'

'So threats have been made against her?' Beckham said. 'What do I have to do with it? Leave me out of this shit.'

'Let's say she's in the middle of a disagreement with her superiors. They've threatened to kill you.'

Beckham scoffed. 'What's it to her?'

'She was willing to ruin her life to keep you alive.'

Beckham stared.

'Let me be more specific,' Slater said. 'I was one of her closest allies. She was willing to double-cross me and kill me to save you.'

'Then what are you doing here?' Beckham said. 'Come to get your revenge?'

'No. We made up. I trust her again. I'm on her side. I want you alive, too.'

'That was fast.'

'Only way to be in our world.'

'So what is this, exactly?'

'I'm going to need you to come with me.'

Beckham looked down at himself. 'You think I have a choice? You can do what you want with me.'

'I want you to do it willingly.'

'How real are these threats?'

'Very real.'

'Tell me exactly who you are and what you do,' Beckham said. 'I'm sure it'll violate all sorts of agreements. But if you want me to trust you, then you need to trust me.'

'I was a government black-ops killer up until two days ago. Now I'm just a killer. A vigilante. Think of it as an unceremonious separation — myself and my colleague broke up with the secret world. Violetta decided to come with us.'

'So the government wants me dead?'

'Just the shadowy parts of it.'

'Great.'

'I'm the best of two bad options,' Slater said. 'You're your own man. You make up your mind.'

Beckham looked around the room. There was a bed, and a small television, and a pair of armchairs for visitors facing that television, and a tiny kitchenette that clearly hadn't been used in years, and an amalgamation of assistance equipment for his crippling disability.

Then Beckham turned back to Slater, as if he was surprised Slater hadn't moved.

'What?' Beckham said. 'You think I have any sort of attachment to this place?'

Slater nodded his understanding.

Beckham said, 'Whatever keeps me alive — do that. I don't care what it takes.'

Slater nodded again.

That's all there was to it.

He crossed the room, took Beckham's wheelchair by the handles, and guided it towards the door.

Tapping into automatic reflexes, he stopped the chair in its tracks as soon as they reached the door and skirted around, sliding the Glock out of its holster. He pushed down on the handle and swung it outward, slowly, keeping the gun raised, sweeping the corridor outside with the barrel.

Empty.

He leant out through the doorway and looked down, then up the corridor.

There was a pair of tall serious men six feet away from the doorway.

Heart-wrenchingly close.

One had a Beretta M9 in his hand.

The other had a syringe.

75

They made an odd trio, crammed into a tight row in the cabin of the tractor-trailer truck.

Jason King behind the wheel.

Violetta LaFleur in the middle seat.

Joshua Banks on the far side.

King made the introductions. 'Violetta, Josh. Josh, Violetta.'

'Pleasure,' Banks said.

'Likewise.'

Banks said, 'You two are probably the most wanted individuals in the country, right?'

'Probably,' she agreed. 'We'd argue it's unwarranted.'

'You would, wouldn't you?'

'Can we trust you?'

'If there's one thing I hate more than enemies of the state, it's human traffickers. Let's deal with this, and then we'll talk.'

King said, 'You'll be talking to thin air. After this we're gone. That was the agreement.'

Banks nodded. 'And what exactly do I tell my superiors?'

'There was a commotion at the mansion,' King said. 'Gunshots. A cacophony of them. You moved straight in, but the truck got away. That's the last you saw of it. If all this goes to plan, then a massacre in the desert will make headlines in a few days time. This truck will be found on the scene. You don't know anything. You didn't see where it went.'

'That makes me look incompetent.'

'It's a whole lot better than admitting you aided enemies of the state.'

'They might not believe me.'

'Then you'd better be convincing.'

King entered the address Quinn had given him into his phone's GPS, and threw the truck into gear. It rumbled out of the courtyard, leaving the walled property behind. They were out of Emerald Bay within minutes, on the Pacific Coast Highway in the dead of night, with the wind howling in through the sliver of a gap in the driver's window. King had rolled it down a crack to air the cabin of Quinn's stench. When King had picked him up off the driveway, he'd inhaled the aroma of stale sweat coating the man's skin.

Salty perspiration generated by fear.

It had never, and would never, make sense to King.

If you were going to make yourself supremely uncomfortable, why do it in the pursuit of selfishness? Quinn would have no doubt worked through his fear and delivered the truck to its owners and run off with hundreds of thousands of dollars, but what good would that have done him? He'd still be miserable, still be uptight, wound into a ball of chronic stress. Constantly looking over his shoulder, constantly searching for the next criminal opportunity to keep himself afloat.

King was constantly uncomfortable, too. But when his

head hit the pillow at night, he always found stillness. Satisfaction in the knowledge that he was contributing to the common good. Satisfaction from the fact that he'd be okay if he died in the process. Quinn had died terrified and full of unrest, because everything had been banking on reaching the pot of gold at the end of the rainbow. King was happy risking it all without the prospect of reward, because he was content with his own actions.

That was the difference between him and the people he hunted.

It always would be.

There was little conversation as they finished their southward journey on the PCH and turned east on the Ortega Highway, aiming for Mission Viejo and beyond. The hills rose, and the suburbs turned to bare dry chaparral. The plains undulated under the night sky. The vastness became apparent, and the lights of the coastline faded away, replaced by the odd new housing development buried in the spectacle of the mountains. The GPS guided them in the direction of Perris, out into the emptiness of the desert beyond the hills.

King and Banks knew little about each other, but they didn't talk. Now was not the time for superficial conversation, and almost all conversation they could think of would be superficial.

It didn't matter what they'd done in the past, or who they were as people, or how long they'd served their countries, or what they enjoyed doing in their spare time. It would only serve to humanise each other, and there was no need for that.

They were bracing for war.

Violetta, although not a field operative, understood the dynamic better than anybody. She'd handled operatives like them for most of her professional career. It took ruthless objectivity, clear-headedness, and a refusal to ever be reactionary, which meant she stayed just as quiet as they did.

When there was twenty minutes left in their journey — at least according to the navigation software — Banks broke the silence. 'Tell me everything Quinn told you about what we're going into.'

'It's a ranch-style compound,' King said. 'Unspecified number of *sicario*s, but he mentioned perimeter guards manning the walls, more guards on the ground inside, and maybe even a couple of roving crews in the surrounding area in armoured SUVs.'

'Whole lotta manpower.'

'It's the Baja cartel,' King said. 'What were you expecting?'

'Not for them to be involved in this,' Banks said. 'That's for sure.'

The mountains fell away.

The desert spread out before them, so vast, so empty.

Violetta said, 'Pull over.'

King looked across. 'What?'

'You heard me.'

'Why?'

'Just pull over.'

He sensed her tone.

I need to speak to you in private.

He slowed the giant truck and drifted over to the shoulder. No traffic went past them on either side.

The night was dead.

Banks regarded them warily. 'Everything okay?'

'Fine,' she said.

King left the engine running and threw the driver's door

open and stepped down into the dirt, crushing a weed underfoot.

He heard Violetta follow him out and shut the cabin door behind her.

~

BANKS FOUND himself sealed in a soundproof box, alone for the first time since King had accosted him.

He raised a hand clad in a fingerless woollen glove and touched a dirty nail gently to his inner ear.

A connection activated.

A low voice said, 'Yes?'

'She's here.'

'Thought so. You know what to do.'

'Yeah,' he grunted. 'On it.'

He took his finger away from his ear, and without the pressure the line automatically disconnected.

76

S later targeted the guy with the Beretta.

The more dire threat of the pair.

He locked in and raised his Glock and blew the guy's brains out the back of his head with a single shot.

It was all he had time for.

The second guy — the one with the syringe — rushed him, recognising the fact that he'd brought a needle to a gunfight. The only way to proceed, therefore, was aggression and a total lack of hesitation.

Slater's field of view opened up like he'd been juiced with a massive dose of methamphetamine. The laser focus was the only way he'd survive what happened next. Because the guy was close enough to lunge wildly with the outstretched syringe, his palm enclosed around the barrel, like holding a knife by the hilt. He made the lunging motion even as his partner collapsed with the contents of his skull emptied across the far wall.

Slater threw himself back into the door frame, moving like he'd been electrocuted. He bounced off the wood, taking the brunt of the impact across his upper back. It hurt, but it was a whole lot better than being jabbed with a lethal fluid.

The tip of the needle missed him by inches, displacing air a hair's breadth away from his chest.

He didn't really process it, because if he recognised how close he'd come to death the shock would have made him hesitate. Instead he rebounded and sidestepped the outstretched hand and smashed the butt of the Glock into the bridge of the guy's nose, breaking it clean, making his eyes water involuntarily. The guy swung again with the syringe, but this time he missed by a mile.

Slater had the upper hand.

He figured one unsuppressed gunshot could be attributed to a delivery van backfiring, or some sort of electric panel bursting, or some sort of freak incident, but two gunshots definitely couldn't. So he refrained from shooting the second guy in the face.

Instead he timed the next swing, anticipating exactly when it would finish its trajectory, then he caught the wrist and wrenched it back and plunged the whole needle into the guy's mouth. He felt the spongy sensation of the needle inserting into the guy's inner cheek, and that's when he smashed the plunger down, unloading the contents of the barrel.

He kicked the guy's legs out from underneath him and held him down by the throat as he waited for the fifteen seconds of thrashing and foaming at the mouth to come to an end.

The guy slumped, and his eyes glazed over.

Slater grabbed each man by the collar and hauled both bodies over the threshold, back into Beckham's room.

Beckham watched it all unfold with wide eyes. Slater practically tripped over himself to get back out into the corridor in time.

Seconds later, a flummoxed nurse with flushed cheeks came sprinting around the corner.

Slater flooded his face with manufactured disbelief. 'Did you *see* that?!'

She careened to a halt, her mouth flapping, rendered incapable of speech.

Before she could fully process the brains and blood splattered across the opposite wall, Slater said, 'A fox. It must have got in through a window or something. It bashed its head against that wall right there and then ran off. It made the most godawful sound when it hit its head. Jesus... someone could get hurt.'

The nurse looked at the wall for perhaps a second, tops. Then she said, 'Fuck me,' turned on her heels and ran off to seek assistance. Instinct had taken over. *I can't subdue a wild fox on my own. Especially not a manic one.*

Creating room to overthink is the key to buying time. Slater had been vague enough on the details to instil terror. Her brain was now locked on an endless thought loop — *What do I do? A fox. What do I do?* — instead of questioning how the hell any of that made sense.

Slater backtracked into the room and found Beckham locked in a surreal staring contest with the two bodies — both corpses wide-eyed, both ugly in their death throes, both turning cold.

Slater said, 'Lucky I got here in time.'

'Get me the *fuck* out of here,' Beckham said, unable to take his gaze off the dead men.

'You bet.'

Slater steered the wheelchair with one hand, and kept the Glock raised with the other.

There'd be no more pretending. He didn't care what anyone here thought of him.

He pushed Beckham out of his room, into the exposed corridor, and set off at a manic pace for the front entrance.

77

Hot wind battered them, howling along the shoulder.

King crossed his arms over his chest and said, 'What's up?'

'We hand this over to the government,' she said. 'That's what we do. We leave it all with Banks. It's his responsibility.'

'It's mine.'

'You're a vigilante now, Jason,' she said. 'As am I. You got your revenge on the men that wronged you. It's time to walk away.'

'I've never done things that way. I'm not about to start.'

'They want you and I dead because we know state secrets. That doesn't mean the entire country is corrupt. Just look at your body of work. You think you would have done all those things — helped all those people — for a country that was secretly evil? That's not how it works.'

'I know,' King said. 'I no longer see eye to eye with the people I used to work for. That doesn't mean I should paint them all with the same brush. Right?'

'Right.'

'But how does that change things?'

'Because this isn't you anymore.'

'There's who-knows how many people in that container back there. Their lives are now forfeited. They were to be handed over to a group of people who would have done horrific things to them before killing them and then either crushing or burning the bodies. Am I supposed to let that go?'

'You won't stop the global human trafficking industry with this one operation, and you'll probably get yourself killed. This isn't on you.'

'It is,' King said. 'Otherwise I never would have made it two days in Black Force. I'll never have the mentality you want me to have.'

'I just don't want anything bad to happen,' she said. 'Not when we're this close to getting away.'

'If I leave it with Banks, it'll take him time to call in backup. That's inevitable. That leaves more room for the Baja cartel to wise up. They'll be gone before he gets there. That's provided he even storms the compound in the first place.'

'Why wouldn't he?'

'Because he doesn't have a death wish.'

She stared at him. 'Sometimes I question why the hell I fell in love with you.'

'I'll take that as a compliment.'

'You should. It means I care about you.'

She stood on her tiptoes, planted a kiss on his lips, and then patted him on the stomach with a flat palm. 'Come on. Before I use an iota of common sense or reason.'

He leapt back onto the tractor unit's step, but before he opened the door he turned back to her.

'There are people in this world who deserve to die,' he said. 'That's never going to change as long as I'm alive to do something about it. I hope you know that.'

She stared up at him, perhaps pondering a response.

Then she said, 'I do. But I dread the day your luck runs out.'

'Hasn't happened yet. Maybe that's why you fell in love with me. You know you're trapped in this savage survival-of-the-fittest world forever. Once you've seen it, you can't go back to the way things were. Maybe it was wise to attach yourself to the luckiest guy in it.'

She stared at him.

He said, 'Or maybe it's not luck.'

He winked.

Opened the door, swung in, and let her clamber over his lap to sit in the middle of the cabin.

Banks said, 'All good?'

'All good.'

'We're still laying siege to a compound full of *sicarios*?'

'Sure are.'

Banks gave a curt nod. 'So be it.'

King wrestled with the gearstick and the giant truck rumbled back onto the desert highway.

A civilian observer might have considered them insane. Heading toward what was certain to be a gruelling, vicious firefight, perhaps spilling over into the use of knives and fists and feet, all against hardened cartel killers with beheadings and disembowelments and other various forms of torture under their belts. If only the same civilian could see inside their minds, and what they'd put themselves through to get to the state of stoic calmness they exuded.

Maybe then they'd understand.

They branched off the highway, down an uneven dirt

road that rattled the trailer behind the tractor, vibrating the big wheel in King's hands. They bounced and jolted and bumped over the potholes.

Then they saw it.

The distant outline of a compound — walls and buildings and cars and a big explosive-resistant front gate. In the middle of nowhere, surrounded by chaparral, the perimeter illuminated harshly by floodlights. The Baja cartel couldn't have made the stronghold more obvious if they tried. Soaking it in from a distance, King rippled with disgust at the corruption. All this focus in the news on harmless undocumented illegals when the real culprits from across the border were rich enough to pay off the right people to look the other way.

Banks said, 'How do we go about this?'

'Hide in plain sight,' King said. 'I'm still Liam Kingsley, one of Ryan Duke's crew. Banks — you're a new guy. Duke isn't shy about outsourcing muscle, so it won't be hard to convince them.' King faced Violetta. 'And you're Duke's girlfriend.'

'Why would he send a group of fresh faces instead of coming himself?'

'Why wouldn't he?'

Silence.

Then Violetta nodded. 'He doesn't have to be here. He's a man of efficiency.'

'This is all going to come down to confidence,' King said. 'Just act like you belong.'

He got a pair of nods in return.

They both knew the drill.

They weren't novices in this realm.

One slip-up, one misplaced word, and they'd pay for it with their lives. It was the risk they took on each and every outing. The fact that they did it voluntarily was nothing to scoff at.

King mounted the narrow trail running to the compound's entrance and let the truck's big headlights illuminate the gate in stark detail. A pair of perimeter guards — cartel thugs, through and through — made straight for the tractor unit as it slowed.

King wound down the driver's window as one of them — a thirty-something man with intense blue eyes and a shaved head — leapt up onto the exterior step.

King nodded a wordless greeting.

The *sicario* took out a revolver and stuck the barrel in his face.

78

S later wheeled Beckham through a communal space with bookshelves and a cluster of chairs that could be arranged in circles or rows depending on the nature of the group activity.

He reached the corridor leading to the entrance lobby, and pulled the wheelchair back in its trajectory at the last second. The desperate move kept Beckham out of sight by inches, both of them pressed to the wall beside the big archway.

He'd heard unfamiliar voices.

'Thank you so much for coming,' the receptionist was saying. 'I had no idea...'

A deep male voice said, 'It's not your fault. Which way did he go?'

'To visit one of our residents. Jonathan Powell. Oh, God, don't tell me he was here to hurt—'

'We don't know, ma'am. We'll find out what happened. He's still in there?'

'I haven't seen him since. So, yes, he's probably still...'

She trailed off as her voice was drowned out by rapid,

heavy footsteps. Slater soaked it all in as the footfalls grew louder, rapidly approaching their position, seconds away from bursting out into the communal space and—

Slater iced his veins. These men, whether government employees or not, had come to execute an innocent man with no ability to defend himself. They were lower than scum.

He kept that in mind.

There was a rudimentary attempt on their part to sweep the communal space, but they were too hasty. Everything they'd heard from the receptionist indicated they could catch Slater off-guard in room 52. They weren't *really* expecting him to be lying in wait, so they barrelled into the open too fast, barely taking the time to scan the space with their weapons.

Slater didn't know how many there were — he just burst into motion.

Shot the first man to step into view through the side of the head, showering the opposite wall of the archway with brain matter, and then lashed out and kicked his body to the floor to make room for a follow-up shot. Which went through the face of the second man, knocking him back into the third as the life sapped from his limbs. It gave Slater a half-second to assess features — there were five of them in total, all clad in nondescript mercenary gear, sporting bulletproof vests and thick combat boots and black pants and black shirts. Nothing affiliated to any division of the U.S. government, but being used by them all the same. Maybe active operatives with no morality, called in for an important black op, told to carry out orders with no questions or protests.

The fact that they were here, obeying their masters without a moment's hesitation, said it all.

Slater fired a three-round burst into the face and throat of the third man — the guy who'd caught his dead partner in his arms. Both of them — now lifeless corpses — toppled, exposing the final pair in mid-lunge.

Not lunging for Slater.

Smart.

They dived behind columns on either side of the hallway before Slater could finish them off. Sensing a bad position, he fired a handful of rounds to give himself covering fire as he ducked back out of sight. He sensed Beckham right behind him, silently terrified, hoping like hell this was all a bad dream.

A quick calculation on Slater's part revealed the Glock was out.

He ejected the empty magazine out the bottom of the handle and reached back instinctively for a fresh one.

His fingers grasped at air.

His blood ran cold and nervous sweat leached from his pores.

He patted himself down, all around the waist.

The utility belt he used to store spare magazines had been ripped from his waist, probably when he'd crushed himself into Beckham's doorway to avoid getting nicked by the syringe. Where it had fallen, or how he'd missed it, was entirely lost on him. Adrenaline was a crazy bitch of a drug, and not even a seasoned practitioner like Slater could overcome the occasional mishap. Putting himself into situations like this — volatile, highly reactionary, often tactically improvised — meant it came with the territory.

He maintained a crouch, staring at his feet, running through a dozen different options.

Then he heard murmurs round the corner, drifting down the corridor.

'Is he still there?'

'I don't fuckin' know. You check.'

Slater ran through hypotheticals. These men were more than likely tier-one, but they wouldn't have a clue who Slater was. The five here and the two who'd led the charge would have all been summoned simultaneously to the disability centre. Seven total operatives for an assignment that should have taken one guy at the very maximum. Kill a cripple? How much manpower did that really require?

So maybe, just maybe, the pair up the back might have disregarded arming themselves to the teeth.

The five in the lead could get the job done, right?

Slater chanced a look, peeking round the corner.

He caught them halfway through the act. They'd both stepped out from cover in unison, and they were running for the bodies littered across the carpet beside Slater.

The bodies that had dropped guns.

Slater stepped into view, bent down, and snatched up one of the dead men's Berettas. He got there seconds before the two men did, which might as well have been years in their world. He checked the weapon was ready to fire and then aimed it at the unarmed duo, freezing them in their tracks.

One guy said, 'Cool it. Let's talk.'

Slater kept the barrel trained on the dead space between them, ready to flick the gun to either party and fire at a moment's notice.

Then he sidestepped so he could reach out and grab the armrest of Beckham's wheelchair and pull the whole thing out from behind cover.

So Beckham could see the pair.

Slater said to them, 'Here he is. The guy you came to murder.'

They stared at Beckham, unable to mask the guilt. They were seasoned combatants who'd probably seen war, which meant they'd learned to compartmentalise just as Slater had, but they weren't incapable of shame.

This was their failure, laid out before them.

What was supposed to be a discreet assassination. In and out fast. No witnesses. No judgment.

Now, not only was an enemy combatant judging them, but so was the target in question.

They looked at their feet, one by one.

As if it wouldn't exist if they didn't look.

Own your choices.

Slater shot them once each through the tops of their heads.

He got behind the wheelchair and pushed it through the scene of slaughter, navigating the bodies. He found the receptionist bolt upright in her swivel chair, on the verge of passing out from terror.

He locked eyes with her.

She screamed.

He waited for her to finish.

She sat there, practically catatonic.

He said, 'Nothing I say will make you understand. But know I'm the only person keeping this man alive.'

He gestured to Beckham, and then wheeled him straight out of the Hooper Quadriplegic Centre.

Leaving seven dead men in his wake.

79

King stared down the chamber of the snubnose revolver.

It was a Colt Detective Special, short and fat and guaranteed to blow his brain to pieces at this range. An ineffective weapon for combat, as all old-school revolvers were, but good for making a statement. Which the owner was currently doing.

King said, 'That's not very nice.'

Violetta sat rigid beside him.

Banks didn't say a word.

The thug pierced them all with his baby blue eyes, which settled on Violetta. He said, 'Hello, *mamacita.*'

King said, 'Don't talk to her like that.'

'I talk to her how I want, *ese.* You came here.'

'This is where we were told to come.'

'Were you? Cause I don't recognise a single fucking one of you.'

'I'm Liam Kingsley,' King said. 'Duke would have sent my file over. I'm new.'

The blue eyes pierced him, now. A glimmer of recognition passed over the man's face. 'Maybe you right. Maybe I do know you. But these two...'

He shook the Colt at Violetta and Banks.

King could have ripped it right out of his hands, pistol-whipped him in the face with it, then turned it on him and put one through his temple. It might have taken him two seconds, tops.

But he didn't.

He sat still, tense and ready for anything, forcing an aura of calm.

It was critical.

They needed to get inside before they started a war.

Before anyone could respond, all of them noticed head-lights far behind them — first the trio in the cabin saw them in the side mirrors, and then the gate guard caught them in his peripheral vision and turned to look.

It was a civilian vehicle, not a truck — long and low to the ground — and it was making a beeline for the compound.

An old-school muscle car.

Maybe a Dodge.

Hard to tell in the darkness.

King said, 'Expecting company?'

'Yes, actually,' the guard said. 'A private client. Here for one of the girls in particular. He's right on time.'

'You know him?'

'We've dealt with him before. He has ... a certain arrangement with the boss man.'

'Right,' King said. 'Doesn't make a difference to me. Where do you want the container?'

'Inside,' the guard said. 'But I'll need your weapons first.'

'That's not happening,' King said.

'*Pinche gringo.* Excuse me?'

'This isn't charity. We're not beneath you. We have cargo in the back that you want your hands on. So it's a two-way street. Treat us with respect, and that's how we'll treat you.'

'There are sixteen of us here,' the guard said. 'We can take it by force.'

'Maybe. But we'll kill at least a few of you. And yes, I know how this works — you've got a reputation to uphold. It's worth losing a few men to avoid looking weak. In your world weakness is death. But you'll also lose access to the supply we consistently provide, and that won't make upper management happy.'

The guard bristled on the elevated step, looking King right in the eyes, waiting for him to back down.

King didn't.

Then the guard started truly considering it.

King said, 'I'll do many things, but I won't hand over my weapon. I respect myself too much to submit to you. But if you let us through, you have my word there'll be no problems. We'll get the container out of the trailer, you'll pay us, and we'll be on our way. Simple as that.'

The guard said nothing.

King said, 'Or we go the other way.'

For dramatic effect, he placed his hand on the grip of his weapon.

The guard leered.

He was enjoying this.

He clearly respected confidence.

'Okay,' he conceded. 'But I don't know about letting all three of you in. I only know you, Liam Kingsley.'

Violetta leant forward. 'Honey, if you ever want to do business with Ryan Duke again, you'll let his woman in. And Josh here is his right-hand man. You think he's going to tolerate any bullshit you try to put us through?'

The guard stared at her for a long beat.

Then he drifted the Colt slowly over to aim at her face.

But the Dodge pulled up behind the truck, and the muscle car's engine rumbled in the night, and the guard became aware that he was keeping an important client waiting.

He winked, blew her a kiss, and leapt down off the step.

King breathed out.

The guard signalled, and two men on the perimeter wall ducked into a booth atop the parapet. A moment later, the gates inched open, accompanied by a mechanical whir.

King drove through.

The Dodge followed, stalking its prey.

King thought he made out a silhouette behind the wheel in the side mirror, but it might have been a figment of his imagination.

The tractor unit crossed the threshold and a couple of seconds later the entire truck entered the compound.

Swallowed whole.

80

The night drenched Slater as he wheeled Beckham across the road.

Everything was still.

Ordinary suburbia.

A world away from the bloodbath he'd caused back there. He felt nothing toward what he'd done. No one had died who hadn't fully deserved it. Some residents might have been startled by the racket, but that was necessary collateral.

Now, Slater pushed the wheelchair faster and faster toward the dormant Hyundai across the street. It was too dark to see inside. His stomach had knotted long ago, and he wouldn't dare relax until he knew—

The passenger door flung outward, and Alexis stepped out, Glock in hand.

The knot loosened.

Slater masked a sigh of relief.

'Girlfriend?' Beckham said when they were still halfway across the street. He made sure to keep his voice low.

'Yeah.'

'You're a lucky man.'

'I like to think so.'

He wheeled Beckham right up to the rear passenger door.

Alexis rounded the hood to greet them.

'Hi,' she said.

'Hello,' Beckham said.

'I wish we could have all met under different circumstances,' she said. 'I hope you're doing okay.'

Beckham craned his neck to look up at Slater, then back to Alexis. 'Do you know what your boyfriend did back there?'

Alexis met Slater's gaze, and nodded slowly before turning back to Beckham. 'I saw seven men go in. You two came out. I think I can figure that out for myself.'

'Are you military?' Beckham asked.

'No.'

'Just a civilian like me?'

'Yes.'

Beckham shook his head, still pale, still in a state of shock. He would be for quite some time. The memories of what he'd seen would live with him forever. But it was a whole lot more preferable than being incapable of memory, buried in an early grave.

Beckham said, 'This is madness.'

'Welcome to my life,' Slater said.

He and Alexis got to work helping the man out of his wheelchair, lifting him gently up and placing him in the back seat. They strapped him in, draping the seatbelt over his frail torso. He nodded his thanks, but it was half-hearted. He was distant. Detached.

Slater said, 'Relax. You don't have to be cordial. You're allowed to think I'm a monster.'

'Wouldn't that stick with you? If everyone thought that.'

'I don't care what people think.'

Slater folded up the modified wheelchair and manhandled it into the two rear seats Beckham wasn't occupying. There was no space in the trunk of the i30. Then he got behind the wheel and swivelled to make sure Beckham was settled in okay.

They locked eyes.

Beckham said, 'I don't think you're a monster.'

'I'm glad.'

'I thought you didn't care.'

'Maybe I do,' Slater said. 'Just a little bit.'

'You just saved my life, but everyone's going to think you murdered seven loyal patriotic troops and kidnapped a cripple.'

'People believe what they're led to believe,' Slater said. 'Sometimes doing the right thing is messy. As long as the people in this car, and a certain few outside of it, know who I really am ... that's all that matters.'

After that Beckham went quiet, and they drove for close to an hour in silence, barreling as far away from Stratford Hills as they could feasibly get. Separating themselves from a messy crime scene that would undoubtedly make national, if not international, headlines. After such a prolonged quiet, Slater figured Beckham was in the midst of an adrenaline dump, and might even be fast asleep back there. But when he angled the rear view mirror to check on the man, he found him wide awake, meeting Slater's gaze with an unblinking stare.

Slater said, 'What's up?'

'What happened between Violetta and I was messy,' he said. 'How couldn't it have been? But maybe you're right. Maybe she was doing the right thing all along.'

Slater nodded.

When he shot a glance at Alexis, he was surprised to find her staring at him with a tear in her eye.

Probably remembering what had happened earlier that morning.

Sometimes doing the right thing is messy.

She reached out and gripped his thigh with her hand.

Gave it a reassuring squeeze.

Maybe it would all be okay.

81

The house in the centre of the compound was long and low and enormous, built ranch-style.

It sprawled out across the space, surrounded by a couple of outbuildings — each of them probably home to bunks for the extra manpower. To the right there was a big garage with the roller doors up, home to a number of off-road vehicles and more traditional SUVs. Four mean-looking guys with Hermès caps atop their heads milled around out the front of the garage. A couple of them had AK-47s hanging off slings over their shoulders, and the other two had clearly visible semi-automatic pistols in holsters on the belts of their jeans. All four weapons were on full display.

It was a show of force, designed to intimidate the new arrivals.

It might have worked, had the trio in the cabin not been immune to intimidation.

The blue-eyed guard ran alongside the truck and directed it to pull up in the middle of the space in front of the house. King parked and killed the engine. The huge tractor unit creaked and groaned as it powered down.

Behind them, the Dodge drifted lazily in through the front gate and parked behind the trailer.

The front door of the house opened, but no one came out. King spotted silhouettes in the doorway, milling about with excitement. Probably the underlings, forced to stay back but enthusiastic about the arrival of the precious cargo. There were seven men in sight — the blue-eyed guard, the two guards atop the wall, and the four men with Hermès caps. A sizeable force in an open landscape with no nearby cover. Bad for King and Violetta and Banks. Bad for the cartel, too, but they had more than twice the amount of troops, and they were all expendable.

The blue-eyed guard beckoned.

King unclasped his seatbelt, popped the door and slid out of the cabin.

'Wait here,' he murmured over his shoulder as he exited. 'Stay frosty.'

'What was that?' the guard said, twirling the snubnose revolver on his finger with a shocking lack of trigger discipline.

'I just told them not to do anything stupid,' King said as he stepped down into the dirt. 'It's a little tense, after all.'

The guard shrugged. 'I'm not tense.'

Then he aimed the Colt at King's chest.

He smiled, exposing artificially white teeth. 'Are you tense?'

'No,' King said.

'You look it.'

'You should take my pulse,' King said. 'You, on the other hand ... you're coked to the eyeballs. What are you right now — 140, 150 beats per minute? You look *jacked*.'

'I'm fine, *gringo*.'

'Uh-huh.'

But the guard squirmed regardless. It was the equivalent of telling someone not to think about a white elephant. King even mentioning the man's pulse — which was naturally elevated anyway — must have shot it through the roof, because the vein on the side of his neck started pumping and he reached up and wiped his forehead with his sleeve.

Which only made him more fidgety.

The compound effect, live in the flesh.

The guy jerked a thumb toward the back of the trailer. His palm was slick with sweat. 'Get to it.'

King nodded. Started running through possibilities, trying to determine when would be the best time to catch them off-guard.

Not for a while, he concluded. They were too spread out, too heavily armed. Violetta and Banks were still in the cabin, out of position, not ready for a quick-draw firefight. The night was hot and oppressive and rife to leach stress from pores. King shrugged off a nervous stab of energy, trying to calm himself, trying to wind down.

In stillness, he could find his opportunity.

Then he turned to make for the back of the truck and saw the Dodge's driver door swing open.

A man stepped out.

Grizzled.

Old.

Long grey hair swept back off his forehead.

A face like steel.

Everything made a lot more sense. King thought about how odd it was that an ex-Navy vet who ran a small-time leadership company had been tasked with providing security detail for one of the wealthiest and most powerful men in the United States. Jack Coombs had never fit the bill. It should have been obvious from the start. He was being used by Sam Donati the whole time, perhaps forced to work at a heavily discounted rate. Donati must have been getting considerable expertise for pennies on the dollar to bother using Coombs at all. But why?

Because Jack Coombs had a guilty secret.

A compulsive urge he had to keep away from the public eye.

King wondered how the conversation had gone.

Donati: *You're a dirty old man with dirty wants and needs. But you're in luck. I bring girls over from Eastern Europe. It's part of my business. You can take your pick when they get here. You can do what you want with them. But you give me all your expertise, and all your connections, and you work for me for free. How's that for a deal?*

King looked into the old man's eyes.

That was a deal Jack Coombs would have agreed to in a heartbeat.

But now there was a bigger problem.

Coombs was now looking at the only delivery driver on the planet he knew damn well wasn't part of the criminal underworld.

King cocked his head, and so did Coombs.

They recognised each other.

King thought, *Who's going to talk first?*

82

Neither of them said a word.

Understanding rippled in the air around them.

There were unspoken revelations hovering there, invisible and menacing.

The corners of Coombs' mouth tilted upward.

A wry smile.

The old man said, 'Are you going to tell them or should I?'

'I thought we might avoid that,' King said.

He tried to alert Coombs to the presence of the Glock at his waist, clearly visible in its holster.

The old man saw it, then said, 'I think not.'

The wry smile amplified.

Petty revenge for King botching the Moscow job, for almost ruining Coombs' vital connection to the pipeline, for nearly stripping him of the vice he needed to satiate.

Keeping him from a steady supply of Eastern European sex slaves.

Coombs turned to the perimeter guard, and said, 'This man right here is—'

The rest of the speech wasn't necessary, because there was only one potential outcome, so King fast-tracked Coombs along his chosen path by taking out his Glock and shooting the man once in the head. The long mane of grey hair snapped to the side, and his neck jerked from the whiplash, and he fell awkwardly into the dirt.

The *thump* of his body hitting the ground was the equivalent of a starting gun, firing a shot to initiate all-out war.

Banks had already vaulted out of the cabin and landed in the dirt beside the tractor unit. As soon as Coombs died, he brandished the M4A1 carbine rifle that had been sitting on his lap the whole time and unloaded on the *sicarios* in the Hermès caps.

King saw him peppering silhouettes with clusters of bullets out of the corner of his eye, and before he could blink four men were dead. He expected nothing less from a fully prepared, razor-sharp DEVGRU operative.

King in turn executed the three guards closest to him at blistering speed. He put a round through the face of the blue-eyed man — the body smacked into the dirt beside Coombs — then turned to the two men along the parapet and nailed them with shots until they both fell, one clutching a fatal wound in his throat as the other simply dropped stone dead on the spot, a cylindrical hole in the centre of his forehead.

Violetta leapt from the cabin, landed beside King, and used her Beretta to fire a trio of shots at the open front door of the ranch-style house. A shriek of either pain or surprise came from within, but King barely registered it. His hearing was reeling from the barrage of unsuppressed rounds, particularly from Banks' carbine.

Savouring a second's respite, King ejected the half-empty mag and slammed a fresh one into the handle.

Violetta's covering fire had bought him precious time.

Not much.

An inexperienced combatant would waste it thinking and planning and calculating.

He simply sprinted for the front of the house.

The front deck was aproned by a thick row of xeriscaping, and King slid to a halt behind an enormous drought-resistant plant he couldn't identify. It wouldn't stop bullets, but it shielded his mass entirely, and for those vital seconds no one was looking. Everyone inside was cowering from follow-up shots.

King crouched and put his head down and waited.

Then shots blared from the second storey windows, only a dozen or so feet above his head. They weren't aiming at him, though. They were aiming at Violetta and Banks, now safely behind cover on the other side of the truck.

King leant backward and saw them right above him, practically leaning out the windows. Three men — one per window.

King aimed and fired, aimed and fired, aimed and fired.

Three dead.

One body fell out and crashed into the sand in front of the house, and the other two fell back inside.

King dived laterally, crab-crawling a dozen feet along the row of landscaped shrubbery, avoiding the follow-up shots he knew would come his way. And they did, predictably reactionary, tearing apart the plant he'd been cowering behind seconds earlier. But now he was a world away, and his mindset became ice, and his thoughts fell away, and all he saw was tunnel vision. A wrecking ball in human form.

Still prone, he sandwiched himself between a pair of desert plants and got a clear view of the front doorway and found two men bundled up together in a supposed rush to riddle the enemy with lead.

Except all they riddled with lead was a native plant.

King aimed the Glock — methodically, surgically, and shot one in the chest, then the other. These two weren't wearing protective clothing, so he didn't bother with head-shots. They collapsed limply atop one another, forming a makeshift barricade in the doorway, and King saw it all laid out before him and kept deathly still, so still he might as well have been part of the landscaping.

Because he knew what was coming.

A hotheaded adrenaline-fuelled *sicario* eventually spotted the barricade of corpses and figured he ought to use it as cover, so he did just that. King only had to wait ten calm seconds before he spotted movement behind the bodies, and then he simply unloaded all the remaining rounds in the magazine through the doorway. Corpses are terrible bullet-stoppers, and at least a couple of lead parcels got through the dead flesh and slammed home against the living.

An inhuman shriek rose from the entranceway.

King reloaded again, leapt to his feet, and sprinted through the front door.

He found the third *sicario* writhing in a pool of his own arterial blood and put one through the top of his head to put him out of his misery.

Then he took a breath.

Three dead here.

Three dead upstairs.

Seven dead outside.

There are sixteen of us here, the perimeter guard had said. *We can take it by force.*

'Not anymore you can't,' King muttered.

Three left.

He settled into berserker mode and advanced into the darkened house.

83

He should have remembered how the cartel functions.

All sixteen of the occupants couldn't be foot soldiers. There had to be a hierarchy, a chain of command, which meant top dogs. But that was far less reason to worry. It's easy to slack off at the top. It's easy to convince yourself you're invincible. So when King swept the whole corridor and stepped out into a large communal living space and found the last three members sitting bolt upright on the sofa with an entire bowl of cocaine in front of them, he wasn't surprised.

Absolute power might corrupt absolutely, but a little power can do the trick also.

Not one of them was a shade over twenty-five. Two guys, one woman. She was dressed in skin-tight leggings and a tube top that pushed her breasts up, but there was nothing superficial about her. Her eyes were the eyes of a killer. She had to be, to be sitting where she was, ordering the rest of them around. She'd draped a leg over the skinny guy with the mop of unruly black hair on the left, and not even King's arrival had made her take it off. The other guy was a little further away from them, a little beefier, fat in the face and red in the cheeks.

King understood.

The skinny guy was where the nepotism lay.

He was the son of someone important. King drew eerie parallels to a kid named Rico he'd met a few months ago, the scion of a cartel over the border. Rico had lashed out needlessly at Slater, and ended up paying for it with his life. Slater hadn't killed him, but the nature of their profession usually made that sort of thing inevitable.

Now, King regarded this kid sitting before him.

Even weaker than Rico.

He was trying to shrink into the corner of the sofa, as if he could turn himself invisible on a whim. There was no aggression or confidence in his eyes. King turned to assess the girl and realised her eyes were flooded with those very things. The fat guy on the right was a hanger-on, unimportant in the grand scheme of things.

The girl was the ringleader.

King sat down on the footstool in the middle of the room, facing the couch.

The girl tried to look smug.

King said, 'Is this the part where you convince me there's more guards?'

'Of course there are,' she spat.

'I got them all.'

'You sure?'

'Uh-huh. Thirteen.'

'There's fifteen.'

'No,' he said, looking right at her. 'There isn't.'

She didn't lose any of the arrogance, but she relented. 'What are you hoping to achieve?' She reached out and tilted her boyfriend's chin up, trying to give him some dignity, trying to make a man out of him. He couldn't have been any older than nineteen. She, on the other hand, had to be in her mid-twenties. She said, 'Do you know who this is?'

King said, 'No. But I know he doesn't want this life.'

The kid looked at him, his eyes hollow, his face blank.

She said, 'Of course he does. He's—'

'If you're going to rattle off a name,' King said. 'I don't care. I'm sure his surname means something. Speed this story up.'

'He is the heir to the throne,' she said. 'Señor Álvaro is his father. You kill him, you start a war with the whole Álvaro clan. Do you understand what that means?'

'I've started wars before,' King said. 'It doesn't bother me.'

'You clearly don't understand.'

'Oh, I understand,' King said. 'He'd rather do something else. Anything else, really. Whatever doesn't involve killing a bunch of people and then dying young. Because that's what happens to most of you. I'm sure he's buried brothers and sisters and aunts and uncles. But you ... you're grooming him for the throne. You're the one who wants it. What's your name?'

'María.'

'María, what will you do once you get it?'

'His name is Damien Álvaro, and you will—'

'If it mattered,' King said, 'he'd tell me himself.'

Damien Álvaro seemed like he'd rather be anywhere else. And not just because a hulking executioner was across the room with a loaded semi-automatic pistol. He had unmistakable nihilism in his eyes. As if he was silently telling her, *See what I told you? I don't want this. I never did. And now here we are.*

King said, 'Damien, what's going to happen to me if I put a bullet in you?'

Álvaro looked at the floor.

King said, 'Now's your chance. Tell tales of your family's power. Tell me everything.'

María opened her mouth.

King aimed the Glock at her face.

She quietened.

Damien just slowly shook his head, his eyes squeezed shut, his face pale.

King thought, *They still think I'm a monster.*

They don't know this is Judgment Day.

He turned to María and said, 'I'm here for the container that just got dropped off. I'm willing to let you all go if you look the other way. There's some valuable goddamn women in there. I could get a pretty penny for them. How'd you pull that deal off?'

María leered, sensing opportunity. 'Wouldn't you like to know?'

'Don't push your luck.'

She shrugged, opening back up, seizing the moment. 'Damien here doesn't think it's *savoury*. But it's good for business. And it gives this one—' she pinched Damien's cheek, '—a solid rep. Doesn't it?'

She spoke to him like someone spoke to their pet.

King realised what he needed to do.

He raised an eyebrow, and half-smiled, embracing the malevolence. 'I *knew* it. I could see in his eyes he was a pussy.'

Damien kept looking at the floor.

María laughed, keeping her leg draped over him. 'You're

smart. It's okay. I'm bringing him round. He'll get there eventually. But, yes, take the container. There's a lot more where that came from. I think that's a fair trade, don't you?'

King nodded. 'Yeah.'

Then he turned to the fat guy with the red cheeks. 'What about you? You going to miss the supply?'

The red cheeks brightened as the little psychopath smiled.

'Nah, man,' the kid said. 'I can go a few weeks without. Been a wild ride for the last year, though. You'd better enjoy yourself when you run with what's inside. Prime eye candy.'

King laughed.

The fat guy laughed.

María joined in.

Damien looked at the floor.

King stood up, wiped the smile off his face, and shot both María and the fat guy once each in the forehead.

84

Neither had the chance to react. They slammed back against the sofa and froze in seated positions, their wide eyes glassed over.

Damien finally looked up.

Genuine surprise on his face.

King said, 'You can disappear. They'll chalk it up to an abduction if everyone else in this compound is dead. They won't look for you for very long. They'll assume you were taken and tortured and killed and then buried.'

Damien stared blankly.

King said, 'Or you can run back to Daddy, and he'll give you a new gig like this, and the same thing will happen eventually. It might be someone like me, or it might be a rival cartel. The outcome's the same.'

Damien managed an imperceptible jerk of the chin — it might have been a nod.

King said, 'I didn't need to ask you a thing. I can read people. You never wanted this life but you felt trapped in it. Your girlfriend made the decisions for you, and you were slowly getting desensitised to it all. You were coaxed toward a cliff edge. You nearly went over it. This is your out. Take it or leave it.'

Damien said, 'How can you be sure I'll make the right decision?'

The first time he'd uttered a word since King had arrived.

He barely had an accent. His English was impeccable.

'Because if you weren't going to,' King said, 'you never would have asked that question.'

Then King looked around, morose. He added, 'And I've killed enough people tonight.'

He walked out.

vicious gust of desert wind blew in through the open doors and shattered windows as he made for the entrance.

The house's foundations creaked, protesting the elements.

At least it wouldn't bear the burden of caring for new residents for quite some time.

King stepped outside and surveyed the scene of destruction. There were bodies everywhere — scattered across the dirt, resting against bullet-riddled vehicles. Violetta was by the truck, her gun still raised, ever vigilant. Her face was flustered but her eyes were focused. She saw him emerge, and palpable relief washed over her. He nodded to her — *it's done* — and she lowered the weapon.

Banks was on the other side of the truck, still in the zone, rolling corpses onto their backs with the toe of his combat boot and checking for signs of life. As King stepped down off the porch, he looked up and nodded with satisfaction.

Compound cleared.

King approached. 'Well, now I feel stupid.'

Violetta said, 'Why?'

'I kept the container in the trailer because I thought we'd have to present it long before we shot up the place. Then our cover got blown way early, and we still pulled it off. So it was an unnecessary risk all along.'

Violetta looked at Coombs' body. 'Speaking of cover being blown ... who the hell is that?'

'The guy who sent me to Moscow,' King said. 'Slater's old instructor.'

Violetta stared at the dead man, and then at King. 'That's why I pressured you not to take civilian gigs.'

'I'm sorry I didn't listen.'

She stopped, taken aback. She must have been expecting an argument.

Clarity cleared his head as he looked at her. 'What? You want me to put up a fight? I made a bad judgment call. End of story.'

She nodded, somewhat reserved. 'So we're done? This is finished?'

King regarded the trailer. 'We'll take the container to a police station. Somewhere commercial. Somewhere well-known. Laguna Beach, maybe. There's no way the cartel owns cops in good neighbourhoods. Out here, that's where they have control. In the places most people don't have the nerve to stick their noses.'

'People live out here,' Violetta said.

'This place is as obvious as it gets,' he said. 'Anyone who's seen it hasn't had the backbone to do a thing about it.'

He surveyed the dead, and added, 'Just one of many problems I'm looking at.'

'Problems you solved,' Violetta said.

Banks had been lackadaisically sauntering up behind

her throughout the conversation. King had barely noticed him. The guy was focused on his carbine, checking it had come out the other side of the onslaught in one piece.

Now, only a couple of feet from Violetta, he closed the gap in the blink of an eye and had his Beretta drawn and pressed to the side of her head before King even realised what had happened.

She opened her mouth to gasp, and he clamped a gloved palm over it and wrenched her close.

King drew his Glock and locked it onto Banks' forehead, but that had clearly been expected.

Banks said, 'Can't solve this problem, buddy.'

'What the fuck are you doing?'

'You might be able to outsmart a cartel foot soldier in a standoff,' he said. 'Not me.'

'I—'

'You shoot me, she dies. Simple as that.'

'You die too.'

'I know,' Banks said. 'Isn't this fun?'

'Again,' King said, 'what the fuck are you doing?'

'I respect you. Soldier to soldier. They wanted you both, but you did a good thing here. I'm not some tyrant. I know evil when I see it. You wiped out evil here.'

'You helped.'

'It was your idea,' Banks said. 'You get the credit.'

'So you despise what you see here, but you don't care about her?'

'Trust me, I'd prefer it didn't have to go this way. But I got orders. I'm not about to disobey orders.'

'You were going to.'

'All a ruse. I'm a patriot. I asked them to pick — her or you. They picked her. She has a thousand secrets in this little head of hers that you don't have. So I'm going to leave with her. Please don't do anything stupid.'

'You're not ready to die.'

Banks half-smiled. 'Bad luck, my friend. I'm perfectly willing to die. And your shot leads to my shot. You know it does. Look at my finger on the trigger. That'll spasm, the moment I die. You shoot me, you're killing your girlfriend.'

Violetta didn't move a muscle. Her eyes, wracked with tension, said everything.

Not now.

Not this close to the finish line.

King said, 'You could have said we escaped before you could get your hands on her.'

Banks shrugged. 'Then I'd be lying. I'm a man of my word.'

'I thought you were decent.'

'I am,' Banks said. 'You might like to paint me as the bad guy, but this isn't sunshine and rainbows. Hard choices have to be made. Be objective, King. Ask yourself — if you were upper management, would you willingly let her go with everything she knows about them? The greater good, blah blah blah.'

'She knows nothing about them,' King said. 'She's told me that herself.'

'She knows enough.'

King lowered his Glock, recognising it was futile.

The wind howled.

Something under the hood of the truck hissed, the engine mechanics still powering down from the long drive.

King said, 'Then it's a good thing I heard the call.'

Banks hesitated. 'What?'

'When I lay down next to you outside Duke's mansion. I grabbed your wrist.'

'Yeah.'

'I slipped something under your glove.'

'No you didn't.'

'Then how did I hear what you said when we got out of the truck?'

Banks stared.

The tension built.

The air froze, despite the desert heat.

King said, 'I slipped something else under there, too.'

Banks didn't react.

But his eyes flickered toward the woollen hem of the glove on his right hand.

The hand clutching the gun.

It wasn't enough to act. King's gut churned, and the rest of his insides seized, and a cold fell over him he wasn't familiar with. The cold of defeat.

He met Violetta's gaze and tried to convey how sorry he was with his eyes alone.

Then Banks' gaze floated past his glove, past King even. Over King's shoulder. He was staring at the house. King's speech had thrown him off ever so slightly, and now something had distracted him on top of that.

King didn't have time to turn around, but he knew it was Damien that had emerged from the ranch. The skinny kid with the mop of hair must have seemed like an apparition in the desert night to Banks. Especially considering the fact he thought King had cleared the compound.

Still meeting Violetta's gaze, King gave an imperceptible nod.

She wasn't an elite combatant. She didn't have superhuman reflexes. She knew all Banks was experiencing was a brief flash of cognitive dissonance, a momentary spark of confusion.

But she went for it anyway, which made her braver than anyone King had ever met.

She jerked out of his grip, hard.

He fired.

The first shot missed, passing an inch past her head.

She fell away from him.

He got the gun halfway up and shot her.

King blew his head apart.

86

He moved so fast he caught her before she hit the ground.

Skidded through the dirt and wrapped his arms around her and lowered her gently to the earth.

His heart hammered.

His whole world stopped.

She landed in his arms, her eyes closed...

...and her face contorted in pain.

Pain.

Pain was good.

You can't feel pain when you're dead.

It was the slowest second of his life. He saw each millisecond pass, the whole time unimaginably tense, every muscle locked, every fibre and sinew vibrating with uncertainty. He checked her body and neck and face, searching for the point of impact, searching for the wound that might spell—

A red patch on her arm, rapidly expanding.

The bullet had gone through the bicep and come out the other side.

Clean entry and exit.

He fell off her and collapsed onto his back, panting hard, an infinite weight off his chest.

He thought he'd known relief before that moment.

He realised he'd never come close to the true sensation.

She panted, too. They'd both dumped their adrenaline hard. King gave thanks he'd wiped out the compound before the standoff with Banks. He figured he didn't have the energy to stand, let alone fight.

Eventually he sat up. She lay there, staring up at the night sky, keeping pressure on her arm. She knew exactly what to do. She'd practically stemmed the bleeding already. Her first-aid training was unparalleled.

Her voice low and shaky, she said, 'You didn't have a bug.'

'No shit,' King said. 'But when else would he have talked to his handler? Either you or I were with him from the moment we approached him. Except for when we got out.'

'That didn't work, though. He wasn't distracted enough.'

King pivoted, still sitting in the dirt. He looked back over his shoulder. Damien was still there, shoulders slumped, hair flipping side to side in the wind. He was cold and unnerved and terrified of the solitude that awaited, the new life he would have to build for himself, the new identity he'd have to forge. And now he was doubly shocked by the brief gunfight he'd witnessed.

The kid had no idea how his appearance had saved everything.

King nodded a silent thanks to the kid, which he knew would go uninterpreted.

He didn't care.

He knew his mercy had saved Violetta's life.

She looked at the kid, too. They were far enough away to

be out of earshot, especially with the wind. She said, 'You missed one.'

King said, 'No I didn't.'

She looked at him. 'He's young, and he's here. You know what that means.'

'He's the boss?'

'Precisely.'

'He's no boss.'

'His father is someone important, obviously.'

'So he should be held accountable for his father's business?'

'He's here,' Violetta said. 'How many containers do you think he saw come in? How many times do you think he watched his men force themselves on the slaves? Not to mention the ordinary business of the cartels — drugs, guns, extortion, murder. He was witness to all of it. He did nothing about it.'

'It's not that simple.'

'It is. Not to mention he's a witness.'

'It's not,' King said, lowering his voice. 'You haven't seen the side of humanity I've seen. You think people just start evil? They're corrupted over time, each and every one of them. He was being corrupted — by all the people around him, by the fact he couldn't do anything to stop it, by the knowledge of what his family does, by the life he sees no way out of.'

For the first time, she truly looked at him. Saw past the stereotype. And King thought he saw her register that something was different. This kid had no ambition. Nor was there relief on his face — he seemingly didn't care that he'd been spared.

Violetta said, 'You think he'll find a normal life? This is all he's known.'

'He can try,' King said. 'We owe him that much. If he hadn't walked out when he did, Banks' first shot would have gone through your skull.'

She stared at him. 'You're sure?'

'I'm sure.'

He got up and helped her to her feet in turn. They dusted themselves off and took a moment to survey the bodies. Joshua Banks, Jack Coombs, and a compound of *sicarios*.

Seventeen dead, in total.

She said, 'Is this the way you thought it would go?'

'Not even close. But at least it resolved everything.'

She said, 'Almost everything.'

The trailer loomed over them.

King nodded. 'Let's get to it.'

He vaulted up through the open driver's door, into the seat he'd been forced out of minutes earlier.

All those minutes ago.

Back when everyone was alive.

It was a strange world he lived in, and he'd never fully adjust.

Violetta rounded the hood and got in beside him. The cabin felt enormous with just two people in it. King worked the ignition and listened to the behemoth rumble slowly to life. Through the windshield, he watched Damien sit down on the porch, taking stock of what had happened here.

King executed a sweeping three-point turn in the courtyard and drove the truck out through the open gate.

Objective cleared.

87

The truck plunged into anonymity as soon as it mounted the highway back to the coastline.

Just another set of headlights in the night.

Nothing to do with the scene of slaughter in the rear view mirror.

Violetta got on the phone immediately. They were both balls of tension, their sanity threatening to unwind if they received bad news. Violetta no doubt more concerned about Beckham, King more concerned about Slater. But not by much. There was equal worry for the party in general.

And they both knew, if one was dead, the other likely was too.

Because Slater would go down fighting to avenge Beckham — that's the way he was wired. And if Slater wound up dead before he reached the Hooper Quadriplegic Centre, then Beckham's fate was sealed also.

King sensed the phone pressed to her ear, but she wasn't speaking. He focused on the unchanging highway flying past underneath the truck and nothing else.

The knot that had found its home in his gut returned with full intensity.

Then he heard a tinny voice from the speaker, muffled by Violetta's ear.

She said, 'Do you have him?'

An answer came.

She said, 'Is he hurt?'

Another answer.

She said, 'Alexis. She's okay too?'

A single syllable that could only have been, *Yes*.

Violetta breathed out, and so did King.

She said, 'Okay. Still good to follow the plan we discussed?'

Another, *Yes*.

She said, 'Speak soon.'

She clicked off.

King bowed his head to the top of the wheel. When he finally sat up, he shook his head. He could see her in his peripheral vision, staring vacantly out the windshield, wondering what might have been.

Which made him think.

He said, 'I was stupid.'

She said, 'Why?'

'I hadn't seen combat since New York. I don't think I fully believed in myself. So I gave up on the idea of storming in there and letting loose with bullets straight away. I thought I'd have to present the human cargo first, prove my presence in the compound was justified. Then flip the switch and start executing them silently. Berserker mode would have been the right choice, because it meant I could have left the container out of it.'

Violetta said nothing.

King turned to her. 'If we all died back there, no one

would know. The women would be sitting in that container, helpless. I'm a moron for bringing them back into danger when I'd already got them out of it.'

She said, 'All "what-ifs." You didn't fail. They're alive.'

'But I didn't trust myself,' he said. 'That can't happen again.'

She stared. 'You think it's because of the hiatus you took?'

'Quite possibly.'

'Then what are you saying is the solution?'

'Work harder. Do more.'

'Isn't that why you abandoned the government? So you could do less?'

He shook his head. 'Never. I can't stop. I'm going to do things my own way. But I didn't know if you'd be along for the ride. I need to know if you're okay with that.'

She sat, pensive and still.

He said, 'I think Slater's in the same boat. I don't think we want our talents to go to waste.'

She said, 'There's nothing to stop me from continuing to handle the pair of you.'

Music to his ears.

'So that's the way forward?' she said. 'A vigilante crew?'

'Like old times. Only a little more organised.'

She didn't respond.

He said, 'Unless you have other ideas.'

'I'll be honest — I did. Until this. I know what's in that container back there. I can't sit back and allow things like that to keep happening.'

'Welcome to my mind.'

It felt good, he had to admit.

Unity.

Mutual understanding.

They spent the rest of the trip in silence. Adrenal fatigue hit hard, making them feel they were moving through quicksand. King was a little better accustomed to the sensation than Violetta, but that didn't make it any easier. He settled into autopilot and went through the motions, following the GPS route back through the mountains toward the Pacific. Then he navigated the coastline until he was finally made to stamp on the truck's brakes outside a giant cream building with brick columns and a tall archway above wooden double doors.

Over the doors, a sign illuminated by an overhead light read: CITY OF LAGUNA BEACH POLICE DEPARTMENT.

Violetta said, 'You think this is the way to go?'

'What else can we do?' King said.

She nodded her understanding.

They didn't share another word. They got out, went to the back of the trailer, and King opened it up. The container rested within, neatly settled on low supports. He vaulted up onto the trailer bed and set to work on the exterior locks. He made quick work of them. They were designed to be opened from the outside, not within.

He swung the door open.

There were twelve of them in total, huddled up in a nervous group against the rear wall. They must have sensed the truck coming to a stop with some measure of finality. The space in front of them was cool — that's what the refrigeration was for, to ensure they didn't suffocate. Mattresses had been arranged in neat rows against each of the longer walls — six per side. There were bedsheets and duvets and pillows in cases. MREs — military ration packs — were stacked in equal towers next to each bed, alongside multiple gallon water containers. Up the rear of the container, lidded plastic buckets served as toilets, complete with a makeshift privacy screen.

King paused a beat to truly admire their resolve.

The women were all dirty and dishevelled and riddled with stress, but they hadn't let their surroundings mirror the fear they'd been crippled by. Throughout the whole journey they'd kept the space as clean as they could, even though he was sure every part of them wanted to descend into nihilism.

They hadn't wavered, not even in the face of their worst nightmares coming true.

There was nothing more impressive.

And they were strong now. They glared at him from across the container, daring him to lay a finger on them.

He pointed a thumb at himself. 'Police.'

No one budged.

They'd been lied to before.

He said, 'You're safe. Trust me.'

Violetta appeared beside him. She regarded the contents of the container and winced in horror. She couldn't help it. The role of handler involves a necessary detachment from the field. When you see the consequences, when you hear them, smell them — it's so much more real.

Too real to process.

King knew Violetta was imagining exactly what would have happened here had they not interfered.

King was wondering that too.

Wondering what might have happened if Jack Coombs and his dirty secrets hadn't wandered into a bar in Koreatown.

Days ago.

It felt like years.

It always did.

Violetta steeled herself, and then pointed to her own chest, and said, 'Police.'

Something about the presence of a female inspired trust. Not fully, and each of the women moved with a certain amount of scepticism, but it was progress. A woman at the front stepped forward, in her twenties, with pale skin and delicate features and black hair and wide eyes. She kept her gaze locked on Violetta and walked towards her.

Which opened the floodgates.

King and Violetta helped each of them out the back of the trailer, where they milled around on the asphalt opposite the police station. A couple of them stared up at the big sign, but most of them stared at their feet. Violetta leapt down to console them as King helped the final few out of the container.

The last woman out was tentative. She held back as the rest of the group dispersed, silhouetted at the rear of the space.

King hovered in the doorway and beckoned her out.

She stepped forward.

It was the girl from the surveillance photo.

Eastern European. Naturally beautiful. Long blond hair. The secretarial garb was gone, replaced by dirty tracksuit pants and a sweatshirt.

Full circle.

King said, 'Do you speak English?'

She shrugged. 'A little. I needed it for work.'

'Then you speak for them,' he said. 'When you get inside, you tell them exactly what happened. Give them all the details you know. Drop the name "Donati Group." The investigation will do the rest. You'll be returned home as soon as possible.'

'Where are we?'

'A police station in California.'

'I do not trust police.'

'There's too many of you,' King said. 'There's no chance of a cover up here. We're in Laguna Beach. The whole station would have to be corrupt to hide it.'

She looked at him, deep bags under her eyes, cynicism in her gaze.

Her look said it all, revealed her distrust of authority.

All police are corrupt.

King said, 'Not here. I'm sorry for what happened to you. But here is different.'

She didn't move.

He said, 'This will make the news. If it doesn't, I'll know something's up. Then I'll come handle it.'

She looked at him again.

Again, her look said what her mouth didn't.

I've heard many empty promises.

He said, 'Trust me.'

She took a step forward.

He led her out of the container and said, 'Let's get you home.'

88

Officer Eddie Ma was tired to the bone.

A cliche, for sure, but that's what it felt like — the switch to the night shift was killing him, one miserable stack of paperwork at a time. He checked his watch for the millionth time, but it was only eleven. He lowered his head to the desk and saw visions of being cocooned in bed, binging a Netflix show, eating takeout, with no goals and no responsibilities.

Seemed like bliss.

And fantasy.

He picked up a fresh stack of evidence reports that needed filling out when someone banged on the front doors of the station. His desk was closest to the entrance, and he couldn't deny he welcomed the break in monotony, so he rose on creaky knees and made his way out of the work-space and into the hallway. He made sure to bring his service weapon just in case, but he didn't figure he'd need it.

Probably just some harmless junkie.

He unlocked the door, swung it open, and came face to face with an enormous man in dirty clothes. The guy was dressed in tight-fitting black khakis and a black long-sleeved shirt, but they couldn't hide his powerful physique. He had hands and feet like bricks. His fingers and the tops of his hands were caked with dirt and sand, but that didn't mask the cuts and bruises and swelling underneath. His messy brown hair was matted to his forehead, above eyes like steel and a strong jaw.

He looked like he'd been through hell, but he stood tall regardless, keeping his chin up and his shoulders back.

Eddie said, 'Can I help you?'

The big man said, 'I'm a delivery driver. I do most of my work at the ports. I think I picked up the wrong container. I heard banging on the inside. I opened it up, and, well...'

The guy stepped aside.

His mass had filled Eddie's field of vision, and now with an unobstructed view the officer could see the dozen women huddled in a tight pack on the sidewalk below the portico. They were dirty, too, but nowhere near as bedraggled as the big driver. There was nothing about their presence that conveyed what their fate might have been, but Eddie's mind ran wild. He thought of containers, and smuggled girls, and all the horrors that sort of business led to.

It was like someone had closed a fist around his guts.

His instincts kicked in, and he fell back to rehearsed practices.

He turned to the driver, already thinking of the questions he'd ask the witness.

The guy wasn't there.

Eddie realised he'd spent far too long transfixed by the group below.

Only a few seconds, but that was enough, because there was no way the guy was a delivery driver.

Eddie had already pieced that together.

He sensed shuffling behind him, and knew the rest of the night shift officers would be materialising, sniffing out the commotion at the front of house.

Soon there'd be pandemonium. A moral uproar.

A dozen trafficked sex slaves in Laguna Beach.

Strangely, Eddie wasn't tired anymore. Fatigue falls away when you've got a worthy mission. He was, above all, an officer of the law. He was green, for sure, but that didn't make him naive. There'd be challenges — this was the first of many — but he'd handle them as justly as he could manage.

He ushered the girls inside.

89

Hours later, King sat behind the wheel of a Mercedes-Benz CLA250.

Violetta sat beside him.

The Benz was only a year old at best, and stood out over most of the other traffic putting in the overnight miles, but the choice had been deliberate. If you're going to steal a car, steal it from a wealthy neighbourhood. They can afford it, and they're more likely to have insurance. Steal an ordinary vehicle and you could ruin someone's life. King had used that methodology for close to a decade, and hadn't felt a shred of guilt.

After all, it was a minor inconvenience for the owner of the car, but for King it was usually life and death.

They only needed the stolen ride for a few hours, anyway. It'd give them a head start cross-country until Alonzo came through with what they needed. Then they'd dump it, torch it, and when the owner woke up and reported the theft to the authorities it'd already be far too late. They'd gone north all the way to Santa Clarita and then turned inland, gunning it north-east toward Victorville.

On the long road to Vegas.

The pre-determined rendezvous point, at a nondescript Airbnb in the outer suburbs, far from the Strip.

Now, Violetta dialled a number. She sucked in her breath as she did, anticipating the call that would spell their fate.

They had reassurances.

But that didn't mean much when they were wanted fugitives, at the top of the shadow world's shit list.

The call connected.

She put it on speaker so King could listen in.

Alonzo's voice resonated through the Merc's sleek cabin. 'Yeah?'

'We're all clear,' Violetta said. 'On our end, and on Slater's. Everything went according to plan.'

'Everything?'

She instinctively looked down at the bandages wrapped tight around her arm. 'Basically. Could have been a whole lot worse.'

'That's always the case, isn't it?'

'Are you okay with doing this?' she said. 'You know what it will entail.'

'A few polygraphs?' Alonzo said. 'That's all they have to work with, and I can beat those things in my sleep. They're bullshit. They measure your stress response to questions. If there's anything this job taught me, it's how to stay calm in stressful situations.'

'Thank you,' she said. 'From the bottom of my heart.'

'Spare me,' Alonzo said. 'I owe you. You fought for me my whole career. You didn't go anywhere without dragging me along for the ride. It's set me up for life.'

'Because you're the best.'

'And I also consider myself a good man. So your secret's safe. No matter what.'

'If they find out...'

'They won't.'

'Hypothetically.'

'I'm a software engineer,' he said. 'All I do is plan for hypotheticals. There's no scenario where they'll find out. What I've done is untraceable, so all they have to work with is the suspicion that I was involved in your disappearances. And suspicion is baseless. They can question me all they want. There's no scenario where I break.'

'You don't know how low they're willing to stoop.'

'I've considered every hypothetical,' he said. 'I'll be fine.'

Violetta fell quiet.

'And besides,' Alonzo said, 'they need me. You said it yourself. I'm the best.'

King chuckled at that.

'Hey, Jason,' Alonzo said.

'You're a good man,' King said. 'Thank you.'

'Least I can do.'

'What are you going to without me?' Violetta said.

'Something tells me I'll manage.'

She smiled.

King said, 'You're sure this is bulletproof?'

'I'll pretend not to be offended that you even asked.'

'Understood.'

'So what's left to do?' Violetta said. 'Give you the go-ahead?'

'I'm sitting at my computer,' Alonzo said. 'The go-ahead is all I need.'

Silence.

Then Alonzo said, 'Done.'

King gripped the wheel tight to ride out a wave of relief,

and stared through the windshield at the desert whipping past on either side of the highway.

A free man once more.

Alonzo said, 'The four of you can go anywhere, do anything. My contact in Vegas will sort you out with the physical documents, but your identities are sacrosanct. No one at any level of the government — surface or shadow — knows of their existence. Same goes for Beckham Lang. His application at the Rentarío Paralysis Centre in Henderson has been processed and accepted in their system. They're expecting him in three days time under a whole new identity, which gives him time to learn his new details. As for you four, no photo identification software will work on your new ID photos. I've altered what subtle traits needed to be altered. No one will know the difference. And lastly I've wiped all trace of what I've done from every system our beloved Uncle Sam has access to.'

Neither King nor Violetta said a word.

Alonzo continued. 'As for the money ... it was me who followed the trail to Slater's accounts. I doubt anyone else could have managed. So I wiped the trail and buried his accounts under additional layers of secrecy that he wasn't knowledgeable enough to think of. It's untouchable now. You have all your money. A little over four hundred million, to be precise. You can do as you please with it.'

The silence stretched out.

Alonzo said, 'Go. Be free. Enjoy yourselves.'

Violetta said, 'Somehow I don't think enjoying ourselves is on the cards.'

King managed the slightest head shake. It was strange that the smallest gesture conveyed the largest impact, revealing what he was destined to do until the day he died — fight.

Violetta stiffened in the passenger seat.

Alonzo sensed the hesitation and said, 'You know it's not too late. There's a way to salvage all of this. The upper echelon isn't all the way corrupt. They will listen to reason. They'll listen to the three of you, if you all come back. There's a hypothetical where everything goes back to the way it was. If that's what you want.'

King said, 'No. This time, Alonzo, there isn't.'

Violetta said, 'It's the principle. We're done serving a country.'

Now it was King's turn to fall quiet.

A deep admiration stirred in his chest.

Violetta said, 'We're individuals. Not drones. We'll do it our way.'

'You're really on board with this?' Alonzo said.

She looked at King. 'I really am.'

'Then I wish you Godspeed.'

'Thank you again,' Violetta said. 'Best of luck, my friend.'

'You, too.'

The line went dead.

Silence.

Overwhelming silence.

King said, 'So that's it?'

Violetta said, 'That's it.'

Simple as that.

New lives. New identities. New futures.

King stepped on the gas. It didn't matter as much if they were pulled over now. No system could identify them. They were a well-off couple with a Benz in a country of over three hundred million people.

Ghosts in the wind.

King accelerated into the night.

90

E ven though he'd known it was coming, the news took Slater by surprise all the same.

We're in the clear.

No one will ever find us.

We can start again.

They'd been driving for two full days since receiving word from Violetta — through Tennessee, Oklahoma, Texas, New Mexico, and Arizona. Now they branched off I-93 onto I-11 as they crossed the state border into Nevada, taking it up past Boulder City and into the sleepy suburban city of Henderson. They trawled through residential streets, passing rows and rows of identical houses with cream walls and ochre roofs. Xeriscaping dotted the middle strip of each street. It was early evening, and the lowering sun had both elongated the shadows and drenched the suburbs in golden light.

According to the GPS, their destination was two streets away.

Slater had to admit the knowledge was jarring.

Both he and Alexis had got to know Beckham Lang over

the previous forty-eight hours, and they'd both concluded separately that they'd never met a tougher soul. What Slater did paled in comparison to Beckham's reality. Sure, he put his body and health on the line in the name of vigilante justice, but at least he still had the ability to feel pain, to experience movement and exertion. Beckham had spent a decade trapped in the prison of his own body, and yet his morale had never wavered.

Not once.

Earlier that morning, Slater had asked him how he dealt with it on a day-to-day basis.

Beckham had said, 'I separate tasks.'

'What?'

'It's a concept I read about in some book, right before I was paralysed. I can't control what happens to me, and I can't control what people think about me. All I can focus on is what I *can* control, no matter how broken I am, no matter how much I'd love to play the victim. Playing the victim isn't a task that benefits me in any way. What benefits me is persevering. So I separate everything I can potentially do into the tasks that have positive outcomes, and then I do only those things. I have no expectation of anything else. It helps me stop thinking about what could have been, because that's useless, isn't it? We're living in this reality. All I can do is improve my circumstances as much as I can.'

Slater was taken aback. He'd said, 'That's a good theory. But to put it into practice...'

'Takes determination. Takes relentlessness. You'd know.'

Slater knew.

Now, he pulled into the parking lot of the Rentarío Paralysis Centre. It was a long low building, the whole exterior painted white.

From the back, Beckham said, 'Home?'

'If you want it to be,' Slater said.

Beckham smiled wryly. 'Oh, so if I don't like it, you'll become my full-time carer?'

Slater shrugged. 'We can find another place if you don't—'

'They're all the same,' Beckham said. 'Trust me.'

Both Slater and Alexis spun in their seats so they could speak to him face-to-face.

Beckham said, 'This is my life. There's no point ignoring reality. I need a place like this. It doesn't matter how fancy it looks or feels. It's not like I can feel it anyway. Like I said, all I can focus on is what I can control. Like my happiness.'

Slater didn't know how to respond.

Alexis said, 'I want you to know you've changed my perspective on life.'

Beckham looked over. 'I'm glad. Now get me inside before I change my mind and go back on all this inspirational bullshit.'

Slater laughed, and levered himself out of the driver's seat, and stood tall and spread his arms wide and stretched his body, all his muscles wound tight from endless hours of driving.

The evening was warm, and the atmosphere was pleasant.

No one was hunting them.

If they were, they'd never find them.

Life, for the first time in a long time, was simple.

Four parking spaces down, the front doors of a Ford Mustang with tinted windows opened.

King and Violetta stepped out.

Slater walked over and outstretched a hand. King slapped it and pulled him in, and they hugged tight for a single second. That was all they'd allow. They had oversized egos to nurse, after all. Then Slater moved to Violetta and hugged her, too. She grabbed the back of his head and pulled him down and whispered, 'Thank you,' in his ear.

He didn't say, *You're welcome.*

He didn't say anything.

He'd never been one to rely on gratitude.

He did things because they were the right things to do.

He went back to the Hyundai and, together with Alexis, helped Beckham out of the back seat. They put him down in the modified wheelchair Alexis had reassembled, and adjusted his position until he seemed comfortable enough. Then Beckham craned his neck to look past them, to meet the gaze of his ex-girlfriend.

Slater and Alexis took the cue, and wandered over to King. All three of them stepped aside and busied themselves with nothing.

Violetta went to Beckham with tears in her eyes.

91

King didn't try to get within earshot.

He respected Violetta too much for that.

He went with Slater and Alexis to the other side of the Mustang, where they milled about making unnecessary small talk to fill the silence. That way, even if Violetta and Beckham were speaking in raised voices, nothing would float over to them and ruin their privacy.

But he kept shooting glances sideways.

He couldn't help it.

She was squatting by the wheelchair, staring him right in the eyes, and he was staring right back. They were speaking animatedly. There was no hostility there. He seemed at peace, which contrasted what he'd heard about the grudge the man held. Violetta seemed like she understood.

There were tears, but they weren't tears of sadness.

The conversation lasted twenty minutes. King didn't postulate as to what it involved. The decade the pair had spent apart must have exacerbated the issues — at least, that's what King thought. But he couldn't get over the lack of animosity, especially from Beckham.

Finally Slater noticed, and muttered between frivolous small talk, 'I think Beckham forgave her on the way here.'

King said, 'After all this time?'

'It was something I said.'

'What?'

'"Sometimes doing the right thing is messy."'

King paused.

Thought about it.

Realised he'd never heard a truer statement.

He said, 'That's all it took?'

Now it was Slater's turn to glance at Beckham. 'He's one of the most unique individuals I've ever met.'

Alexis nodded her agreement.

King turned to her. 'How are you holding up?'

'Better than expected,' she said. 'Given the circumstances.'

'Your family is safe. Alonzo's work is second to none. He's thrown a virtual blanket over them. They won't be found.'

She nodded. 'I know. It's not about that.'

King hesitated.

Then he understood.

Before the brief settlement in New York, his life had been a freight train of constant motion for as long as he could remember. As had Slater's. To them, an upheaval of their surroundings was barely cause for raised eyebrows. Each of them had taken the events of the last few days in their stride — given their pasts, it was only slightly out of the ordinary.

Alexis was a civilian. A few days ago she'd held a job, socialised with work friends, been deeply set in the routine that confines so many to a certain chain of actions, over and over and over again until the day they died.

Which was human nature.

It took a certain level of madness to do what King and Slater did.

And she'd willingly come along for the ride.

That was nothing to scoff at.

King said, 'It gets easier.'

She reached out and took Slater's hand. 'Even if it doesn't, it doesn't matter.'

King didn't immediately respond. He looked all around the parking lot, watched the sun finally dip behind the row of houses opposite the disability home. The golden light dimmed a touch.

He said, 'How the hell did we end up here?'

Slater said, 'Could be worse. Could be dead.'

'Always a plus.'

He turned one final time and saw Violetta exit her crouch, bend down, and touch her forehead to Beckham's. They both had their eyes closed. One last moment of connection before their new lives began. It didn't faze King one bit. There was no room in his heart for jealousy.

Never had been.

When they parted, she wheeled him toward the entrance doors.

King, Slater and Alexis all instinctively stepped forward — the natural impulse to assist.

Violetta looked at them and shook her head.

They all stepped back.

Understanding.

Beckham nodded a farewell to the three of them, and his gaze lingered on Slater. King knew, then and there, that Slater's words had stuck with the man. Whatever they'd said to each other, it would affect them both long after they left this parking lot.

Then Beckham was gone, vanishing into the centre.

Violetta came back out fifteen minutes later. She looked like she'd lived a decade since she'd first approached Beckham.

She walked up to the three of them and said, 'Funny how life unfolds, isn't it?'

Slater said, 'What did you talk about?'

King knew better than to ask.

She looked at Slater, but didn't answer.

Alexis squeezed Slater's hand.

Slater understood, and shut his mouth. Probably made a mental note not to ask again. What was said was between Violetta and Beckham, and nobody else.

King said, 'How do you feel?'

She sighed. 'Good, all things considered. I never thought I'd see him again. I never thought I'd get the chance to talk things through.'

Then she looked at Slater. 'Thank you. For whatever you said to him.'

Slater opened his mouth, but Violetta held up a hand.

She said, 'I don't need to know.'

Another moment of understanding.

Then respectable silence.

They stood that way for close to a minute, as if trying to shake themselves from a lucid dream. But it was very real, and it had all unfolded exactly like this, so eventually they peeled off in pairs — Slater and Alexis heading for the Hyundai, King and Violetta for the Ford.

They'd rendezvous at their temporary stronghold and work from there.

And do what? King wondered.

All in due time.

He took the passenger's seat, and Violetta drove. It was a short ten-minute journey to the Airbnb they'd rented under a false, untraceable profile.

Violetta ran her hands along the wheel before she threw the car into reverse.

King said, 'What?'

She said, 'Ever wish you had a normal life?'

'No.'

'Good,' she said, and stepped on the accelerator. 'Me neither.'

92

S later and Alexis arrived in Spring Valley first, a couple of miles west of the Strip.

They used the gate code the owner had provided through the Airbnb app to access what was practically a compound. The walls were high for a private residence and the grounds were considerable, although they hadn't been tended to in quite some time. Most of the grass was dead, and patches of dirt riddled the lawn. The house was impressive, though — a one-storey sprawling homestead made of brick with a sand-coloured tile roof. The weak light of dusk gave the setting an idyllic aura.

They pulled the Hyundai to a halt in the courtyard, got out, and found the key under a pot plant on the front porch, just as the instructions conveyed. They unloaded what meagre possessions they had, dropping them in a sizeable living area with an open bar and an eighty-inch television mounted to the wall.

Then they waited.

Slater leant on the back of the sofa and said, 'If you ever want out of this life, tell us.'

'And go where?' Alexis said. 'My old life doesn't exist anymore.'

'But you can start fresh,' he said. 'With your new identity. You can be normal. You don't have to do ... what we do.'

'I made the choice,' she said. 'I don't go back on my word.'

'Is this what you want, though?'

She moved to him, and sat down on his thigh. 'Yes. It is.'

Fifteen minutes later, the low rumble of the Mustang's engine reverberated through the compound, and a minute after that King stepped inside.

'What was the hold-up?' Slater said.

Violetta answered that wordlessly when she came in with two jumbo bags of electronic goods from a tech store.

'New laptops,' she said. 'And a bunch of other stuff.'

She dumped it all down on the great slab of wood that constituted the dining table, and set to work arranging it into the foundations of a makeshift intelligence centre. It would never be as good as the real thing, but they didn't need the real thing.

All they needed was enough to work.

King looked around. 'So this is home.'

'For now,' Violetta said. 'Until we grow tired of it.'

Slater said, 'I think we should clarify a couple of things before we settle in.'

She looked up from the mass of hardware. 'Like what?'

She seemed disgruntled. She was supremely efficient — just like King, just like Slater. They'd been in the house for three minutes, and already were slotting the pieces into place to establish it as their base of operations.

In that sense, Alexis was the most human of them all.

Slater said, 'I was the first to step away. I kickstarted all of this. I need to know the pair of you are in it for the same reasons.'

King stared at him. 'Where you go, I go.'

'That's not an answer.'

'We understand,' Violetta said, straightening up, suddenly recognising the importance of the conversation. 'We're all on the same page. It was impossible for you to continue your role officially, and the same goes for King. There was too much oversight, too many chefs in the kitchen. It didn't gel with how the pair of you operate. You see problems, you fix them. When the shadow world was sourcing the problems, you constantly questioned them. Which meant you were always clashing with me, because I was the one handing down the orders.'

'Exactly,' King said.

'I always tried to look at the big picture, too,' Violetta said. 'It's a great concept, in principle. But it doesn't work on the ground floor. I saw it with my own eyes.'

She turned to Slater.

'When they asked me to help get rid of you,' she said. 'That was for the greater good.'

'Which makes sense,' Slater said. 'They can't have all their operatives going rogue when they please. They need to set an example. They can't make exceptions.'

'But that just couldn't be,' she said. 'The moment I started conspiring to keep you alive, I realised what you two had been telling me all along.'

Slater said, 'To *really* follow the greater good, you need to be a ruthless sociopath.'

'Which I'm not,' she said. 'None of us are.'

'So no government,' King said. 'No oversight.'

'I'm done,' she said. 'Speaking for myself. I can never go

back. Not after what happened. If we're going to do this, we do it independently.'

'Like mercenaries,' Slater said. 'But working for ourselves.'

'Precisely.'

King said, 'Until when?'

They all looked at him.

He said, 'Is there a finish line?'

Slater said, 'Not for me.'

Violetta said, 'I'll never be able to live a civilian life. I'm too far gone.'

'Good,' King said. 'Just checking we're all on the same page.'

'For as long as our bodies hold up,' Slater said. 'We do this.'

Violetta nodded.

King nodded, too.

Alexis was quiet.

The missing piece of the puzzle.

Slater turned to her. 'I don't take back what I said earlier. If this is too much...'

She said, 'It sounds like you're trying to get rid of me.'

'That's the last thing I want,' he said. 'But you know what I did for you yesterday. I'm willing to do it again, if that's what you want. If you leave, it'll crush me. But you deserve to do what you want.'

'I want this,' she said. 'The civilian life never felt right. I felt like an imposter in it. Here, I feel ... nothing. The tiny voice in the back of my head that always poked and prodded ... it's gone. I don't know what that means. But it's a step in the right direction.'

Slater soaked it in.

It was the first time she'd revealed part of what made her tick.

She added, 'If we do this, I don't want to sit on the sidelines.'

King stared.

Violetta stared.

Slater said, 'You don't have—'

'Training? Experience?'

He didn't say anything.

Alexis said, 'Then consider what happened over the last few days my initiation. Look at me. Do I look rattled? Sure, I can't break bones or hit a target with a pistol. But I think I've proved I can handle stress better than anyone. If you need me for anything, I don't want you to hold back. I don't want to be the damsel in distress.'

'You're not,' Slater said. 'You're far from that.'

King added, 'And we can teach you to break bones. We can teach you to shoot straight.'

Slater glanced over.

King said, 'What?'

Slater said, 'You're right. We can.'

All four of them looked at each other. They were positioned like four corners of a big square, and now they tightened the space between them, stepping closer. Slater went to the dining table, picked up one of the Glocks, crossed the space, and pressed it into Alexis' palm.

Slater said, 'Now we're all outlaws.'

King took a deep breath and said, 'Home sweet home.'

KING AND SLATER WILL RETURN...

Visit amazon.com/author/mattrogers23 and press **"Follow"** to be automatically notified of my future releases.

If you enjoyed the hard-hitting adventure, make sure to leave a review! Your feedback means everything to me, and encourages me to deliver more books as soon as I can.

And don't forget to follow me on Facebook for regular updates, cover reveals, giveaways, and more!
https://www.facebook.com/mattrogersbooks

Stay tuned.

BOOKS BY MATT ROGERS

THE JASON KING SERIES

Isolated (Book 1)

Imprisoned (Book 2)

Reloaded (Book 3)

Betrayed (Book 4)

Corrupted (Book 5)

Hunted (Book 6)

THE JASON KING FILES

Cartel (Book 1)

Warrior (Book 2)

Savages (Book 3)

THE WILL SLATER SERIES

Wolf (Book 1)

Lion (Book 2)

Bear (Book 3)

Lynx (Book 4)

Bull (Book 5)

Hawk (Book 6)

THE KING & SLATER SERIES

Weapons (Book 1)

Contracts (Book 2)

Ciphers (Book 3)

Outlaws (Book 4)

LYNX SHORTS

Blood Money (Book 1)

BLACK FORCE SHORTS

The Victor (Book 1)

The Chimera (Book 2)

The Tribe (Book 3)

The Hidden (Book 4)

The Coast (Book 5)

The Storm (Book 6)

The Wicked (Book 7)

The King (Book 8)

The Joker (Book 9)

The Ruins (Book 10)

Join the Reader's Group and get a free 200-page book by Matt Rogers!

Sign up for a free copy of '**BLOOD MONEY**'.

Meet Ruby Nazarian, a government operative for a clandestine initiative known only as Lynx. She's in Monaco to infiltrate the entourage of Aaron Wayne, a real estate tycoon on the precipice of dipping his hands into blood money. She charms her way aboard the magnate's superyacht, but everyone seems suspicious of her, and as the party ebbs onward she prepares for war...

Maybe she's paranoid.

Maybe not.

Just click here.

ABOUT THE AUTHOR

Matt Rogers grew up in Melbourne, Australia as a voracious reader, relentlessly devouring thrillers and mysteries in his spare time. Now, he writes full-time. His novels are action-packed and fast-paced. Dive into the Jason King Series to get started with his collection.

Visit his website:

www.mattrogersbooks.com

Visit his Amazon page:

amazon.com/author/mattrogers23

CPSIA information can be obtained
at www.ICGtesting.com
Printed in the USA
LVHW111919131120
671648LV00003B/532